Please feel free to send me an email. Just know that my publisher filters these emails. Good news is always welcome.

S.G. Sonysa — sg_sonysa@awesomeauthors.org

Sign up for my blog for updates and freebies!
sg-sonysa.awesomeauthors.org

I0565239

About the Publisher

BLVNP Incorporated, A Nevada Corporation, 340 S. Lemon #6200, Walnut CA 91789, info@blvnp.com / legal@blvnp.com

DISCLAIMER

Praise for Broken Hearts

The story has an awesome story line and you are an
amazing writer.
Broken heart is one of the best story I've read till now. So
please keep writing like this.
-Vidhi

Broken Hearts is an amazing unique book, it brings out all
the emotions from a being; happiness, sadness and mainly
excitement. I just simply loved this book.
-Uzmaa Qadri

The book Broken Heart is just amazing. The storyline is
very different and unique and can't be found anywhere else.
Moreover, the writing language is just splendid. The way all
the emotions are conveyed gets me goosebumps. It's just
awesome!
-Rajlaxmi Shinde

A book that truly shows the chemistry between two people.
I think its great how the author has presented Hailey and
how she grows as a person.
-Aysha Guthus

If you want a book that make you feel every emotion in a
matter of a few chapters then this is perfect for you. It's
well written and overall such a great read, you honestly will
have an internal sturggle to put it down.
-Sobia Syeda

Broken Hearts

By: S.G. Sonysa

BLVNP

ISBN: 978-1-68030-978-2

Table of Contents

Remained strong when lightning struck,
Didn't fall when fate smacked,
But crumbled into dust,
Due to broken trust.

This book is dedicated to all those people who didn't give up on life,
but stayed strong and fought back.
And now they're empowering others to do the same.
Thank you.

FREE DOWNLOAD

Chapter One

A Life-Changing Decision

Hailey

I was sitting in my room near the window, reading my favorite book, which was full of mystery and thrill. I loved reading books before going to bed because they kept me from recalling all the horrible memories in my past that haunted me every night.

I shivered thinking about last week's nightmare. In it, I was crying hysterically at something my mom said, and then the world collapsed under me as I fell into darkness.

I wanted to keep reading and finish the whole book before going to bed, but it seemed impossible to continue because I was so sleepy. I closed the book and put it on my study table before I got up from my chair.

The glowing full moon outside my window caught my eye, and I stared at it. It looked beautiful, spreading light in the darkness of the night. Suddenly, the rustling of the trees in the garden made me jump. I looked outside but couldn't see anything or anyone. Before something would appear and scare me, I decided to go to bed.

I jumped on my bed and pulled the comforter up to my chin. The softness of the new sheets felt so nice, making me sigh in contentment. I snuggled my face in the pillows and drifted into a dreamless slumber.

My mother's screams woke me up. I looked around, and my eyes landed on the wall clock; it was half past twelve. I heard the shattering of glass and jumped from the bed, running out of my room to search for my parents and granddad.

The angry voices of my mom and granddad led me to my granddad's study. The door was ajar. Taking advantage of it, I silently slipped inside. I found my mom standing in the middle of the room crying and mumbling something. My dad was sitting on the couch and staring at the floor like it was the most interesting thing in the world.

I didn't know what was going on and I was scared to find out. I noticed anger and worry etched on my granddad's face while he was busy glaring at my mom. They didn't know I was standing in the corner and watching everything.

Finally, I found the courage to open my mouth. "What is happening? Mom? Dad?" I asked them.

Their heads snapped in my direction, and their eyes stared at me with terror. My mom met my gaze and I felt myself freeze. Her eyes were filled with hate, as she looked straight at me. I feared for my life at that moment.

In my sixteen years of existence, I never saw this much hate for me in my mom's eyes. I was used to her disappointed glances, but this glare felt dangerous like it promised to inflict me an unimaginable amount of pain.

My father noticed the look on my mom's face and shook his head.

"Hailey, go back to your room," my dad said.

I was about to turn around and leave the study, but my mother's angry voice stopped me dead in my tracks.

"No! She should know what is going on in this house. Emily left us because of some stupid promise your grandfather made years ago to his best friend," my mom yelled, making me freeze.

I couldn't believe my ears.

My sister left! Why would she suddenly leave the house? What happened?

I asked my mom. "Why did she leave?"

My grandfather heaved a sigh and stood up from his chair. He took long steps, and within seconds he was standing in front of me.

"Hailey, when I was young, I made a promise to my best friend. Now, he is on his deathbed. He wants me to fulfill my promise before his death," my granddad said.

I was more confused after hearing what my granddad said. I didn't understand how it was connected to my sister leaving the house.

My mother noticed my confusion and said, "Tell her the truth!"

My granddad glared at my mom then turned back to me.

"My friend and I made a promise that someday, we will unite our families by arranging a marriage between our first grandchildren. Now, that he is not well and dying in the hospital, his family contacted me. They want me to fulfill my side of the promise before my friend's death. He wants to see his grandson happily married to my granddaughter before dying," my grandfather said.

I looked at him in shock. Now, it all made sense. That was why Emily ran away in the middle of the night. She had always been against marriage, and an arranged marriage was something she would never do. She always wanted to become a model and marriage meant the end of her modeling career.

"Why did you tell them that Emily would marry their son? She is eighteen, and it's too early to get married. She has her whole life ahead of her to spend the way she likes. Please don't ruin it by forcing her to marry a man she barely knows. Please, I beg you! Stop this nonsense so she can come back home," my mom said.

"What do you want me to do, Melanie? Do you want me to refuse them or tell them that I can't fulfill my friend's last wish?"

My mother's eyebrows scrunched up at his words. A few moments later she started smiling cryptically my way. I felt nervous while staring at her. With slow predatory steps, she approached me.

"I think Hailey is the better candidate to marry off. She doesn't look that young. She has good height and weight. She will look perfect as the wife of your friend's grandson," Mom said and gripped my arm.

I was shaking with fear, but her grip was so tight, making it impossible for me to move.

"If she marries your friend's grandson, you will be able to fulfill your friend's dying wish, and I will get my daughter back in this house." She suggested.

My eyes widened, and I instantly paled. My hands started shaking violently in anxiety, but she tightened her grip on my arm, digging her nails and making me hiss in pain.

"Are you out of your mind? How can you suggest something so absurd?" My dad was in a rage.

"This is the only solution. Believe me. It's best for all of us, even for Hailey," my mom said looking at me.

I felt tears brimming in my eyes, and they were ready to fall.

"She is sixteen, Melanie. She is younger than Emily if you haven't noticed," my grandfather said.

My mom's grip on my arm loosened.

"I don't care how young she is. I just know she is not Emily, my blood, my real daughter. And it's time for her to repay me for taking care of her all these years instead of making Michael leave her outside some orphanage," Mom yelled.

I went numb after her words registered in my mind.

Why was she saying this? Did it mean she was not my real mom?

"Melanie, why have you done this? It is not the right time to inform her all about the past. You promised me that we would not discuss this with her until she turns eighteen," Dad yelled.

At that moment, I forgot how to breathe. It meant whatever my mom said a few seconds ago was the truth. I was not her flesh and blood. I was not her real daughter.

Was my dad even my birth father? Was he?

"Yes, I promised that I will not tell her anything until the right time comes. But I think this is the best time to talk about your past, Michael," my mom said with nonchalance.

My dad looked at her in utter disappointment. The betrayal that he was feeling after my mom's revelation reflected on his face.

"Hailey, look at me," my father said, walking towards me and cupping my face. "I wanted to tell you this before, but then we decided to wait until you become mature enough to understand it. I am your dad. You are my own flesh and blood, but Melanie is not your real mother. Your real mother died giving birth to you."

I stopped breathing after what my dad said. My world collapsed, and I felt like falling into a dark hole.

"I was already married to Melanie and had Emily when I went to England on a business trip. There I met your mother and fell in love with her. Then one day, I found out that she was pregnant. I didn't know that the doctor informed her that there might be complications during the birth. She kept that information to herself and stayed positive. She decided to bring you into this world. The doctors tried their best to save her, but she died a minute after you were born."

I gasped and pulled away from my dad's grasp. It felt like he ripped my heart out.

He continued, "I informed Melanie about my infidelity, and about you. She was angry and hurt when she found out that I cheated on her. But after some time, she forgave me because of Emily's and your future. Melanie accepted you and me. She is just angry at the moment," he said to me.

He thought she was only angry. I wanted to tell my dad that she was not only angry but that she also hated me. No one deserved a cheating husband and his bastard child from another woman. At that moment, I understood her constant jabs and hatred towards me.

I deserved her hate and Emily's hate.

Oh, God! I destroyed their happy family by intruding.

All my life, I thought this woman was my mother. Even when she called me a freak and constantly sent me hateful glances, I never doubted that she wasn't my mom.

I remembered when I was small; she played with me, took care of me, and fed me with her own hands. But when I turned eight, she stopped doing anything for me, and I started spending more time with grandma. From that day onwards she never showed any affection to me. But I still loved her.

I was completely silent absorbing everything in. My dad looked defeated, and grandfather was deep in thought. My mom was staring straight at me still waiting for my answer.

"Michael, I forgave you a long time ago and accepted her. Now it's her turn to do something for me. I want my daughter back in this house at any cost. Emily and I cannot tolerate her presence here anymore," mom said.

And at that moment, I realized that she really wanted me to leave. Her last statement made me choose my poison, and I decided what I needed to do next. I was already standing on the edge of a cliff, but she finally made me jump and fall.

My voice was emotionless when I announced my decision.

"Mom is right. I will marry your friend's grandson instead of Emily," I said to my grandfather. "Please, ask Emily to come back home. She deserves to live here more than me," I said, turning towards my mom.

"Thank you so much, Hailey. I'll stay grateful to you for this sacrifice." She smiled at me.

I left and ran back to my room as fast as I could and locked my bedroom door. My eyes were misty from the tears pooling in them. I flung myself on the bed and hugged my pillow tightly. The tears that I had been holding back started falling from my eyes soaking the pillow.

I cried for my dead mother and for my father's infidelity. But mostly for the decision, I made a few minutes ago without thinking about the consequences. Thinking about my past and future, a sob broke out from my chest.

*   *   *

Chase

After my last class, I decided to go to the hospital to visit my granddad. He had been preparing me for the day that he would leave me all alone in this world.

I was running towards my car when Jack called me.

"Hi, buddy. We are leaving for practice. Are you coming?" Jack asked me.

"I have already talked to coach about skipping today's practice. I need to visit Granddad."

"Okay. See you tomorrow." Jack turned to leave with the team.

I got into the car and started driving to the hospital.

I still remembered the first day my granddad taught me how to play soccer. At first, I was not able to throw the ball in the goal net, but he made me practice and told me that one day I would be able to do it. Now, I'm on the NYU soccer team and one of the best players on the team.

My granddad became my best friend as my dad had always been busy with business meetings, and my mom stayed out with her friends enjoying her life. My twin sister and I used to stay at home with Granddad, and he would make us dinner then played with us.

My mom had always been controlling. She was very specific about what I needed to do to stay on her good side. She was the one who decided where I should study and what I should choose as my major.

My twin sister, Kate, quickly turned into the girl my mother wanted her to be. She took fashion design because of Mom even though she wanted to become an artist. Her passion for painting and drawing had diminished due to the constant pressures of her studies.

I parked my car and made my way inside the hospital, taking the elevator to the second floor where my granddad had been staying for the past two weeks. Instead of recovering he had become weaker.

I opened the door to his room and slipped inside silently. My granddad was sleeping peacefully. I sat on the empty chair beside his bed and placed my hand on his fragile one. His hand used to be so tough and strong, but now, it felt soft and lifeless.

When I looked at his face, he opened his eyes and stared at me. He moved his hand up and removed the oxygen mask from his face.

"Granddad, why did you remove this?" I asked him, trying to make him put it back on his face.

"I want to talk to you, son." He stopped me from putting the oxygen mask on.

"Okay. I'm listening, Granddad," I said.

"Chase, I have this friend, and we made a promise to arrange... arrange a marriage between our first grandchildren." My granddad stared at me.

I didn't know what to say at that moment.

"I want you to marry his granddaughter. This is my last wish, son," he said, clutching my hand.

"Granddad, I..." I was about to remind him that I'm still in the last year of my bachelor in business administration but he cut me off.

"Please, Chase. Do this for me. I want to see you married before my death," he said.

At that night, I made the decision that would change my life forever.

Chapter Two

Did I Make The Right Decision?

Hailey

I woke up after hearing the constant knocks on my bedroom door. Groaning, I sat up on the bed and rested my head against the headboard then shut my eyes to block the light. The knocking on the door stopped, and I sighed in relief.

I felt an immense pain in my head. My eyes were sticky and swollen. I cracked open my eyes and tried to clear my throat but ended up coughing violently because of the dryness. I ran my tongue over my lips and felt the cracks on them.

Slowly, I opened my eyes and looked around my room. My eyes went to my pillow, which was damp with tears and just like that everything that happened last night came crashing. I wanted to sleep again when I recalled what happened last night. I never wanted to wake up again.

Last night was like some horrible nightmare that turned into reality really fast. Everything was still vivid in my memory. I hoped that I could forget everything and continue with my boring life but even that seemed hard to do at the moment.

Yesterday, I found out that I lost my real mother the day she gave birth to me. And the one that I had looked up to as my mother for the last sixteen years was not my real mother. I was not her real daughter, her flesh, and blood. Even more so, I turned out to be the product of my dad's infidelity. And lastly, the revelation that my biological mother's death was because of me left me in so much pain.

If I had died with my mother that day, I wouldn't be in so much pain right now. I got up from the bed feeling my muscles ache and made my way to the vanity table. I stared at myself in the mirror, and I cringed at how horrible I looked. My eyes were red and puffy from crying all night. Even my face looked a little swollen, and on top of that, I had a runny nose.

Did I make the right decision last night?

Even my inner voice didn't answer my stupid question.

I recalled the time I had spent here in this house with this family. I wondered why they were so kind to provide me a house to live in, instead of leaving me at some orphanage or giving me up for adoption. Even Melanie, let me called her Mom. My dad did his best to provide me a great life. He put a roof over my head. He provided me with clothes and had me educated.

Then I heard the knock at the door again and went to open it. I found mom or should I say stepmom standing outside.

"Can I come in?" my stepmom asked.

I nodded my head, and she entered my room. I shut the door and looked at her, suddenly feeling nervous in her presence.

"I came here to apologize for my behavior last night. I'm sorry that you had to find out about your mom and dad that way," she said.

I felt somewhat happy after hearing her apology and thought she might be here to tell me that I didn't need to marry anyone to repay her.

"And I just want you to know how grateful I am for what you are doing for your sister. She really appreciates your sacrifice and is thinking about forgiving you for what you and your mother did to our family," she said, and my hopes died.

I nodded my head solemnly.

"Your dad and granddad are not happy with my idea. They want to tell his friend's family how young you are so they won't pursue the marriage and wait for a few more years. But now, it's your responsibility to convince them and make them lie about your age. My daughter and I cannot live with the constant reminder of Michael's infidelity anymore," she said, making my heart froze.

She wanted me to ask my father and grandfather to lie to other people about my age. I opened my mouth to tell her that I couldn't possibly convince my dad and grandfather to do it, but she took hold of my hand.

"Hailey, I know it's difficult, but you have to do this for your sister. Tell them how you enjoy the idea of early marriage, and happily ever after with your husband. Convince them that this is what you want, and you are not doing this because of me. I know you, Hailey. I know your words have magic on them. Do this for your sister and me," she said, kissing the center of my forehead.

I felt the tears brimming in my eyes at her words. She really wanted me to leave this house.

"I will try to convince Dad and Grandfather to lie about my age," I said, and she hugged me.

"You will look so pretty in your wedding dress. I am sure of it." She then left my room.

For the first time in my life, I saw admiration and love for me in her eyes. I didn't know if she was pretending, or it was real, but I liked the feeling it gave me.

In sixteen years of my existence, she never showered me with love like she showered Emily, but she didn't abuse me either. She would always glance at me with disappointment in her eyes and taunted me with my appearance, but I thought it was because she cared about how I looked.

Emily and I were never close, and I thought it was because we were so different from each other in looks and mind. While I loved studying, she hated it. I loved being in comfy casual clothes, but she despised them. Even her nightgowns were fancy and made up of silk with frills.

She never treated me like a sister, but in my mind, I admired her because of her beauty and perfection. She was always confident, which I lacked tremendously. Emily acted like a queen in school, and people worshiped the ground she walked especially the boys.

Because of her, other kids started bullying me. One day, she pushed me on the floor in the hallway for other students to see and laugh at my misery. The other students started pushing me too, and that was how "push Hailey" trend started in school. Amazingly, other students were more creative. They would make me trip in class, in the bathroom, in the cafeteria, and how could I forget the school grounds.

I was always a timid and submissive girl. I never liked fighting back for anything even if my life depended on it. With each passing year it got worse, and soon other students started playing horrible pranks on me, which left me with injuries. Each day at school became hell for me, and I wished death upon me than attending school.

I had to hide all the abuse from my parents and grandfather because Emily blackmailed me. If I would ever open my mouth, her friends would cut my tongue. She was a senior, and she had a lot of friends especially scary boys.

Until the fifth grade, I was able to hide all the pain and traces of abuse on my body. But, when sixth grade rolled in, I was beaten by a few guys and girls in the parking lot. I was waiting for my dad to come and pick me up and that was when those boys and girls attacked me. They told me it was my punishment for telling my dad that I didn't want to go to school because other students treated me badly.

It was Emily who found out and punished me by sending her friends to beat me. They broke my right leg, and my jawbone got fractured. I had a head injury too, and that landed me in the hospital for weeks.

My dad was the one who found me broken, beaten, and unconscious on the school grounds, bleeding to death. I was rushed to the nearest hospital, and during the checkup, doctors found many old bruises on my body and informed my dad.

After that incident, my dad forbade me to go to school and hired a home tutor for me. I was a shy girl, but getting homeschooled turned me into an antisocial, awkward girl or as Emily liked to call it; a freak. Whenever Emily's friends would come over for a sleepover, they called me names and told me how ugly I was. They told me I look fat and I should lose some weight.

At first, I didn't believe them. But slowly, they successfully drilled it into my head, and I started believing that I was a freak. I stopped making an effort to change myself and do something to look beautiful because I realized a long time ago that whatever I did, it wouldn't stop people from calling me ugly, fat, and freak.

Between Emily and me, she had always been everyone's favorite and in the spotlight because of her beauty and style. I tried a few times to mingle with the family, but they always pushed me back by making a snide remark on my clothing or on my awkward communication skills. They would make jokes about me and laughed while I sat there in front of them with a fake smile on my face.

They never realized that they were breaking me from the inside, breaking my confidence, my will to speak, and my ability to interact with people. Later, I stopped talking to anyone. I would just nod my head in answer or did anything they wanted me to do for them without complaining. It saved me from the pain.

I used to think that I was useless to this family, but now, I knew how important I was for my mom and sister at this very moment. She asked me for the first time ever to do something for her that would make her proud. And I wanted to do it for her, to make her happy and proud of me, even if it meant getting married to a stranger.

I was always the extra ugly piece of their perfect house. If this was their way of throwing me out, then I should accept it. Also, I didn't have any right to stay in this house anymore. They didn't even want me. I knew their lives would be a lot better without me in the picture.

Sighing, I made my way to the washroom and decided to take a shower. After the shower, I changed into my sweatpants and a baggy shirt. Then I combed my hair and put them in a high ponytail. I heard knocks and made my way to the door. I opened it and found my grandfather and dad standing outside with grim faces.

Smiling brightly at them, I opened the door wider and invited them inside.

"We are here to talk to you, Hailey," my dad said.

I nodded my head and waited for them to say something.

"Hailey, I love you, and I know you are hurt at the moment. That's why you made that decision last night," my dad said, and I grew still.

"You don't have to do anything that you don't wish to do. I will talk to Melanie and ask her to change her mind. If she cannot accept you after all these years, then you shouldn't stay in this house. I can rent an apartment, and we will shift there."

I wanted to hug him and ask them to take me away from this house and this life, but my mom's word reminded me what I needed to do. I needed to convince them instead of agreeing with this.

"No, Dad you are getting everything wrong about Mom. She is still my mom, and I love her. This morning she came to apologize to me and told me to do whatever I want. She was the reason why I said yes to this marriage last night. But now, I'm taking responsibility for my decision. I have always wanted to get married at a young age, and now, I have the opportunity," I said, trying to look convincing.

Both of them shook their heads at me.

"I cannot believe this. You are lying, Hailey," Dad said.

"Dad, I don't want to stay in this house with you, Emily, and Mom. I want to make a new life with new people. Let me get married to this guy so I can try to become someone on my own. I am sure grandfather's friends are nice people and won't hurt me," I said, feeling my heart bled.

"They are nice people, and the boy is great, too. But I don't think you should make this decision so soon." Grandfather rose to his full height.

"Your friend doesn't have much time left. And I'm not making this decision under any pressure. It just feels right to do," I said, feeling my voice crack at the end.

My grandfather looked pretty convinced, but dad had doubts.

"Hailey, you need to understand that whatever I did in the past, I did to protect you," my dad said, sounding guilty.

The hurt and guilt were clear in his voice, making my own heart ache for him. I wanted to hug him and tell him it was alright, but it wasn't. I was still hurt. Not even in my wildest imagination had I thought that one of my parents would turn out to be my stepparent.

My body stilled, and my hands hung loosely on my sides. It was difficult to tell them how I felt about this situation, but I tried.

"Dad, I forgive you. I understand why you did it. I am just in shock, and really hurt that you hid something so important from me for this long," I said. "But, I still love you, and I am happy to know that you are my real father," I said the last part with a small awkward smile.

A sad smile graced both of their faces.

"I will inform them that you agreed to get married to their son. You are still young, so they might change their mind and decide to wait. I'm sure you will change yours with time," grandfather said.

"Don't tell them that I am still sixteen. Lie to them. Tell them that I am eighteen."

They looked at me with horror.

"Why?" they both asked in unison.

"Dad, I want them to think I'm an intelligent, young girl and not a high school girl. Please, dad, granddad. Do this for me." I begged them while tears flowed from my eyes.

They looked at me in shock when I started to cry, but I was desperate to get rid of mom and Emily. I knew if I stayed here, they wouldn't let me live in peace.

"Okay. We will tell them that you have recently turned eighteen," my dad said, wiping my tears.

I hugged him.

"It looks like I have a wedding to arrange," Grandfather said, leaving the room.

My dad and I smiled. I felt like my granddad knew why I was doing this, but he didn't really want me to stop.

"Thank you, Hailey, for forgiving me. You are the best daughter a father could ask for," Dad said.

I nodded my head, controlling the tears.

"They are really nice people and rich too. I met them last week. Mr. and Mrs. Edwards have two sons and two daughters. The son they want to marry off is twenty, and his name is Chase. He is a handsome young man and is studying in NYU. It's his last semester before he graduates. I have heard a lot of good things about that family and their son. I'm sure they'll keep you happy and safe," my dad said, and I hugged him again.

"I know Dad. And I'm glad you and Granddad accepted my decision."

Deep inside, my heart broke into tiny pieces knowing that there was no escape now.

Chapter Three

Wedding

Hailey

[Two weeks later]

I stared at myself in the full-length mirror. The girl staring back at me didn't look like the plain girl I had known all my life or like the girl I was just two weeks ago. She was different from my boring, plain self. She looked beautiful with her brown hair tied up in a chignon. A few tendrils framing her heart-shaped face, and her lips were painted in a beautiful shade of pink, making them look naturally fuller. Her face was healthy and glowing, making her look fresh and beautiful. Her cheeks were rosy, giving the appearance of natural blush.

She was dressed in a pure white chiffon and lace dress. The bodice was made up of lace, wrapping around her chest like a second skin, while the skirt was flowing down to her feet in a silky mess.

I looked at the girl in the mirror, and my eyes caught the shiny pendant dangling from the white gold chain clasped around her neck. Unintentionally, my hand moved up to my neck, and I gripped the pendant while still staring at the girl in the mirror who was no one else but me.

I was the one dressed in an elegant wedding gown. I was about to get married and start a new life with a stranger in just a few hours. The mere thought scared me, causing my grip to tighten on the pendant as if seeking some kind of support. The presence of something that was so special to me instantly relaxed the turmoil inside me.

This piece of jewelry was valuable to me because it belonged to my biological mother who gave birth to me sixteen years ago and wearing it today made me feel that she was here with me, hiding somewhere but watching me take the biggest step of my life.

My bedroom door opened, making me turn around to see my dad.

"Dad, how do I look?" I asked him.

He smiled at me lovingly, and said, "You look beautiful like your mother."

"You really loved her." I saw the emotion in his brown eyes.

"I still love her, and I love you. Don't ever think that you are an unwanted child because I am glad that I have you as my daughter," he said and placed a kiss on my temple.

My dad grimaced as a tear rolled down from my eye, leaving a wet trail on my face.

"Please, honey. Don't cry. It will make your eyes red and puffy. It wouldn't look good when we take your wedding pictures," Dad said, picking up the tissue from the vanity table and drying my face.

I gave him a watery smile.

He smiled, and said, "Let's go. We need to leave for the chapel."

I nodded my head and held out my arm to him. He led me down to where others were waiting for me. After we were all settled in the car, the driver took us to our destination. When the car stopped, my dad and Emily helped me in getting out of the car without ruining my dress.

Emily arrived a week ago when she heard that she didn't need to marry anyone and no one was forcing her anymore. She decided to come back and see for herself if it was true.

When I stepped out of the car, my body started quivering, and to hide it, I clasped my dad's arm. He gave my hand a reassuring squeeze, and we made our way inside the chapel. With every step I took to enter the chapel, my heartbeat accelerated to the point where I felt my chest would burst open at any moment.

Despite all the nervousness, I continued walking down the aisle towards the nave of the chapel where the priest and a man in black tuxedo were standing. I couldn't see the man's face because he had his back to me.

When I reached the center, my dad cleared his throat, making the man turn to me.

With my abnormally beating heart, I took the risk and glanced at him, freezing the moment my eyes landed on his face. The first thing that came to my mind was that this good-looking, almost perfect man was Chase Edwards. I stared at him, taking in all his features, from his straight nose to his perfectly crafted sharp jaw and the arrogance he had on his face. Then, my eyes went to the mass of shiny brown hair on his head. It looked messy like he had been running his fingers through it all day. Then my brown eyes connected with his sterling grey ones, which were filled with hidden anger and hate urging me to run away from him and this chapel with the intention of never coming back. I couldn't fathom why a good-looking man like him would ever agree to marry someone like me who was plain and naive.

My dad nudged me, telling me to stand beside the man, but my legs were wobbly, making it difficult for me to make my way to him. A man in a dark blue suit patted Chase's shoulder and murmured something in his ear, which in return made him clench his jaw. I was ready to lift my dress and make a run for it when Chase extended his hand towards me. I was caught off guard by his stunning looks again, and his act of giving me his hand for support. It made me think that maybe he would not abandon me like other people in my life did. My hopeful nature made me thought that maybe he would be different from other people and would always be there to support me whenever I needed him.

I extended my shaking hand and placed it in his, which was large and strong compared to my soft and small one. He grasped my hand tightly and pulled me towards him. His iron hold on my hand was hurting me. I forced myself not to hiss in pain. When I was beside him, he dropped my hand as if I had burned him. I was sure no one noticed his hostile behavior towards me, so I ignored it, feeling hurt I faced the priest.

The priest started saying something, but I wasn't hearing him. My eyes were cast down, staring at nothing in particular but I was thinking hard about the consequences of this arranged marriage that I would have to face. I couldn't change my mind now. If I refuse, my dad and granddad would be humiliated in front of these people and guests.

The priest's voice brought me out of my thoughts.

"Do you, Hailey Watson, take Chase Edwards to be your lawfully wedded husband, to have and to hold, from this day forward, for better, for worse, for richer, for poorer, in sickness and health, until death do you part?" the priest asked.

His words sounded jumbled in my mind, but one thing was clear: He and everyone in the chapel were waiting for my answer.

I took a deep breath and mumbled softly, "I do."

The priest's head tilted towards Chase, who was standing beside me stiffly, his face set like stone.

The priest repeated the same lines to him. "Do you, Chase Edwards, take Hailey Watson to be your lawfully wedded wife, to have and to hold, from this day forward, for better, for worse, for richer, for poorer, in sickness and health, until death do you part?"

"I do," he said.

His husky voice made me shiver.

"Please exchange the rings," the priest said, making me freeze.

I turned to see Emily with a small velvet box in her hand. A thick platinum band was snuggled inside of it. I picked it up with trembling hands and waited for him to extend his hand. When he extended his hand, I hastily pushed the ring onto his finger.

Chase had a similar band in his palm, but it had a tiny diamond in the center. I extended my shaking hand, allowing him to trap my finger in his strong grasp and slid the ring on harshly.

My hand dropped to my side, and Emily had a satisfied grin on her face. I didn't know why she was suddenly so happy. Maybe it was because she was finally free or because she witnessed his insensitive actions and my pain made her happy.

The priest's announcement pulled me out of my thoughts. "By the power vested on me, I now pronounce you man and wife. You may now kiss the bride," the priest said.

The simple word *kiss* made my legs wobble. I never thought about the part where I would have to be kissed by my husband. My heart was drumming in my ears because of my nerves. I had never been kissed before. Let alone stayed in the presence of a boy or a man for longer than a minute, other than my dad and granddad. The mere nearness of a stranger made me want to scream "bloody murder" and make a run for it.

I was proud of myself for remaining composed for so long in this chapel full of strangers, but the idea of a kiss turned my world upside down. I wanted to experience something beautiful: a kiss like the ones in the stories, but I was scared of my reaction, and I might embarrass myself in front of everyone. If he kissed me and I did something wrong, he might dislike me more. In the past half hour, I had already concluded that Chase Edwards didn't like me at all, or maybe he was just angry because he was bounded by marriage at a young age. But whatever reasons he had, it was clear that he was not happy.

I took the risk of glancing around the chapel and saw everyone staring at us, waiting for us to do something worth cheering at after enduring the boring ceremony. I looked at Chase's face, which looked torn between pushing me down and doing what everyone expected of us.

Suddenly he took a step forward, leaving a centimeter's space between us and leaned his head down. I had been anticipating this moment since the first time I read how beautiful it felt to be kissed by your husband, but I was cursing myself for being so inexperienced and nervous at the same time.

I searched my mind for all the information I had learned from the romantic novels I got the chance to read a few months ago while hiding from the prying eyes of my librarian who forbade me from touching any book that wasn't an encyclopedia.

I waited to feel his lips on mine with my heart pounding at a hundred miles per hour. But I never felt them because he had curled them in his mouth so he would avoid touching my lips. There was no kiss, just the presence of his mouth near mine. It looked like he was kissing me. His breath fanned over my cheek, and his jaw touched the side of my chin, but I just kept staring into his eyes as he did the same.

I would definitely hyperventilate from the closeness of his strong, hard body if I wasn't too shocked and hurt by his actions. Everyone applauded, clearly missing what just happened between us. He moved away from me, breaking the eye contact while sending me a glare as if telling me to keep my mouth shut.

I felt an ache in my heart, making me want to cry. But I had to keep standing straight and pose like the happy newlywed bride I was supposed to be. I had long accepted that I was not made for love so I thought his rejection wouldn't hurt me this much, but it did. I felt like he had reopened the old wound in my heart.

Afterward, we left the chapel, and I had to share the ride back home with Chase. He was busy typing something on his cell phone, ignoring my presence for the entire fifteen-minute ride.

My granddad was feeling generous, so he had arranged a very nice reception in our backyard. The celebration lasted for two long hours. The guests we invited were immediate family and friends: just a few of dad's friends, and my uncle and aunts who were as happy as Emily to finally get rid of the freak.

After spending long hours watching other people dance and enjoy the celebration more than me, I was fed up and ready to bolt to my room upstairs. At that moment, my mom came to remind me that I needed to get changed out of my dress because I would be leaving in an hour for New York.

I was aware that I had to leave earlier than the rest because I needed to meet Chase's granddad to receive his blessing and show him that we respected his wish and fulfilled it. Mom came and helped me to my room because it wasn't easy for me to walk up the stairs in my gown and heels. When I reached my room, I thanked my mom, and she left me alone.

I hurriedly stripped off my wedding dress and got changed into simple jeans, a loose black off-the-shoulder top that looked comfortable for traveling. Almost everything that I owned was loose except for my undergarments.

When I went downstairs after getting dressed, I noticed my bags were already in the trunk of the cab while Chase was standing there. He had also changed into simple jeans and a white shirt and was looking impatient.

I hugged my dad and granddad. They both placed a soft kiss on my head, making me want to cry, but I held back my tears. I loved my dad and granddad; leaving them felt more difficult than I thought. Despite all the harsh words my mom had thrown at me last week, I hugged her and kissed her cheek. Emily made no effort to hug me nor did I. Her eyes were full of hate as if she was cursing me as I slid into the cab beside Chase.

That day, I left my old self at my house with hope in my heart that I might make this new family love me. And I made a wish that hopefully Chase Edwards would be the first one to fall in love with me.

Chapter Four

The Beginning of Something New

Hailey

When we landed in New York, the driver was waiting for us outside the airport to take us home. He took the bag from my hand and put it in the trunk of the car. Chase got inside the car after dropping his bag on the ground for the driver to put in the back with mine.

I glared at his back for being rude to me then got inside the car. Chase stayed busy with his cell phone, avoiding me again. I stared at the tall buildings for a while then dozed off because of exhaustion from the wedding.

Next thing I knew, someone was shaking me brutally, making me groan and slap the hand on my shoulder away.

"Wake up! I don't have time for this." I heard an angry voice.

Groaning, I opened my eyes and found Chase staring at me in anger. In seconds, I was awake and out of the car. I looked around the neighborhood, and the beauty took me off guard. The beautiful two-story white house in front of me had a vast garden and gave out a peaceful and calm vibe.

Chase took our bags from the driver and made his way towards the house. I followed him like a lost puppy. Suddenly, he stopped outside the door and searched his pants' pockets then pulled out a key. He unlocked the door and went inside without even bothering to invite me in.

I was hurt by the way he was behaving. I was not expecting him to accept me as his wife in one day, but he could at least welcome me in his house. It looked like my dream of happily ever after was not going to come true any time soon.

I could understand that he wasn't ready for such a huge life change neither was I, but we had no choice other than to accept our fate. At least he should be thankful that he had spent twenty years of his life with his family who loved him and gave him the freedom to do everything. Unlike me who stayed cooped up behind the walls of my room and tried everything to feel accepted by my mom and this cruel society.

I entered the house and shut the door. When the lights were switched on, I gasped at the expensively decorated living room. Everything in the house looked extravagant and perfect.

I was pulled out from my daze when I heard Chase's voice.

"Follow me. Your room is upstairs," Chase said, making his way upstairs with our bags.

I nodded even when I knew he wasn't looking at me and followed him upstairs. After the long flight of stairs, four rooms came to view. Passing by the first three rooms, Chase made his way towards the last room in the left corner.

He twisted the doorknob and pushed open the door. Then he stepped inside with my bags and switched on the lights of the room.

I stared at the room with my mouth agape.

He faked coughed to catch my attention. I turned to face him with the horrible blush gracing my cheeks in embarrassment at my shock.

"This is your room. The room on the right corner is mine," he said, sounding irritated.

"Thanks for showing me the room," I mumbled, looking down at my sneakers feeling scared to make eye contact with him.

He was quiet for a second and stared at me with narrowed eyes, making me look up.

"You're welcome. Now I hope to catch some sleep. And if you want anything, don't even think of disturbing me," he said with a glare.

I nodded my head in a silent okay.

"Be ready at ten tomorrow morning. We need to go to the hospital to visit my granddad," he said.

"Okay," I mumbled.

He gave me one last lingering glance then left me alone in my room. I let go of my breath that I didn't realize I was holding while he was here.

Why did he scare me so much?

Oh God! How was I going to stand in front of him and talk to him without cowering back in fright?

I shrugged my shoulders and took a quick glance at my new room. I realized that I liked it more than my old one. This room was large and beautiful than the one back at my home. The cream-colored walls and baby pink curtains were great in contrast. It was too girly for my taste but who was I to complain.

My eyes went to the very comfortable looking queen-size bed in the center of the room, calling me to sleep on it like a baby. But I decided to unpack first. I dragged my bag to the center of the room. After twenty minutes, I was done unpacking all the stuff that I brought here with me for tonight and placed everything in the closet.

My other stuff would be delivered tomorrow, so I didn't have a lot of things with me. I just had some necessities and clothes in the bag, and it didn't take much time to unpack.

I looked at the silk pajama shorts that my lovely half-sister put inside my bag with the note stating that I should show my fat body to my husband so he would divorce me. Good thing we were not sharing a room. I had no other option but to wear the pajama shorts if I didn't want to sleep naked. I picked up my white tank top and shorts then made my way towards the washroom to take a shower.

The washroom was large and pretty nice with a white and pink theme. There was a large bathtub on the side inviting me in. Changing my mind, I filled the bathtub and lay inside feeling my muscles relaxing in the warm water.

After the bath, I wrapped a fluffy towel around my body, and another one on my head then put moisturizer on my body. When I was done applying moisturizer, I got changed into my undergarments then put my pajama shorts and a white tank top on.

I dried my hair with the towel because my hair dryer was something that I thought wasn't important for one day and packed it with my other things that would be here tomorrow. And asking Chase for a hair dryer meant disturbing him and risking my life, so I had only one option, and that was to towel dry my hair.

I opened the window of my room and breath in New York's air, which made me sneeze instantly. My eyes roamed around the neighborhood, for a few seconds I took in the beauty of other similar fancy large houses.

When I felt my eyes dropping, I made my way towards the bed then flung myself on it. The feel of soft silky sheets under me instantly made me fall into a deep slumber.

[In the morning]

I woke up to the loud banging on my door. It took me a few minutes to sit up on bed and recall where I was. When I heard an angry voice calling my name, I was up from the bed in seconds and running towards the door like my life depended on it or in my case it really did.

I unlocked the door and opened it to find Chase standing outside with a scowl on his face. I was breathless from running.

He opened his mouth to say something but stopped. His eyes moved up and down, staring at me from head to toe and his mouth opened then he closed it.

I was so scared of him, so instead of staring back at him, I averted my eyes.

The cold, chilly air came through the open window and made me sneeze. Chase snapped out of the trance he was in and looked at my face. He clenched his jaw and opened his mouth again.

"It's already 9:00 am. We need to leave in half an hour if we want to make a stop for breakfast before going to the hospital, so get ready." He ordered with a glare.

I nodded not able to say anything to him.

Chase looked like he already showered. He was dressed in a black t-shirt and jeans. His attire was casual, but just like yesterday, he managed to look perfect.

Wow! It was already a day, and he didn't dispose of me last night. I was off to a good start then!

I closed the door when he disappeared from my sight and sighed in relief. Then my eyes landed on my night attire.

Bloody hell! He saw me in shorts! Would he divorce me now?

My mind told me to crawl under the bed and die there, but I was more scared of getting scolded again by Chase. I hurriedly went to the washroom and did my routine. Then I got changed into the first thing I got my hands on, which happened to be my black jeans and cream wool jumper. I put my hair in a ponytail then went downstairs to find Chase sitting on the couch in the living room. He was tapping on his cell phone, probably messaging someone.

I didn't want to disturb him, so I coughed. He didn't look at me, so I coughed again, but this time loudly.

"Do you have some contagious lung disease?" Chase asked me.

I stared at him in bewilderment then shook my head. Chase rolled his eyes at me then put his cell phone in the pocket of his black leather jacket and got up.

He walked closer to me, making me feel uncomfortable.

"Are you mute?" he asked me.

I shook my head, and he raised his eyebrows at me.

"No, I am not mute."

"Then why were you coughing instead of informing me that you are ready to go?" he asked me.

My eyes widened, and I opened my mouth to explain.

"I… I thought you were." I tried to tell him, but he interrupted me.

"Forget it. You'll take the whole day to speak," he said, turning around and walking towards the door.

Coming out of shock, I realized that I needed to follow him outside if I wanted breakfast.

He seemed arrogant and rude. I felt scared around him, and my mind would shut off. His all hard and angry demeanor made me scared, but the feminine side of me got me distracted with his stunning looks.

I locked the door behind me and found him waiting for me inside a shiny black car. I got in and put my seat belt on. When we were settled in the car, he started driving to some place for breakfast. I kept my eyes on the road or sometimes looked out of the window to stare at the scenery. The car ride was so silent, and I was ready to fall asleep again if he didn't stop the car outside the cute small café.

We got out of the car and made our way inside the café to have breakfast. Chase selected the corner booth for us to sit. The waitress approached us with menus, and she handed Chase one while I waited for her to give me the other menus. She stared at him dreamily and didn't hand me the menus, but Chase didn't notice her.

"Hailey, take a look at the menu and order something for you," Chase said, handing me the menus.

I stared at him dumbly because it was the first time that he said my name, and it sounded really sweet to my ears.

"I know what I want, so order for you," he said, pulling me back to reality.

I nodded my head happily, and with a quick glance at the menu, I ordered coffee with lots of whipped cream and some chocolate pancakes.

Chase ordered some sausages and sandwiches with black coffee. I couldn't even think about drinking a black coffee. The mere smell and look of black coffee made me shudder. I liked my coffee sweet with rich cream and milk.

We were waiting for our food to arrive when I thought of striking a conversation with him. It was really difficult to find the right topic to initiate a conversation with Mr. Stone Face. Yes, I had given him a nickname that would be stuck with him until he would change and show me some emotion to convince me that he was indeed a real human and not made up of stone.

Before I can think of a much interesting thing to say, I opened my big mouth and said, "It's a very nice place. It smells like coffee."

And there I went embarrassing myself again because of my stupid mouth incapable of striking a nice conversation. I was busy cursing myself in my head when my stomach growled and embarrassed me further. I was sure he heard it, and my cheeks started to feel hot.

I stole a shy glance at his face, and my eyes got stuck. I was mesmerized seeing a semblance of a smile on his face. It was something like a slight twitch of lips similar to a smile, but it was beautiful nonetheless. I was staring at him completely amazed. My mind started to imagine how a full smile would look on his face.

Yesterday, when I saw him for the first time, I realized that he was handsome and had great features, but the constant scowl on his face dampened his looks a little bit. It made him look dangerous.

The waitress came back with our orders and placed it on the table. The smell of pancakes and coffee instantly filled my nose, and I wasted no time devouring my breakfast like I was some starved person.

"This place is my granddad's favorite. We used to come here every Sunday after football practice when he was healthy," Chase said.

I was shocked that he was talking to me and sharing something about himself with me. Discretely, I turned my head to look if someone was standing behind me, but I didn't find anyone. When I was sure that he was actually talking to me, I cleaned my lips with a napkin.

"It means this place is special and full of memories," I said.

He nodded his head and said, "We used to spend a lot of time here. This place has both happy and sad memories of my granddad and me."

Then he took a sip of his coffee.

"Recall the happy memories. They will make you smile," I said.

He stared at me, and I stared back at him.

I was informed that his granddad had not been in good condition for some time. Doctors had hardly given him a week.

We finished our breakfast, and Chase paid the bill.

It took us fifteen minutes to reach the hospital. The large board stated that it was St. Martin Hospital. We made our way to the elevator. Chase knew the floor and room number of his granddad's room, so we didn't make a stop at the reception to ask.

When we were outside the room, Chase turned towards me.

"Hailey, when we go inside, we must look happy," he said.

I nodded my head understanding his need and gave him a reassuring smile. He took my hand in his and laced our fingers together. My heart started doing a somersault, and a blush appeared on my cheeks. He looked at me, and I smiled.

Maybe I made the right decision that night by agreeing to this marriage.

Chapter Five

My Dream Family

Hailey

When we entered the hospital room, the first thing that came to view was a fragile old man lying on the bed with different tubes and wires attached to his body. He had an oxygen mask on his face, helping him to breathe. When we moved closer to his bed, we realized that he was sleeping. His breathing was slow and came out as a gasp.

My eyes started to sting with tears while looking at him. The state he seemed to be in, reminded me of my grandma. I was ten years old when my grandma died, leaving me all alone in this huge world. She was my only best friend, my savior, and my mentor. She took care of me like my real mother would have if she were alive today. My grandma was always there for me, not my stepmom. My stepmom stopped playing the role of a Mom when I turned eight, and Grandma had to take her responsibility.

I was devastated after my grandma's death, and I spiraled into depression. I was so close to her, and her death tore me apart. The school was already hell, and after her death, I started sinking into depression because I had no one to console me. Later, I started having nightmares. They were horrific, and they would appear almost every night. As usual, I hid it from everyone, and the condition got worse. My pleas and screams turned so loud at nights, and that was how mom and dad found out. I had no other option but to tell them the truth.

After that day, my dad took me to a psychologist. I was diagnosed with MDD (major depressive disorder). I had to attend a session every week to get better. The nightmares decreased gradually, but they never disappeared completely. I still had a fear of losing people that I loved, and whenever there was death, my mind took me back to the past. Sadly, I couldn't control my mind while I was asleep.

I was pulled out of my thoughts when Chase said, "Granddad, wake up. We are here to meet you."

Slowly, his granddad opened his eyes and looked at Chase in confusion. Chase smiled at him and tilted his head in my direction. His granddad followed Chase's gaze and looked at me.

I gave him a wide smile, and said, "Hi."

He removed his oxygen mask and put it on the bed. I walked closer to him.

"Who is this pretty girl?" he asked him.

"She is Hailey Edwards." Chase placed a hand on my back and pulling me towards him.

My heartbeat accelerated hearing my changed last name.

His granddad's eyebrows scrunched up in confusion, so Chase said, "She is my wife, Granddad."

His granddad's eyes widened, and then a smile broke on his fragile face.

"Are you David's granddaughter?" he asked me.

"Yes. I am his granddaughter." I smiled at him.

"Great, come sit here," he said, telling Chase to move and making me sit on the chair beside his bed.

Chase narrowed his eyes at his granddad's antics then grumbled something in annoyance. I stifled a giggle at Chase's expression, catching his attention. He glared at me, and I fell silent.

"Hello, I'm Joseph. David and I used to study in the same high school," he said.

"I'm Hailey." I placed my hand on his fragile ones.

He smiled, and my heart swelled looking at the happiness in his eyes. If Chase agreed to marry me because of his granddad's happiness, then the smile on his granddad's face was worth everything.

"I hope my friend didn't point his old pistol at your head to make you marry my grandson," he said, making me laugh.

"No. He didn't use any villainous tricks to convince me to marry your grandson. He left the decision to me, and I did what I felt was right to do." I glanced at Chase.

Chase stared at me, and I found myself spellbound under his intense gaze, forgetting where I was.

"Good. I must say I am very happy with both of your decisions. If his grandma were still alive, she would be ecstatic to see you both bound in a beautiful relationship," his granddad said, snapping me back to reality.

His granddad noticed how Chase was still zoned out from the conversation.

"He is a bit off, but I assure you, he could be nice when you talk about his favorite sports: soccer. If you find him sad or upset just put anything made of chocolate in front of him and let the sweetness of the dessert work its magic."

I memorized it. It was the first thing that I got to know about Chase Edwards.

"He can get upset about small things like a small kid, so you can scold him if he doesn't listen to you," his granddad said with a mischievous smile.

"Hey! Don't feed her lies."

His granddad and I laughed.

Then his granddad started to tell me embarrassing stories of Chase and his brother, Cameron. I couldn't stop myself from laughing at every story his granddad shared with me. They were hilarious.

"Now you know what to expect from your children in the future," his granddad said.

I didn't get his joke and glanced at Chase to find him blushing.

The nurse came to check on Joseph and gave him his medicine. After a few minutes, he was asleep, and we decided to leave.

$$* \quad * \quad *$$

When we came back home, Chase went straight to his room, leaving me alone in the living room. I switched on the TV and watched my favorite movie *Tangled*. The movie ended after two hours then I went to my room to freshen up and change into something comfortable.

I changed into my grey sweatpants and black dolman sleeve cold shoulder top then sat on my bed with the book that I didn't finish the night I found out that my life was a lie. The woman I tried to impress my whole life wasn't my real mother, and I was a product of my dad's affair. I stopped myself from thinking further about that night and started reading the book.

My stomach growled, and I checked the time on the wall clock to see that it was already three o'clock in the afternoon. I was hungry, and I didn't know if I should ask Chase for anything. Whenever he was around me, I felt scared and ended up doing something stupid.

I decided to go to the kitchen and find something to eat. I went downstairs and hoped that my mother-in-law wouldn't get angry with me for snooping around her kitchen without her permission.

I found some milk, cheddar cheese, a pack of macaroni, and chicken. When I was a kid, I used to help my grandma in the kitchen a lot, so I knew my way around it.

I put the pot filled with water on the stove and boiled the macaroni. I cooked the small pieces of chicken with some salt and black pepper. Then I started to prepare the sauce by melting butter in a saucepan over medium heat. I stirred in flour, salt, and pepper until it was smooth. Slowly, I poured milk into the butter-flour mixture while continuously stirring it until the mixture was smooth and bubbling. Then I added cheddar cheese to the milk mixture and stirred until the cheese was melted.

When the sauce was ready, I put the cooked macaroni and chicken pieces into the sauce then simmered it for a minute. I dished it out in the serving bowl and stared at it. It looked good, and I hoped it would taste good too.

Should I go and ask Chase if he wanted to eat?

He would probably throw the plate in my face if I disturbed him. I shook my head and dismissed the thought of asking him, but then I thought again. It is basically his house, his food, and I should ask him even if he would get mad at me.

I made my way upstairs and knocked on his door, but he didn't answer, so I twisted the doorknob and peeked inside. Chase was sitting on his bed with some papers and books spread around him. His head was bobbing up and down, and that was when I noticed, he was wearing headphones. He looked busy, and I didn't want to distract him.

Suddenly, his eyes snapped up and caught me staring at him. I gulped scared to death. He narrowed his eyes at me and removed his headphones then placed them on the bed. He got up from the bed and made his way towards me.

"What are you doing here?" he asked in a stiff voice.

"I... I came here to... uh, ask you if you want to have lunch." I stuttered.

He intimidated me, and I didn't know why. It was the first time that I was alone with a guy, and probably that was scaring me.

He frowned then glanced at the wall clock in his room, and his eyes widened.

"I am really sorry. I was busy with the assignment and forgot about lunch. Give me five minutes, and I'll order something for you," he said, looking upset.

"No."

He frowned.

"No?" he asked, scrunching his eyebrows in confusion.

I found his reaction cute.

"I have... prepared pasta. Do you want to... eat with me? If you don't, I can bring it for you here," I said, stuttering.

"No thanks. I am not hungry."

I nodded my head and went back to the kitchen sulking. I wasn't even expecting him to join me and eat with me.

I put some pasta on my plate then took a bite. It tasted good, and I was happy. After a few minutes, I heard footsteps coming down, and Chase appeared in the kitchen. I was frozen and stared at him.

He made his way to where I was sitting on the stool near the kitchen counter and sat across me. Then he glanced at the pasta and picked up the spoon. He put some of the pasta on the empty plate and then started eating it.

I was beyond shocked and forgot I was eating before he walked into the kitchen.

Oh god! What if he didn't like it?

"He will throw it on you," my mind taunted.

He didn't complain, and I relaxed a bit. We ate in silence.

"Did you make this?" he asked me, catching me off guard.

"Yes."

He stood up, and said, "It wasn't bad."

Then he left the kitchen before I could say anything to him.

It wasn't bad meant it was good. He complimented me, and it made me smile like a Cheshire cat. The smile didn't leave my face even when I was washing the plates and cleaning the kitchen.

Around six o'clock, my in-laws arrived. They were now sitting in the lounge with me.

My father-in-law smiled and asked me, "Did you meet my dad?"

"Yeah, Chase took me to meet him in the morning. He was very nice and friendly," I told him honestly.

My mother-in-law asked me, "Did you like the room? I decorated it myself."

"I loved it! Thank you so much for giving me such a beautiful room." I kissed her cheek.

She looked at me lovingly, and said, "No. You don't need to thank me, dear. You are like a daughter to me, and it was just a simple decoration."

For her, it might not be a big deal, but for me, it was very special. I was never pampered by people like this before, so least to say I was extremely happy receiving so much love. The tears brimmed in my eyes when I realized that she could be the mother figure in my life that I didn't have all these years. I could experience how it felt to be loved by people.

I looked at her and thought maybe this could be my dream family that I wished all these years to have.

[A week later]

I had been married to Chase Edwards for a week, but my life didn't change that much. Except that I didn't receive snide remarks here and there from Emily anymore.

I was in my father-in-law's study. He told me I could borrow books from his library. His study room had a large collection of romantic books, which belonged to Allison. Allison was Chase's elder sister who I had yet to meet. My father-in-law told me she took some of her favorite books with her when she got married, but there were still some here in his study.

Now that I was in the study, I realized that they were placed on the top of the shelf. I tried to reach them, but my 5"4' height made it impossible for me. I ran my eyes around the study to search for something that would give me a few inches to allow my hand to reach the top. My eyes landed on a small stool in the corner, and I dragged it to the shelf. Putting my right foot on the base of the stool, I tried to stand on it, and after a few attempts, I succeeded.

I read the titles of the books and smiled, but then I heard a creaking sound and glanced down. My face paled. The stool was about to break under my weight, and that made me nervous. I wanted to hit my head for being so stupid. I looked at the books in my hand and put them back on the shelf. Before I could get down from the stool, it broke, and I fell down on the floor.

In the process of saving myself from the fall, I scraped my hands and elbows. They started to bleed. The tears brimmed in my eyes, and that was when the door of the study opened. Chase entered looking confused.

"What's going on here?" he said, walking towards me, and I wiped my tears.

I didn't want him to see me as a kid, so I didn't tell him how I fell down, and I stopped crying like a baby.

He knelt down and looked at me suspiciously.

"What are you doing here?" he asked me.

"I was just looking for some books to read." I tried to get up and flinched at the pain in my hand.

He looked at the broken stool and then he looked back at me. He started to laugh, and I forgot about the pain, staring at his face in awe.

"You tried to reach those books by standing on the broken stool and fell down," he said, making me flustered with embarrassment.

"You are so small. You should have asked someone else instead of trying to reach them yourself. Did that stool even help you reach the books?" He offered me his hand.

I placed my hand on him, but when he tried to pull me up, I cried in pain.

He stopped pulling me and knelt back down to look at my foot.

"Are you feeling pain in your foot?" he asked me, and I nodded.

Then his eyes landed on my elbows and hands that were bleeding. He cursed under his breath then picked me up bridal style. My heart started to beat faster at the closeness of our bodies, and my face felt hot. I was numb to my body's reaction.

He put me on the study table.

"Don't move. I'll be back in a minute," he said, making his way out of the study.

After a few minutes, he came back with the first aid kit and placed it on the table beside me. He opened the first aid kit and took out the alcohol wipes, and cleaned the scrapes, and cuts then put an ointment on them.

Then he took my foot and pressed the swollen area.

"Ouch." I hissed in pain.

"It's not broken. You might have twisted it when you fell down," he said then pulled out a nude color sock.

"What's that?"

He rolled his eyes at my question.

I was wearing a skirt, so he moved it up to my knee easily then pushed the sock on my swollen foot.

"This is a compression sock. Wear it for a day or two, and it will help reduce the pain," he said, patting my knee.

I felt shivers where he touched my skin.

I smiled at him, and he stared at me with the same intensity. Everything froze around us, and we stared into each other's eyes. My heartbeat accelerated. Our faces were getting closer.

Suddenly, his cell phone rang, and he pulled it out from his pocket.

"Yeah, I'm coming out in a second," he said on the phone

My smile vanished when I realized he was leaving. I wanted to spend some time with him.

Chase didn't leave right away. He remembered about the books. Without any support from the broken stool, he picked the books from the top of the shelf then placed them on my lap.

"You better not try something like this again. You might end up hurting yourself badly. Take a rest if you want to start walking on your foot again," he said before leaving the study.

I was just staring at him in daze and confusion. He helped me, and in his own way told me to take care of myself.

It made me happy. The care he showed a few seconds ago messed up my heart, and I wanted to hear the same care in his voice again.

His smile was contagious. I wanted to see him smile more around me.

Chapter Six

Pain of Losing a Loved One

Hailey

It had been a week of living with the Edwards. Everyone in the house had been very nice and friendly with me except Kate. Kate was Chase's twin sister. She always gave me death glares, which scared the hell out of me. She made snide remarks about my appearance and clothing. For me, she was like a second version of Emily.

Every morning I would wake up at eight so I could see Chase before he left for his classes. I hurriedly got ready and went downstairs to the kitchen to give my mother-in-law, Eva, a helping hand.

When I reached the kitchen, she was almost done preparing breakfast. I asked her if she wanted me to set the table and she nodded with a small smile.

I took the coffee tray from her hands and put them on the table.

It had become my routine to help Eva in the kitchen while she prepared breakfast for everyone.

I picked the coffee cups and placed them on everyone's side of the table. Kate liked to drink orange juice during breakfast. Everyone took their seats at the dining table.

"Good morning," I said with a small smile.

My father-in-law replied. "Good morning, dear."

"Good morning," Chase said, and I smiled then put the plate of toast and cheese omelet in front of him

Kate didn't reply to me. Sighing, I picked the bowl of cereal and put some milk in it then started eating.

We all ate in silence. After breakfast, my father-in-law left for the office. Chase and Kate went to their rooms to get ready.

I was cleaning the table when they appeared, ready to leave.

Kate was wearing black jeans with a white crop top and knee-length black boots. Her straight brown hair was left open, and her face was flawless as always. There was a black bag dangling on her shoulder while she was busy talking to someone on the phone.

Then my eyes moved to Chase. He was wearing a dark blue fitted shirt with blue jeans. His face was perfect, clean, and handsome. His brown hair was a mess, making him look like he had just rolled out of bed. The sneakers he was wearing were black with some white logo on it, a simple black bag hung over his left shoulder.

My mother-in-law told me that Chase and Kate were both studying in NYU. Kate was studying fashion design while Chase was studying business and it happened to be his last year, more like there was three months left before his graduation.

They both said goodbye and left in a hurry as they were getting late for their classes.

After cleaning the kitchen, I went to the backyard, which was kind of a small decorated garden. It was the part of the house that I often went to. I loved reading in the peaceful and calm atmosphere it offered.

I took the empty chair in the corner and sat down on it. When I opened the book, I found myself lost in the story.

The book I was reading didn't belong to me. It was Chase's elder sister's book. She didn't live in this house with us because she was already twenty-eight years old, happily married, and had two beautiful kids.

It was evening when I finished reading, so I got up from the chair and made my way inside the house. My mother-in-law was watching TV, and when she saw me, she asked me to join her. I didn't tell her that I was tired and wanted to rest instead I sat down beside her.

After one hour of watching her favorite show, she asked me to help her in the kitchen, and I did without complaining. She told me that Amy, her maid, was on leave because her cousin died and she will be back soon.

When dinner was ready, I excused myself and went to my room. I took a shower then blow-dried my hair. I took out my blue jeans and red full sleeved top from the closet and changed into it. Then I went downstairs and heard the doorbell. I opened the door and found Chase and Kate standing there.

I took a step back and opened the door wider, making room for them.

"Hi," I said and tugged a strand of hair behind my ear.

Kate entered first, purposefully hitting my shoulder with her bag and making me stumble back, but Chase's arm circled around my waist and stopped me from falling.

I stared into his beautiful grey eyes. They were simply magnificent.

"Sorry," Chase said, removing his arm and helping me to gain my balance back.

"It's okay," I mumbled.

I shut the door then we made our way to the kitchen.

"Hi," Chase said, planting a kiss on his mom's cheek.

"Hi. Go freshen up and come downstairs before the food gets cold."

He nodded and went to his room.

Chase came downstairs changed in a fresh set of clothes. He told his mom that his dad called and said he couldn't join us tonight for dinner.

When I was done setting the table, all of us took our seats and started eating. We were almost done eating when Chase's cell phone rang loudly.

He picked up his cellphone and said, "Hello, Dad."

Suddenly, he was up from his chair and mumbled a hasty "okay" before ending the call.

"Mom we need to go to the hospital. Granddad needs us," he said, looking scared and upset.

I started to worry about him, but I couldn't do anything more than stare at them. In a few minutes, he and his mom left for the hospital, leaving Kate and me alone in the house. Kate and I waited for them to come home, but they didn't come back.

After hours of waiting, Kate was sleepy and went to her room while I stayed in the living room, waiting for them to come back. At some point, while waiting, I must have dozed off because when I woke up, it was midnight. I heard the noise of someone entering the house and sat up on the couch. I rubbed my eyes to see clearly and found Chase staring at me with a dazed look on his face.

"Why are you sleeping in the living room?" he asked me.

"I was waiting for you to come back."

He looked taken aback at my response.

"I am going to my room. Mom and Dad need some time alone so they might come home late tonight. You should go to your room and sleep there," he said, making his way upstairs.

I nodded my head, but I wanted to know what happened.

"How is your granddad?" I asked him.

"He is gone. He left me." His voice sounded hollow.

I was shocked and looked up at him, but I found him standing on the stairs, making his way to his room. I wanted to go after him and comfort him. I wanted to tell him that everything would be alright, but I knew he needed some time alone.

After doing my night routine, I changed into my nightshirt and pajamas then went to my bed. I fell asleep thinking about Chase and what he must be feeling at the loss of his grandfather.

The dream started with me standing in the middle of a beautiful garden. It looked familiar, but I couldn't remember where I had seen this place. Then my eyes caught a silhouette standing behind the tree, hiding someone from my view.

I took a step forward and looked closely to see my dead grandma standing there. I stepped faster towards her, but she started running away from me, making me follow her deep into the forest. I followed her into the deep woods, but some kind of force pushed me down on the sticky mud of the forest. Then I heard the ear-piercing scream of a woman, and my eyes snapped open.

I was breathing hard and looked around the room, taking in my surroundings. I was in my room, not in any woods, but my body was trembling with shock.

"It was just a dream, Hailey. Just a dream!" I repeated the same words in my head hundreds of times to calm myself.

I pulled off the quilt from my body and got up from the bed. My throat felt dry, so I looked for a water bottle and found it sitting empty on my bedside table. I groaned in frustration because now, I had to go downstairs to get some water.

Opening my bedroom door, I made my way out of the room but stopped dead in my tracks when I heard weird noises. I followed the noise, and they took me to Chase's bedroom. I twisted the doorknob and entered his room to see him standing on the balcony dressed in shorts.

He didn't notice me, and I stared at his bare muscled back in astonishment. I had never seen a barely dressed man before if you don't count the time when I accidentally entered my cousin's room, and he was lying on his bed only in shorts, but he was eight years old. I guess he was more embarrassed after the incident.

My eyes followed his strong biceps but the sight of him turning around and repeatedly throwing punches at the black bag hanging in the middle of his balcony disrupted my train of thought.

The expression on his face was murderous as he threw punch after punch. I noticed the rigidness and tightness of his muscles. My eyes moved from his arms to his hands and widened in horror.

Bloody hell! He was BLEEDING!

Without thinking twice, I rushed to his side and placed my hand on his biceps making him freeze under the touch of my extremely cold hands.

"Chase, please stop." I pleaded him, staring into his angry eyes.

His body relaxed, allowing me to assess the injury of his hand. I felt sick to my stomach when my eyes caught a large slit in the middle of his palm, bleeding. My hands started to shake, but I pretended to be calm. His right hand was heavily bruised, bloody, and swollen.

I didn't know where he got that slash from, but my question was answered when I saw a broken vase on the floor on the left side of his bed. I dragged him to the right side of his bed and forced him to sit. Then I went downstairs to search for the first aid kit, and when I found it in one of the cabinets, I ran back to his room.

I knelt down on the floor and took his hand in mine then cleaned it with some wet towels that I fetched from his washroom. Then I poured some alcohol on the cut. Chase hissed in pain. I felt the tears brimming in my own eyes but I held them back. I applied the ointment on his cuts and wrapped the bandage around them. My horrible past taught me how to patch up cuts.

I looked up at his face. His face was free from any sort of emotion except pain. My heart was crying for him, and I wanted to do something to make him forget all the pain. I hugged him, and he stiffened in my arms. I waited for him to feel some comfort, but his body was still rigid like a statue. I pulled away from him and got up to leave the room when he stopped me.

He hugged my waist, snuggling his face into my stomach and that was when I felt him shaking and crying. The tears I was holding back started to spill out. My hands went to his head, and I ran my fingers through his hair to calm him down.

I didn't know how long I stayed still and let him cry while holding on to my waist. He was like a little kid who didn't want to let go. After some time I found myself stepping away from him and pushing him on the bed.

When he was lying on the bed, I pulled the quilt on his body and sat beside him.

"Chase, go to sleep," I mumbled, making him close his eyes.

"Don't go."

I sat beside him and pulled the quilt over my body. He placed his head on my lap and closed his eyes. My hand was shaking, but I took the risk and started running my fingers through his soft hair. He said nothing to stop me, silently crying on my lap.

Later, he fell asleep while I stayed awake. When I was sure, he was in a deep sleep I removed his head from my lap and placed it on the pillow then I slipped out from the bed.

I was not sure why I did that, but I placed a soft kiss on his forehead.

"The pain will go away with time. You just need to be strong. And I know you are really strong." I mumbled.

Picking up the broken pieces of the vase, I dumped them in the trash can and cleaned the floor so he wouldn't get hurt because of the broken vase when he woke up in the morning.

I didn't see him as a wimp for crying in pain over his granddad's death. I felt like he trusted me enough to show me his honest emotions, and it was his way of giving me a chance to be with him when he was in such a fragile state.

I knew very well how it felt when someone you loved left you.

I was glad that he allowed himself to break down in front of me because keeping all these emotions pent up in his heart would make him miserable, just like it did to me.

Chapter Seven

No, You're Not Alone

Hailey

I woke up in the morning and remembered how Chase broke down in front of me last night. Getting inside the washroom, I hurriedly showered then changed into my black trousers and white top.

I went downstairs and saw my mother-in-law working in the kitchen.

"Good morning," I said to her.

"Good morning, dear."

I looked around and saw a bowl of cereal and glass of juice in the tray.

My mother-in-law saw me staring and asked, "Hailey, dear, do you want to eat cereal?"

"No, I was just looking," I said.

"Oh, this breakfast is for Chase. He has a fever, and he can't come down for breakfast, today."

I instantly became worried. I wanted to go to his room, and check how he was, but then he might not want to see me after last night.

"I'm taking this tray to Chase's room. Please turn off the stove for me," she said, and I nodded.

If I went to see him with the breakfast, there would be fewer chances of him getting angry with me.

"Eva, I can't find the file that I put on the bedside table yesterday. Did you put it somewhere?" My father-in-law yelled from his room.

My mother-in-law rolled her eyes and handed me the tray.

"Hailey, please take this to Chase's room and make sure he eats everything," my mother-in-law said, walking to her room.

I stared at her retracting figure and the tray in my hand. After turning off the stove, I made my way upstairs to Chase's room.

I knocked twice, but when he didn't open the door, I twisted the knob and went inside to find him asleep on the bed.

Should I go back downstairs and tell her that he was asleep or wake him up?

I walked closer and placed the tray on the bedside table then put a hand on Chase's shoulder to wake him up.

When my hand came in contact with his skin, I realized he was burning.

I searched the medical box and found some Advil. I put them on the tray and shook Chase's shoulder. He groaned and grabbed my hand.

"Chase, wake up," I whispered.

He opened his eyes and looked at me.

"Hailey, what are you doing here?" he asked me, closing his eyes.

"I brought breakfast and medicine for you."

He groaned and turned his back to me.

"Chase, you have fever. You need to take your medicine. Please, wake up," I said, making him turn back to me.

He glared at me then sat up on the bed. The quilt that was covering his body fell around his waist, and that was when I remembered that he was shirtless.

Did I blush?

Yes, I did.

"Has anyone ever told you how annoying you are?" he said.

"Many people told me I'm annoying, awkward, and silly."

He shook his head at me and rubbed his hands on his face in irritation then glared at me.

"You are stupid too," he said with a roll of his eyes.

I didn't know what I should say to him when he seemed so cranky.

"Umm, breakfast," I said, picking up the tray and placing it on his lap.

He looked at his hands that were wrapped with a bandage, and I averted my eyes. I hoped he didn't remember anything about last night.

He picked up the spoon and started eating, but after a few minutes, he pushed the tray away.

"You need to finish it," I said.

His jaw clenched in pain when he tried to pick the spoon again. Taking the spoon in my hand, I put it near his mouth. He looked irritated, but let me feed him silently.

When he was done eating, I put the two tablets of Advil in his palm, and he gulped them down with a glass of juice.

I was ready to leave when he took hold of my wrist and pulled me back to the bed.

"You're stupid if you believe people when they say you're annoying, awkward, and silly," he said.

I froze. His face was so close to mine.

"Then who should I believe?" I asked him.

"Ask that question to yourself, and you will know the answer."

I nodded my head and got up. My heart was beating frantically, glancing one last time at his face; I flew out of his room and went straight to my room.

My heart was still racing, and I shut my eyes to calm myself.

[Two days later]

It was the funeral of his granddad. He seemed sad and silent all day.

We went home after the burial, and the visitors had been coming for support and comfort. Everyone looked sad over the death of Mr. Joseph Edwards. I heard that he was a great husband, dad, and granddad for his grandchildren. People loved him and respected him with their hearts.

My eyes went to Chase. He was sitting alone in the backyard on the bench. I handed the cup of tea to Amy, our housekeeper, and made my way out to the backyard. I sat beside Chase on the bench, and he blinked back his tears.

"Everything is going to be alright," I said.

He stayed silent for a few minutes.

"I don't know how to accept that my granddad wouldn't be here for me anymore," he said.

I felt the tears brimming in my eyes, but I held them back.

"When my grandma died, I thought there will be no one for me anymore. I will be forever alone, but am I alone, Chase? I have my dad, your parents, and you," I said to him.

He placed his hand over mine and squeezed it, lightly.

He didn't say anything, but his small gesture warmed my heart, and we stayed in the backyard with our hands intertwined until the evening approached.

When the stars appeared in the sky, I said, "Do you know when someone dies they become a star?"

"I don't believe that." He looked at me like I was lying to him.

"I do believe that the good people become stars after death," I said. "Look, that's my grandma on the left and the center one is your granddad. On the right of your granddad is your grandma and that shiny star on the far right is my mom," I said with a smile.

He looked at me in confusion.

"Your mom is alive, Hailey," he said, and my heart dropped.

No one knew that Melanie was my stepmom.

Should I tell him the truth?

"Melanie is my stepmom," I told him.

His eyes widened, and he stared at me in shock.

"What? But I thought she was your real mother," he said.

"My whole life I didn't know that she was my stepmom. But one night, I found out that my real mother died giving birth to me. Emily and I are half-sisters."

"I didn't know that." Chase looked at me with a frown.

"I didn't share it with anyone because I don't want people to pity me," I said, hiding my face with my hair.

"I'm sorry about your mom." Chase lightly squeezed my hand.

"I don't even know if I look like her or my dad."

"I think you look like your mom because your dad has a beard and silver hair while you have smooth skin and brown curly hair," Chase said.

I laughed at his logic, and he smiled at me.

We both looked up at the stars, and they shone brighter tonight.

[Two weeks later]

After two weeks, the atmosphere in the house was still mournful. I didn't get the opportunity to spend time with Joseph, but I was sad and hurt by his death. His death had triggered my old nightmares again. They were even more horrible now, keeping me awake every night, or if I fell asleep, they would come back to haunt me again. I hadn't been getting any sleep because of these terrible nightmares.

Chase and my father-in-law looked a lot better now. Both of them were the most affected by the news of Joseph's death as both men were close to him. He loved all his grandchildren, but Chase had spent a lot of time with him and had a great bond with him.

I looked up at myself in the mirror and saw dark circles under my eyes. Lack of sleep showed on my face. I felt fatigue because of not getting any sleep from the past week. I walked to my bed and slumped down on it then picked up a book. I decided to keep reading the book all night to stay awake. To avoid getting horrible dreams, I had been trying different tricks to stay awake.

Back home, whenever I got these nightmares, my father would buy me the prescribed medicine that helped me sleep. I stopped taking my medicines and antidepressants since last year because of the improvement of my condition.

Now that I had started getting these horrible nightmares again, I needed them to go back to sleep. I remembered the name of the medicines that I should be taking, but I didn't bring the prescription with me and without that the pharmacy wouldn't allow me to buy those medicines.

And if I would ask anyone in the house to give me a sleeping pill, they would ask me questions like why I needed them to sleep. I would be forced to tell them the truth, and they might send me back to my dad. If I went back to my dad, mom and Emily would kill me this time for meddling in their family.

I shivered thinking about Emily and Mom, and their hateful glares if I ever went back to their house.

Somewhere in between reading the book and thinking about not falling into sleep, I closed my eyes, and I was instantly asleep.

This dream started differently from my last dream. I saw the chapel where I got married to Chase, but this time he was holding me close with a beautiful smile on his face when he leaned down and mumbled something in my ear, which made me smile.

I looked happy, and the guests were staring at us with smiles when suddenly there was a loud scream. I turned my head to look at Chase and realized that he had vanished. The place where he was standing now had a puddle of blood. My eyes went to my wedding dress, which was stained with blood too, and that was when I screamed loudly.

I was harshly pulled out from the dream when I felt someone shaking me violently. I opened my eyes and blinked a few times to remove the blurriness. I felt someone wiping my tears from my face, and I opened my eyes to find Chase crouching near my bed. His eyes were fixed on me while his right hand was resting on my cheek. He looked worried and tired.

"Hailey are you alright?" he asked me softly, making me close my eyes in bliss.

I was glad that he was perfectly fine and with me in my room.

What?

Without thinking much, I pushed the quilt from my body and threw my arms around his neck, making him fall onto his back on the floor with me on top of him. He was too shocked at my reaction to say and do anything. Even I was shocked at my own actions, but seeing him alive and healthy made me so happy that I couldn't stop myself from throwing my arms around his neck to hug him.

We were in a really awkward position. My legs were tangled with his while my head was resting on his chest. His chest was really comforting and bare. Oh, God! I didn't notice that he wasn't wearing a shirt before I threw myself on him.

My face started to heat up, and my eyes moved from his chest to his face that was still frozen in shock. I pulled away from him with lightning speed, and he sat up on the floor with a dazed look on his face.

Did he hit his head on the floor?

I felt so embarrassed with my stupid actions and took a shy glance at his face, but my traitorous eyes fell on his chiseled chest again, making me blush. It looked hard and sculptured, but when I hugged him, he felt so soft.

With the reminder of feeling his skin under my palm, I felt tingles in my hands.

My eyes went to my alarm clock on my bedside table, and I frowned.

What was he doing in my room at three in the morning?

But did I question him? No, I didn't because somewhere in my mind I was still scared of getting scolded by him. I hated it when he scolded me. But I loved it when he smiled at me, which happened rarely.

Chase said something I didn't hear because my eyes were stuck on his lips. They were so pink and beautiful. The upper lip was thin, and the lower one was plump.

"Hailey are you okay?" he asked me in his husky voice, snapping me out from studying the structure of his lips.

I nodded my head dumbly.

Chase looked hesitant but asked me, "Why were you screaming and crying in your sleep?"

My eyes widened at the mention of my screams. It meant that he was here in the middle of the night because of my screams.

"Did you wake up because of my screams?" I asked him.

"No, I was awake, working on an assignment then I heard you screaming and came here to check on you," he replied.

"Oh. It was just a bad dream, nothing to worry about," I said, getting up from the floor.

A frown appeared on his face, and he looked unconvinced.

"Do you want to talk about it?" he asked me.

I felt something warm spreading in my heart at his soft, concerned voice making me want to hug him again, but I refrained myself from doing anything stupid again.

I shook my head and said, "No. I am fine now. Thanks for waking me up."

He opened his mouth then closed it. It was like he wanted to question me further, but stopped himself from prying.

"Good night," he mumbled and left the bedroom.

After that, I didn't dare fall asleep and stayed awake all night.

When it was eight in the morning, I got ready for the day and went downstairs.

On the breakfast table, Chase kept glancing at me weirdly, which made me extremely uncomfortable during the entire breakfast. I felt like I had something on my face, which he wanted to clean. It was weird.

After the breakfast, he left for college with Kate. My boring day started with me doing my usual tasks.

My father-in-law asked me if I wanted to continue college, but I told him that I didn't want to go to college. In reality, I still had to finish high school before I would be eligible to join college. I had to lie to them about my age, my education, and my past.

I was never weak in my studies and never got bad grades in any subject. When I was at school, my teachers were happy with me. But they never realized what happened during lunchtime. They didn't know how Emily's evil friends waited for me in the washroom to beat me because that was where I used to hide to save myself from their abuse.

I shook my head to escape from all the horrible memories of my past that still lingered in my mind.

*   *   *

After dinner, my father-in-law called me into his study and told me that I needed to continue my studies this coming semester, which would start after three months. He told me he would support me and wanted me to study further. I didn't know how to tell them the truth and how they would react.

I wanted to tell him that I couldn't do what he wanted me to do, but at that moment, I had no choice other than to nod my head.

Around 10:30 pm everyone went to their respective rooms to sleep. And like last night I stayed awake in my room, reading a book. When I started to feel sleepy, I quickly got up and went to the washroom. I splashed cold water a few times on my face to get rid of the sleepiness.

Then a thought struck me. Caffeine helped to prevent sleep, and it meant I should try drinking coffee. It might be more effective than these methods.

Slowly, I opened my bedroom door, tiptoed downstairs, and entered the kitchen.

Pulling out the coffee beans from the cabinet, I started preparing coffee for myself. When the coffee was made, I poured it into a large cup and turned around to see a shadow near the wall. I wanted to scream and run back to my room, but I stayed frozen with the coffee cup in my trembling hands.

The shadow moved closer, and my heart jumped in my chest like a bloody basketball. I closed my eyes, scared to death.

"Relax Hailey. I didn't mean to scare you," Chase said.

I opened my eyes and stared at Chase in confusion.

He glanced at the coffee cup in my hand.

"You're drinking coffee at this time," he said in confusion.

I didn't know what to tell him, so I stayed quiet.

He took a deep breath and said, "I know you have been having horrible nightmares since last week. Last night, your scream was louder than any other nights, and I had to wake you up."

I was shocked at his words.

"How do you know this?" I asked him.

"Actually, I have been working on my assignment every night for the past few days. That's why I heard you screaming and came to your room the other day to wake you up," he explained.

I did not only wake him up the previous day, but I had also been disturbing him every night for the whole week. I felt ashamed and guilty for disturbing him.

He startled me by taking the coffee cup from my hand. Then he laced his fingers with mine and dragged me upstairs to his room. I didn't know why he was taking me to his room. When we were inside his room, he placed the coffee cup on his bedside table and turned to me.

I thought he would lecture me to stop disturbing him every night, so before he could start, I said, "I just... ah, I am sorry for disturbing you every night. They are just stupid nightmares, appearing every night. I was... ah, trying to stay awake to avoid them. I am really sorry. Please, don't get angry at me for this."

I felt like crying at the end of the statement. I didn't know why I embarrassed myself in front of him every time. I stared at the floor waiting for him to get angry with me, but he surprised me by putting his fingers under my chin and making me look up.

"I am not angry with you, Hailey. I want to help you get rid of these nightmares," he said softly.

Butterflies erupted inside my stomach at his words, creating a fuzzy feeling. He cared for me. My husband, who I thought would hate me forever for coming into his life unwelcomed, actually cared for me and wanted to help me in chasing away my nightmares.

"The nightmares are really horrible that's why you are resisting sleep," he said.

I nodded my head and stared at him. I felt something different in my heart for the first time. I didn't feel scared of him. I felt like I wanted to hug him and thank him for his concern for me. I felt special.

Tonight something changed in me.

"I have something to help you," he said, walking back to his bedside drawer and pulling out a small box.

I looked at him curiously.

"Come closer," he asked me, and I did.

There was a beautiful long chain in the box. He picked it up, and I saw a shiny purple stone locket dangling in the middle.

I stared at it in bewilderment.

"When I was five years old, my grandma gave me this chain because I used to feel scared at night and couldn't sleep alone. She told me that she will keep an eye on me through this stone and protect me. I wore that necklace every night and stopped feeling scared. She knew the stone had no power to scare away my nightmares, but it was a belief that my grandma put in my head that she was looking after me while I sleep at night. I kept this locket with me even after I stopped feeling scared because it's a special gift for me. Now it's yours," he said, pulling the chain over my head and letting the pendant rest in the center of my chest.

My emotions were flying everywhere after what he shared with me. I still couldn't believe that he had given me something that was so special to him. I touched the purple stone and looked up at him to see a smile on his face.

I thought I fell in love with him at that moment. I fell in love with the purity of his heart, with his beautiful smile, with his kind and caring nature, and obviously with his handsome face.

I tried stopping myself from throwing my arms around him, but I failed and hugged him tightly. My hands were wrapped around his waist, and my head was resting on his chest above his heart. The rhythmic sound of his breathing felt music to my ears. I wasn't expecting him to hug me back, but he put his arms around my shoulders and hugged me.

After a few minutes, we pulled away from each other. There was an awkward silence between us, and a broad smile was etched on our faces.

"Thank you for giving me something so special," I said, touching the stone pendant.

He moved forward then kissed my head. I looked up at him in shock then turned back and left his room before my heart could melt.

When I entered my room, I closed the door and slid down on the floor with my back still pressed on the door. I smiled and pressed my hand to my mouth before I would erupt into giggles or shouted to the world that I loved Chase Edwards.

After that night, I was sure that I would sleep well, but I didn't know that the reason would be my new dreams.

Chapter Eight

Welcoming Cameron

Hailey

The house was in chaos since morning because Cameron would be coming back today from his boarding school.

Cameron was Chase's younger brother, and he lived in a boarding school in Grand Forks, North Dakota. He was in the middle of his midterm examination when his granddad died, and because of that, he didn't come home to attend the funeral. I heard that he was really sad when he heard the news about his grandfather's death and wanted to come home for his funeral, but his school administrator didn't grant him permission to come home.

Now that his examinations had ended, he was coming back home for a month long vacation.

I did not meet him before, so I didn't know much about him, but what I heard from my mother-in-law was that he was quite immature and a prankster.

She also told me that Chase and Cameron were not very close. I heard when they were all kids Kate used to hurt him so he wouldn't play with Chase. I thought the twin bond between Chase and Kate didn't let anyone come close to both of them. They were inseparable as kids.

My mother-in-law had requested me to bake lemon tarts because it was Cameron's favorite dessert. I was quite good at baking, and the credit for that went to my grandma. Amy helped me in the kitchen, but she had other chores to do so she left. I was left alone waiting for the tarts to bake.

The alarm beeped indicating that the lemon tarts were done baking. I slipped my pink baking mittens on and pulled out the tray from inside the oven then set it on the counter to let it cool.

I would have baked chocolate chip cupcakes today if my mother-in-law hadn't requested me to bake lemon tarts. Actually, chocolate chip cupcakes were Chase's favorite, and I loved baking them for him. I remembered his granddad told me how much Chase liked everything with chocolate, so I started baking chocolate chip cupcakes.

Last week, I served some cupcakes during breakfast. He didn't know who made them and thought it was from some bakery. He kept eating them while saying how good they tasted.

I felt giddy when I heard his praises. So it had become kind of a daily routine for me to bake chocolate cupcakes for him. I had noticed whenever Chase found cupcakes during breakfast, his eyes turned alive, and his face morphed into happiness.

I was daydreaming again about Chase and his beautiful smile when the sudden noise of someone clearing his throat startled me, causing me to jump. My hands slipped and landed on the hot tray. I hissed in pain and looked up to see the culprit who caused me this stupid burn, but I found myself frozen on the spot. Someone was standing in front of me with a gun in his hand targeted on my head. His face was covered with a black cloth except for his pretty blue eyes and brown hair.

At that moment, I was scared out of my wits.

I panicked and looked around the kitchen in the hope of finding something to scare the guy, but to my utter luck, I didn't find a single thing, not even a butter knife to stab him in the eye.

He suddenly moved closer to me, scaring me more.

"Don't come close or I will…" I searched my brain for a good threat that will scare him off.

"You'll what?" he asked me, sounding amused.

"I'll throw this hot lemon tart on your face." I inched my hand near the lemon tart.

"You are so cruel, but you have a very innocent face. Do you use this innocent face to deceive people?" the stranger asked, walking closer to me.

I kept my mouth shut because clearly my threat didn't affect him and my words would only amuse him.

"And for your information lemon tart is my favorite," the guy said, looking at the lemon tart then glancing back at me.

"Not extremely hot, I guess? Do you want to taste it hot this time? It will burn your mouth," I said sarcastically.

I was never sarcastic, but today it came naturally.

"I would love to taste it if you promise to feed it yourself in my pretty mouth," the stranger said, taking another step closer and blocking my way so I couldn't run out of the kitchen.

"Stop there."

He rolled his eyes at me and took my hand where it was burned. The small red mark was clear. He traced his finger on it, making me hiss in pain.

Before I could shout for help, he asked me, "Who are you?"

I was baffled at his question, I had been living here for months, and he was asking me who I was.

"Well, are you not going to answer me?" he asked me.

Instead of answering him, I glared at him in anger and encouraged myself to give him a piece of my mind when he rudely interrupted me by placing his finger on my lips.

His thumb ran over my lower lip making me shudder while his eyes pierced through mine.

"How sad, a pretty girl like you is going to die today," he said, pointing the gun at the center of my forehead.

I closed my eyes ready to meet my maker. After facing so much in life, this was how I was going to die because of some stupid burglar who entered the house and wanted to get rid of me.

If I died today, I would regret not telling Chase how much I loved him and wanted to spend my life with him. The only good in this situation was that maybe after all this time I would finally be free from all the pain and could meet my mother in another world.

I waited for the pain, but the pain of getting shot in the head never came, and I opened my eyes. My breath hitched when my eyes landed on the brown haired blue-eyed boy. He was standing so close to me, and his face was so near that I could clearly see his long lashes and plump lips. The mask that was hiding his face was now ripped off. His eyes flickered from my eyes to my lips for a millisecond, and I sucked in a breath.

Suddenly, the realization dawned on me that this boy was not a burglar, but Cameron.

"Cameron?" I said his name.

"Oh, God! Your face was priceless," he mumbled and started laughing.

The first thought that came to my mind was this boy didn't know how to make a first impression. From now on I was going to dislike him for lessening ten years of my life by scaring me to death.

Then an awesome plan formed in my head to get my revenge on him for his stupid prank. I started to pretend that I was crying because what he did has scared me. It was my first time to fake crying, but I just had to imagine the most emotional scene of my book and that brought tears to my eyes, automatically.

Now I had his complete attention. He was looking at me in complete panic.

"Hey, are you alright? Why are you crying?" he asked me.

I didn't answer him and continued fake crying some more. The tears did the trick, and he started rambling, "It was just a prank, a joke. I'm not going to harm you. Please, stop crying. I'm sorry. Just stop crying, pretty girl."

Cameron looked quite ready to beg me if I continued my act. Before I could tell him that it was only a joke, he hugged me, and I was not expecting a hug.

I turned frozen due to shock. Well, if it helped you to understand my situation better then let me inform you that I had never received a hug from anybody except obviously Chase, which happened just two weeks ago and I was still getting used to everything.

After a few seconds, he pulled away, and I started laughing. Now he was the one who had a priceless face. The confusion was clear on his face. He looked shocked and realized what I just did with him.

He smiled in amusement while my laughter turned into giggles. And that was when his mother entered the kitchen and squealed with happiness at the sight of her son.

She hugged him and dragged him out of the kitchen into the lounge where Chase and Kate were playing a video game. Hearing the commotion, my father-in-law also came out from his study and hugged his son. I was just watching the family reunion with a satisfied smile on my face.

Everyone in the family hugged him and asked him a few questions, which he answered with a smile.

Then he turned to his mom and said, "Mom, you didn't introduce me to this beautiful girl."

My face exploded with a blush at his compliment because no one had ever called me beautiful, not even Chase.

Suddenly everyone was silent and was looking at him.

"Cameron, I told you that we have a new family member in our family," my mother-in-law said.

"Yeah mom, you said something like that, so who is she?" He was frowning this time.

"Cameron, actually Chase got married a few months ago. She is Hailey, your brother's wife," my mother-in-law said with the smile.

He stared at me in complete shock and then glanced at Chase. Chase clenched his jaw in anger like his mother just insulted him by reminding him of the marriage. Cameron, on the other hand, looked hurt, maybe I imagined it.

Cameron then smiled, and said, "I guess congratulations to both of you. Hailey, it is nice meeting you," he said, staring at me.

I nodded my head and mumbled, "Thank you."

With that said, he went upstairs to his room.

Chapter Nine

Getting Ready For My First Party

Hailey

I was staring at the TV and remembered the month Cameron and I spent exploring New York. For the whole month, Cameron and I were inseparable. He became my best friend, and I was given a chance to experience something I had never experienced before: friendship.

Every day, he would take me out to see new places. The first day, we went to Central Park then we ate dinner in Cameron's favorite fast food place. The second day, he took me to The Empire State Building, which was beautiful. Another day, we went to Manhattan Skyline, and that was how I spent the whole month with him and experienced new things in the world.

The last day of his stay here was eventful. He took me to see the Top of the Rock, and we stayed there until sunset. Around eight o'clock we had dinner in a nice restaurant.

I still remembered what happened that day when I came back.

[Flashback]

I entered the house with a silly smile on my face because of Cameron's stupid joke. I never felt so happy in my life, and no one ever attempted to make me happy, but Cameron did, and it meant the world to me.

I was going upstairs to my room when I felt a presence behind me. I turned around and found Chase looking at me with anger. He took a step forward, and I took a step back from him. It went on until my back was plastered to the wall. He took that as his advantage then trapped me there, by placing both of his hands on each side of the wall.

"I've noticed how you've been spending a lot of time with my brother," he said, sounding bitter.

I felt my heart pounding at the nearness of our bodies. I could feel his breath fanning my face. He looked angry and jealous.

"I... I went to see the Top of the Rock then..." I said, stopping in the middle of my narrative.

"What Hailey?" He gritted his teeth.

"Then we had dinner," I said, waiting for his response.

"From now on, you will not go with him anywhere, especially not on dinners." He stared into my eyes.

I nodded unable to speak under his commanding gaze. He was scaring me, and I hated that I felt scared of him.

"Answer me," he said.

"I w-will not go anywhere with Cameron," I stuttered.

"Good," he said, staring into my eyes.

I was waiting for him to step back and leave but he kept staring at me. I didn't know what came over me and why I did what I did, but I kissed his cheek.

Chase's eyes widened, and I was ready to melt in shame at my brazenness.

"I'm sorry for going to dinner with Cameron. I didn't know it will make you angry," I blurted out while Chase was still staring at me with wide eyes.

Chase took a step back from me and looked around like he was expecting someone to come out and tell him it was a prank.

"No, I... I'm not angry at you. I just don't like... it when you both go out," he said, putting his hand over his mouth.

I stared at him in confusion. Why didn't he like it when Cameron and I went out? My mother-in-law told me that Cameron and Chase were not a fan of each other, but I didn't know Chase would react so mean towards his brother.

Cameron was such a sweet soul.

Chase took a step back from me and left me. I shook my head then went to my room.

*　　　*　　　*

From that day until today he had been ignoring me like I had some contagious disease. I didn't mind if he ignored me, but he had been playing with my heart. He would smile at me one minute and would glare at me the next.

"Hailey, can you take this hot chocolate to Chase's room. My poor baby has been studying all day for his upcoming exams." My mother-in-law handed me a mug. "Good night," she said, patting my shoulder and leaving me in the kitchen with the mug in my hand.

I wanted to tell her that she should take this hot chocolate to her son's room because he had been ignoring me and I had been avoiding him after the embarrassing incident, but I stayed silent.

Sighing, I went upstairs to his room and knocked on his door, but he didn't open it. I was ready to go back down when he opened the door.

His hair was tousled, and his grey eyes were sleepy. He was standing shirtless in front of me, dressed only in his dark blue pajamas. Suddenly, my throat went dry, and my hands started shaking.

He looked baffled to find me standing outside his bedroom at ten in the evening.

"Hot... hot chocolate," I said, offering him a mug.

He looked at it but didn't take it.

"Put it on my bedside table," he said, stepping away from the door.

I nodded my head and entered his room then placed the mug on his bedside table.

My eyes went to his messy bed where few books, sheets, and pens were scattered around. I glanced at Chase who was yawning. He looked too sleepy to clean his bed himself.

I turned to him and saw his eyes dropping due to sleep.

"Do you want me to make your bed?" I asked him.

"No, I will do it myself." He yawned.

"It's fine."

I removed the books, papers, and pen from his bed and placed them on the study table in his room then I arranged his pillows.

"It's done, you can sleep now," I said and turned around to find him gazing at me.

I felt uncomfortable under his intense gaze. He took a step forward, and my heart started to beat faster.

When he was standing mere inches away from me, he said, "Thank you."

I nodded my head at him, and then he did something, which left me shocked.

He placed a kiss on my left cheek, and I shut my eyes. The feeling of his soft lips on my skin made me shiver from inside. He didn't remove his lips for a few seconds letting me relish this new feeling. I felt my legs wobble and then butterflies erupted in my tummy.

When he moved away, I opened my eyes and found him staring at me with a smile on his face.

"Good… Good night," I said and escaped from his room.

When I was inside my room, I touched my face where he kissed me and smiled.

*　　*　　*

Chase

I woke up and sat on the bed then my eyes landed on the empty mug of hot chocolate that Hailey brought last night for me. I smiled thinking about her. She was so innocent and pure. Her reactions were amusing, and I loved it when she blushed. She thought I didn't notice the shy glances she threw my way, but I did. I noticed how she looked at me and took care of all the small things that I liked and disliked.

Hailey might not say that she liked me, but her actions betrayed her. I could see that she had started to develop some feelings for me and I might have started to feel something for her. I didn't know what I should call these weird feelings. When she blushed at my single glance, I liked it. And when she went out with Cameron, I hated it.

I didn't know when she made me addicted to her attention. I hated it when my parents didn't give me the attention that I needed. My mom used to keep herself busy with her friends and going out with them while leaving my other siblings and me to be looked after by maids or Granddad. My father always stayed busy in running the business deals, but he would take weekends off for the family.

My siblings and I grew up without receiving attention from our parents. Cameron turned into a rebel and gained all the attention he wanted from our parents.

But I knew as well as others that he didn't deserve the kind of attention that he gained. When they realized that they couldn't control him from becoming the person he was turning into, they sent him to boarding school.

On the other hand, I never rebelled against my parents or their rules. I tried to gain my parents' attention by being the perfect son they wanted. I had never done anything that they didn't want me to do. When I secured the seat in NYU and selected business as my major, I finally got my parents attention. My father started to ask me to accompany him to his office. I got the chance to spend time with my dad, and mom started to stay home. She realized that it was time to free Granddad from extra responsibilities and took part in the household chores.

I loved my parents. They were not bad parents, but they made thousands of mistakes while raising us. They never let me decide for myself. The day I was born they decided that I would pursue a business like my dad and granddad. They never allowed me to make my life plans. Instead, they told me what I was supposed to do with my life and what I was not supposed to do.

When my granddad told me his last wish about seeing me married, I wasn't prepared. It was new for me, something unplanned and I felt scared because somehow I had become the guy who feared the unplanned. This marriage with Hailey made me fear about my future plans, and it scared me.

What would happen if my life wouldn't go according to the plan my parents made for me?

The feelings of attachment with Hailey, enjoying her company, or getting distracted because of her were never included in the life my parents planned for me. I was supposed to graduate and take over my dad's position as CEO of Edwards Investing Company after his retirement. He was preparing me to become a man he would feel proud, and my granddad trusted me that I would make him proud like my dad did.

My mother loved me because I never did anything that she didn't want me to do. Hailey was never part of the plan, and I needed to keep it that way. I needed to stop all these silly feelings towards her. I didn't want to get distracted from the main goal of my life.

My parents' dreams were more important than my own. Hailey was nothing but a beautiful distraction, and she would destroy me if I didn't push all these feelings away.

*   *   *

Hailey

I was in my room reading when Kate barged into my room.

"Dad wants you to come downstairs," she said then left.

I went downstairs to the living room where Kate, Chase, and my in-laws were sitting.

Chase looked really angry. His jaw was clenched while he was staring at the floor. Kate glared at me like everything bad that happened in this world was my fault.

"You asked for me?"

"Yes, Hailey. We need to leave today for Chicago to attend Kate's painting exhibition tomorrow morning. She can only bring two people with her, so Eva and I have decided to go with her. We will come back tomorrow evening," my father-in-law said.

"Chase needs to attend a very important party, and we don't want you to stay alone here late at night." My mother-in-law added.

"I can manage one night alone if there are no ghosts in the basement," I said.

My in-laws looked at me then laughed loudly.

"Yes, I know you are an intelligent girl and can take care of yourself, but we think you should go with Chase to this party. It's time he introduces you to his friends as his wife," my father-in-law said.

I glanced at Chase, and he narrowed his eyes at me like telling me to say no to his dad. Instantly, I understood that he had no desire to take me with him to this party.

"I don't like parties. I will stay at home," I said.

"Sweetie, you should go to this party with Chase. It's a great chance for you to meet his friends. I'm sure Chase will take care of you and Kate will lend you a dress. I think she wouldn't mind doing your makeup." My mother-in-law smiled.

Kate eyed me from head to toe then said, "Sure, I will do her make-up and lend her my dress because I don't want my brother to feel embarrassed when he introduces her to his friends."

I had no choice but to agree to go with Chase to the party.

Kate dragged me upstairs to her room and shouted at me.

"Remove that stupid ponytail and red hairband from your head," she yelled, making me jump and remove the ponytail and hairband hurriedly.

I let my waist length hair fell down on my back and looked at her.

"I think we need to go to the salon. They will give you a haircut and do something to improve that face of yours. You're not a case I can handle alone," Kate said.

She talked on the phone for a while before dragging me downstairs. She picked up her car keys and then we went to the salon.

The salon owner, Lilly, knew Kate, so she approached us.

"Hello, dear," Lilly said to Kate.

"Hello, Lil." Kate kissed her on both cheeks.

I stared at them. Lilly was dressed in a black skirt and red silk blouse. Kate mumbled something in her ear then Lilly looked at me from head to toe.

"Girls, we have a target to achieve," Lilly yelled and clapped her hands to gain the attention of the other workers.

A few girls dressed in black pants and black shirts came to me and dragged me into a room. After that, I didn't remember much as to what happened to me. I screamed in pain when they waxed my legs and face. Lots of tears were spilled when they shaped my eyebrows and cut my hair.

For the whole hour, I was in extreme pain because of all the pulling and whatnot.

Finally, after an hour of torture, they let me look at myself in the mirror. When I looked at myself in the mirror, I couldn't believe that the girl staring back at me was the same Hailey.

My hair was cut in many layers framing my face. The length of my hair was shorter than before, and it was shiny and glossy. My skin was glowing because of the mask they put on my face earlier. My legs and hands were looking smooth, and I felt nice.

"Hailey, stop looking at yourself like that," Kate said.

I looked at my feet feeling nervous.

"Thank you, Lilly, for helping me," Kate said then paid a hefty amount for all the services.

When we reached home, she dragged me out of the car and took me to her room.

I was standing in her room, staring at her rummaging through her closet for a perfect dress for me. She pulled out few of her dresses and told me to try them on. I put the dress on then she assessed me with hawk-like eyes and made me turn left and right.

"They do not look good on you, Get changed into this one," she said, telling me to change into the black dress.

When my eyes landed on the black dress, I took a step back.

"I can't wear that dress," I said.

Kate glared at me, and asked, "Why can't you wear this dress?"

"It is really short, and it doesn't have sleeves."

"Hailey I will pinch you hard if you don't get into this dress in the next minute," Kate said, throwing the dress on my face.

I gulped and went to get changed. The dress had a sweetheart neckline which was covered with jewels, displaying my cleavage. The dress hugged my entire frame like a second skin. It was too short for my liking.

Kate just smiled at me evilly.

"I must say, Hailey. You look good in this dress, but I suppose that's only because this dress is quite pretty and expensive," Kate said while I was pulling the dress down from my thighs and up from my chest so my breasts would not spill out.

I looked at myself in the mirror and stopped. The dress made me look like some model from a magazine Emily used to have.

When I tried to touch my hair, Kate glared at me, and it scared me. She was like a ticking bomb waiting to explode.

Kate pushed me on the chair in front of her vanity table and started doing my makeup. After fifteen minutes, she stopped stabbing my eyes and told me to take a look at myself.

I gazed at myself in the mirror. My hair was left open in loose curls, and my lips were painted red. She shaped my eyes with black liner and put something on my lashes to make them look thicker and longer. My face was *looking smooth and glowing. I was looking pretty.

Kate handed me black wedges and told me to walk in them. She eyed me from head to toe then smiled looking satisfied.

She took out her bag from the closet then started packing her things for the exhibition.

When she was done with her work, she walked to me and leaned closer.

"If I find a single dirty spot on my dress and scratch on my wedges then I will throw you out from this house," she said in a slow, dangerous voice. "Is that clear?" she yelled, scaring me.

"Yes." I nodded frantically.

"Good," she said, patting my head like I was a puppy.

Now I thought there was nothing that could stop me from attending my first party.

Chapter Ten

Mesmerized By Her Beauty

Chase

When Mom, Dad, and Kate left for Chicago, it was already 7:30 pm. I was supposed to be at the party by 7:00 pm so I went to my room to take a shower. After showering, I changed into my jeans and black shirt, leaving the first two buttons of my shirt undone.

I combed my hair and ran my hands through it a few times to give it a messy look. After putting on my shoes, I went downstairs. I picked up my car keys ready to leave when suddenly I remembered that I was ordered to take Hailey with me.

Hailey was nowhere in sight so for a second I thought of leaving for the party without her. Then I groaned thinking that if I left her here tonight, my parents would not like it at all.

"Hailey, where are you? I'm going to be late! If you're not ready yet, then I'm leaving without you." I yelled.

I heard fast footsteps coming down the stairs, and that was when my cell phone rang indicating that I had a message. Retrieving my cell phone from my pocket, I checked it to find a text from Kyle. I was busy with texting him back when my eyes caught sight of smooth, bare, long legs in front of me.

I put the cell phone back in my pocket and dragged my eyes up to see the owner of those beautiful legs, but my eyes landed on the beautiful breasts hardly leaving anything to the imagination.

Suddenly, I was nervous to look into the eyes of this beauty but finally moved my eyes up to see her face. My breath hitched when my eyes landed on her face. I was blown away by her gorgeous face and sexy looks. I couldn't believe my eyes. She looked mesmerizing. I was immobile with my mouth slack just staring at her like some stupid lovesick puppy.

I didn't know Hailey could be this sexy. I could tell she was cute, innocent, sweet, and shy but sexy was something that I could associate with Hailey.

Was she really the same girl I married a few months ago? The girl who wore baggy clothes and always smiled at me like a fool?

Then my traitorous eyes made their way to her sexy legs again. The mere sight of them made me imagine the unmentionable things I could do while these beautiful legs were wrapped around me. It started to make my mind hazy.

Her pretty face was covered in makeup, which I didn't like at all because she was quite pretty herself without the support of all this makeup. But even the makeup couldn't hide her innocence. It was still clearly showing on her face.

I felt captivated by her mesmerizing beauty. Her red lips called me like a siren. Suddenly, I felt like someone slammed a baseball bat on my head to remind me that I wasn't supposed to feel this. I should stop feeling anything, and she should too. She was a beautiful distraction, and I needed to push her back to stay focused on the goals my parents had set for me.

I was not supposed to get attracted to her or to find her cute and sexy. I should stop thinking inappropriate things. I shook my head to get rid of any absurd thoughts.

She glanced at me biting her lower lip nervously, and that was enough to make my heart flip. I wanted to feel those lips and kiss them, but this stupid fear of what would happen in the future made me took a step back.

"She is your wife, and it means she belongs to you. You can kiss her," the devil whispered in my ear.

No. I shouldn't kiss her. If I kissed her, it meant I would be raising her hopes. I would be giving myself a chance to be loved. I would be destroying my planned future with my own hands. My parents wanted me to graduate then take over the business, and that was my priority.

Now I had to act like an ass to push her away. I wanted her to hate me. I didn't want to make her feel like we could work this arranged marriage out. I knew I had been acting like an ass since she came here to live, but it was because I didn't like her before.

But now I had to act like an ass knowing that we could not work this out because I shouldn't make this relationship my priority and should focus on fulfilling my parents' wishes before anything else. I wanted to decide how I would live my life and who I would spend my future with, but I couldn't let my parents down.

She might be the girl for me, or she might not be, but right now it was not the time to worry about that. If we continued this relationship, in the end, it would break us both beyond repair.

To hurt her and make her hate me I said the cruelest words that came to my mind, "Why are you wearing that dress? It is revealing your fat figure. Didn't you see yourself in the mirror after wearing that dress? It looks terrible on you."

Instantly, her face turned pale, and her eyes lost all the shine they had on them earlier.

I felt guilty and wanted to take my words back. I wanted to tell her how gorgeous she looked in the dress and how much I wanted her, but I needed her to hate me.

If I would keep saying sweet things to her, how would I make her hate me?

She gazed at me with her big brown eyes then stuttered, "I... I am sorry if you... you want me to change I can do it. Just give me a few seconds."

"I'm running late for the party. My friends are waiting for me," I said, trying to sound irritated.

"I didn't pick the dress myself. This is Kate's dress, and she told me to wear it. If you are running late, you can go. I will stay here." She looked down at the floor.

Her eyes were filled with tears.

I had never seen her so sad before even when I talked rudely to her. But tonight, I thought I crossed the line.

"It is not like I care about how you look. Just come with me and make sure you keep your mouth shut at the party," I said.

She nodded. Her eyes were wide like I had scared her. I didn't want her to feel scared of me.

I had no idea why she never got angry at me, yelled at me, or cursed me when I said rude things to her. I wanted her to fight with me and argue with me so I would have some valid reasons to do all these things.

We both stayed silent on the way to the party. When we arrived outside my friend house, I parked my car at the empty spot and stepped out of the car. She stepped out of the car and followed me into my friend's house. I went to the poolside where the party was arranged. I glared at the guys who were staring at Hailey.

What was I going to tell my friends when they ask me about Hailey?

Sam, Kyle, Clara, and Michael were standing near the bar, drinking.

"Hi, guys. Sorry for coming late." I went and greeted them.

"It is fine. The real fun hasn't started yet," Sam said.

Clara came to me and hugged me.

The boys of my group looked at me with raised eyebrows when she mumbled, "Hi handsome."

"Hi Clara," I replied.

Clara and I had been friends since kindergarten. Also, she used to be my neighbor until her dad bought a new house a little far from my place.

Sam asked me, "Chase. Who's this pretty girl standing behind you?"

That was when I realized that Hailey was standing behind me and I still hadn't introduced her to my friends.

I turned around to find Hailey tucking the traitorous tendrils of her hair behind her ear. Her act was so simple and innocent, yet it left me breathless. Her eyes were downcast like she was scared to look at people in the eye. She had an uneasy look on her face.

Clara, Sam, and the others waited for me to introduce her.

I cleared my throat, and said, "She is Hailey, the daughter my mother's best friend. She is staying in our house because her parents are out of the city for some meeting."

Hailey's head snapped my way when I was done introducing her. The hurt, pain, and betrayal were clear on her face.

My friends still looked confused, so I decided to elaborate the lie I created to make them believe.

"My mother insisted I take her to the party that's why I brought her here with me," I said, patting Kyle's shoulder when he came to stand beside me.

"Hello beautiful, I am Kyle." Kyle extended his hand.

She looked at me in the eyes like silently asking my permission. I nodded, and she placed her small hand in Kyle's large tan hand, shaking it.

"It is my birthday party. Chase is my best friend, and I am glad he brought you here tonight," Kyle said, making her smile.

I was sure that I was not the only one who got starstruck when she smiled. Sam, Michael, and Kyle looked surprised when she smiled innocently. Her smile was truly beautiful like it would light up your world in seconds.

"Happy Birthday," she said softly, making Kyle smile.

"Thanks." Kyle had a shy smile on his face.

Sam pushed Kyle and took hold of Hailey's hand.

"Hi, I am Sam. Chase and I have been friends from fifth grade," Sam said, and I rolled my eyes.

Hailey nodded her head and mumbled, "Hi."

I glared at Sam. He was my friend but a certified player in our group of friends. He knew better how to charm girls and lured them to do what he wanted because of his good looks.

"Hailey, you are really beautiful. Are you single?" he asked her, still holding her hand.

I clenched my jaw at his stupid habit of flirting. I wanted to push him away from her and told him to keep his hands to himself, but I controlled my temper.

"I... I am-m..." Hailey stuttered.

I interrupted her before she would drop the "married" bomb on my friends.

"She is not interested, Sam. She is here on vacation, and her parents are very strict. She's not allowed to date until she'll turn twenty-five so please remove your hand," I said, making him glare at me.

"Is he telling the truth?" Sam looked at Hailey.

She nodded her head looking at me like I just told her I murdered kittens in my past time.

"Your parents are not here, Hailey. And as much as I know, Chase is not your dad, so I don't think it's any of his business to state your parents' rules to you. Let me give you a tour of the party," Sam said with a smirk, which I felt like eradicating with a punch.

I didn't know why I was feeling so angry towards Sam when I knew it was nothing more than a harmless flirt.

"Sam, she is off limits. Leave her alone," I said harshly, and this time I caught Clara's attention.

Her eyes went to Hailey and me like she was solving some puzzle.

"Oh c'mon man. I just want to be Hailey's friend and give her company all through the party," Sam said, smiling at Hailey.

Hailey looked really anxious. I could see her hand trembling, and she was biting her lower lip again. I guessed that she was feeling uncomfortable surrounded by new people.

"I think Sam should give her a tour. Chase won't mind it if I keep him occupied," Clara said, kissing my cheek and winking at Sam.

My jaw clenched when Sam smiled and placed his hand on Hailey's bare arm then dragged her with him. She held my gaze until she was out of sight.

I was angry at Sam, but I knew he wouldn't hurt her.

Clara gave me a drink, and I chugged it down. It burned my throat but instantly calmed me down.

"Let's dance," she said, dragging me to the dance floor.

I always felt like Clara assumed we could be more than friends someday, but for me, she could never be more than a friend. From the start of college, she had been acting weird, and my friends told me that they thought she had a crush on me.

I was dancing with her when she pressed her body to mine intimately.

"Clara, what are you doing?" I asked her.

"I'm dancing," she slurred in my ear, pressing herself again.

I could feel every curve of her body and her rigid breathing.

"It's not appropriate for friends to dance like this," I said, creating space between our bodies.

"Why?" She took a step closer and planted her lips on mine.

I was not expecting her to kiss me. My mind froze. Her hands snaked around my neck and pulled me closer, pressing our bodies.

I was a little drunk myself, and she was reeking of alcohol. Her lips felt nice, soft but eagerly invading my mouth. I shut my eyes, and Hailey's beautiful face appeared in front of me. A few seconds later I realized that I was pulling her closer and responding to her, but when I opened my eyes and found Clara, I pushed her back.

I was kissing her because I imagined Hailey at her place.

"Sorry Clara," I said, taking a step back and leaving her on the dance floor, confused.

Why did I see Hailey's face when I was kissing Clara? Did it mean that I loved her?

I felt someone following me, so I turned around to see Clara staring at me intensely. She pushed me on the wall, smashed her lips on mine, and started kissing me hungrily.

I pushed her away and yelled, "Clara, what is the matter with you?"

She looked at me with her hooded eyes. They were filled with lust.

"Chase, I like you. I like you so much. Please, don't push me away. In a few months we will be graduating then you could move out from your parents' house. We can live together," she said.

I was shocked at her words, but I realized that she was too drunk to even know what she was blabbering.

"Clara, we'll talk about this when you are sober," I said, leaving her standing there.

I went to the kitchen to drink something to calm myself and found a few boys in my college making drinks.

"Hello, buddy. Do you want something to drink? We have vodka shots, tequila shots, and martini," the one with a long hair asked me.

I thought his name was Quinton. He was waiting for me to answer.

"Anything will be fine," I said, and he handed me the glass.

I took the shots, one after another and let myself get drunk. The boys and I talked about random things, and after some time they left me. I was going to take another shot when I heard the loud shouts and whistles coming from the backyard. I followed the noises, and it led me to the center of the backyard.

I was shocked at what my blurry eyes were seeing. Hailey was dancing on the top of the table while girls and boys were making appreciating noises and giggling at her moves.

Hailey looked like a hot mess. Her brown hair was flying in the air as she was bobbing her head left to right. She was swinging her ass on the beat like a pro.

I walked closer to find that her dress had risen up from her knees and showing her ass. Her every move was making boys crazy including me. Her breasts were ready to spill out from her dress any moment, clearly leaving nothing to the imagination.

"Oh, girl. You are so hot! Where have you been all my life?" a boy said, breaking me out of my shock.

I realized that I was not the only one getting a free show of how my wife looked like under the plain dresses she wore every day.

"Hailey, what the hell are you doing?" I asked her in an angry voice, but the music drowned my shouts.

The bastards around the table were hungrily running their eyes on my wife. I wanted to punch them for staring at her lustfully.

A guy whistled and moved his hand to touch her ass, and that was when I pushed him to the ground. Everyone around us froze. I picked Hailey from the waist and placed her on the ground.

"Are you out of your mind?" I asked angrily.

She gave me a dazzling smile, and my eyes widened as realization dawned on me. I sniffed her mouth for alcohol, but she only giggled.

Sam came to me, and said, "Man, she knows some sexy moves that just made me want to f**k her right here."

My jaw clenched at what he said, and I punched him in the face. He fell down on the ground.

"I will kill you if you ever think of touching her," I yelled. "What did you make her drink?" I asked him.

"Sam didn't give her drinks. It was Britney. She gave her drinks and lied that they were fruit punch," a girl said, looking at Sam's injured face.

He was sprawled on the ground groaning in pain and cradling his jaw.

I cursed myself for being stupid and leaving Hailey alone with these people. I took her arm and dragged her to the main area. I collided with Kyle on the way.

"Where are you going in such hurry?" Kyle asked me, rubbing his arm.

"I'm leaving. Hailey is pretty drunk, and I think the shots I took in the kitchen started working their magic on me."

Hailey started to dance again, so I had to put my arm around her waist to pull her closer.

Kyle's eyes went to Hailey's leg, and I pulled her short dress down to hide her legs.

He cleared his throat, and said, "Wait here. I am calling a cab for you guys."

"Thank you, buddy," I said, and Hailey giggled.

I glanced at her, and she smiled at me innocently.

"Stop being cute, Hailey," I said, groaning when my head whirled around due to the number of drinks I consumed earlier.

The cab arrived after five minutes, and Hailey and I stumbled in the back seat. I gave the address to the cab driver while holding Hailey's hand in mine.

Suddenly, she leaned towards me and kissed my cheek. I stiffened under the feel of her soft lips on my skin. I glanced at her and found her staring at me with her brown eyes. They were shining like diamonds, and I loved the mischief in them.

On the way home, her head remained on my chest just above my beating heart while my arm stayed around her waist to make sure that she was safe and warm.

Chapter Eleven

I Don't Want To Stay Alone

Chase

When we arrived at the house, I paid the driver and helped Hailey out from the car. She stumbled at the first step then got her balance back before she could've fallen flat on her face. She blushed red when she saw me staring at her with an amused smile.

I shook my head at her and realized that she was sober enough to walk her way to the door. I unlocked the door, and she followed behind me closely. Once we were inside, I shut the door.

The house was completely dark, making it impossible to see anything, so I switched on the light. When the lights were switched on, my eyes landed on Hailey. Her back was pressed on the wall while she was struggling with the straps of her wedges. She had a pout on her lips like a cute little kid.

Shaking my head with a smile, I walked to her and kneeled down. I swatted her hand away and unstrapped her wedges then pulled them off of her feet. My eyes got the stuck on her bare legs making me uncomfortable. To divert my attention, I looked at her face

She smiled at me and started wiggling her toes with a giggle. I didn't know why I smiled at her instead of glaring. Maybe it was because of those drinks, or I was finally going insane around her.

I got up and stared at her. She stared back at me, making me feel something weird in my heart.

I never enjoyed giving her the cold shoulder, but that was the only way to keep her at arm's length.

She made her way towards the stairs and stumbled back. If she stumbled again, she could hurt herself or worse she could break her leg before she reached her bedroom. So I did what any sane person would do, I picked her up bridal style and started making my way upstairs to her room.

She did something unexpected, and I halted. She circled her arms around my neck then slowly started running her hand through my hair and snuggled her face into my neck and breathed me in.

"You have very soft hair, and you always smell so good," she mumbled, running her nose into my neck then teasing me by placing her lips there.

I shuddered at the touch of her lips on my skin. My legs wobbled, but I continued the journey to her room.

On the way to her room, she kept snuggling her face into my neck and running her nose leisurely, making it difficult for me to walk while carrying her. Every move she made intensified the need to kiss her, but at the same time, I was preparing myself to leave before anything happened between us.

Finally, we reached her room, and I was glad that I didn't have to feel the torture of her soft hands in my hair anymore. I made my way to her bed and placed her there. I was ready to leave her room when I heard a weird noise.

I turned back to her and switched on the lamp on her bedside table. She was the one making noises. I sat beside her on the bed and pried her hand away from her mouth to see her stifling her cries.

At the sight of tears dripping from her eyes, I panicked.

"Love, are you hurt? Did something happen at the party?" I asked her. Concerned, I checked her head and hands for any injuries. "I shouldn't have left your side. I'm sorry Hailey. Please answer me! Do you want me to take you to the hospital?" I asked her, cupping her face in my palms.

She stopped crying and whispered lightly in my ear, "You called me love."

I glanced at her confused. "I did."

"But everyone hates me: Melanie, Emily, Kate, and you. Everyone hates me. I know I am not made to be loved. I deserve to be hated so don't call me love," she said.

I felt my heart breaking by looking at this beautiful, innocent girl who was thinking that she deserved everyone's hate.

"I don't know about the others but I can assure you that I don't hate you," I said.

"You don't hate me." She looked confused.

"No, I don't hate you."

"I don't hate you either. I really love you, but it is a secret," she mumbled in my ear.

I was shocked at her confession. She loved me. I mean I knew that she had obviously developed a crush on me in the past few months, but love. I never thought that she could be in love with me all this time when I was just an arrogant jerk. The way she acted around me. The way she secretly stared at me when she thought that I wasn't looking at her.

I glanced at her and saw the sadness in her eyes. They were swollen from crying. Her head hung low like a kid, a very cute one I must say.

"Good night," I said, getting up from the bed ready to leave.

"Chase, don't go. Please don't leave me. I don't want to stay alone. Everything scares me." She clenched my arm like her life depended on it.

I didn't have the heart to leave her alone like this.

"Go change. I'll wait for you here," I said.

She nodded her head solemnly and went to her closet. She pulled out her nightshirt and started unzipping her dress. Her zipper got stuck, and she awkwardly angled her arms to get to the zipper on her back.

I didn't know I was looking at her until I realized she needed help. I got up and made my way towards her. I took hold of the zipper of her dress and moved it downwards. My knuckles were brushing on her smooth bare back. I didn't even notice that my movements were slow until I felt her shiver.

The dress fell down from her body and pooled around her legs. When she turned to me, my throat went dry. She was wearing plain black undergarments, which looked beautiful against her pale skin.

I thought I had drunk too much to think straight. I needed to get out of this room and ran far away from here before something happened between us, which we would both regret later.

I made a mistake by looking into her eyes. Her eyes held me captive. They were begging me to love her instead of leaving her like others. Despite trying my best to move and leave that room, my legs became frozen. She took a step closer to me, and I took a step closer to her.

"You're beautiful, Hailey. You are made up to be loved," I said, caressing her cheek.

"Then why don't you love me?" She had tears pooling in her eyes again.

Instead of answering, I planted my lips on her. She stilled until I started moving my lips. Her arms circled around my neck pulling me closer and my arms went around her waist. She was copying my actions innocently proving that it was her first kiss.

I didn't know how long we kept kissing, but when we pulled apart, we were breathing heavily.

She looked at me with wide eyes. Her eyes went to my lips then she bit her swollen lower lip. It was hard to watch and not kiss her again, so I kissed her again, pressing her back on the closet. Her breath hitched when my clothed body pressed her bare body intimately. I sucked her lower lip into my mouth making her gasp and gaining the opportunity to invade her mouth. Her sweet taste made me hungry for more. I didn't know how I would be able to live without kissing her every day after this.

Her every stroke and every move were making me hungry to have her. We pulled away from each other taking in some oxygen. I put my head on her neck, calming my breath. Then I ran my nose in the same motion she had done earlier on the stairs while I was carrying her.

She shuddered at my actions, and I smiled.

"You taste better than anything in this world," I said, placing a kiss on her neck.

She made a noise of approval, and I started showering kisses on her neck. She moaned loudly when I sucked the skin of her shoulder. My hands went to her waist pulling her closer to me while her hand held my biceps tightly. I moved back to her lips and bit her lower lip lightly, seeking permission to enter my tongue into her mouth. Her mouth tasted like freshly ripened strawberries, making it my favorite fruit from now on.

Her moans of pleasure filled the room. Her hands were rubbing the back of my neck, encouraging me to deepen the kiss.

Due to the mutual need to breathe, we pulled away from each other. My forehead rested on her while our breaths mingled.

I could see the growing passion between us and the love in her eyes was firing up with every touch. I had never seen something this beautiful and never felt this much pleasure kissing someone. There was no match for her kisses in the world.

Her cute face was an open book showing how much love they held in it for me. The word love actually stirred something inside my heart making me want to feel her love even if it was only for tonight.

Whatever sanity I had left a few minutes ago left my mind at that moment.

I picked her up and lay her on the bed. Then I started kissing her again like a starved man. Her taste was making me dizzy, and her delicious lips were responding to me, trying to match my actions. My lips moved to her neck where I started sucking, feeling her pulse beating under my tongue. A loud moan emerged out from her making everything hazy around us.

Her hands were frantic, tugging at my hair and sinking her nails into my flesh.

I was so lost and far in that moment of passion that I didn't feel the small amount of pain she was inflicting on me. At that moment, I forgot that I was supposed to make her hate me. I was not supposed to let my guards down and let myself get captured by this sinful little angel.

All rational thoughts flew from my mind, leaving my body to do the work.

I bit her earlobe lightly, making her arch her back.

"Let me love you, Hailey," I whispered.

"Please, love me." She closed her eyes.

It was the last thing that I remembered before losing myself completely inside her that night.

Chapter Twelve

Sore Muscles

Chase

The next morning, I woke up to the constant ringing of my phone. I tried opening my eyes, but the pain in my head was killing me, making it impossible for me to open my eyes. I shut them tightly and massaged my head with my fingers, groaning in pain.

When I was finally able to open my eyes, my eyes landed on Hailey. Her head was resting on my chest, and her brown hair was sprawled on the pillow. For a second, my mind turned blank. Everything around me turned blurry, making it impossible for me to think properly.

I blinked my eyes to make sure I was not dreaming and imagining everything, but to my utter dismay it was real, and she was really sleeping beside me.

My eyes widened when they landed on her naked torso. I shot up from the bed and removed her head from my chest.

"Shit," I cursed under my breath and realized she was waking up.

Everything that happened last night started to play in my head like a movie. I glanced back at her and cursed myself for being so dumb and letting my body control me.

"Shit, Chase what have you done?" I asked myself.

My phone started ringing again, making me look around for my clothes. I found them on the floor near the bed. I picked up my jeans and pulled out my phone from the pocket to see four missed calls from my dad.

I called him back and told him everything was alright, and we were waiting for them to come home. Then hurriedly, I put my pants on and picked up my shirt.

I was buttoning up my shirt when my eyes fell on Hailey. She was now sitting up on the bed, massaging her head with one hand while she had no idea that she was completely naked and revealing her beautiful body for my hungry gaze. Even at that moment, she was looking like some sexy model posing for a fashion magazine.

Slowly, she opened her eyes and looked at herself. Her eyes widened, and she quickly bunched the sheets in her fist and pulled them to her chest, hiding the view of her mesmerizing figure.

Shit, Chase! Why the hell are you staring at her? Are you still in a drunken haze?

Her eyes made contact with mine, and I sucked in a harsh breath. The look of confusion and distress appeared on her face, and her gaze begged me to explain everything to her, but I didn't have the answers of her questions, so I fled out of her room, leaving her alone.

I went straight to my room and pulled my hair in frustration. I was already regretting losing control last night. I was sure that she would also regret it later when she would realize what happened between us last night.

Shit! I really had ruined everything.

Then I remembered that my parents and sister were on their way home, and I needed to look somewhat presentable to receive them. I made my way to the washroom to take a shower and to get rid of the traces of everything that happened last night.

*　　　*　　　*

Hailey

[The same morning]

I woke up when my head jerked. I sat up and moved my hand to lightly massage my head. I had a killer headache, and I was feeling dizzy. The overwhelming need to vomit rushed inside me and I opened my eyes to find myself completely naked under the sheet. Hurriedly, I bunched up the sheets in my fist and pulled it up to my chest to hide my body.

I was panicking inside. Hundreds of questions were swirling around my head.

Why was I naked? Why my head had killer pain like someone had repeatedly hit it with a sledgehammer? What happened last night? Why couldn't I remember coming back home?

I forced my mind to remember something, anything that would answer my questions, but again I came up blank. I felt an immense pain in my head when I tried to remember everything again.

I recalled Chase's hateful words that he threw at me before taking me to the party and the way he introduced me to his friends telling them that I was the daughter of his mom's best friend. My brain reminded me how he was dancing with that girl and smiling at her and how much it pained me.

I was really hurt seeing him so happy with another girl. She was perfect in every way slender figure, long blonde hair, and small waist where Chase's hand was resting while they were dancing together.

A girl was sitting beside me at the party. She offered me something to drink, and I took it without asking her what it was. It tasted like orange juice so I gulped it down and instantly felt myself relaxing. That was my last memory. I didn't remember anything after that, and I couldn't recall how I came back home.

I glanced around the room to see Chase standing there buttoning his shirt. I frowned at his presence in my room. He never came into my room so what was he doing here?

He looked up and our eyes connected. His grey eyes widened at the sight of me, and he halted.

I opened my mouth to ask him how we came back home last night, but before I could have said anything, he sprinted out of the room leaving me confused with my own questions.

This time I felt the bile rising in my throat, and I ran in the direction of the washroom. I emptied my stomach there, coughing violently. I felt light-headed, so I sat down on the washroom floor to relax my wildly beating heart and to regain some energy. My body was aching everywhere, and I felt extremely tired.

After a few minutes, I got up and walked to the basin to wash my mouth. I caught my reflection in the mirror. My hair was a wild mess, but weirdly my skin was glowing. My usual dull brown eyes had some kind of spark in them.

My eyes moved on my body, and I caught the pinkish purple marks on my neck. Those marks were everywhere on my body. My eyes traveled to my breasts, and I found the same purplish marks there too. I touched them and felt a minor pain.

Maybe they were bug bites or some kind of skin allergy.

I shrugged my shoulders and picked up my toothbrush. I brushed my teeth then leaned down to spit it in the washbasin, and that was when I felt pain in my lower region.

Ignoring it, I washed my mouth and decided to take a shower. I took a hot shower, which relaxed my sore muscles. The water soothed most of the places, but the pain in my lower region didn't reduce.

After the shower, I dried myself with a long white fluffy towel and looked at the bruises that were still there. I would give them a few days if they wouldn't go away on their own then I would tell my mother-in-law, Eva, about it.

I searched my closet for comfy clothes that would hide these nasty bruises too. I found my black high neck shirt and paired it with my black and green checkered skirt. I didn't have many clothes, and that was because my mother never spent a penny to buy me new clothes.

When I was changed into clean clothes, I decided to clean my room, which looked like a tornado occurred here. I was making my bed when my eyes landed on the sheets. There was a small amount of blood on the sheets. I didn't understand where it came from, but I changed the sheets with a clean one and then placed the comforter on the bed.

My eyes roamed around and settled down on my bra, which was lying on the floor at the bottom of the bed. I picked it up from the floor then put it in the laundry basket.

Kate's dress was also lying on the floor near the closet, and I picked it up. I checked it upside down for any stain or rip, but when I didn't find anything I sighed in relief. Folding the dress properly, I placed it on the chair in my room and went downstairs to the kitchen to find some Tylenol because the pain in my head was killing me.

After searching the kitchen cabinets, I found the medicine box. I popped two tablets into my mouth and gulped them down with water.

I felt tired, and my sore muscles were protesting whenever I tried to move. I decided to go back to my room and take a nap.

On the stairs, I collided with Chase. I was about to fall down when his arms circled around my waist to steady me. I looked up to find him gazing at me with wide eyes. Then he stepped back with a look of disgust on his face.

Before I could thank him for saving me from falling on the stairs, he ran out of the house.

I stared at the closed door for a few minutes then continued to make my way up to my room.

When I was inside my room, I shut the door and drew the curtains closer to block the sunlight and fell on my bed pulling the comforter up to my chin.

The way Chase acted this morning really hurt me. He wasn't friendly to me, but until today he never showed that my presence disgusted him.

Did I embarrass him at the party? Oh, God! I got drunk last night! That was why I couldn't remember anything!

That explained a killer headache and sore muscles, but I didn't drink anything except the fruit punch or juice that girl gave to me. It meant that was not a fruit punch or juice, but something that contained alcohol and it made me forgot everything.

I felt tears forming in my eyes at the thought of me doing something embarrassing in my drunken state which embarrassed Chase. The tears started to spill from my eyes when I thought how he used to dislike me and now my presence disgusted him.

I was pathetic. I knew I shouldn't have gone to that party.

"Oh, God! Please don't make him hate me more, please." I begged God, sobbing into my pillow, and at some time during all the crying and begging I fell asleep.

Chapter Thirteen

Seeking Apology

Chase

On the stairs, I collided with Hailey. She was about to fall back when my arms circled around her waist to steady her. She looked up at me and found me gazing at her with wide eyes. I felt ashamed for letting everything happen between us last night. I didn't plan to sleep with her when we were both under the influence of alcohol. I shouldn't have let the alcohol control my mind.

Before she could ask me anything, I stepped back and removed my arm from her waist. I took one last glance at her sad face and left the house to go to Kyle's place to pick up my car.

I rang the doorbell and waited for Kyle to open the main door.

"Hey man. What are you doing here so early?" he said, yawning.

"I came here to take my car and realized I forgot my keys last night in your house." I entered his house to see a bunch of girls and boys sleeping in the lounge.

"Why do you still look drunk?" I asked him.

"I drank last night, but my appearance has nothing to do with the alcohol. It's because of drugs."

"What do you mean by drugs? Man, have you started doing drugs?" I looked at him shocked.

"You are not funny Chase. Everyone got drunk last night, but it wasn't because of alcohol. It was because our food and drinks were spiked by Quinton's gang buddies. They took revenge for the prank we played on them last time by changing the size of their shorts before the match," Kyle explained.

They made the drinks for me last night. It meant they were spiked too.

Shit! Shit! It meant Hailey and I were not only drunk but drugged too.

"How do you know all this?"

"The boy with Harry Potter spectacles found them mixing drugs in all the food and beverages," Kyle said, slumping down on a chair.

"I was drugged last night. F**k," I yelled.

"We were all high. Someone could have robbed us all last night." He chuckled.

I glared at him, running my hands through my hair desperately thinking how to fix the situation.

"Shit! Buddy, did you sleep with someone like Clara slept with Sam?" he said.

"What? Clara slept with Sam?"

"Yes, stop yelling. Innocent drugged people are sleeping here," Kyle said, looking at our friends and some strangers sleeping dead on the floor.

I couldn't believe that after confessing her love and whatnot, Clara slept with Sam. Well, it proved how temporary her love was.

"Do you know where my car keys are?" I asked him.

"I don't know man. Where were you last time?"

"I was in the kitchen," I said and looked around the kitchen counter.

After searching around, I found my car keys under the table. I picked them up then turned to Kyle.

"I want to tell you something about the girl that came with you last night," Kyle said, looking nervous.

"What do you want to tell me about her?"

"Britney thought Sam was attracted to her, and she got jealous. She gave her the spiked drinks."

I felt beyond angry after hearing the information.

"I want to find Quinton and his gang, then kill them. Do you know where they are?" I asked him.

"I don't know. But they might be staying at Malinda's place."

Malinda was like a gang leader. She sold drugs and did a lot of wrong things. Whenever Quinton and his buddies did something like this, they went to hide under her wings.

I took a step to leave, but Kyle stopped me by placing his hand on my shoulder.

"Going to Malinda's place means getting yourself killed. You don't know when the police will raid her house and that is very dangerous."

He was right, and I didn't plan to die soon. So I didn't push through with my plan, and I bid him goodbye.

"See you tomorrow, Kyle," I said and left his house.

On the way back to my house, I kept thinking about last night, which was nothing but a blur of images in my head.

Now I knew why Hailey and I ended up sleeping together last night. Why I had no control over my body to stop me from loving her. My plan to make her hate me was doomed from the start, but now she might hate me all her life for sleeping with her when we were both not in our right minds.

The whole drive back to my house I cursed my fate and luck.

*   *   *

Hailey

I felt someone gently shaking me, and I woke up.

"Hailey, dear wake up." I heard my mother-in-law's voice, waking me up.

I opened my eyes and found her looking at me with concern. I groaned and closed my eyes, shielding them from the bright light in the room.

She said something, which I didn't understand. My head was pounding, making it impossible for me to keep my eyes open so I fell asleep again without a care in the world.

Next, when I woke up, it was already morning. The bright rays of the sun were coming into the room through the open slits between the curtains.

Groggily, I got up from the bed then pulled the curtains close. My body was still sore in some places, and every muscle was aching. Despite the pain and tiredness, I made my way to the washroom and did my business. When I was washing my face, I saw dark circles under my eyes. Sighing in disappointment, I walked out of the washroom and opened my closet. I pulled out my grey sweatpants, black tank top and a black hoodie then got changed into them.

I went downstairs for breakfast.

"Good morning." I took the empty seat beside my father-in-law.

"How are you feeling Hailey?" my mother in law asked me.

"I'm much better than yesterday, but my muscles are aching."

Chase started coughing.

Kate gave a glass of water to Chase, and he gulped it down while staring at me with wide eyes. I didn't know what I had done to make him act so weird.

"When did you all come back?" I took a bite of the pancakes.

"We came back yesterday around two in the afternoon," she said.

My eyes widened at what she said. It meant I slept the whole day.

"You didn't come downstairs, so I came to your room to wake you up for dinner, but found you burning in fever. I gave you some medicines. Thank God, you're now feeling better," my mother-in-law said.

"I don't remember when you came to my room, but thank you for giving me medicine. They really helped."

"You had a high fever maybe that's why you don't remember anything," she said.

I nodded my head and started eating again. Suddenly, Chase got up and left the dining hall for college without giving me a single glance. Kate followed behind him, sending me a small glare.

With a heavy heart, I tried to swallow some food but gave up after a few bites.

His impertinence and uncaring attitude were hurting me. I liked it when he smiled at me or at least glanced at me like he cared for me.

[*After three weeks*]

I was baking chocolate cupcakes because it was Chase's favorite. I had already prepared his coffee the way he liked it.

I would take these to Chase, and tell him how sorry I was if I had embarrassed him at the party. Yes, that was my famous plan to seek his forgiveness. I hoped this trick would make him talk to me.

It had been three weeks, and he hadn't uttered a single word to me. I had tried many things to make him talk to me again, but nothing had worked so far.

Two days ago, I went to his room with his coffee, which Kate ordered me to deliver to him. He shut the door in my face after taking his damned coffee, but I was not angry with him. I was just hurt because of the way he was acting after the party.

Chase avoided me at all cost. He wouldn't even talk to me or reply to me if I asked him how his day was. After that night when he gave his grandma's gift, I thought he had changed, and our loveless marriage might become a real marriage. My stupid heart fell in love with him because I thought he cared for me.

Inside he was breaking me. I had a feeling that something bad was going to happen if I didn't solve this situation quickly. I didn't remember what happened at the party that made him hate me and avoid me like this. I really wanted to know so I could apologize to him, but my stupid brain was still blank about everything that happened.

I should wait until his graduation. I would talk to him about everything after his graduation dinner.

Sighing, I thought about myself and the weird sickness that I had been feeling the past few weeks. Constant nausea and dizziness were making me tired. A single bite of food was making me throw up. My emotions were all over the place. One minute, I felt like crying, and the next minute I would be puking my guts out.

Sometimes, I felt extremely hungry and found the need to eat everything. Yesterday, I finished half the jar of cucumber pickles, which I used to hate all my life.

Suddenly, Kate entered the kitchen and brought me out of my thoughts. She opened the refrigerator and pulled out a tub of chocolate ice cream. My mouth watered at the sight of my favorite ice cream. I wanted to eat it, but I was scared of Kate and couldn't ask her to share some with me.

I never did something like this before but today was an exception. When she left the kitchen after filling her bowl with ice cream, I took the ice cream tub out of the refrigerator and dig out a few scoops of ice cream for me and put them in a bowl.

The cupcakes were ready, so I pulled them out from the oven and placed them on the kitchen counter to let them cool down.

I sat on the kitchen counter and started eating chocolate ice cream. The creamy taste of ice cream felt heavenly in my mouth soothing the ache in my heart from Chase's constant disregard.

Why did I fall in love with him?

He was the most difficult person yet the softest man I had ever met. He didn't like to show his soft side much, but whenever he did, he made it hard for me not to love him.

I was enjoying the ice cream while daydreaming about Chase. I didn't notice when Kate entered the kitchen and saw me eating her ice cream. She looked at me and started fuming like a bull ready to attack.

At that moment, I knew I was going to die. She looked ready to kill me.

"Hailey, how dare you eat my ice cream without my permission? You know I don't like sharing my things with anyone," Kate shouted at me, making me jump off the kitchen counter.

"I… I'm sorry. I like chocolate chip ice cream, and I thought I can eat it."

"You thought you can eat it and I won't notice. You thought I am a fool. You're so dead, bitch," she said, pushing me to the ground.

I fell on my butt, twisting my ankle in the process.

The pain exploded in my ankle and tears started to blur my vision. The memories of those bullies in school who used to push me to the ground and bathroom floor started to play in my head, making me panic.

I didn't know she would get this angry if I ate her ice cream. Now, I was regretting eating her damned ice cream.

We heard footsteps coming down the stairs.

"What's going on here?" Chase asked.

"She ate my ice cream. You know I don't share my ice cream with anyone. She didn't even ask me before eating it." Kate was ready to slap me, but Chase stopped her.

"Kate, I will get you a new tub of your favorite ice cream. Now go to your room and leave Hailey alone," Chase said, making her glare at me.

She walked to Chase.

"Brother, I am doing this because you are asking me to leave her alone. Otherwise, I know a lot of ways to make her learn how to ask for permission before taking others' things without their permission," Kate said then left.

"Hailey, why do you do things that make people dislike you? Next time don't eat anything that's hers."

His words were a stab to my heart.

"I'm sorry for doing things which made you dislike me. I'm really sorry for everything," I said, looking at my feet.

When I looked up, Chase wasn't there. He left me without saying anything.

I sat on the floor and cried my heart out.

Chapter Fourteen

Graduation Dinner (Part 1)

Hailey

The house was in chaos today because we were preparing for Chase's graduation. His mom and Kate had prepared all his favorite food.

His family invited my parents tonight to be a part of this celebration. My dad, mom, and Emily would be coming here in the evening. I was really happy that my dad was coming. I hadn't seen my dad for three months, and I missed him. I was sad that Granddad wouldn't be able to come because of his health issue. The doctor didn't allow him to travel so far.

My best friend was also coming on leave for a weekend. I felt excited to see him after a month. I knew you were wondering who I was calling my best friend and how the nerdy, antisocial girl now suddenly had a best friend. Cameron was actually someone who didn't think that I was some weird creature that came to earth from some planet to complete my punishment for treason. He was the one I liked to call my best friend.

Before, I never thought and cared that I had no friends, but when I became friends with Cameron, I came to know the real meaning of friendship. He was the first person to understand me and who genuinely enjoyed my company as much as I enjoyed his. He sometimes acted a little cocky, but that was what made him a fun guy. I cherished his carefree and confident personality.

Chase and I still hadn't cleared the issue between us. I wanted to know what I had done at the party or after the party that made him so angry at me that he had stopped talking to me.

Why I didn't remember anything was still a mystery.

I planned to finally talk to him after dinner so we could stop this useless fight. Our relationship wasn't good before, but it was friendly enough to give me hope that someday he would start liking me. Now it felt like everything was falling apart.

I felt the bile rising again, making me rush to the nearest washroom. I had been sick for few weeks and felt nausea all the time. Sometimes, the mere sight of food and its smell made me want to puke.

I told my mother-in-law about the constant vomiting and fatigue. She told me that I must have eaten something bad that upset my stomach. She made me chamomile tea, which soothed my nausea for the time being, but it didn't completely go away.

For the past few weeks, I had been eating crackers and light food like oatmeal, bread, and veggies and drinking juices instead of coffee because its smell irritated my stomach.

Tonight I knew there was going to be so much food and I would have to eat with everyone at the dinner table. I just hoped that I wouldn't embarrass myself tonight by throwing up at the sight of all the food.

I helped my mother-in-law here and there with the stuff of arranging things, and when we were done, it was already evening.

The bell rang, and I ran to get the door because I knew it could be my dad. I opened the door, threw myself into my dad's waiting arms, and hugged him.

"Dad, I missed you so much."

"You've no idea how much your dad missed you, my little girl," my dad said, kissing my head.

I pulled away from him and hugged my mom. I didn't hate her nor loved her after what she had done, but I respected her for my dad's sake. She surprised me by pulling me into a warm hug, making me feel like she missed me.

"What the hell are you wearing?" Emily hissed in my ear

I looked at the plain black sweatpants and white shirt that I was wearing.

"What's wrong with my clothes?" I asked her.

"Oh God, everything is wrong with your clothes. Don't tell me this is what you are going to wear tonight." Disgust was clear in her voice.

"Why would I wear this for dinner when I have a beautiful dress in my room for tonight?" I said with a smile.

Emily's face dropped.

I had a beautiful dress that Allison bought for me for tonight's dinner. Allison was Chase's older sister. She was nothing like Kate. She had two cute kids; a boy who was four and his name was Chris, and a small two years old girl named Susan. Her husband was also very nice and friendly. They both looked perfect with each other, and I could see how much they were still in love after five years of their marriage.

I showed my parents to the guest room so they could freshen up and left. I went to my room to get ready for dinner. I plugged the hair straightener to heat it up and went to the washroom. I washed my face and applied some makeup, which was also courtesy of Allison.

After applying makeup, I straightened my hair and left it open. When I took a final look at myself in the mirror, I felt proud of myself for making myself look presentable enough for tonight's dinner.

I heard a whistle and turned around to find Cameron standing in my bedroom. I ran to him and hugged him.

"Hi, how are you? When did you arrive? And how did you get inside my room? Did I forget to lock the door?" I asked.

"Hailey, stop with the questions. I'm fine. I came half an hour ago, and you forgot to lock your door." He shook his head with an amused smile. "I see you are all dolled up tonight. Was all this effort for my brother?" Cameron asked.

I rolled my eyes at his comment.

Chase didn't even look at me. It didn't matter if I dolled up or not because he wouldn't notice me.

"But you want him to notice you," my heart said.

I shook my head and realized that I was extremely nervous for tonight's dinner. Something didn't feel right.

Cameron noticed my internal battle, and said, "Don't be nervous Hailey. You're looking very beautiful, and everything is going to be alright."

"Thank you, Cam. And you're looking pretty... nice."

He smirked at my compliment then smiled amusedly. I knew he was controlling himself from laughing at me. Seriously, who complimented a guy with pretty nice? Apparently, I did.

It was just too embarrassing and a jab to a man's manliness. Argh! What was I saying? I groaned at my stupid thoughts and hid my face with my hands.

Cameron cracked into laughs and wiped his imaginary tears.

I glared at him, and muttered, "Jerk."

But he just smiled at me.

"Excuse me, at least call me a handsome jerk. And if you will continue doing interesting things like this, then I am sure I wouldn't get bored tonight," Cameron said.

I rolled my eyes and dragged him downstairs.

Cameron went to the back garden where we had arranged dinner while I made my way to the kitchen to check for the last time if everything was ready for dinner.

"Is everything ready?" I looked at the dishes.

"Dear, everything is ready. Don't worry about it and go enjoy," Amy said with a smile.

I smiled at her and left the kitchen.

Chapter Fifteen

Graduation Dinner (Part 2)

Hailey

The dinner was going great. Dad and my father-in-law were talking about politics and business, which was quite boring for my mother and my mother-in-law to listen to, so they started talking about some new turkey recipe.

Emily and Kate looked pretty engrossed in their discussion about the new designer and model that walked on the ramp this year in Victoria Secrets' fashion show.

Allison and her husband were busy pulling Cameron's leg and teasing him constantly about his secret girlfriend that he had been hiding from everyone.

Chase was standing with them, smiling at their childish bickering.

I was in the kitchen helping Amy in heating up dinner. Amy was their housekeeper who was on leave when I came here, but now she had returned. She set the table and went back inside. I called everyone for dinner.

Everyone settled around the table, and I got the seat across Chase. The plates and dishes were being passed to one another, and I couldn't stop myself from staring at Chase. He looked handsome as always in fitted black button down shirt and jeans.

I didn't expect him to start loving me, but I wanted him to at least like me enough to glance at me. I didn't know why but I craved for his attention. Just one glance and his smile was enough to make me happy.

Was it too much to ask from one's husband?

"Hailey, snap out of daydreaming and start eating before your food gets cold," Allison said.

I smiled and put some salad and a small piece of baked chicken on my plate. I made the baked chicken for Allison's kids on her request, but that was the only thing I could eat during dinner. I was hoping that no one would notice my plate.

I ate salad then cut the baked chicken in small pieces and stabbed it with the fork then put it in my mouth. On the third bite, I felt my stomach flip. At that moment Allison eyed my plate.

"Hailey, why are you eating kid's food?" she asked me.

"Hailey is eating kid's food because she is still a kid." Emily laughed sarcastically.

"Hailey is eighteen. Eighteen means she is not a kid," Cameron said to defend me.

I cringed knowing that it wasn't the truth

"She is not eighteen. Didn't she tell you that she is sixteen?" Emily said, making everyone freeze around me.

I wanted to say that I was going to be seventeen soon as my birthday was near but I stopped myself.

"Oops! I think you all didn't know this. Sorry, sis." Emily had a smug smile on her face.

My heart stopped beating. I felt ashamed to look everyone in the eye. My head started to spin, and I closed my eyes.

"Is this true Hailey?" Chase asked me in an angry voice.

He stood up from the chair and threw the spoon on the table.

I looked down at my hands. They were shaking in fear. I glanced at mom, but she averted her eyes.

Taking a breather, I got up and looked at everyone in the eye.

"Yes, I'm going to be seventeen soon. I lied to you all about my age."

"I can't believe this. I'm married to a kid. Don't you know how old I am? Why did you agree to get married to me? Why did you lie to us about your age?" Chase demanded, slapping the table in anger making my heart jump in my chest.

"I was planning to tell you everything," I mumbled.

"When were you planning to tell me this?" Chase shouted again.

My body started to shake. I felt my temperature dropping, and my hands turned cold.

"Chase you are scaring her. Now, she is your wife, and you cannot change it," Allison said.

"I can change it, and I will change it." Chase hissed.

I blinked my eyes to stop the tears that were pooling in my eyes at his harsh retort.

My dad looked at me with guilt and shame in his eyes. I didn't want him to blame himself for my misery. I felt ashamed for the lie that I asked him to tell. I opened my mouth, but a sudden headache and dizziness made me clutch the table. I refrained myself from falling down on my knees as my body was shaking with anxiety.

My eyes landed on Emily. She had a satisfied smile on her face. I concealed the tears that burned my eyes by shutting them for a moment.

"Chase, you need to calm down. It's a family dinner to celebrate your graduation, and we have guests. We will discuss this matter after dinner," Chase's dad said.

Chase glared at me then sat back down on the chair beside his dad. His face was red with anger.

Cameron was staring at me like I betrayed him by hiding the truth. And I felt guilty for hiding the truth from him.

Chase looked at me like he was disgusted with me after hearing the truth. I felt pain in my heart again. I wanted to run far away from everyone's questioning gaze. I didn't want to explain anything to anyone. I didn't want them to find out that no one in this world cared for me and I had to agree to this marriage to get away from my stepmom and half-sister's house.

I decided to escape from the scrutinizing gaze of the people around me.

"Please excuse me," I said and got up from the chair.

I was about to leave when Allison pulled me back to the chair.

"Let's finish dinner first. You haven't touched anything other than salad," Allison said, putting something on my plate.

I glanced down at the plate and words came out of my mouth before I could've stopped them.

"Oh, God. Why is this so green?" I said, looking at the green pasta.

I felt the bile rising again. Putting a hand on my mouth, I got up from the chair and ran towards the nearest washroom, which had to be in the living room.

I threw up everything I tried to eat during dinner. After puking my guts, I washed my mouth and took a glance at my reflection in the mirror. My cheeks looked sunken from the constant puking and lack of food. The tears that spilled from my eyes during vomiting were dried on my face.

I looked pale and tired. I closed my eyes then heard a knock on the door.

I didn't find the energy to speak.

"Hailey are you alright?" Allison asked me from outside.

"I'm fine." I lied when I was actually exhausted.

After a few minutes of sitting on the floor and concentrating on calming my breath, I got up and splashed some water on my face. When I came out from the washroom, I took a lungful of breath.

Amy came running to me. "Are you alright dear?" she asked me, handing me water.

I took the glass of water and gulped down some.

"I'm fine," I said.

"Miss Kate made the green sauce pasta."

I closed my eyes and thought she was not going to let go of this easily. I needed to apologize to her. I prepared myself to receive her hateful glare and taunts. I made my way outside to the garden. My mind was begging me to run back to my room and never come out.

I reached near the table and found Kate crying on Chase's shoulder.

When everyone noticed me standing there, they fell silent. Kate's eyes snapped to me.

"You... you always ruin my mood. You knew that I made that pasta for Chase that's why you pulled that stunt. I hate you. I hate you so much," Kate yelled at my face.

I opened my mouth to apologize to her when Chase decided to intervene between us.

"First, you lied to us about your age and now you do this. Did you plan to ruin my life with your presence? I'm not going to forget my graduation day ever because you have made it so special by ruining it," Chase said.

The anger was clear on his face.

"Stop doing things that make me and others hate you more each day. You should be ashamed of yourself for lying to us and making us fools for so long," he said, gripping my shoulder.

His words started to play around my head, "Stop doing things that make me and others hate you more each day. You should be ashamed of yourself for lying to us."

I should be ashamed. I should stop doing things that made others hate me.

"Apologize to Kate for the stunt you pulled earlier, which hurt her," he said, gritting his teeth.

I just stared at him in complete silence.

Cameron got up from his seat and made his way to me.

"Brother, I think that's enough. Don't make a big scene out of a small thing. It's not your forte. Kate is enough to create drama," Cameron said.

"Shut up, Cameron. Don't put your nose in my business." Chase sent daggers my way.

My father-in-law interfered before a fight could break between the two brothers.

"Boys, stop," Chase's dad said, glaring at Cameron and Chase.

Cameron glared at Chase and clenched his jaw.

Emily smiled and took a sip of her drink. She was enjoying everything that was happening.

"What did I say, Hailey? Apologize to my sister then apologize to everyone for lying." Chase hissed in anger.

I felt something breaking inside me with every word that came out from his mouth. I literally heard the shattering of my heart and felt the pieces dropping into the pit of my stomach. His anger was not the one that hurt. It was his words, and they knocked the breath out of my lungs. I started to feel like someone just left me to die on the shore, where I was drowning in helplessly.

I would've apologized to Kate and tackled this situation with more dignity and confidence if Chase hadn't interfered and broke my heart.

The line "stop doing things that make me hate you more each day" kept replaying in my head, slashing my heart, again and again, making it bleed until I was gasping in pain. He broke every ounce of confidence I had gained in the past few months and made me feel worthless like before.

My heart was bleeding, and I felt like dying from inside. But I put my mask on, my face devoid of emotion. I looked Chase straight in the eye.

"I'm really sorry, Kate. It wasn't my intention to offend you, and I'm sorry for hurting you," I said to Kate. "I'm sorry for lying and hiding my real age from all of you. My parents are not responsible for this lie. I'm the only one you should blame for this," I said then took a deep breath. "Chase, I hope you'll forgive me for everything that I have done so far to make you hate me more each day. I'm really sorry for ruining your day," I said, looking at Chase.

Before anyone could see the tears falling from my eyes, I turned around and ran to my room. I locked my bedroom door and threw myself on the bed. Putting my face on the pillow, I cried.

The tears soon turned into loud sobs. I wished that I had a normal life where I wouldn't have to play the role of unwanted wife.

I married him hoping that he would give me a beautiful future, and hoped he was different from other people. I thought someday he would love me, but now I knew it was just my silly imagination. I fell in love with him thinking that he was different.

Now, it looked like I was wrong about him and I was only chasing false dreams. He hated me, and he would always hate me just like all those kids who hated me in school for being different, freak, loser, and dumb.

I cannot change myself, and they were not going to love me the way I was.

Many people had broken my heart before, but Chase had taken the top spot on my list. I loved him with all my heart and stupidly, blindly believed that he cared for me, but tonight he showed me that he didn't.

The tears were falling down from my eyes and wetting the pillow under my head.

I closed my eyes, wishing that I would never wake up.

Chapter Sixteen

Guilt

Chase

After Hailey ran inside the house and left us alone in the backyard, we were silent until Allison said, "Chase you were extremely rude to her. She looks sick and earlier when I went after her: I heard her throwing up in the washroom. You scared the poor girl so much."

Before I could say anything, Cameron interrupted.

"He wasn't rude. He was a complete ass. He yelled at her like she has no feelings. She is human Chase, not your punching bag, who you can hurt whenever you want. Most importantly she is your wife," Cameron said, staring at me.

He emphasized the word "wife," and I cringed internally.

Then he turned to Kate and glared at her.

"Kate, please grow up dear sister and stop creating drama out of petty things."

"Cameron, go inside right now," my mom said.

"I'm leaving because I don't like to sit with people who've sticks shoved up their asses." He stood up.

I clenched my jaw.

"Cameron, go inside," my dad said.

He left and went inside the house.

I just shook my head and left them without saying anything. On the way out, I picked my car keys and went for a drive.

For a few minutes, I drove here and there carelessly without any destination in mind. Then my eyes landed in an empty park where I used to come with my granddad and decided to stop there.

I parked the car and step out of it then made my way inside the park. The park was completely empty. I sat down on the bench near the water fountain and stared at the moon above.

I didn't know what I had done in my life to deserve this kind of fate. In my twenty years of life, I had done everything that my parents and granddad wanted me to do. Then why was I getting punished by fate?

I wasn't prepared for marriage, but I said yes to make my granddad happy. I wanted to be a doctor, but my parents wanted me to study business.

My entire life, I did everything to make others happy and did nothing to please me.

I didn't know Hailey, but when I saw her on our wedding day, I thought she was a perfect definition of an angel dressed in a beautiful white wedding gown. She looked so innocent and pure.

During the wedding ceremony, I assured myself that what I just felt for her a few minutes ago wasn't attraction but a reaction to seeing her for the first time.

After the wedding, I started to give her the cold shoulder, but it didn't change her natural friendly attitude with me. My feelings for her started to change. I used to dislike her presence in my house, but then I became addicted to her innocent, shy glances and her attention.

I started noticing her and every small action she made. She made a special place in my heart when she stayed with me the night I found out that my granddad left this world. I remembered her sweet voice whispering calming words in my ear. I remembered the feel of her soft fingers running through my hair.

After that night, everything changed in my heart. I started to crave for her attention, but before I could create my place in her life, Cameron stayed for a vacation. He became her friend, and I distanced myself from her. It gave me time to sort my feelings. I thought it was fine with me if she wanted to spend time with him. I tried to push every thought of them back in my head, but it became impossible.

I started to keep tabs on her and my brother. I hated it when she laughed with him. I hated it when she would enter the house with a smile plastered on her face and the reason for that smile was Cameron.

One day, I realized that it was jealousy. I felt jealous of my own brother because she had been spending time with him instead of me, and he was the one receiving all her attention. I cornered her and told her that I didn't want her to go anywhere with Cameron, and that was the day she kissed my cheek. My body went still when she planted her soft lips on my cheek, but my heart was somersaulting in my chest.

When I went back to my room, I touched my cheek. Her lips left a lingering feeling on my skin. My heart felt warm, and there was a silly smile on my lips.

I didn't know what was happening to me. I was confused about my feelings towards her. Then, I realized that I needed to stop all those feelings before I ruined everything.

I pushed her away from me that night of the party but ended up loving her. I found myself captured by her beauty and innocence. The time I put in creating boundaries between us was useless because it only took her simple confession to break them.

I never felt something like that before for anyone. I didn't know how it felt to be in love. Every new feeling scared me and to avoid getting hurt, I pushed her away again and ignored her for the whole month.

But did I stop feeling the same about her after ignoring her for a month? No, I couldn't stop my feelings, which was growing more every day.

Despite not talking to her all day, I still smiled thinking about her. Every night she would come in my dreams, and I would recall the sweet taste of her lips on my tongue. I could never forget the sensation of her lips on mine. Her innocent face in ecstasy was something that would always stay in my mind as my most beautiful memory.

I never felt such a special connection with any other girl before. They always felt temporary and left something unsatisfied in my soul. But that night Hailey filled the void in my soul and joined our hearts together. She took my heart and ruined me for anyone else.

I was planning to apologize to her tonight for avoiding and ignoring her for a month. I wanted to ask her for forgiveness and start fresh, but the truth about her age that was revealed tonight ruined the desire to be with her.

Now, I felt disgusted with myself for sleeping with her even when it was because of those drugs. I hated it for thinking that we could turn this loveless marriage into a real full of love marriage.

I couldn't understand why she agreed to get married to me when she should be worrying about graduating from high school, instead of staying in my house and playing a role of my wife.

I didn't know if I hated her for lying or I hated the truth of how young she was, and I couldn't be with her knowing the truth.

I knew what I had done tonight with her wasn't right, but it was the best way to finally make her hate me and let her go.

Chapter Seventeen

Alone

Hailey

[Morning after]

I woke up with extreme pain in my head. I sat up on my bed and rested my head on the headboard. My eyes were still shut due to the pain in them from crying all night.

Then I felt the sudden urge to throw up, and I ran in the direction of the bathroom. I emptied all the contents of my stomach then rinsed my mouth. I brushed my teeth to get rid of the vile taste of vomit. After that, I decided to take a shower and unzipped the dress, letting it pool down on my feet. I got inside the shower, and the cold water soothed my burning body making me sigh in relief. When I was done showering, I wrapped the towel around myself and opened my closet. I pulled out my inner wear and put them on. Then I pulled out the hair dryer and plugged it in.

After I was done drying my hair, I looked at my pale face and swollen eyes in the mirror. Chase's words started to replay in my head making me shut them in pain.

I hated myself for loving him. I hated myself for letting my stupid heart fell for him. He broke me, hurt me, and treated me like there was nothing between us.

Couldn't he see how much I loved him?

I moved to go back to my room but stumbled due to the excruciating pain in my head. I tried to hold myself together, but everything around me started to fade. Then slowly, I fell down on the floor. My eyes rolled back in my head and breaths turned into gasps after that darkness consumed me.

*   *   *

Chase

[Morning after]

When I came downstairs for breakfast, I found Amy and my mom working in the kitchen.

"Where is everyone?" I asked my mom.

"Your dad left for the office because he has very important meetings lined up for today. Kate went out for breakfast with some friends. Cameron is still sleeping, I guess."

I was hoping that she would continue and tell me about Hailey, but she didn't say anything about her.

Amy placed my coffee and plate of toast and fried eggs in front of me.

I took a sip of my coffee and cringed because it wasn't perfect like Hailey made it. In those three months she had made me addicted to the coffee she made and how could I forget about those delicious cupcakes. Almost every morning, she served me these together turning my boring breakfast into a heavenly one.

If she hadn't prepared coffee for me, it meant she still hadn't come down for breakfast.

I was about to take my first bite when I stopped. She was sick last night. The thought of her made me worry. I checked the time, and it was ten in the morning. She usually came down around nine.

I hesitantly asked my mom to confirm my suspicions.

"Mom where's Hailey? I mean she's usually with you when you're in the kitchen making breakfast," I said.

My mom raised her eyebrows at me.

"She hasn't come down this morning to help me with anything. I think she's embarrassed to show her face after lying to us," she said.

After hearing that, I got more worried.

I got up, and said, "I am not hungry."

My mother gave me a weird look but said nothing.

I went upstairs to Hailey's room with the spare keys of her bedroom in my hand. I knocked loudly on her door twice and waited, but she didn't open the door.

My heart started to beat faster. Different types of scenarios started playing in my mind. What if she had hurt herself after last night's incident? What if she was too sick to even move and open the door or answer?

If something happened to her because of me, how would I be able to forgive myself?

Without dwelling on the thoughts of what ifs, I inserted the keys and unlocked the door.

I pushed open the door and went inside. The first thing my eyes landed on was a messy bed that was empty. I walked to her bathroom and knocked on the door, but again I didn't receive any answer from her. I pushed the door open and found her sprawled down on the bathroom floor in her undergarments.

I kneeled down and called her name, but she didn't open her eyes. Her face looked extremely pale, and her lips were almost white, not in their natural pink color, which I loved.

My heart broke at the sight of her motionless body in my arms. I picked her up bridal style and took her out then carefully placed her on the bed.

I picked up a glass and rushed to the washroom to fill it with water. Then I came back out. I splashed some water on her face to wake her up, but she stayed unconscious.

Then I went back down to inform my mom about Hailey.

"Mom, I found Hailey passed out in her room. We need to take her to the hospital," I said to her, picking my car keys from the table.

"What? You found her passed out on the floor?" She got up from the chair.

We went to her room so she could look at her.

"I'm dressing her into something appropriate. Go call 911," she said.

She walked to the closet and picked out a simple white summer dress and hurriedly dressed her in it.

I dialed 911 and informed them of the situation. The ambulance arrived in ten minutes, and the paramedics checked Hailey. They said her blood pressure had dropped really low and she needed to be taken to the hospital. Mom rode in the ambulance with Hailey, and I went to the garage to take out my car then followed the ambulance.

When we arrived at the nearest hospital, Hailey was immediately taken to the emergency room.

My mom and I followed them to the ER.

An hour had passed, but the doctor hadn't informed us of anything except that she was fine and they were running some tests to find the reason why she passed out earlier.

I was extremely anxious and worried about her. When the doctor came out from Hailey's room, my mom and I were instantly by her side.

She looked at the reports in her hand and then said, "Hi, I'm Doctor Ashley. What's your relationship with the patient?"

"I'm her mother-in-law," my mom said hesitantly.

"Oh, that's great. I have good news for you."

My mom and I frowned.

"Your daughter-in-law is pregnant," the doctor said.

When her words registered in my mind, my world tilted upside down. My body went numb. Everything around me slowed down, and I stumbled back.

How could I be so stupid? Why didn't I think about this? What had I done?

Oh, God! She was pregnant with my child.

I had ruined everything for us.

"Are you sure that she is pregnant?" my mom asked the doctor.

"Yes. I'm sure. Hailey is almost four weeks pregnant and here are her reports. She just has a very bad case of morning sickness that's why she is so weak and fainted. I have written some medicine to tame down nausea and vitamins to keep her and the baby healthy. You can take her home, but I recommend complete bed rest at least for 2 weeks as she is quite weak at the moment."

My mom awkwardly smiled, and said, "Thank you."

The doctor handed my mom Hailey's report and prescription.

When the doctor left, I fell down on the nearest chair and looked down at my feet. Everything had changed. She was now pregnant and hated me for what I had done last night and how I had treated her all these months.

A shudder went through my body at the thought of confessing everything that happened between us to my parents. It gave me a mini seizure.

*   *   *

Hailey

I tried to open my eyes, but the bright light made me shut them instantly. I groaned and opened them again to see the white ceiling and walls. I shot up from the bed and looked around. My room didn't have white colored walls. I glanced at myself and found an IV sticking in my left hand.

What was I doing in the hospital?

Then I remembered how I fainted in the morning.

Oh, God! Did I have some kind of fatal disease? Was I dying? Was that why they brought me to the hospital?

I felt like crying at my fate for being so cruel.

Before I could dwell on my thoughts, my mother-in-law stormed inside. She looked at me in anger and disgust.

"Get up. We're leaving," she yelled, making me jump in fright.

I looked at the IV attached to my hand and then I looked up at her.

She made a noise of irritation then roughly removed the IV from my hand. The place where the IV was attached started to bleed, and I felt the pain in my hand. Tears brimmed in my eyes at her harsh action.

She glared at me, and I got up from the bed.

I looked around for my slippers but couldn't found them anywhere.

"Don't waste time," she said, getting out of the room.

I silently followed her out without slippers.

People looked at me confused, and I hid my face by looking down at the white tiles of the hospital floor.

When we stepped out of the hospital, we found Chase waiting for us in his car. I risked a glance at Chase and found him staring at me. We were both frozen then I averted my eyes from him and got in the back seat of the car. He started driving towards the house.

We reached the house, and my mother-in-law pulled me out of the car, roughly.

"Mom, I need some time alone. I will be back soon," Chase said, getting back in the car and left us.

After Chase left, she dragged me into the house.

I was so scared of her because her actions were screaming danger. If she weren't holding my wrist so tightly I would have considered running to my room and locking myself inside.

She dragged me to the living room where Kate was resting on the couch and watching something on TV.

When she saw us, she got up, and said, "Mom. Is everything alright?"

She let go of my wrist and sat down on the couch. I took a glance at my wrist and found three harsh red marks due to her death grip.

She gave me a cold glare, which could freeze the whole country.

"Kate, go call your father and tell him to come home immediately." She ordered Kate.

Kate opened her mouth to ask her why but thought better of it.

My legs trembled from standing, and I moved towards the couch to sit, but I was stopped by my mother-in-law.

"Did I give you the permission to sit? Keep standing," she yelled.

I retraced my steps back and stood still.

Kate finally got the courage to open her mouth.

"Mom, what's going on?" Kate asked.

That question made my mother-in-law so angry, and her head snapped to me. I moved my foot left to right and glanced at her again to just receive another cold glare from her.

"Kate, I'll tell you what's going on. This merely 16-year-old girl is four weeks pregnant, can you believe it?" she said with her hand pointing at me.

After I heard her, the first question that popped into my mind was how I could be pregnant?

Pregnant as in there was a baby inside me.

Holy cupcakes! How? When?

That question just made me want to faint again and never wake up.

"She is pregnant," Kate repeated, snapping me out from my train of thoughts. "Mom, I told you what kind of a girl she is but you didn't believe me. Emily told me everything. How this girl was caught fucking a boy in the janitor's closet and got suspended from school. After that, her father homeschooled her because of daily complaints from school about her immoral activities," Kate said, looking at me.

I couldn't believe that Emily would go so far in hating me and told lies about me.

"Is it true Hailey?" my mother-in-law asked.

"No, it's not true." I looked down at the floor.

"She is a liar, Mom. She is not even Aunt Melanie's real daughter. Her mother trapped Emily's dad knowing he is married and got pregnant with her to gain money from him. Now she is doing the same thing her mom did. She has become pregnant so her stay in here will be permanent. She just wants to enjoy a lavish life, which only Chase can give her. I doubt the child she is carrying is even Chase's child because he never liked her," Kate said.

My hands turned cold after hearing her. The look on my mother-in-law's face was giving me goosebumps.

"Is it true, Hailey? Are you a product of your dad's infidelity?" she asked me.

I didn't know how to answer her without breaking down in front of her.

"Tell me, girl!" she yelled, and my body started to tremble again.

"Yes."

"It was a mistake that I did not believe you, Kate," she said glaring at me. "Now tell me, who is the father of this child you are carrying?" she asked me.

My mind was jumbled up with questions. What did she mean by, "who is the father of the child I am carrying?"

Before I could comprehend what was happening, I felt a very hard slap on my right cheek. The force of the slap made me stumble back, and I fell down on my bottom on the floor.

The tears pooled in my eyes and the metallic taste of blood filled my mouth.

At that moment, the main door opened and Chase and his dad entered the house. The tears furiously rolled down from my eyes and my right cheek felt numb and swollen because of the slap.

Chase's eyes landed on me, and he came running towards me then kneeled down. He assessed my face and wiped my tears.

"What happened?" he asked me.

I looked at him and blinked my eyes to get rid of the blurriness.

"Eva, what's going on here?" my father-in-law asked.

"Look at this William, and you'll know what's going on here." My mother-in-law slapped some papers on my father-in-law's hand.

He read them silently and looked at us in shock. Then my mother-in-law suddenly pulled me up from the floor roughly.

"I'm asking you one last time girl. Tell me who the father of this baby is before I completely lose my mind." She threatened me.

I didn't know anything myself.

What was I supposed to tell her? What should I tell her?

My legs started to tremble from the effort of standing. I felt a hand on my back and looked to my left to see Chase standing beside me with his jaw clenched.

Tears were now blurring my damn vision. The pounding in my head that subsided earlier came crashing back making me want to puke all over the place. But I refrained myself from doing anything that would make my mother-in-law angrier at me.

Kate suddenly said, "Mom, I think this slut will not open her mouth easily. You should beat her with the whip granddad used on the ranch to tame the wild horses. I'm sure she will tell you willingly who the father of this bastard child is."

At her words, my face went pale, and my whole body started to shake in fear of getting beaten by a whip.

I looked down at my feet to hide the tears, which were now flowing freely from my eyes.

My mother-in-law was about to slap me again when Chase caught her hand and pushed me behind his tall figure. I sneaked a quick look from behind to see him and his mom standing frozen and staring at each other.

"Why are you stopping me? She is carrying another man's baby," she said, and my eyes widened.

Why would she say something like that?

My father-in-law finally came out from his shock and dragged her away from Chase and me.

"Eva, control your temper. We need to handle this situation with a cool mind and through communicating, not with hands or whips," he said.

Chase slipped his hand into my trembling hand and gripped it.

"Kate, never use those words in my presence again, or you'll be responsible for my actions. Now go to your room," my father-in-law said with a glare.

Kate took a glance at his father, and quickly said, "Sorry Dad."

Then she left the living room and went to her room.

"Dear, please go to your room and take some rest," my father-in-law said to me.

I turned to leave, and Chase turned like he wanted to come with me.

"Son, come with me to my study," Chase's dad said.

Chase glanced at our intertwined hands and then relaxed his grip, removing his hand. Without looking at him, I ran upstairs to my room and locked the door so no one would ever come inside and hurt me again.

I slid down on the floor with my back pressed on the door and started thinking about Melanie. I always thought she was my real mother, but she turned out to be my stepmother. The good thing was that she never abused me physically at least. She would make fun of my fashion sense, hurt my feelings, and made me feel insecure about myself, but she never inflicted physical pain. In that house, Emily was the only one who inflicted physical and emotional pain.

When I started to live here, I thought Eva was sweet as she was treating me like a daughter for the past three months. I never thought she would hate me so much once she found out that I was an illegitimate child. I never thought she would hit me so hard and broke my soul again making me recall all the memories of abuse I endured during my childhood.

I touched my swollen cheek and flinched when it stung. I licked my chapped lips and tasted the metallic taste of blood.

The tears started spilling from my eyes. At that moment, I felt so alone in this world, utterly and completely alone.

Chapter Eighteen

Claiming What's Mine

Chase

When we reached the house, we got out. Instead of going inside with them, I told Mom I needed some time alone and got back in the car then drove away.

I glanced at the furious expression on Mom's face, which cleared one thing in my mind, that she didn't like the news of Hailey's pregnancy.

I was only a few blocks away from the house when my cell phone rang.

"Hello, Dad." I picked up my dad's call.

"Hello, son. Your sister called. There is an emergency, and your mom wants me to come home," Dad said, and my heart fell.

"Dad, I am not at home but I'm going back there, and I think you should come home too. I need to talk to you about something."

"Okay, son. I'm coming," Dad said, understanding that if I was asking him to come, it meant I really needed him.

We both arrived at the house at the same time.

"What did you want to talk to me about?" he asked me.

"First, let's go inside, Dad."

I unlocked the door, and we entered the house. My eyes landed on Hailey sitting on the floor. Without thinking much, I ran towards her and kneeled down.

"What happened?" I asked her, looking at the bruise on her cheek and blood oozing out from her lower lip.

She glanced at me and blinked, trying to get rid of the tears.

"Eva, what's going on here?" my dad asked my mom.

"Look at this William, and you'll know what's going on here." Mom slapped some papers on my dad's hand.

I knew they were Hailey's report. Dad read them silently then looked at us in shock.

Then my mom suddenly pulled Hailey up from the floor roughly, and I got up too.

"I'm asking you one last time girl. Tell me who the father of this baby is before I completely lose my mind." She threatened her.

I was confused by her question.

What did she mean by who the father of her baby was?

It was obviously me. Did she think Hailey cheated on me?

I looked at Hailey's trembling form and placed a hand on her back to provide her support. I couldn't understand why my mom would accuse this innocent girl of cheating. She had done nothing wrong. It was only my fault that got us in this situation. I clenched my jaw thinking about Quinton who put drugs in the food and drinks, which led us here.

Kate's voice brought me back to the situation at hand.

"Mom, I think this slut will not open her mouth easily. You should beat her with the whip granddad used on the ranch to tame the wild horses. I'm sure she will tell you willingly who the father of this bastard child is," Kate said.

At her words, Hailey's face went pale, and her whole body started to shake in fear. She looked down at her feet to hide the tears, which were now flowing freely from her eyes.

I wanted to yell at my sister for sprouting rubbish, but I stopped when I saw my mom was about to slap Hailey again. I caught her hand and pushed Hailey behind me to hide her from my mom's view. She was frozen, and so was I. We were staring at each other's eyes.

"Why are you stopping me? She is carrying another man's baby," she said.

I didn't know who put the lie in her head that this child was not mine.

My dad came out from the shocked state and dragged mom away from Hailey and me.

"Eva, control your temper. We need to handle this situation with a cool mind and through communicating, not with hands or whips," he said.

I slipped my hand into her trembling one and gripped it.

"Kate, never use those words again in my presence, or you'll be responsible for my actions. Now go to your room," he said with a glare.

Kate took a glance at him, and quickly said, "Sorry Dad."

Then she left the lounge and went to her room.

"Dear, please go to your room and take some rest," Dad said, looking at Hailey.

I turned to leave with Hailey because I wanted to talk to her and apologize to her for my mom's actions, but dad stopped me.

"Son, come with me to my study."

I glanced at our intertwined hands, and then I let go of her hand. Without looking at me, Hailey ran upstairs to her room, and I turned to my father.

*   *   *

When we were inside his study, Dad locked the door and took a seat on the couch and patted the side telling me to sit beside him. I did.

"Chase, do you want to tell me something?"

I wanted to tell him, but my mouth suddenly felt dry.

"Do you know who the father is? Because son, I'm lost here," my dad said, sighing.

I opened my mouth to say something then closed it.

"In three months, I have never seen her talk to anyone other than family. She has no friends here, and I don't think she has ever gone anywhere alone," my dad said, rubbing his forehead.

He looked tense, and the worry was clear on his face.

"If you think I don't notice then let me tell you something. I have noticed how that girl always looks at you with love in her eyes. How she waits for you to come home and glances at you secretly. Kate, your mom, and I know she loves you. You have tried your best to push her away, son, and you crossed every line last night by insulting her in front of her family. I know you didn't want this marriage, but that girl doesn't deserve your hate and your mother's slap. She doesn't deserve being called names and especially not in front of you. You need to take control of your life son. Hailey is your responsibility," Dad said, placing a hand on my shoulder.

After hearing him, my throat felt clogged with emotions. I knew he was right about everything.

I didn't know if I would ever be able to reciprocate her feelings with the same ferocity. But I was sure about one thing that I cared for her and our unborn child. And I would do anything to protect them both. They were both the most innocent creature I have met in this world and didn't deserve to be hurt.

I had to stop thinking like a stupid, careless boy. I had to take responsibility for my actions.

"Dad, it's me... I'm the father of the baby," I said.

He didn't ask me for explanation or pressured me for details. I was grateful for that. I knew my dad. He could read me like an open book and understood me better than anyone.

My dad patted my back, and said, "Son, congratulations. I know you will become a great dad but remember to take care of the mother of your child as well. Do whatever you think is best for your child and your wife. You have my full support."

I hugged him tightly like I used to do when I was a kid.

"Dad, thank you," I said to him.

He ruffled my hair and smiled at me.

"Let's go. We need to tell your mother before her mind forms more stories," he said.

I nodded my head and followed him to the lounge where my mom was sitting on the couch, and Cameron was standing in front of her.

"Mom, what happened? Why do you look so stressed?" Cameron asked.

Before she could say anything, her eyes landed on us. She raised her eyebrows in my direction.

I knew my words would break her dreams. I had ruined all the plans for my future, and my mother would be most affected with this.

I took a deep breath, and said, "Mom. I'm the father of the baby Hailey is carrying."

She stood up and looked at me.

"Son, can you repeat what you just said?" Mom asked.

"Mom, the baby is mine. I know it's difficult to accept everything, but you've to accept it. And don't even try to touch Hailey again."

She looked at me in anger then left the room. My dad followed her to their room.

Cameron stepped in front me, and asked, "Did Mom really hit Hailey?"

I nodded my head.

Cameron looked panic and worried at my answer.

"Where is Hailey?" he asked me.

"She is in her room."

He ran upstairs towards her room, and I followed him. When we reached outside her room, Cameron knocked at the door, but she didn't answer. Then he tried to unlock the door, but it didn't budge.

"Go, Chase. Fetch the spare keys right now," Cameron told me.

I ran back downstairs and brought the spare keys then gave them to him.

When we pushed the door open, my breath was knocked out of my lungs.

Chapter Nineteen

Cameron and Allison

Cameron

When Chase came with the spare keys, I took them, and said, "I think you should give her some space. I'll go first."

He nodded and stayed behind. I pushed the door open and went into the room. Hailey was sitting on the floor. Her head was resting on the foot of the bed. I kneeled down to wake her up but stopped when my eyes landed on her face. Her cute chubby cheeks had a handprint on them and looked swollen. Her lower lip was split open, and a small amount of blood was still oozing out. I felt sudden anger at my mother for hitting Hailey like this.

I shook her shoulder lightly to wake her up. Suddenly she opened her eyes and looked around, scared then her eyes landed on me.

Tears filled her eyes, and she flung her arms around my neck and hugged me tightly. "Cam, I don't know anything? Why... me?"

I rubbed her back to provide her some comfort, and replied, "Hailey, I'm here. I promise you no one is going to hurt you again. Now, calm down."

After a few minutes or sobbing and mumbling incoherent things, she finally untangled herself from me.

I got up from the floor and turned back to realize that Chase had left already. I helped Hailey got up from the floor, and said, "You need to wash your face."

She nodded and went inside the washroom.

I decided to go to the kitchen to bring some ice to her swollen cheek. When I came out from Hailey's room, I found him leaning on the wall.

I asked him, "What are you doing here?"

"I just want to know how she is. She hasn't eaten anything this morning," Chase said in worry.

The concern he was showing angered me.

"Oh, so now you're worried. Where were you when mom slapped her? She has a swollen cheek and split lips because you're a loser who cannot stand up against his mother for his wife. Stop being her puppet," I said.

At my statement, guilt and sadness appeared on his face, and instead of saying anything he left.

I went to the kitchen. I took a bowl and filled it with Hailey's favorite charm cereal and milk. Then I made a cup of hot chocolate for her. Lastly, I took out some frozen peas from the fridge and arranged all the things on the tray and went back to her room.

When I entered the room, I found her curled up on the bed.

In a low voice, I said, "Hailey, sit up. You need to eat. I have your favorite charms and hot chocolate here."

She sat up, leaning her head on the headboard. But she looked so broken, and I wanted to beat my brother to the pulp for making her so sad.

I put the pack of frozen peas on her cheek, and she hissed at the coldness of the ice. I laughed at her cute face, and she gave me a murderous glare.

I just made an innocent face, and her lips twitched upward in a small smile. When the swelling on her cheek has reduced, I pulled off the bag of frozen peas.

She took the bowl from my hand and started eating. But her face stayed emotionless. I was upset at the sight of her so just to lighten up her mood, I started making jokes, and she actually laughed at a few of my stupid, senseless jokes.

When she was done eating, I gave her the hot chocolate. She drank half the cup then handed it back to me. I applied some ointment on her split lips and told her to sleep.

Like a little kid, she curled up on the bed again and hid her face in the blanket.

I wanted to help her. I wanted to see the smile on her face again, which reminded me of Mia. Mia was my best friend who I lost three years ago. I shouldn't think about her right now.

I closed the door of her bedroom and went to my room. I was thinking about what to do to bring back the smile on her face? Then suddenly, a light bulb went off in my head and the best idea to cheer her up came to my mind.

I called Allison, my older sister, and told her everything. Allison agreed to come for a visit in the evening to distract Hailey.

I opened my closet and searched for the box. When I found it, I opened it and took out all the money that I had been saving up to get my favorite sports bike, which dad refused to buy me.

I wanted to buy it before I would come home permanently from the boarding school, but it could wait. Now I needed the money to proceed with my plan to make Hailey smile. I called my friend Mike and asked him to pick me up.

When I came back from shopping, I found Allison sitting with mom on the couch.

"Allison come with me." I pulled her up from the couch and dragged her upstairs to Hailey's room.

Hailey was still curled up lying on the bed and probably crying.

I switched on all the lights of her room, and yelled, "Surprise! We have something for you."

She sat up on the bed and rubbed her eyes to wipe the tears then looked at me with a smile.

"Hi." She mumbled.

"Hey. How are you feeling?" Allison asked her.

"I'm fine."

But I knew she wasn't fine.

I jumped up on her bed with the gifts, and said, "C'mon, open them."

She moved lazily, sluggishly and opened the first bag that contained the box of chocolate that she liked and a very cute, fluffy white teddy bear holding a heart. In the center of the heart "smile" was printed in bold letters.

She giggled and hugged the bear tightly.

"Thank you, Cam," she said, kissing the bear.

I nudged her to open the other bags, and she rolled her eyes at my eagerness but opened it.

And boy she wasn't just giggling anymore. No, she was squealing, jumping with happiness and believe me it was worth all the money.

She looked at me with a shocked expression on her face, and asked, "You got me a laptop. A laptop! Really?"

Allison and I both glanced at each other and smiled at Hailey's reaction to getting a laptop. For other people in this house and me, the laptop was no big deal. Everyone in the house had their own laptop, mobile, and other gadgets to use except her. I was literally shocked after knowing that. I mean, c'mon, we were living in the twenty-first century. Everyone had their own laptop and cell phones. So today, I thought, *"Why not give her a laptop, which she can use whenever she wanted. It'll entertain her when she'll miss me and need a friend."*

She thanked me, again and again, it was like she forgot about what happened today, which was good.

I asked her if she wanted to learn some new functions of this laptop. She eagerly nodded her head, and I showed her some new apps and functions.

"Hailey, I need to go and pack my bag because I'm leaving tonight. Take care," I said after some time, hugging her.

She nodded.

"I'm going to miss you, Cam. Please, come back soon," she said, hugging me back.

Then I left her with Allison in the room.

*   *   *

Allison

After Cameron left us in awkward silence, I glanced at Hailey.

"Are you really fine?" I asked her, staring at her swollen eyes.

She nodded, but her eyes were telling another tale.

"I heard you're expecting. I hope you don't mind Hailey, but it's really difficult to understand. How and when did you both become this close? Did Chase confess his undying love or was it just attraction between you guys that lead you both to have sex? And why didn't you guys use protection? Did you both plan to have a family? These questions are jumbling up in my mind so please tell me," I asked her.

She looked hurt, confused, and mostly broken. Different emotions played on her face in those sixty seconds. She moved closer to me like she was going to tell me some secret.

"Allison, you are like an older sister to me. Do you trust me when I say that I don't have any answers to your questions?"

I was confused by her answer.

"What do you mean, Hailey? Just tell me when did you both have sex?" I asked her.

Her face suddenly exploded with a blush. She looked embarrassed and shy.

"I... I don't know how to say this, but I don't know anything. I have no idea how I became pregnant," she said.

I was shocked and scared to ask her anything anymore.

"Hailey, do you mean to tell me that you don't know what lovemaking means? What goes on between husband and wife in the bedroom after marriage?"

"I don't know anything but I read a few things from books, and they didn't make any sense," she said with innocence.

"Have you been living under the rock your entire life? Why didn't your mother tell you and give you the safe sex talk?" I asked her.

I was appalled at her mother for not giving her daughter a proper education.

Hailey looked so flustered and tears brimmed in her eyes. Instantly, I regretted what I said a few seconds ago.

She glanced at me, and said, "My mother and I weren't close to each other. Emily was always too busy to spare me time. I had no friends, and I was dumb in class, so maybe that's the reason I'm so clueless about simple things, which everyone knows. I was homeschooled and didn't learn things like other teenagers, so to say that I was living under the rock was right."

I didn't know what to say after hearing her. I was beyond frustrated and angry at everyone. We were living in the twenty-first century, and still innocent people like Hailey existed.

"Hailey, I'm guessing you never had a boyfriend," I said.

At my question, she flushed again, and her small act confirmed my suspicions.

"I never had a boyfriend or any involvement with a boy... uh." She looked so embarrassed while saying that like it was a crime.

A girl could spend thirty years and stayed a virgin. I didn't mind, but she should have known about this.

I just didn't know how to explain everything to her, but I tried. I explained everything to her then she told me she didn't remember having sex. I cried at her answer.

"Hailey, did you sleep with Chase?" I asked her.

"No, I didn't sleep with him. I sleep in my own bed every night."

At that moment if someone asked me to jump down from the Eiffel Tower, I would have listened.

"Hailey, please try to remember." I begged her.

"I don't remember anything," she said, shutting her eyes.

I looked at her with pity and sadness. I was angry at fate.

"If you ever need me, then please, don't hesitate to call me. Take care of yourself and the little one growing inside you. You need to be strong and to think wisely from now on." I kissed her head and left her room.

I found Chase sitting on the bench in the backyard and went outside to talk to him.

My mind was full of questions, which only he could answer. I quietly sat beside him on the bench.

He glanced at me then sighed.

"Chase. I… uh was with Hailey in her room, and we talked about this entire situation," I told him.

He looked at me with his eyes wide open but kept his mouth shut.

"Chase, I know it's your personal life, but I don't get it. When did you get attracted to Hailey? When did you both become so close to each other? I mean we noticed how you treated her all these months," I asked him.

The emotions of guilt and regret appeared on Chase's face at my questions.

"Promise me, Allison. You won't tell a soul what I'm going to share with you," he said, staring into my eyes.

I nodded my head, and said, "I promise, Chase. Whatever you're going to tell me will stay between the two of us forever."

He was satisfied with my answer, and said, "You remember Hailey and I went to this party when Mom and Dad left for Chicago with Kate?"

I nodded my head, and he continued.

"A few boys spiked the drinks and food with drugs. I thought I was drunk and she was too. We had no control of our bodies, and one thing led to another thing. After that, we ended up in bed. And I have been avoiding her since that day. I felt guilty, and I was embarrassed to talk to her," he said, looking at his feet.

I gasped after knowing that they were drugged when everything happened between them.

But if Chase remembered that night then why didn't Hailey remember anything?

"Oh God, Chase! Hailey doesn't remember anything. She has no idea what happened between you two," I yelled in shock.

"What do you mean she doesn't remember anything? We were both drugged, and I was drunk too, but I remember everything. Then why doesn't she?" he asked me.

I shook my head, and said, "She doesn't have any memory of the night you spent together. She is confused and blank."

Chase rubbed his face with his palms and shook his head.

"It means she was drugged with something that leaves no trace of memory when you wake up in the morning," Chase said in disbelief.

"No, it means someone wanted her to forget everything in the morning. Someone deliberately gave drugs to her that night."

Chase cursed under his breath.

"Yes, Al. It was Britney. She is obsessed with Sam, and when he was giving more attention to Hailey, she got jealous. She wanted to hurt her that night. And that's why she was given that specific drug to make her forget everything," he mumbled and pulled his hair in anger.

"I'm so sorry, Chase," I said, putting my hand on his arm.

I pitied my brother at that moment. He looked so lost and heartbroken.

"I don't know what to do to make everything okay. It seems like whenever I love someone their life gets destroyed," he said.

I knew he was blaming himself for everything,

"You need to focus on your heart, Chase. Stop listening and looking at things from others' perceptive and find your own. Let your heart guide you."

He hugged me like he used to do when he was a kid.

Chapter Twenty

I Will Live For Him

Hailey

[Two months later]

It was midnight. Everyone was sleeping soundly in their rooms, but I was wide awake in the night like an owl.

My nights were mostly ruined courtesy of my weird cravings. Tonight, I was craving for some ice cream. The craving was not weird this time, but the timing was. I felt like someone was sending images in my mind, making my mouth water at the thought of ice cream.

I had a habit of doing weird things, so at that moment, I did the weirdest thing I could think of and closed my eyes then started praying loudly.

"Please Santa, I know it's not Christmas, but can you give my present before Christmas? I don't want much, just some chocolate chip, vanilla, strawberry, and cookie dough ice cream," I said loudly, standing beside my window and looking up at the sky.

I went back to my bed and slumped down on the bed with a pout on my face when I didn't see Santa coming.

"Tell me baby boy what should mama do. What do you say, baby, should we sneak out from this fancy prison and have some fun? Would you like to have an adventure with your mom? Huh?" I said, placing my hand on my baby bump.

I loved talking to my baby. It was not weird, okay, a little bit weird. I knew he cannot answer me yet, but I could assure you that my boy was a good listener.

You must be wondering why I called my baby a boy. Actually, I had a dream last Sunday, where Chase and I were in the garden playing with a very cute little boy. It was a beautiful dream and awakened hope inside me. Since that day, I had been calling my baby a boy.

I hoped he was a boy because if my baby turned out to be a girl, it would be awkward on my part after his or her birth as I had been calling him a son.

I looked at the walls and sighed. I hadn't left this room since the day my mother-in-law found out about my pregnancy. She had cut me out of the family. She wouldn't allow me to eat with anyone. Amy would bring my meal to my room every day.

Amy told me when Chase or my father-in-law would try to see me Eva would create lies to stop them. She would lie to them and say that I was sleeping or taking a nap so they wouldn't come to see me.

Eva, my mother-in-law, told me like really told me to my face with a cold glare that she never wanted to see me out of my room. The great thing was that she still took me to the doctor for monthly check-ups and I wondered why.

Thinking about her, always made my heart ache. Before everything, she was sweet to me and treated me like a daughter. I respected her and thought she would fill the space of motherly love in my life, but that dream was shattered really fast when she slapped me that day. Now, I knew she hated me, and I didn't like her as much as I used to like her.

I didn't get it. Why did my life have to be so difficult? Why did I have to go through all these problems and humiliation?

Sometimes, I felt like I was a puppet for everyone to use, and they moved my strings however they wished.

It was like I didn't have any wishes or any dreams of my own that I wanted to live up.

Whenever I closed my eyes to get some sleep, I felt like I was drowning in an ocean and it was getting harder to breathe underwater. I felt like I wouldn't be able to surface back and given a chance to escape this cruel world. But then there was always a shadow pulling me out of the water and making me breathe.

And I thought it was my baby, my son because when no one would need me, he would need me. He would always need his mother's love and care, and I decided as long as he needed me I was going to live. I was going to live for him. He was my last hope for life and for my future.

I didn't know what would happen when my baby would be born. Although Chase had accepted this baby, he hadn't shown much care in this past two months. He still avoided me, which hurt me more. I understood it was a lot to take in for him, and he was scared. But at this moment I needed his support because I was scared too.

Two months ago, when Alison told me about sex, believe me, I had a little seizure. My heart literally stopped beating for a few minutes. Then I read little more and understood how one got pregnant. After learning that, my face exploded in blush, and I started choking. When Amy came to give me food, she was so worried. She told me my face looked likc someone tried to murder me by squeezing my neck.

I was seriously not ready to believe that Chase and I did something like that. And he remembered everything while I forgot every single detail.

I wanted to remember everything about that night. After I knew what lovemaking meant, I assumed that it happened on the night of the party because that morning I found myself naked on the bed. The bruises I found on my body, which I thought were bug bites were actually love bites or hickeys. Whenever I thought about that night my face heated up, and a shiver went through my whole body.

*   *   *

Chase

I was walking to my room when I heard her voice.

"Please Santa, I know it's not Christmas, but can you give my present before Christmas? I don't want much, just some chocolate chip, strawberry, vanilla, and cookie dough ice cream," she said.

I frowned at the word Santa in her prayer.

Why would she ask Santa for ice creams?

I didn't know if Santa heard her or not, but I did.

I picked up my car keys and went to the nearest mart and bought strawberry, chocolate chip, vanilla, and cookie dough ice cream tubs. I came back home and went to the kitchen. I pulled out a large bowl from the cabinet and placed it on a tray. Then I put scoops of all the flavors of ice cream in it.

I put the tubs of ice cream into the refrigerator so she could finish them later. I made my way out of the kitchen with the tray in my hand and went upstairs to Hailey's room then knocked on her door. I didn't know why I felt so nervous and why my heart was beating like crazy.

When she opened the door, I stared at her with my mouth agape. She was wearing very short pink cotton shorts, which were revealing her beautiful legs for my hungry gaze, and a white singlet which was molding her perfect body. Her hair was on top of her head in a messy bun showing me that she didn't put any effort to look this attractive.

I didn't know she would be wearing something too sexy when I decided to come here. It was midnight, but she looked radiant and flawless. Her skin was glowing and looking beautiful. The small baby bump was also peeking out from her singlet, and my heart flipped.

I averted my eyes and looked down, but her beautiful smooth legs came into my view, and I gulped. Suddenly, the weather seemed hot to me, and I felt the urge to sit under the air-conditioner.

She stared at me with her mouth agape. She seemed to be in shock at finding me outside her bedroom.

I cleared my throat, and said, "I... uh... I bought some ice cream."

I showed her the ice cream bowl in my hand. She pinched herself on the arm and hissed in pain.

Her face turned red with blush, and then she said, "Uh... ple-please come inside."

I went into her room while she shut the door behind me.

I handed her the bowl, and she took it from me. Her hand lightly brushed against mine and I felt electric shocks where our hands touched. She looked so nervous.

She said, "Uh... we should sit on the bed."

I nodded my head and sat down on the bed. She picked the pillow then placed it in front of her and sat across me. I didn't know what to say to her, but I had to start somewhere.

"You should start eating your ice cream before it melts," I said, cringing internally at my words.

She looked at me then started eating, but her eyes were still fixed on me like I would disappear any minute.

"How are you?" I asked her.

"Fi-Fine."

It was really awkward to talk to her after two months.

"How did you know I wanted to eat ice cream and especially these flavors?" she asked me, catching me off guard.

I searched my mind for some lie but came up blank.

"You were talking to yourself, and I heard it," I told her the truth.

Her face instantly turned red like a tomato. I was mesmerized for a second, staring at her cute face. Then I mustered a little courage to ask her about the baby.

"How's the baby doing?" I asked her.

She smiled from ear to ear at my question.

I had never seen such an honest smile on anyone's face before.

"He's doing very well. Sometimes, he would upset his mommy by making her throw up and not letting her sleep. But other than that he is a good baby," Hailey said, looking at her stomach.

The love in her eyes for that unborn child made my heart ache in pain for hurting her in the past.

"Huh. How do you know it's a he? It can be a she, you know," I said.

"It's a boy. I'm sure. You can say it's a mother's intuition." She smiled. "Do you want to look at his picture?" she asked me with a hopeful face.

I was confused by her question but nodded my head.

She got up from the bed and walked to her nightstand then pulled out something from a file. She came back to me and handed me a piece of paper. When I looked at the paper, I realized it wasn't some random piece of paper. It was a sonogram that clearly showed a baby.

I looked at the sonogram in amazement. I couldn't believe that Hailey and I created a baby. Suddenly, my heart felt the need to protect this little thing from all the bad things in the world. It was a completely new feeling for me.

Finally, I peeled my eyes off of the sonogram and looked at her. There was a full smile on her face. She seemed to be in love with the sonogram as she was staring at it with her brown eyes. She placed her hand on mine and sat down beside me.

"Look, baby, your dad is staring at your picture in amazement," she said, looking at the baby bump.

"Do you think he hears you?" I tried to hide my smile at her innocent action.

"Yes, he hears me. He hears everything. He is even listening to us talk to each other at the moment, but my voice is clear to him than yours," she said with a sweet smile.

"And how do you suddenly know so much about babies?" I was suddenly curious.

She bit her lower lip then looked around.

"I have a laptop. It helps me learn new things and keeps me entertained in this room," she said with an enthusiastic smile.

"When did you get the laptop?" I was bewildered.

"Cameron gave me this laptop before leaving for the boarding school," she said, looking hesitant.

I didn't know if I should feel jealous of my brother for getting her a laptop, which she finds so useful and makes her happy, or if I should beat myself for not thinking about getting her one before him.

"Are you angry?" she asked me.

I was about to answer her when she interrupted me.

"I'm sorry. I didn't ask Cameron to buy me a laptop. He gave me this as a gift. And I'm glad I have something to spend my day with or else I would have become insane by staying locked up all day in this room alone. The doctor told me during my last visit that walking and fresh air is good for the baby, but your mom won't let me go out," she said, looking sad.

I couldn't believe my ears at her statement.

Why would mom stop her from walking and going out?

"Hailey, I am not angry at you or Cameron. I'm glad he bought a laptop for you," I said, and she looked up at me.

"You are not angry at me?"

"No, I am not. Tell me, why wouldn't Mom let you go out?" I asked her.

"She told me that she doesn't want neighbors to find out that I am pregnant. If they found out about this, she wouldn't get selected for the head of society next month," Hailey mumbled.

I felt a pang in my heart at her words. I didn't realize my mom could be this selfish and cruel.

Hailey loved my mom from the day she came to live here. She was always there for my mom, helping her and working beside her. Now Hailey needed her, and she was not there for her.

I looked at her and found her staring at the floor deep in thoughts.

"Do you want to take a stroll in the garden?" I asked her to bring a smile back to her face.

"You want me to take a stroll in the garden at 1 am?"

"Yes, and you just said it is good for a baby," I said, leaving no space for argument.

She got up and put her slippers on.

"It's cold outside. You should wear something warm," I said.

She froze then turned to me and stared at me like she couldn't believe her ears.

I coughed to pull her out from the shock.

She made her way to the closet and pulled out a knee-length black jacket and put it on. Then we made our way downstairs and went to the garden, which was located at the back of our house.

She closed her eyes then took a deep breath. It gave me the chance to stare at her without getting caught. I felt my heart skipped a beat at the flutter of her eyelashes.

"It feels amazing," she mumbled, opening her eyes.

"What?" I was confused.

"It feels amazing to breathe in the open air and to stare at the full moon," she said and pointed the finger at the moon.

I looked up, and my eyes landed on the bright full moon surrounded by small stars.

"Yes, it is beautiful," I said, looking up.

"Do you know I love stars and the moon?" She was smiling.

"I can guess by the way you talk about them."

"Well, they shine and brighten up the path in the night for people to find their way back home."

"Like you." I found myself saying.

She looked at me baffled.

"Yeah, like you. When you smile, everything brightens up." I elaborated.

She suddenly went silent, and I cursed myself for being stupid and upsetting her.

"I don't think my smiles brighten up anything for anyone," she mumbled lightly.

"Hailey, you shouldn't think like this about yourself. Your smile is beautiful. You are beautiful," I said to her.

She stayed silent, and we continue walking. Then, after two rounds, she stopped and turned to me.

"I want to go back to my room. I'm tired," she said.

I wanted to spend more time with her, but I understood that it was too early to ask so much of her.

"Okay, let's go inside," I said following, her.

When we reached her room, she went inside and took off her jacket. She took a step towards the closet and stumbled, but I caught her by the arm.

"Are you alright?" I asked her concerned.

"Yes, I'm fine." She sounded sleepy.

I looked at her, and she didn't seem like she could walk to her bed, so I picked her up bridal style.

"Chase, what are you doing?" she asked in a panic, clutching my neck like she did that night.

"I am taking you to bed."

"I can walk, you know."

"I know you can walk, but not at the moment," I said, making my way towards her bed.

She gazed at me with confusion.

I laid her on the bed and pulled off her slippers. I was about to leave when her words stopped me.

"Don't you want to say goodnight to our son?" she asked.

I turned back to her and sat down on the bed.

She understood my confusion because next thing I knew my hand was placed on her baby bump.

"It's your dad, and he wants to say good night to you," Hailey said.

I felt my hand shaking with the anxiety.

"Talk to him." She mouthed.

"Your dad loves you. Good night, buddy," I said.

Hailey smiled warmly at me, and my heart swelled.

"Hailey, I am sorry. I am sorry for being an assh*le. I am ashamed of the way I acted all these months. I know I wasn't there to protect you that day when my mom hit you, and I am sorry for that. It wasn't your fault. You shouldn't be the one to receive her anger because I deserve it. You are the kindest person in this world, so if you can find it in your beautiful heart to forgive me, I will not disappoint you again. Can you forgive me, Hailey? Can you give me another chance?" I asked her

I was waiting for her reply, but when I didn't get one, I looked up to find her asleep.

I smiled and kissed her head then got up. She snuggled deeper into her pillows, making me chuckle. I put the quilt on her then switched off the lights leaving her night lamp on.

"Goodnight, love," I mumbled, closing her bedroom door.

I went to my room and lay down on my bed.

"Will she forgive me?" I asked myself aloud.

Hailey was the sweetest girl I ever met and had a beautiful heart. She would forgive me.

Thinking about her I fell asleep.

Chapter Twenty-One

Best Birthday Ever

Chase

My dad asked me to join him at the office today as he wanted me to do my internship in his company so he could prepare me in replacing him as CEO after his retirement.

I was getting ready for office when I heard a knock at the door.

I opened the door, and my breath was knocked out of my lungs.

Hailey was standing outside in a red dress. Her brown hair was open resting on one shoulder. There was a light tint of pink on her plump lips, and my eyes got stuck on them.

She shrugged then flipped her hair. For a minute I thought I was dreaming.

"Hailey, is everything fine?" I asked her in a trance.

She took a step closer to me then another. She didn't stop until she was standing a breath away from me.

Suddenly, my heart started to hammer inside my chest.

"Amy told me that you are going to the office today," she said.

My eyes went to her moving lips again, and I felt the urge to kiss them.

"Yes," I said.

"I came here to say best of luck." She bit her lower lip while staring at me.

"Thanks."

"I forgive you."

"What?" I thought I heard her say that she forgave me.

"I forgive you, Chase. I will forget everything that happened in the last few months, and we can start anew if you promise me that you will be a good dad to our baby," she said.

Tears welled up in her eyes.

"I promise to be a good dad for our baby. I promise, Hailey," I said and cupped her face in my hands.

She was leaning towards me, and I felt her lips touching mine. I closed my eyes, and my hand went to her waist then I pulled her closer.

She gasped, and I smiled.

Our lips didn't move, but I felt contentment in my heart at the touch of her heavenly lips on mine.

I traced her lower lip with my tongue, and she closed her eyes.

Before we could properly kiss, we heard the shattering of plates and pulled away from each other.

Amy was standing there with her mouth agape. She had happy tears in her eyes while she was staring at us in awe. I knew the moment she met Hailey that she had developed a motherly feeling for her.

"I'm sorry. I brought breakfast for you, but I am leaving," she said, picking the shattered pieces of plate from the floor.

Hailey was blushing so hard while my heart was still beating wildly in my chest.

"I should leave. You must be running late for the office," Hailey said, tugging her fallen lock behind her ear.

"No, I mean I am not running late."

"Chase, we are running late, son," my dad yelled at that moment, embarrassing me for life.

"I think I should go."

Hailey nodded.

When I left the room, I heard her giggling, and it put a smile on my face.

The rest of the day in the office went well. My dad didn't put much workload on me as it was my first day as an intern. My office colleagues were too hesitant to talk to me. They were already seeing me as their future boss.

I didn't want to appear too eager to go home in front of my dad, but I was internally begging him to give me permission to leave. It was already eight in the evening. All the workers had already left the office. But dad was still going through some files, and I was checking the time every five minutes.

"Son, let's go," Dad said, and I jumped up.

"You look too excited to go home. Did you not enjoy your first day here Chase?"

I cursed myself for appearing too happy to leave the office.

"Dad, I really enjoyed my day here even though you didn't let me do much. You know, I have been coming here for the last twenty years, just not as an intern but as your son," I said.

Dad smiled at me warmly. Dad's driver, Clark, was waiting outside. He opened the car door for us, and we got inside the car. The ride home felt so long.

When we arrived home, I got out of the car without wasting an extra second.

Dad gave me a weird look, and I smiled at him. We went inside the house, and I found Mom sitting on the couch in the lounge watching TV.

"Hi, Mom," I mumbled.

Then I went upstairs and knocked at Hailey's door. I waited for her to open the door and greet me with her beautiful smile, but she didn't come out.

I went to my room with a sulk.

I got showered and changed into my sweatpants and white V-neck t-shirt. I heard a knock at my door and went to open it with a smile to find Amy standing there.

"Madam is calling you for dinner," Amy said.

"Amy, you have been with us for last five years, so please calling my mom 'madam,' at least in front of me."

"She will kill me if she heard me calling her anything else," Amy said sarcastically.

"I bet she will." I made my way downstairs.

Kate, Mom, and Dad were sitting at the table waiting for me. I sat beside Dad deliberately skipping a seat next to my mom, which Kate and Dad noticed.

"Did you call Hailey down for dinner?" my dad asked Mom.

"Yes, I called her down, but she didn't feel well, so she asked me to send her food to her room."

My mom had been lying to my dad, and she did it again today. I hated it. I didn't know what my mother's problem was. *Why was she treating her like a stranger?*

I got up, and my parents looked at me.

"Where are you going, Chase? You haven't eaten anything yet," my mom said.

"I'm going to my room. I am not hungry."

"Are you fine, son?"

"I'm fine Mom. I ate in the office, so I am not hungry," I said, leaving the table.

Instead of going to my room I went to Hailey's room. I knocked on her door, and she told me to come in.

I entered, and she looked up at me in shock. A strand of spaghetti was hanging out of her mouth.

"I can come later if you want." I stopped myself from laughing at her cute face.

"No, you can stay if you want," she said and swallowed the spaghetti.

I walked to her bed and sat down in front of her.

The spaghetti was looking delicious, and I was hungry as I hadn't eaten anything for hours.

"Do you want to eat some?" Hailey asked me innocently.

The offer was too tempting, but it wouldn't be nice to eat from her share.

"It is too much for me to eat alone and I have another clean fork," she said, showing me a clean fork.

I grabbed the fork, and she moved closer to me. I twirled some of the spaghetti and took my first bite. She smiled and started eating again.

"How was your day at the office?" she asked.

"It was good. I learned how to work with a workaholic boss."

She giggled.

"Your dad doesn't seem like a workaholic. He comes home for dinner."

"He used to be a workaholic, but he has changed."

She nodded.

"I will not become a workaholic for my child. I will come home on time and take him or her to the park to play," I said to her.

"You will play with her or him?" I could hear the astonishment in her voice.

"Yes, I will play with our child. I will teach him or her how to play soccer," I told her. "Do you like any sports?" I asked her.

A sad smile appeared on her face.

"I like sports, but I never learned how to play any of them," she said.

"Then you can read bedtime stories to him or her because I know you like reading."

She smiled brightly and said, "That I can do well."

We talked then talked some more and didn't realize it was already midnight.

"Good night baby," I whispered in her ear and placed an innocent kiss near her lips

She gasped, and I smiled at her innocent action.

I pulled away from her and found her eyes were shut tightly. I coughed. She opened her beautiful eyes and looked at me.

"Good night," she mumbled shyly.

I left her room with a wide smile playing on my lips. It was one of the best nights of my life.

*   *   *

[Four months later]

My days had changed and my nights as well. I was spending my nights talking to Hailey about our baby and getting to know her.

We would talk, read, and watch movies together every night. Sometimes she would fall asleep on my shoulder, and I would stay awake memorizing every one of her features.

With each passing day, she was becoming prettier, and I found myself falling for her. Her innocent actions, her sweet blush, and her eyes were making me crazy for her.

Nothing happened after that mere kiss four months ago, but it didn't mean I didn't dream about feeling those lips on mine again every night. But I was giving her a chance to move this relationship at her pace. I didn't want her to feel like I loved her only for one thing because that was not true. I loved everything about her.

I was going to enter the kitchen to tell Mom that I was going out with Nick, but stopped dead when I heard Mom and Kate talking about Hailey. It wasn't my intention to eavesdrop on their conversation.

"Mom, I'm telling you Hailey is a tramp. She trapped Chase by getting pregnant like her mom did. We all know Chase wasn't giving her any attention, so she seduced him and got pregnant," Kate said.

"I know Kate. You are right. He has been talking to her more, spending time with her too. He even started lying to me about small things. She is trying to steal my son's loyalty from this family. She is changing him and distracting him from his goals in life." I heard my mom say.

"Do you know how we can stop him from ruining his future? I don't even believe it's his baby."

"Yes, I don't believe it's his baby. And I know how to stop him from ruining his life," Mom said.

"She is in her third trimester of pregnancy. We cannot even get her an abortion."

"I asked the doctor if we can get Hailey an abortion. She said it could be done, but there are some risks."

"What kind of risk?" Kate asked.

"Serious kind of risk. Like Hailey can die during the process or the abortion will do some permanent damage to her, and she wouldn't get pregnant ever again."

"So have you decided to get her abortion?"

"I have not made the decision yet."

I couldn't believe my ears. *Did they just discuss murdering my child and my wife so casually?* The girl who never uttered a hateful word against them even after what they did to her. Now, they were planning to hurt her again. I couldn't stop the rage building inside me and entered the kitchen.

Kate and Mom stared at me with shock written all over their faces.

"Chase do you want something son?" my mother asked hesitantly.

"Yes, Mom I want something. Actually, I want many things. But first, I want you both to stop interfering with my life." I was so angry at them.

My mom's face turned red in anger.

"Watch your tone with me. How dare you talk to us like this?" she asked.

"I'm talking to you like this because I don't know you anymore. You're my twin sister, and you are my mom, but do you care about me?"

"We care about you, Chase," they said in unison.

I laughed sarcastically.

"That's why you were planning to kill my wife and my baby?" I asked them.

They stared at me in shock.

"We were not planning anything." Mom lied.

"I heard everything Mom. You just told Kate what the doctor said about getting Hailey abortion."

"I was just telling her the doctor advised abortion as she is really young to bring a life into this world." Mom tried to feed me lies again.

"Mom, stop lying," I yelled. "How could you guys talk about getting her abortion this easily? I have spent twenty-one years of my life with both of you, but believe me, I never thought that you both could be this cruel. I never thought that you could plan to murder my child, your son's child." I felt dejected.

How could they do this to me?

They both stayed silent.

"Tell me, Kate, Mom. How can I make you both believe that the baby Hailey is carrying is mine?! I'm the one who didn't use protection, and I'm responsible for everything," I said, taking a step closer. "Please for God's sake accept that your son is not a saint, and he can very well make mistakes. I can do wrong things like any other human being. I already hate myself enough for the way I treated Hailey. Now, you are making me hate my existence for being your son. It's hard to believe that you are a mother yourself. Getting Hailey abortion will ruin her life as well as mine."

"Chase, I thought you don't want the baby," my mom said.

"Why wouldn't I want my own child? Please, I beg you, stay away from Hailey. Leave her alone and let her live."

"You are accusing us. She is turning you against your own family."

"Mom, she is not turning me against anyone. You have no idea how pure and innocent she is. If something happened to her or my child then remember you will lose me too. I'm going to protect my child and Hailey with my life," I said.

The thought of killing an innocent unborn child disgusted me. I was so angry that I wanted to smash everything on my way out. I was barely controlling my rage.

I walked out of the kitchen and picked up my car keys on the way out. I closed the main door and left the house to calm myself down.

How could my mom talk about hurting Hailey?

Hailey was the girl who never disobeyed her and from the first day loved her. When did my mom become this heartless that she could think of killing a baby?

Hailey and I had been getting close because of the baby. I knew a lot of things about her now: about her life before she married me; about her past, which no one knows; and the reason why she agreed to this marriage.

I also found out that we had a lot of things in common. Hailey was an intelligent girl. She was not into gadgets and internet like us, but she was a walking encyclopedia.

She was an angel with a beautiful face and personality.

What made me worried was her innocence. She needed to become strong and independent to survive in this world. I wanted her to fight with me when she thought I was acting like an ass. I needed her to learn to protect herself and voiced out her concern.

I knew I cannot change her easily, but I would stand beside her as a shield until she learned to protect herself without my support.

I understood now that she needed my protection and my love. Her heart had been broken so many times in the past.

I couldn't tell when I started to realize what I felt for her was nothing but love. I had fallen in love with her.

I didn't care about the past anymore. I was not going to curse my fate anymore for pairing me with a teenage girl. I was going to accept her and my fate with all my heart. I was not fighting a lost battle anymore. She was meant to be my life partner as I was meant to be hers, and this was my life now.

I felt weird when I found out I was going to be a father, but not for a second had I wished of getting rid of the baby.

First time in months I felt content with my life. I was happy that I had a beautiful wife and a baby on the way. I knew Hailey, and I still had a lot to learn about each other to develop a relationship like normal couples had. And for that, we would need to go on dates and spend time together.

I planned to make her fall in love with me again and make her mine forever.

My phone rang, and I picked it up.

"Hello," I said.

"Today is Hailey's birthday you dumbass. Don't tell her that I told you about it. Just pretend you know it already." The line went dead.

I realized the voice belonged to none other than my stupid brother. I laughed.

Cameron was different from me. He was a rebel and enjoyed disobeying our parents while I was the one who wouldn't do anything without our parents' permission. I respected our parents a lot and followed their rules with eyes closed; on the other hand, Cameron liked breaking the rules and doing exactly what my parents forbade him to do.

I always admired his courage and rebellious nature because I lacked it. From the day I was born, my parents had decided what they wanted me to do. I was selected to run my dad's business in the future. They portrayed the image of this perfect man with a perfect future, and I had spent my whole life working to become that guy.

My life was ruled by my parents and especially my mom. She would decide everything for me: where I would study, and who I would become friends with. I felt glad for standing up against her today and stopping her from hurting Hailey.

If Cameron got to know what I had done today, he would definitely laugh at my mom's face and would tell me to join his rebellious group of teenagers.

I loved my brother despite the fact that we were so different in many things.

What did he say? Today was Hailey's birthday!

How the hell did Cameron know this when I didn't know it was her birthday today?

My jaw clenched in anger, and I wanted to call him back to tell him to stay away from my wife. But then he did help me by telling me that today was her birthday.

What should I do?

I should surprise her. No, I should take her out somewhere. It could be our first date. I could arrange something romantic for us.

I started with making a reservation. I called the restaurant that arranged birthday dinners and served the best cuisine.

After the reservation was made, I went to the boutique to buy a dress for Hailey.

I was looking around for something, which will fit Hailey as her belly has rounded pretty nicely in the past seven months.

"Hello, sir, how can I help you? Are you looking for something specific?" The salesgirl came to my assistance.

"Uh, I'm looking for something that's not body fitting," I said, staring at the figure-hugging dress on the dummy.

She frowned at me in confusion.

"My wife is pregnant."

"Oh, how far along is she?" she asked with a polite smile.

"Seven months."

"Okay. Give me a few minutes, and I'll show you some of our collection that will be suitable for your wife," the girl said and went inside the storeroom of the shop then came out with four dresses.

She showed me the first one that was in red color with a low round neckline. I didn't like it. The second one was dark blue with jewels around the waist, and short on the front. It was nice but not what Hailey would wear. The third one was a simple green dress with a brown belt, and I shuddered, remembering how Hailey reacted at the green colored pasta on my graduation dinner.

The last one was in purple color. It was floor length and looked perfect for Hailey.

"Sir, it has a sweetheart neckline, and it's loose from the belly. Your wife can easily wear it," the boutique worker said.

"I'm buying this one." I then walked to the counter while she packed it for me in a large box.

Then I went to the jewelry store and bought a gift for her then drove back to the house. I entered the house and didn't find my mom and Kate anywhere in sight.

I went upstairs and knocked on Hailey's door.

She opened her bedroom door and looked at me in confusion.

"Hi," I said and entered her bedroom, pulling her with me and closing the door behind us.

She was dressed in a plain blue shirt and pajama shorts.

"What are you doing here?" She was fidgeting with the hem of her shirt.

"I will answer you, but first tell me where Mom and Kate are," I asked her.

"Your mom told Amy that she is going to her friend's house and Kate also left with her friends a few minutes ago."

I nodded my head and looked at the box in my hand.

"Uh… This is for you," I said, giving her the box, which had a dress inside.

Hailey looked at me weirdly then peeked inside the box. She pulled out the dress and stared at it.

Her mouth was opening and closing like a goldfish.

"Thank you." She mumbled blushing.

"You're welcome. You need to get change into this dress right now."

Her eyes widened. She stared at me like I just confessed to her that I murdered kittens in my leisure time.

"I'll wear… it some other day," she said, looking flustered ready to put the dress back inside the box.

I shook my head.

"Get changed into the dress, Hailey. We are going out," I said, dragging her to the washroom. "Go get ready." I didn't give her a choice except to get changed in the dress.

She nodded at me and went inside the washroom.

I went back to my room and pulled out my blue slacks and grey blazer with a white shirt to wear underneath. I got changed into them hurriedly. I pulled out my shoes and put them on. I sprayed some cologne on me and went back to Hailey's room to find her changed into the dress.

My jaw dropped and touched the ground when I looked at her.

She looked enchanting in that dress; the purple color looked beautiful against her pale complexion. The dress hugged her chest perfectly, showing a teasing amount of cleavage.

Hailey was staring at herself with an uncomfortable look on her face while she was trying to pull the dress up to hide her cleavage. I hid my smile and walked closer to her.

She had no idea how sumptuous she looked while doing that.

I ran my eyes up and down, gazing at her beautiful face and the baby bump, which was clearly showing from underneath the pleats of the dress.

"You're looking gorgeous, Hailey. You don't need to hide and feel uncomfortable," I said, standing behind her.

She glanced at me with a shy smile.

"Let's go," I said, taking her hand in mine.

Then my eyes landed on her feet. She was wearing flip-flops.

"Hailey, why are you wearing flip-flops?" I asked her.

"I don't have any good shoes to go with this dress." She looked down at her feet.

The smile she had on her face earlier disappeared.

"Okay, wait here, I will come back in a minute," I said, leaving her room.

I sneaked into Kate's room and opened her closet then searched for flat shoes that would look good with Hailey's dress.

After looking at my sister's expensive shoe collection, I finally found the silver shoes that look comfortable enough for Hailey and would match her dress too.

Picking those shoes, I went back to Hailey's room and placed them in front of her.

She put the shoes on and glanced at me.

"Now, you look perfect," I said.

I took her hand in mine and led her out towards my car.

"Where are we going?" Hailey asked me after getting inside the car.

I strapped the seat belt and said, "We are going on our first date."

Her eyes widened.

"Da-Date?" she stuttered.

"Yes. I just realized we never went out on a date. I mean that's what people do before getting married." I took a glance at her while driving.

She nodded her head and looked out from the window.

The drive to the restaurant was peaceful. When we arrived at the restaurant, I pulled out a blindfold.

"Hailey, I'm going to blindfold you," I said.

She gave me a nervous glance but nodded in consent.

I helped her get out of the car then covered her eyes with the blindfold.

"You can't see anything right?" I asked her to make sure the blindfold was working fine.

"Yeah, I can't see anything." She touched my shoulder, clinging to me for support.

I took her inside the restaurant, where I had arranged a birthday surprise for her. I removed the blindfold from her eyes, and she stared at the table with her mouth ajar.

Her eyes brimmed with tears but she blinked them back.

"Happy seventeenth birthday, Hailey," I mumbled in her ear.

*   *   *

Hailey

"Happy seventeenth birthday, Hailey," Chase mumbled in my ear.

I wanted to cry my eyes out after looking at the cake and all the arrangements.

"How do you know that today… is my birthday?" I whispered.

Instead of answering me, he kissed me on the forehead, and said, "Let's just celebrate and forget about everything else."

I nodded because I was dazed by the spell he put on me.

My brain was in awe at Chase's efforts. Everything on the table looked delicious and extravagant.

He put a knife in my hand, and I cut the cake.

Then everyone started singing happy birthday, and rose petals fell on us from the ceiling.

I laughed looking at Chase. His head was covered with rose petals while mine was still pretty clean. He touched his head and dusted the petals off.

"Well, I think I'm standing on the wrong side," he said, looking up.

I laughed again.

A few petals were still stuck in his hair, so I removed them.

"Thank you," I said and kissed his cheek.

His face turned a little red, and I smiled staring at him.

I took a slice of the cake and fed him some. Then, I turned back to slice another piece, when I felt something wet on my cheek. I touched my cheek with my hand and found some frosting.

Chase chose that moment to snap a picture of me. He was laughing at my shocked face.

"Why did you put frosting on my face?" I asked him in confusion.

"It was for the picture, Hailey." He then proceeded on wiping the frosting off my face with a tissue paper.

Chase pulled out a chair for me and then food was served to us at our table.

I enjoyed the pasta, steak, and salad. I felt like Chase had ordered everything the restaurant had.

"I'm so full," I said, eating the last piece of cake.

"Me too." Chase groaned.

I giggled looking at him.

"You shouldn't have ordered so much," I said.

"Um, you are right. I think I was just too excited to notice that."

He was more excited than I was and it made me wonder. *When did I win his heart?* All this time, he had a beautiful smile on his face while he talked to me.

"We should leave now," I said, looking at the restaurant.

"Yeah, you're right. I'm such a fool. You must be tired after sitting here for hours." He stood up ready to leave.

I stood up from the chair and walked to him.

"I'm not tired. I just don't want to sit," I said.

He surprised me by leaning down and kissing me on my cheek, but it was too near to my lips. When he pulled away, I tried to calm my heart.

Then we left the restaurant. After fifteen minutes of driving, Chase stopped the car outside a beautiful park.

"If you are not tired would you like to spend more time with me?" Chase asked me.

I nodded my head then we went inside the park.

There was a large fountain in the middle of the park, and he stopped there.

"Hailey this is for you," Chase said, placing a small box in my palm.

I looked at him in confusion.

"It's your birthday gift," he said.

I opened the box and gasped at the beautiful diamond bracelet.

"It's beautiful and looks so expensive," I mumbled.

Chase smiled at me, and said, "It is very expensive, but you deserve it. The project I was working for months brought a great profit to the company. Dad gave me my share of the money, which I used to arrange all this for tonight and bought this gift for you. And I saved up rest of the money for our baby."

After what Chase said, the tears I had been controlling came falling down from my eyes, making its way down to my face. I was crying my heart out with hiccups.

"I'm sorry, Hailey. If you don't like the gift, I can buy you something else," he said, pulling me towards him and rubbing my back.

His stupid, sweet words made me cry harder.

"I love it, and it's beautiful. Thank you, Chase, for making this birthday so special for me. No one has ever done anything like this for me before," I said between the hiccups.

"Then you should put on this bracelet." He took the box from my hand, pulled out the bracelet, and tied it around my wrist.

He kissed the back of my hand and looked at me. I found myself taking a step closer to him. Our faces were so close. I could feel his breath.

"Thank you. It was the best birthday ever," I mumbled again.

"You deserve all the best things in life." He stared at me with his sterling grey eyes.

I closed my eyes and planted my lips on his. Chase turned frozen.

I didn't know what I was doing, so I pulled away. My heart was racing, and I was scared to open my eyes again, but I did.

Chase was staring at me with wide eyes. I took a step back and turned my back on him. The feeling of embarrassment made me want to never look at him again.

Suddenly, he caught my wrist and made me turn back. I didn't have the confidence to look him in the eye after what I had done. Chase put his fingers under my chin and tilted my head up.

I still refused to look at him.

"Look at me, Hailey," he said, making me glance at him.

My breath hitched when I saw how close we were standing again. He leaned lower and placed his lips on mine while his arm went around my waist pulling me closer.

He kissed me slowly and sweetly while I followed his actions. My hands went around his neck to pull him closer to me. The simple, sweet kiss turned passionate when his tongue entered my mouth exploring and devouring me.

He smiled at me when I tried to copy him.

The kiss was exactly like the one I read in books; passionate, sweet, and sensual at the same time. I felt fireworks around me, and butterflies exploded in my stomach. I even felt a kick inside.

Kick!

I pulled away from Chase. We were breathing heavily.

I looked at my stomach, and Chase stared at me in confusion.

"The baby is kicking," I mumbled shyly.

Chase laughed lightly and placed his hands on my belly. He felt the baby kicking, and he stood there in astonishment.

His eyes shining with tears, but he blinked them back.

When his eyes connected with mine, he smiled and ran his thumb in a circular motion on my belly.

"I think our baby gets possessive when his parents kiss," Chase said, looking deep into my eyes.

I laughed at his assumption, but he was pretty serious.

He planted his lips again on mine and took me back to heaven.

Chapter Twenty-Two

Everything Is Perfect

Chase

[Two months later]

I was lying on the couch in the living room while a football match was playing on the TV. My eyes were on the match, but nothing was making sense.

I heard a pain-filled scream and jumped up.

At first, I didn't realize who was screaming, but when I did, I ran as fast as possible for me towards Hailey rooms.

I pushed open the door and barged inside to find Hailey sitting on the bed and screaming.

"Shit! Hailey what's happening. Are you alright?" I asked her concerned.

"Chase, I am feeling contractions. We need to go to the hospital."

I stared at her in shock.

She gave me a murderous glare and gritted her teeth in pain.

"Chase, stop staring. Go tell your mom to come with us. She knows my doctor. Go! GO!" She yelled.

I ran downstairs and knocked on my parent's door. My mom came out while tying a gown and looked at me in confusion.

"What are you doing here Chase?" she asked me.

"Mom, Hailey told me to get you. She is in pain. She is feeling contractions." I told her.

Mom gave me an irritated look.

"But her due date is next week. Why is she feeling contractions now?" she mumbled.

We went upstairs to Hailey's room, and her head snapped in our direction.

She still looked in pain, and I felt my insides flipped at the sight of her in so much pain.

"Hailey, what's this drama? If you're in pain, then take some painkillers and sleep." Irritation was evident in my mom's voice.

"It is not drama. I'm really feeling contractions. We need to go to the hospital like right now, or I'll deliver the baby right here," Hailey said, and my eyes widened.

I was not going to let that happen.

"Hailey, I have four kids, and I know more than you. So please lay down. The pain will go away with time," my mom said.

Hailey glared at my mom with pure hate and gritted her teeth.

"I know you had three pregnancies. But I'm not a stupid girl who doesn't know the difference between pain and contractions. I'm telling you that we need to go to the hospital." She yelled.

My mom looked shocked at her outburst.

"Mom if Hailey is telling us that we need to go to the hospital then we're going. If you want to come with us, then please go change," I said.

"Okay, let me get changed into something appropriate." She turned and made her way back to her room.

I nodded and glanced at Hailey. She was wearing a loose baby blue gown, which ended at her knees.

I took her hand in mine and made her stand up then put my hands on her knees. I picked her up in bridal style and made my way downstairs.

I placed her on the couch in the living room while we waited for my mom to come.

"Chase, please go back to my room and bring the blue colored bag. It is under my bed. We need to take that with us," Hailey said.

I nodded my head and went back to her room. After finding the bag, I came downstairs and found my mom dressed in jeans and shirt. I picked the car keys and went to the garage to take out the car. I parked the car outside the house then went inside to get Hailey.

I carried her out to the car and placed her in the back seat with her bag.

My mom and I got settled in the car. Then I started to drive, praying that I wouldn't crash somewhere as my hands were shaking.

I was so damn nervous like I was the one who was going to deliver the baby.

*   *   *

It was 3:00 am. Hailey was still inside the room with the doctor and my mom.

When we reached the hospital, the doctor told us that Hailey was indeed feeling contractions, and she would be delivering the baby in an hour. An hour ago the doctor told me that they would come get me when Hailey was ready to deliver.

I didn't really know if I wanted to go inside. I had been listening to Hailey screaming for hours, and they were horrifying like she was dying rather than delivering a baby. I felt a shudder run through my body when I heard another scream.

The nurse came to me with a plastic gown and cap and told me to wear it. I hurriedly put the gown and cap, and then she took me inside the delivery room.

Believe me, it was a horrific scene. The doctor was looking down at Hailey, telling her to push. Hailey was panting and screaming due to the pain and holding the bed tightly with her hands. Even her knuckles were turning pale because of her tight grip.

I thought of leaving the room before I would faint or something, but her agony filled screams startled me making me run towards her and hold her hand.

When the baby was delivered, Hailey dropped her head on the pillow. The tears were streaming down her face.

I was just dumbly staring at the baby who was covered in blood and waiting for the damn doctor to give him to the nurse.

"Congratulations sir! You're blessed with a baby boy. He has five fingers in each hand, five toes on each foot, and one little thing every boy should have. He is perfect," the doctor said, dangling my baby in front of me with an excited smile. Then he slapped him on his bottom, which made him cry loudly.

"His voice sounds perfectly alright," the doctor said.

I was so ready to beat the shit out of that man for making my son cry, but Hailey was gripping my hand, and it stopped me.

Then the nurse took him from the doctor to clean him.

"Chase your grip is too tight," Hailey whispered.

"What?" I was still in a daze.

"Your grip is tight."

"Uh sorry," I said looking at her hand, which was turning pale.

"You look more horrified than me."

"I was scared," I confessed.

Her eyes were closed, and I thought she was asleep.

"Everything is fine." I heard her mumbling.

"Everything is perfect," I said.

She fell asleep, and I kissed her head.

The nurse ushered me out and told me to wait outside until they transferred her to the other room.

I was giddy to meet my son and have him in my arms. I was amazed that the baby turned out to be a boy. Hailey told me that she asked the doctor to keep the gender secret. We both didn't know if he would be a boy or a girl.

I heard the door opening and looked up to see my mother coming towards me with a baby. He was the cutest baby I had ever seen. Just by looking at him, I fell in love with his chubby cheeks.

My mom was cooing to him lightly.

I saw the nurse coming out from Hailey's room.

"How's Hailey?" I asked her.

She smiled at me, and said, "Sir your wife is fine. She feels a little tired after delivering this cutie. We are transferring her to her room then you can meet her."

My mom came to me, and said, "I'm going to inform your dad and the others."

I nodded at her, and she left.

They transferred Hailey to a blue and white room. Its walls were covered with balloons. When I went into the room, Hailey had changed into a different gown looking at our baby who was sleeping in the cot that was placed near her bed.

I took her hand in mine and gave it a light squeeze.

She smiled at me, and said, "See a boy."

She was looking smug.

I chuckled at her, and said, "Yes, a boy."

She had bags under her eyes, and she looked tired, so I said, "I will take care of him while you take a nap."

"Promise?" she asked me.

I nodded my head. "I promise. Now go to sleep".

*   *   *

Hailey

I woke up to my son's wails. I looked to my left to find Chase's panicked face. He was staring at the baby and making weird faces to stop him from crying more.

I laughed at him, and he froze. Then he turned to look at me.

Chase rubbed his neck, looking flustered and I found it cute.

"I swear, Hailey. He isn't crying because of me. I was actually trying to stop him from crying," Chase said.

I smiled at him, amused at his explanation.

Before I could say anything, the nurse came inside, and asked, "How are you feeling?"

"I'm feeling fine, just little sore in some places. But I think my son is not fine. He was crying before you walked in," I said, looking at my baby.

The nurse took a glance at him. "Ah, he must be hungry."

"So are you feeling full?" she asked me.

I looked at her in bewilderment.

She probably noticed my confusion, and said, "I'm asking if your breast feels full? Do you want to breastfeed him because he seems hungry?"

I looked at myself and realized that my breast felt heavy. I did read about it in detail that mother's milk is best for almost all babies unless you have some kind of dangerous diseases, which could be transferred through feeding.

"I want to feed him. I have read that mother's milk is best for babies," I said to the nurse.

The nurse gave me a vibrant smile. "Hailey, I think you're going to be a very great mother for this little boy. Let's have you ready for feeding."

She helped me open my gown then wiped my right breast with tissues to clean the area. She picked up my son then placed him in my arms. She held his head and tilted it up so he can easily reach. When he started sucking, she moved away, and he protested at the loss of support. She told Chase to help me.

I forgot that he was still in the room. He took a seat on the chair, which was really close to my bed, and helped me feed our son by holding his head. Then suddenly, it dawned on me that my breasts were showing and that was enough to make me uneasy. I blushed like a tomato while feeding my little bundle of joy. When my baby was satisfied fulfilling his tummy, I made him burp. I had learned that with the help of YouTube videos.

I was embarrassed being naked in front of Chase. I tried buttoning my gown with one hand while making our son burp with the other.

Chase noticed my struggle and got up from the chair to help me button the gown. I felt his hands brushing at my bare and very sensitive breast.

I felt a shudder, and my breath hitched. My eyes instinctively closed.

When I opened them again, I found his face close to me. A slight movement can make our lips touch.

But to my surprise, he was the first one to press his lips to mine. He kissed me lightly, pouring his love and his happiness in the kiss making it the most pleasurable and sensual experience of my life.

I was utterly happy at that moment and contented with my life.

I thought, *"Finally I have my happily ever after with the man I love."*

Chapter Twenty-Three

He Broke My Heart Again

Hailey

I came out from the bathroom after taking a shower and found Chase staring at our peacefully sleeping son. It slipped my mind that I was standing in nothing but a flimsy towel wrapped around my chest.

I discreetly tried making my way to my nightgown that I forgot to take in the washroom with me. But I stopped dead when Chase turned and looked at me.

His eyes bulged out, and I felt like hiding myself. His eyes ran up and down on my exposed body, which made me shiver. The emotions that were playing in his eyes brought the blush on my face, and the room suddenly felt hot. His sterling grey eyes gazed at me intensely, and at that moment I decided to move my Jell-O legs.

I hurriedly picked up my nightgown from the bed and ran back into the bathroom. I closed the washroom door and placed my head on it then took deep breaths to calm my erratically beating heart.

I came out from the washroom, dressed in my nightgown and found Chase standing near the window with his back towards me. I cleared my throat, and his head snapped my way. He opened his mouth to say something then closed it again. He mumbled a hasty good night and left the room.

I frowned, shocked at his weird behavior.

*   *   *

The first day Noah and I came home from the hospital, the whole house was in chaos. Allison decorated my room to welcome my beautiful son into the family. Allison's kids Chris and Susan were the most excited among the group to meet the baby. The minute I stepped inside the house, I was showered with gifts and hugs.

Susan kissed the baby while telling me how much she liked his cousin. Chris kept staring at Noah with astonishment. Whenever Noah would make a face or move his tiny hands, Chris would jump in happiness

I was glad that my son was welcomed into the family with so much love. I never received much love and care from my family, and I was happy that my son's future wouldn't turn out like mine.

Chase had been really supportive. He was taking great care of our son and me. He always had a smile on his face. I told him that I was scared of what kind of a mother I would be to our son. He told me that I would become the best mother there is. His words made me strong, and I stopped feeling low.

My son was everything any parent could ever ask for. I never felt like it was a tough job taking care of him. He had adjusted to the house pretty well and didn't cry when someone else picked him up. I loved his name: Noah.

Chase asked me to name our son, and when I told him that I want to name our son Noah, he was surprised. He told me that he too wanted to name our son Noah but didn't tell me because he thought I should be the one to name him.

I was glad that we both liked and picked the same name for our son.

I heard Noah's small cry and looked at him. He was looking at me with his big brownish grey eyes.

"Do you want your midnight snack buddy?" I asked him, and he scrunched his tiny nose.

I found his every move cute. I took him out of his crib and sat down on the bed then fed him. When he was satisfied, he closed his eyes, and I made him burp. He instantly fell asleep after that.

I woke up at eight in the morning and looked inside the crib to find Noah sleeping. His tiny hands were in a fist, and his mouth was in a cute pout. I ran a finger on his chubby cheek, and he squirmed in his sleep. I giggled then decided to freshen up before he woke up.

I went to the washroom and did my routine then came out and gently pulled my baby out from the crib.

When he was in my arms, he instantly opened his big eyes and stared at me. He made a funny face, and I cooed to him then settled him on my lap to feed him. Then, I got changed into some jeans and a simple white button-up shirt. I was never one to keep up with the latest fashion and trends, so I didn't put much effort into looking like a princess of some state.

I was about to leave my room and get some breakfast for myself when Chase entered the room.

"Good morning," I said to him.

But he stayed silent, and it pained my heart.

His rigid and unemotional state scared me. I started thinking what I had done wrong this time. Before my wandering thoughts led me too far, he brought me back to reality.

"Hailey I uh… I want you to sign these papers," he said.

Hesitantly, I took the papers from him and read them.

After reading those papers, my legs turned weak, making it impossible for me to stand on them any longer. I shook my head not believing it and took a step back. Tears brimmed in my eyes turning everything around me blurry. I blinked them and took deep breaths to calm myself before I would break down in front him.

I looked at him, and his face was emotionless like before. There was no guilt, no regret, and pain in his eyes.

I tried to say something to him, anything and opened my mouth, but I couldn't speak. I felt crushed. The emotions were clogging my throat making it impossible for me to speak. The tears were burning my eyes, but I blinked them back.

"Chase, do you want me to sign them?" I asked him.

"Yes, Hailey. I want you to sign them." His voice was hollow of any emotions.

"But these are divorce papers. I thought you wanted me," I said in pain.

"Hailey, I want you to understand this. I will still support you and Noah financially. You don't have to worry about that. It's just… I don't want to stay wedded to you. I cannot play the role of a husband and help you with the baby. Our marriage was a mistake from the start. You were not meant to be mine, and I was not meant to be yours. If we want to stay happy, we need to stop playing this charade of a happy couple. You can take your son with you because I don't want to play his dad's role."

Did my heart bleed at his words? It did bleed.

"I have already booked your tickets back to Oakland. Your flight is in the evening. Amy will help you with packing," he said.

When it finally dawned on me, I became numb and stopped breathing. His words played around my head like a broken record. I was shocked. I was not expecting this after all these months we had spent together planning our future.

He was the one who gave me hope that I could be loved, that I could be important in someone's life. He was the one who made me feel special, and now he was snatching everything away. He was breaking me, ruining me and my dreams.

I never thought that this man who I had fallen in love with could be this cruel. He proved me wrong today. He was the cruelest person I had met.

The bullies, my stepmom, and Emily broke my pride, my confidence, and my will to live, but this man broke my heart, which I blindly gave him. I never expected anything from Kate, Emily, my mom, and his mom, but I expected the world from him, and he let me down.

Suddenly everything started to fade. My surroundings turned black, and then my world came crashing down.

*　　*　　*

Chase

In the morning, I got a call from the hospital where Noah was born. They asked me to come to the hospital to collect the reports of some tests they did to make sure my son is healthy.

I went to the hospital to fetch those reports.

I naturally felt concerned about the results of the test and decided to discuss it with the doctor. I was assisted by the nurse to the doctor's office.

"Hi, I'm Noah's father. I just want to make sure the reports of my son are fine." I took a seat and handed him the reports

"He is your son," the doctor said.

"Yes, he is my son."

"Sir, the DNA results confirm that you're the father. I mean you don't have to worry. Noah Edwards is your son."

"Excuse me? What DNA results?" I was bewildered.

"Yes, this report contains DNA results," the doctor said.

"What do you mean? I didn't ask this hospital to run a DNA test on my son so why would you run a DNA test? I know he is my son. I don't want any evidence to make me believe it," I yelled and stood up from the chair.

The doctor did as well

"But you signed these papers," the doctor said.

I read the papers, and there was my signature. I recalled my mom bringing some papers and asking me to sign them. To confirm my suspicions, I asked the doctor.

"Who exactly asked you to run this test?"

"Sir, it was your mother. She asked me to run this test because you don't believe that the baby was yours. She told me you want this as evidence," the doctor said, looking scared.

I was beyond shocked at the revelation. Thousands of times, I had told her that the baby was mine.

Why had she done this? Why was she so adamant about proving that Noah was not mine?

For God sakes, my son even looked exactly like me, and she didn't need any evidence to see that.

His face, his eyes, his hair, and almost everything else looked like mine. Even his pictures were so similar to mine that anyone from a mile could guess that he was my son. Then why wouldn't my own mom believe it?

Snatching the damn reports from doctor's hand, I left the hospital.

I went straight home. My mom was sitting in the living room with Kate and an unfamiliar man and woman. Their head turned my way when I stormed inside in anger.

I slapped the reports on the center of the table.

"Why did you ask the doctor to perform DNA test? Why did you feel the need to do this, mom?" I asked her.

"Chase, I just wanted to make sure he is your son." She was looking at me like whatever she had done was right.

"You know what, Mom? Now you have these reports to make you believe he is my son because you clearly did not trust me when I said that he is my son," I yelled.

"That's great. I'm happy if he is your son. He is now our family member, and I don't wish him any harm. Look, Mr. and Mrs. Raves are the best attorneys. They are here to guide us as to how we can claim sole custody of Noah, and you can get rid of Hailey without much effort."

I was beyond shocked after hearing her.

"Who said that I want to divorce her?" I asked her.

"Why don't you want to divorce her?"

"She is the mother of my child, Mom."

"I know. But you need to divorce her and start your life again. I want you to focus on your goals and business. I will take care of your son."

"Mom, Hailey is his mother. She can take care of him pretty well."

"Chase if you don't divorce that girl and throw her away from this house then I will ruin your dad's company."

"How will you do that Mom?"

"She owns fifty-five percent of shares of your father's company. She'll sell the shares to me," Mr. Raves said, handing me the papers.

I read them, and it was true. She owns fifty-five percent of Dad's company, and if she sells them to Mr. Raves, we will lose our company.

"Mom, you cannot do this to Dad," I said.

I couldn't believe my mom would do something like this.

"I will not sign these papers if you don't want me to," Mom said.

"I don't want you to do that Mom."

"Then divorce her."

I did not want Mom to betray my dad. He loved her and trusted her. If he found out what she planned to do with the company that he built with his hard work, I couldn't even imagine what he would feel.

I knew what I wanted to do and what was best for my family.

"I will divorce her, Mom. You don't have to worry. I never liked her, so it's not a problem for me," I said to her.

She smiled at me.

"I knew you would make the right decision. Mr. Raves, I think you just lost a great deal," she said looking at the couple.

They got up and stormed out of the house.

"I'm proud of you, Chase," she said and left the room.

"Chase, I want to tell you something," Kate said.

"Kate, shut up. I don't want to hear a word from you. I don't think you are the same sister who I have spent twenty-one years of my life with. You have changed. Mom has changed you." With that, I left her.

I went to my room to think about this. If I told my dad about this, their relationship would be in danger. Mom could make an issue out of this, and our family would be ruined.

And if I divorced Hailey, we would be the only ones affected. After all this, I thought about Hailey and my son. They wouldn't be safe here. Mom would do anything to drive us apart, and I had no other choice except to divorce her.

Hailey deserved a life with that baby more than me. She was the one who knew how to take care of that small bundle of joy. I had seen how my son slept peacefully in her arms. I cannot separate them ever. I knew what it felt to crave for your mother's attention and I didn't want my son to feel the same.

I knew a baby who was barely a week old wouldn't survive without his mother's care. Hailey could live without me, but she wouldn't be able to live without Noah. She accepted him and fell in love with him. He was her life support to keep her going in this life.

He belonged to her completely. He was her family. How could I snatch that from her?

I couldn't.

I felt the need to talk to Hailey and inform her about my mother's cruel plan. When the night rolled in, I went to her room, but she was in the shower.

I thought of leaving, but my son caught my attention. He was looking so cute while sleeping in his crib. I stared at him in amazement. It was still hard to believe that this little boy was mine. I was so deep in my own thoughts that I didn't realize she was out from the washroom.

When I turned, my eyes landed on her, and they widened. She was standing there wrapped in a small white towel. Unintentionally my eyes followed the beads of water running down from her neck to her chest then disappearing inside the towel.

I averted my eyes before I could go and kiss her. That would only lead us to do something stupid. Her hands were shaking when she picked the nightgown from the bed and ran back inside the washroom.

I waited for her to come out but when she did, I forgot how to speak. She looked mesmerizing. I had to control myself from kissing her. Her knee-length silk white nightgown wasn't helping in any way.

I bid her a hasty goodnight and left her room in a hurry.

Next morning, I received the papers that I requested my dad's attorney to prepare. Before I chickened out again, I went into Hailey's room.

"Hailey, I uh, I want you to sign these papers," I said.

She took the papers from my hand and read them.

After reading them, she looked shocked. Her eyes brimmed with tears, but I couldn't do anything to make her smile.

"Chase, do you want me to sign them?" she asked me.

"Yes, Hailey, I want you to sign them." My voice was hollow of any emotions.

"But these are divorce papers? I thought you wanted me," she said in pain filled voice.

"Hailey, I want you to understand this. I will still support you and Noah financially. You don't have to worry about that. It's just…I don't want to stay wedded to you. I cannot play the role of a husband and help you with the baby. Our marriage was a mistake from the start. You were not meant to be mine, and I was not meant to be yours. If we want to stay happy, we need to stop playing this charade of a happy couple. You can take your son with you because I don't want to play his dad's role."

She was staring at me like I had ripped her heart out by saying that.

"I have already booked your tickets back to Oakland. Your flight is in the evening. Amy will help you with the packing," I said.

After hearing my bullshit, her face turned paler like she had just seen a ghost. Fat tears started rolling down from her eyes making my heart ache. She looked so broken and distraught at that moment making me thought of telling her the truth. I was already regretting my decision, but the thought of her and Noah's safety forced me to keep up the pretense.

Suddenly, she blinked her eyes then they started to roll back. She started falling back as her eyes shut. I ran towards her and caught her in my arms before she hit the floor.

Her body was limp in my arms. Her face was tears stained. I cursed myself for breaking her heart and her trust and giving her agonizing pain.

Picking her up bridal style, I placed her on the bed and kissed her head before leaving her room.

I went to my room and slumped down on my bed. I ran my hands through my hair in frustration that was when I heard my phone ring. I took a glance at the screen of my cell phone and found an email notification. I opened the e-mail and read it.

It was from the Carrington Enterprises, which was the largest company in the US offering internships programs this year. My best friend Kyle forced me to apply for the internship last month, and I applied there.

Mr. Chase Edwards, we have looked at your records and documents you have submitted. Your grades seem to show how talented you are in the business field. We have carefully chosen you as one of the interns in our company. You will need to move to Boston as all the interns would be working in the Boston branch of Carrington Enterprises. Contact us for further discussion and details.

I couldn't believe I got selected as an intern in the largest company in the US. I called Kyle to share the news with him.

"Hey! I just received an e-mail from Carrington Enterprises," I informed him.

"Chase, that's great man! I received an e-mail from them informing me that I got selected as well. We need to move to Boston. Chase, it's awesome! My uncle has an apartment in Boston, which he doesn't use. He told me if I want to move to Boston he will give me that apartment. If you have decided to work in Carrington, then we can share the apartment. What do you say?" He was so excited.

He just gave me hope that there was a possibility for a better future.

"Yes. You are right. I'll call you later," I said and ended the call.

I thought about the whole idea. It seemed like a great opportunity to gain some experience in the real business world without my dad's support.

I could work on my own and build from the bottom. Just like my granddad. He didn't have his father's support when he started the business.

Then I would be able to provide a good future for my son.

Chapter Twenty-Four

Going Back to My Old Life

Hailey

I opened my eyes, but the bright lights made me shut them. I groaned and tried to open them again. I looked around my room and everything that happened earlier played in my head.

I shot up from the bed and looked inside the crib. My son was staring at the wall. I smiled at him, and he did the same. I picked up the divorce papers that were spread on my bed and read them.

I thought with exasperation, *"He left the divorce papers in my room so I would sign them when I woke up."*

I felt rage building inside me, and my hands started to shake. I looked for a pen inside the bedside drawer, and when I found the pen, I signed those papers.

He wanted me to leave him. He didn't want to be Noah's father, and he didn't want us in his life. Then guess what? He was going to have what he wanted.

I didn't need him anymore in my life. I was not the weak girl that I used to be. I would not let people push me anymore now that I was a mother, and I had a son to look after. I would show Chase that I could very well take care of my son without him. I would show him how strong I was. And he could not break me.

I could do anything I wanted to. He didn't even know half about me, and he was going to regret leaving my son and me. I would make sure of it.

I held the papers tightly in my hands and left my room to give him those signed papers. I pushed the door open and stormed into his room.

Chase was talking to someone on the cell phone when he saw me enter. He ended the call.

Before he could say anything to me, I threw the divorce papers on the floor and said, "I have signed these papers. Now, you are free to live your life like you wanted. I don't want your money to make Noah a better man than you."

He was just staring at me with his mouth hanging open.

I was ready to leave, but stopped and said, "I understand you, Chase. I'm really sorry for coming into your life when you didn't want me. I didn't want you either and never wished to be a part of your life. I too think this is best for us."

Then I left his room without giving him a glance. He lost the respect and love I had in my heart for him.

I went to my room and pulled out my suitcases from the closet and started packing my things. Amy came in my room that time and stopped me.

"Please, dear don't go. There has to be some misunderstanding." Amy tried stopping me from putting my things in the suitcases.

"There is no misunderstanding between us, Amy. He hated me from the start, and he never liked me. Now, he doesn't want me and my son after asking me for another chance. It's really easy for him to throw my son and me away," I said to Amy.

She stared at me with sadness in her eyes.

The tears were rolling down from my eyes while I was packing my and Noah's things. Amy helped in packing without saying anything again. I found the bracelet that Chase gave me on my seventeenth birthday and placed it on the bedside table.

I got changed into my denim jeans and cream-colored off-shoulder long sleeves sweatshirt then I changed Noah into his cute blue romper.

Amy came back with breakfast.

"At least eat something," she said.

"I'm not hungry."

"Even if you are not hungry, you have to eat, Hailey. You are a mother who is feeding, and it means you need to keep yourself healthy."

Her words brought tears to my eyes, and I realized by leaving this house I would be leaving Amy too. I hugged her and started to cry. I didn't know how long I cried while hugging Amy, but she pulled away and made me eat some toast and milk then she left.

I scooped Noah in my arms and kissed him on the forehead.

"Don't be sad, baby. Your mom loves you a lot, and she is going to love you till her last breath. And I'm sure your granddad will love you too. He will probably spoil you with so much love." I talked to my son, making him smile.

I chuckled at his cute smile.

I cuddled with Noah then he fell asleep. To kill time, I read my favorite book. After that, I paced in my room when I realized it was evening.

Chase came into my room.

"It's time to leave," he said, looking at me.

I picked up Noah while he dragged my bags downstairs.

Chase's dad entered the house at that time and looked at us in shock.

"Where are you both going?" he asked Chase.

I was suddenly tongue-tied with the emotions I had been feeling all day.

"Hailey, go wait for me outside," Chase said.

I glared at his back but went out.

Then I heard them shouting. His dad was yelling at Chase then he said something, and there was complete silence. After that, I heard the noise of something smashing.

Chase came out. His face was red with anger. He put my bags in the trunk of the car and asked me to give him Noah. I didn't want him to touch my son, but I had to because he was going to put him in the car seat.

Chase put Noah in the car seat, and I helped.

He closed the back door of the car, and at that moment his dad came out.

"I'm leaving," I said, and he closed his eyes for a moment.

I knew he was a very nice man, not at all like his son. He loved me like he loved Allison and Kate.

"I am sorry, Hailey. I am sorry for everything that happened while you were here," he said and hugged me.

"You don't have to be sorry. You did everything to make me feel it's my home."

"I will miss you and my grandson."

"You can come to meet him whenever you want. Will you tell Allison and Cameron? I am going to miss them both a lot," I said, getting in the car and he nodded his head.

After half an hour journey, we finally reached the airport. I was an hour early for my flight, so we went to the waiting area. I thought Chase would leave me alone to wait for the flight, but he stayed and sat beside me.

We both stayed silent. Noah was sleeping soundly in my arms, and I was staring at his face.

"Can I hold him for a few minutes?" Chase asked me.

I was shocked at first and wanted to tell him no, but I did the opposite and placed Noah in his waiting arms.

Noah instantly snuggled into his chest like he knew that it was his last chance to feel his dad's warmth and be near him. Chase kissed his head and murmured something in his ear. My son opened his eyes and stared at his dad. He had a small smile on his lips while Chase was staring at him with tears in his eyes.

I didn't understand why he would feel sad when he was throwing us out himself.

He noticed me staring and masked all his emotions.

We heard the announcement of my flight boarding. I took my son from his arms and turned to leave when he stopped me.

"Hailey." I turned back to find him standing close to me.

Without any warning, he leaned down and planted his lips on mine. He was kissing me, but I didn't respond to him. I didn't respond because I was too shocked. My heart was beating madly in my chest, and my hands were shaking. I tightened my hold on my son so I wouldn't drop him.

Chase pulled away from me, his breathing was erratic.

"Have a safe flight," he said, staring into my eyes.

I turned and left him without saying anything.

When I was inside the plane, traitorous tears rolled down from my cheeks. I furiously cleaned them with my sleeves and kissed my son's head.

Chapter Twenty-Five

Life without Him

Hailey

[Three years later]

I felt a sloppy kiss on my cheek, and it woke me up. I knew who it was from so to have a little fun, I pretended to be asleep.

He kissed my cheek again, and when he realized I wasn't waking up, he made a noise out of irritation. I smiled secretly and peeked at him from half-closed eyes. He had an adorable pout on his face.

I felt bad for upsetting him, but I was enjoying it too much and didn't want to end this charade.

"Mommy please, wake up. I know you're not sleeping. Mommy, you promised me today we'll go out for breakfast. Mommy, open your eyes," Noah said.

He nudged my shoulder lightly a few times then he tried a new trick, which I wasn't expecting at all from him. He took my hand in his and kissed the center of my palm. I instantly got up and caught his wrist with my hand before he could get away.

"You cheeky brat, you know Mommy is ticklish there," I said, pulling him closer.

He smiled at me innocently, but I wasn't letting him go away this time without punishment.

"It's time for revenge," I said and started tickling him mercilessly on his stomach.

He squealed and begged me to stop.

"Stop, Mommy. Stop pwease. I'm sorry," he said, laughing loudly.

It was childish I know, but I tickled him a little more then stopped. I laughed at his cute face, which looked red as a tomato due to laughing so hard. His grey eyes were twinkling with happiness. He gave me a wide smile, which warmed my heart.

I just love him so much. I leaned down and kissed his chubby cheeks.

He launched himself into my arms and kissed me on the right cheek.

"Mommy it's already 9. You need to get ready. I'm starving," he said, looking at his tummy.

I rolled my eyes at the word "starving." He learned that word last week from the movie we were watching and has been using it whenever he wanted to tell me that he was hungry.

Noah was an intelligent child. He could simply memorize a new word and use it in sentences like a pro at such a young age. It shocked everyone but me.

He talked to people confidently without feeling shy. He also knew how to eat on his own despite his young age. Sometimes, it made people curious. They would ask me if I sent him to some particular preschool.

At the age of three, he knew how to tell time, how to read and, how to write his name. He loved reading books, going out to parks, and he loved grocery shopping with me.

I felt him shaking my shoulder, and I looked at him.

"Go, baby, brush your teeth and if you tried swimming in the washbasin again then forget breakfast," I said trying to sound threatening, but he laughed at me.

That cheeky brat was taking my threat lightly. I got up and followed him to make sure he wouldn't do something stupid.

After half an hour, we were both ready in matching clothes. He loved it when we dressed in the same jeans and shirts. Today, we were wearing a white shirt and blue jeans with black jackets to keep us warm.

I picked him up in my arms and went downstairs. I found my mom and dad in the living room. They were having breakfast. I kissed my dad and mom on the cheeks.

"Good morning," Noah said.

Mom picked Noah and placed him on her lap. She kissed his cheek. My parents loved him to death. They played with him, watched cartoons with him, and even read with him.

"Where are you both off to this early?" Mom asked me.

Before I could answer her, Noah said, "Grandma, don't you remember today is Sunday. Mommy promised to take me to the café for pancakes."

Mom looked at him amused.

"Oh, so you think that the café makes better pancakes than me," she said to tease him.

He glanced at me for help, but I shrugged telling him to answer himself.

"No...No Grandma, your pancakes are the best, but the café give them out," he said, making me and dad laugh.

They gave them out means they served breakfast in the open near the lake, which Noah loved. My son loved nature and parks.

We bid our goodbyes to my parents then left the house. I buckled Noah in the car seat and drove in the direction of the café. Light music was playing in my car, and he was bobbing his head side to side.

After fifteen minutes of driving, we reached our destination, and I pulled him out then we went inside. I caught sight of our favorite server, Mrs. James, a cute short lady in her fifties. She liked to give me and Noah extra cookies with hot chocolate, so we both really liked her.

We said our hellos and ordered our breakfast. I was eating and wondering how my life would have been today if Chase and I were still together.

I still remembered the day he divorced me and sent me here to live with my parents. That day was still fresh in my memory.

[Flashback]

When my flight landed in Oakland, I found Melanie and my dad at the airport waiting for me. Mom took Noah from me, and my dad embraced me. I hid my face in his coat as tears were not ready to stop from flowing down anytime soon. They took me home, and I was crying all the way. I felt like my whole life ended. I didn't know what Mom would do to me now that I was back in her house. I was scared for my son's future, but I had nowhere to go except my parent's house.

I spent the whole day crying my eyes out in my old room while lying on the bed and hugging my pillow. Then Mom came into my room and sat beside me. She rubbed my back to provide me comfort, which shocked me.

I opened my swollen eyes and looked at her. She told me to sit up.

"Hailey, your dad is with you. I-I'm with you. Don't worry. We will support you. You need to be strong for your son. He is the one who needs you the most right now. You have to stop crying and move on with your life. Get up and take a shower. Think about a new beginning with Noah and with your family," she said, opening her arms.

I hugged her and cried some more. She asked me to forgive her for the things that she had done in the past. I forgave her that day and forgot everything about my past.

*   *   *

In the last three years, she supported me like a real mother would support her daughter. She told me how Emily left her for modeling and got busy chasing fame. She told me how hurt she was when her real daughter didn't care about her wishes and wouldn't even answer her calls.

Melanie sacrificed her life for her daughter and stayed with my dad for her, but Emily didn't care about her own mom.

Mom felt ashamed of the things she did to me. I thought she took care of my son to compensate for her past sins. Dad and Mom encouraged me to continue my studies and supported me throughout high school and college.

Last year, I graduated from high school with flying colors, which was a blessing to me. Then, I enrolled myself in the nearest best college and continued my studies. I wanted to be a psychologist because I thought it was the best way to help people. I still had to go through years of college to become a psychologist, but that didn't dampen my spirit.

"Mommy, is Dad coming here for Christmas?" Noah had so much hope in his beautiful eyes.

"I don't know, honey, but I will talk to him later tonight," I replied, and he busied himself eating his pancakes.

He had been asking me if he could celebrate this Christmas with his dad.

Yes, he knew that Chase was his dad. As I said before, Noah was an intelligent boy, and one day he found my wedding pictures and asked me who the man was. He noticed Chase had the same color of eyes as his. Noah did look a lot like Chase. It wouldn't be wrong if I said that he was a copy of his father. Even my parents said that there was no point in keeping it a secret, so I told Noah about Chase.

He asked me why his dad didn't live with us, and I lied to him that he lived in another city because of his business.

Now, Christmas was two weeks away, and he wanted to know if his dad would come to celebrate this Christmas with him. But sadly, I still didn't have an answer.

Chase would send Noah gifts on his birthday and every Christmas. Noah asked me who sent him the gifts and I told him that the gifts were from his dad. From that day, he started loving his dad without knowing him in person.

One month after our divorce, Chase came to meet us in Oakland at my parents' house. I let him spent time with Noah, but when he asked to meet me, I refused to see him and talk to him. I wasn't ready to look at him when my heart was still fragile. After losing him, I fell into depression. It was a horrific period of my life, and I didn't want to recall the past events by meeting him.

Chase left after spending few hours with Noah, but he gave my dad a letter and asked him to give it to me.

I still remembered every line of that letter by heart.

Hailey, I know I wasn't a good husband. Believe me, I want to be a good father for Noah. I have opened an account for you in the bank near your house. I want you to use that money without hesitation. I'm not going to visit you or Noah as long as you don't want me to. I know we both want time to heal. But please, I want you to remember me. I assure you that you can ask me for anything any day without thinking twice. I'll be waiting to hear from you.

Now after three years, I really wanted to ask him to come and meet Noah. I couldn't lie to my son anymore. I would have to do this for Noah.

I hoped Chase would not refuse to come meet Noah on Christmas because Noah really wanted to see his dad.

On the way back home, we made a little stop at the ice cream shop. Then we continued our way back home. After spending his whole day playing, he was extremely tired, so I hurriedly gave him a shower then changed him into his comfy night clothes. I laid him on the bed and kissed his forehead. He fell asleep instantly.

I went to the balcony and glanced at my cell phone. I was contemplating my decision of calling him or not. I knew it was now or never. So before I would change my mind, I called him on the number that I took from Allison a few days ago.

I heard the first ring, I thought of ending the call but stopped myself. At the second ring, my heart started to beat faster. At the third ring, I literally stopped breathing, and that was when he picked up.

A whoosh of breath left my mouth. I said, "Hello."

"Hello," a woman replied.

I glanced at the screen of my cellphone to make sure that I had dialed the correct number.

When I realized I had dialed the correct number and a female had answered Chase's cell phone instead of him, my heart stopped beating.

"Uh… Can I talk to Chase?" I asked her.

"I am sorry. He is really busy at the moment."

"Will you please tell him to call me back at this number? I have something important to discuss."

"Who are you by the way?" she asked me and anger was clear in her voice.

"I… Uh… I'm Hailey."

"Okay, Hailey. I really don't care who you are but listen very carefully. Don't call him ever again because I really hate it when his one night stands call him back," she said, and my eyes widened in shock.

Before I could give her answer in the same bitchy way, she said, "And just for your information, I'm Clara, his fiancée," Then the line went dead.

The cell phone that was pressed to my ear trembled in my hand and fell down on the floor.

He has moved on, Hailey. He has replaced you.

Chapter Twenty-Six

Life without Her

Chase

[Three years later]

I was sitting in my office, watching the view of Boston city, and thinking about Hailey. I still hadn't moved on. Every minute, every second of every day I missed her and my son. Sometimes, I wished that I could go to Oakland and tell her the truth.

I still loved her. My heart would call her with its every beat and reminded me that it belonged to her.

I had been trying to become a better person for Hailey and my son. Three years ago, when I asked her to sign those divorce papers, I didn't know I was actually killing myself. After she left, I moved out of my parents' house without telling them anything. I went to Boston and completed my internship at Carrington Enterprises. Also, I enrolled myself in the University to get a higher education, and completed Masters in Business Administration.

Two years and eleven months ago, when I went Oakland to visit Hailey and Noah, she refused to meet me. I spent few hours with Noah and then I had to leave. I decided to write her a letter telling her I wouldn't come back until she would ask me and I was still waiting for her to ask me.

I worked one year for Carrington enterprises then my dad asked me to take my rightful place in Edwards Investing Company. But I refused to work in New York, so I started an office in Boston. Now, after two years, I was a very well-known businessman in Boston. My company was making billions because I worked hard every day to get here. I wanted Hailey to see me as a successful man. I wanted my dad to feel proud of me.

Now that Christmas was fast approaching, I hoped my mother would not insist on me attending Christmas dinner this year. Every year I tried avoiding it. There was no use anyway. My dad would just ask me a few questions here and there then he stayed quiet the rest of the time.

Cameron was a different story. From the day he found out that I had divorced Hailey and made her leave, he hated me with a passion. Now he lived in New York and studied in NYU while running his own studios. If I asked him anything, he would answer me rudely.

Allison was just like before, polite and nice. She still talked to Hailey and told me about her and Noah. She knew everything and understood me.

Chris and Susan loved me and treated me like before. I loved them too.

Kate got married last year to the college bad boy, Evan Thompson and became a mommy to a cute baby two months ago. It would be her son's first Christmas.

At first, I was against Kate getting married to Evan, but she told me that he had changed and really loved her. I called him and had a long talk then I gave my blessing to them. But it didn't mean that we liked each other. Our mutual hatred towards each other showed whenever we were in one room.

Cameron and Evan had built a very good friendship, and both of them loved to gang up on me. They wouldn't let one moment go without making me feel that I didn't have a family and I was alone.

It wouldn't be wrong if I would say that the Christmas dinner or any dinner with my family would always end as a disaster, for me at least.

They were all happy and settled in their lives. They had what Evan called a "perfect life," a wife, a beautiful house, and a son.

My office door opened and it brought me back to reality. I glanced up and found Clara making her way to my table. I groaned inwardly at her presence in my office.

She stood in front of me, wearing a white knee-length dress and black stilettos. Her hands were placed on her waist while she glared at me like I was some kid who had done something bad.

"What are you doing here Clara?" I asked her in annoyance.

"Oh…so I guessed it right, you forgot."

I looked at her and raised my eyebrows.

"What did I forget?" I asked her.

"Argh. Chase, you're impossible. Today we planned to have dinner together because you have no important meetings lined up. You were supposed to pick me up at eight from my house. I waited for you for an hour, I even called you, but you didn't answer. Then I called your secretary, and she told me that you are still at the office."

Her face looked red after she finished her speech. Sometimes, I wondered how she could speak this much without taking a breath, but I refrained myself from asking her anything that would lead me to hear another speech.

Now, I had to take her out for dinner if I wanted to live another day. I picked up my car keys and closed my laptop so she wouldn't see Hailey and Noah's picture on the screen.

"I'm very sorry Clara. Do you have any place in mind where we can go?" I asked her.

I was also starving.

She glared at me and walked out. I followed her. We went to our favorite restaurant and ordered dinner.

"Chase, we have been with each other for a year now. We have known each other for our whole life. My parents want me to get married, so when are you going to propose to me with a ring?" she asked me.

My eyes widened, and I choked on my food.

"Clara, how many times have I told you that I don't feel the same way about you? We are with each other for a year as good friends and nothing else."

"But Chase, the paparazzi have already published news last month about our engagement. You cannot do this to me. It would be so humiliating," she told me.

"Clara, I told them that news wasn't true and you should have done the same," I said.

"Chase, why do you think they don't believe you? They have always seen you with me. You don't go out with any other girl except me. You don't have any girlfriends. Even they have tried making scandals of you with some models. But all the news of you being in a relationship with any model was wrong. Last Sunday in Boston's magazine your name was mentioned in the list of five youngest billionaire bachelors of the year." She said it like it was a very important thing.

"Clara, I really don't care what media or magazines say about me unless if it affects my business or my reputation," I said to her.

She looked mad but stopped arguing. The waiter placed our order on the table, and we ate our dinner peacefully.

When we were done, the waiter approached us with the bill. I gave my credit card, but the waiter came back and told me my card wasn't working. I went with him to the payment counter and left Clara at the table.

I came back after paying them with cash because their machine was not accepting credit cards. The waiter repeatedly apologized to me for the inconvenience, and I assured him it was alright. I went back to the table but found Clara talking to someone on my cell phone.

"And just for your information, I'm Clara, his fiancée," she said then ended the call.

I walked to her angrily and snatched my phone from her hand. I checked who she was talking to and found an unknown number as the last received call.

"Who were you talking to? And why did you say that you were my fiancée?" I asked her angrily.

She looked at me with anger.

"Tell me, Clara," I said, gritting my teeth.

"I was talking to a girl. She said she wants you to call her at that number. I thought she was one of your one night stands and told her that I am your fiancée. Even her name was disgusting, Bailey, Hailey." She made a face.

My heart froze when I heard the name Hailey from her mouth.

Could it be possible that Hailey called me?

"Clara, find a cab for you because I am leaving," I said and left the restaurant.

I went to my apartment and thought if I should call her or not.

I groaned to myself. *Why was I so nervous?* It was Hailey. Why was I feeling like a teenage boy?

"It had been three years, Chase," my mind reminded me.

I dialed her number and waited for her to answer my call. At the third ring, she answered my call.

"Hello," she said in her same sweet voice.

I stopped breathing. I forgot how to speak.

"Uhh… Hello," she said again.

Suddenly, my breathing hitched and I panicked and ended the call.

I tried to calm myself. Oh, God! She called. It meant she wanted to see me.

Then, I remembered what Clara said to her, and I started to curse my luck.

Chapter Twenty-Seven

Surprise

Hailey

My alarm went off, waking me up. I sat up on the bed and groaned. I glanced at Noah sleeping beside me. He looked so cute with his hands under his head and a small amount of drool on his face.

I smiled looking at him and picked the tissue from the bedside table then cleaned his face. I ran my fingers through his silky soft hair and placed a kiss on his forehead.

I loved my son so much. Noah had become my life even though he reminded me of the man who broke my heart and rejected my love.

I felt my heart squeezing at the thought of Chase's engagement. So he had finally moved on and started a new life with another woman.

I didn't need him now, but Noah does. My son was the one who was missing one of his parents, and I knew very well how it felt. I didn't want him to feel the same pain I felt all my life. I would try to talk to Chase again.

Then, I saw the time on my wall clock; it was already 9:20.

Crap! I had to hurry now, or I would be late for class.

I sprinted towards my closet and picked my clothes then went to the washroom. I did my usual routine then put on my clothes and applied a minimum amount of makeup, which consisted of mascara, liner, nude pink lip shade, and light blush to give my skin a little color.

I picked up my bag and checked the contents again to make sure I had all the stuff I wanted for class. On the way out of the room, I picked up my cell phone and black ankle boots. While walking down the stairs, I worked on putting on my boots and strapping them without falling and breaking my neck.

I found my mom in the kitchen and said, "Good morning, Mom. Noah is still sleeping. Please keep an eye on him just to make sure he is sleeping on the bed and not under the bed."

"Hailey you don't have to tell me all these things every time. I know what I need to do. I have been taking care of him for three years now," she said with a smile on her face.

"Sorry, Mom. I just cannot make myself stop worrying about him when I am not around him."

I kissed her on the cheeks

"I know, Hailey. That's how it feels to be a mother," she said with a sad smile.

"When will your class end today?"

"My classes will end around two in the afternoon." I gulped down the juice that was on the table.

"Do you want breakfast?" she asked and offered me some cereal.

"No, Mom. I'm not hungry. I'll eat something after class. Bye."

Julia was waiting for me outside in her car.

I got inside the car, and said, "Good morning."

"Good morning, babe," she said with a smile.

She was wearing a white fitted top and high waist black jeans. Her lips were coated in red lipstick.

"You are looking beautiful, Julia," I said.

"Thanks, but I know I am nowhere near as beautiful as you."

I rolled my eyes at her.

"You only think I am beautiful because I have curves," I said, staring at her.

"Yes, you have curves, which I don't have. And you're looking gorgeous. I am obsessed with your hair and curves. I think I am turning bisexual because of you."

I laughed at her stupid words.

"You're the weirdest person I have ever met," I said, making her glare at me. "Okay, sorry. I have curves that every girl wants including you, and I am supposed to believe whatever you say."

"Yes, you have to believe me because I am always right." She shrugged.

"Yeah. You're always right except that one time when you claimed that the bra store changed your bag and gave you the smaller size when it was you who bought the smaller size to make your boobs look bigger. And that time when you said that black jacket guy had been following you but turned out, he worked at the same place and was just waiting for your shift to end so he will start his shift," I said, making her blush.

"Ugh! Please don't remind me. They were embarrassing. And for your information, I am always right except for those two times."

"Sure."

"No. I think I was wrong that time too when I said Vanessa and Frank are meant to be together," she said, and I couldn't stop laughing after that.

Then for the whole ride, we reminded each other how many times Julia was wrong. When we arrived at the college, we ran to the classroom to make sure we would get to class before our professor.

*   *   *

After three hours of class, I was ready to murder anyone. Yes, the class was that boring.

Julia, Vanessa, Matt, and Ethan were kind to my close friends. Julia and I became friends in high school and decided to go to the same college.

I met with Vanessa, Matt, and Ethan in college, and we all built a pretty good friendship. Vanessa and Matt were dating, and Julia was dating Oliver. Oliver was her high school boyfriend. Ethan and I were the only ones single in the group.

Ethan was very handsome with blonde hair, mesmerizing blue eyes, great height, and strong build. Almost every girl in college had a crush on him except me, Julia, and Vanessa. Ethan was a complete flirt. He slept around, but he was our good friend, so we had no problem with that.

Then suddenly, an image of Chase popped into my head, and I groaned.

"Why are you groaning, Hailey? Did you imagine something kinky?" Ethan asked me with an innocent face.

I hit him on the arm with the book, and said, "Keep your dirty mouth shut."

He just laughed at me.

We were walking towards the parking lot to go out for lunch when I halted on my steps.

"Mommy, Mommy!" I heard Noah's voice and looked to my left to see him running towards me.

And when he ran like that, it meant I am supposed to kneel down and catch him in my arms. I had no other choice but to do so.

There was complete silence in the parking lot. A few people stopped and stared at me.

I stood up with Noah in my arms and looked at them.

"Baby, what are you doing here? Who brought you here?" I asked Noah.

I knew my parents would never bring him here like this unless it was a life or death situation.

Noah gave me a sloppy kiss and smiled at me broadly.

"Daddy is here. We wanted to surprise you," he said, pointing his finger at a man.

I stopped breathing when my eyes landed on the man standing in front of me.

It was Chase. Chase Edwards, the man who made me fall in love with him then ripped my soul by leaving me without any explanation.

He was staring at me with those grey eyes I saw every day when I look at my son. I felt my heart breaking at the sight of him.

Chase looked almost the same in his black jacket and jeans. His hair was cut short on his head, and looking disheveled like he had run his fingers through them. The stubble on his jaw made him look mature, strong, and handsome.

Chase walked in my direction, and I found myself frozen.

"Hi, I brought Noah here. I hope you don't mind," Chase said in his deep voice.

My knees weakened after hearing his voice. I felt like I was sixteen-year-old Hailey again who felt scared of this guy and forgot how to speak in front him.

Maybe I was in shock seeing him after three years?

Oh, God! Why does he still look handsome like before and why does he have the same effect on me after three years?

Before I could say anything to Chase, I saw Brittney making her way towards me.

Shit! She was coming to create a scene.

She smiled at me evilly, and I shuddered.

Brittney was a little messed up in the head. She kind of wanted Ethan, but he didn't want her, and that was where I come in. She thought that I had something to do with Ethan not reciprocating her feelings.

Brittney asked him out in front of everyone last year, and he let her down politely. But she didn't take the rejection very well and made it her mission to degrade me in front of him.

"Hailey, you never told us you have such a cute son." She cooed to Noah while I glared at her. "What's your name little man?" she asked him.

"My name is No-Ah."

"Awe you are really cute. How old are you Noah?" she asked him sweetly.

He showed her three fingers using his right hand while gripping my neck tightly with his left hand.

"Oh…wow! Hailey, you are twenty if I am not wrong, so it means you were probably seventeen when you had Noah," she said, and my grip on my son tightened.

I knew where she was going with this and I didn't want my son to hear her rubbish. I was ready to leave when her words stopped me.

"So did you end up getting pregnant because of a one-night stand? Or you were just sleeping around like a whore," she said in her bitchy voice, and her friends giggled.

I wanted to rip her blonde Barbie hair extensions. But I controlled myself and opened my mouth to put her in her place when Chase decided to speak.

"Miss whatever your name is. You have no right to call my wife names when you are the one dressed like a whore in your barely there shorts and that crop top that looks like a bikini," he said, making all of us gasp in shock.

Oh, God! Chase just did not call her a whore and insulted her clothes.

I thought he was finished insulting her, but he continued.

"Please kindly inform me what's wrong if she has a three-year-old son when she's in her twenties? She has a right to live her life the way she wants," he said, making her gulp.

I was just staring at him with my jaw slack.

"And for your information, we have been married for four years, and I know very well where she sleeps every night. You don't have to worry about that. I would very much appreciate it if you respect my wife and don't try to insult her again by calling her names," he said in anger.

Now Brittney's mouth almost hit the ground. I would have laughed at her face if I wasn't standing there in shock. Brittney blushed in embarrassment and left stomping her feet.

Chase turned to me with a triumphant smile.

Vanessa took hold of my arm, and whispered, "Hey! You never told me that you are married and have a cute son. You never mentioned that Chase Edwards, the CEO of Edwards Investing Company, is your husband. You slay little thing."

"I'll explain everything to you later over a coffee," I said, making her nod.

Then I saw Ethan glaring at Chase with hatred and disgust. He looked jealous, and I was confused by his actions.

He noticed me staring at him, so he averted his gaze. Then suddenly, he turned and left without saying anything.

I knew this would happen if I kept it a secret. I should have told Ethan about Chase. Ethan and Julia knew about Noah, but Ethan never asked me about Chase, so I kept it a secret.

During the second semester, Ethan and Julia visited my house to discuss our thesis, and that was when they met Noah. I introduced Noah as my son to Ethan.

Julia was my school friend and best friend, so she knew everything about Chase and Noah. She was more like a sister to me, and it was her advice to keep my story of marriage and divorce hidden.

No one in college knew about Noah except Ethan and Julia, so it was a shock for everybody.

After hearing Chase, I didn't know what I was supposed to say.

Should I get angry at him for coming unannounced and even bringing my son with him? Or should I thank him for defending me in front of everyone?

Chase reached out and took Noah from my arms into his and said, "I'll be waiting for you in the car."

I wanted to ask him why he would wait for me in the car, but I stayed quiet and turned to my friends.

"Guys it seems like I need to go. Have a great Christmas all of you," I said, sliding my bag on my arm.

I followed Chase to his car. Noah was already buckled in the back of the car in his car seat.

"What are you doing here?" I asked him.

He straightened up, and said, "I'm here to take you home."

"What?"

"I know you didn't bring your car because the breaks were messed up and it's in the workshop, so I came here to pick you up," he said, making my mouth drop again.

How the hell did he know about my car? I looked at him irritatingly.

"I caught a ride here with my friend, and she will drop me off."

"I think she just left," he said, making me turn to my left to see Julia speeding off.

Now he was scaring me. How did he know that I hitched a ride with Julia? And how did he know I was talking about Julia?

I glanced at him suspiciously, and he gave me a dazzling smile.

"I will take a cab," I said.

I was about to open the back door and pull Noah out from his car when he grabbed my wrist.

I suddenly recalled the time when he would grab my wrist like this then kiss my hand. But as fast as I recalled the past, I pulled myself back to the present and snatched my hand from his grip.

"Okay, fine." I got inside the car.

"Put on the seat belt," he said, making me glare at him while I put the seatbelt on.

"Noah, do you know some people look really beautiful when they are angry," Chase said and started to drive.

Noah just giggled making me glance at him with narrow eyes while my face was heating up with a blush.

I glanced at Chase and saw a smile playing on his lips.

I tried to stop myself, but my lips twitched upward.

Chapter Twenty-Eight

Dinner Invitation

Hailey

When we arrived at my house, Melanie invited Chase inside and insisted him to stay for lunch.

Chase agreed to have lunch with us when Noah gave him his best puppy face, making it impossible for him to resist.

I followed Mom to the kitchen. "Mom, did you ask Chase to pick me up from college?" I asked her.

"No, I didn't ask him. He showed up at the door at half past twelve and asked me to let him meet you and Noah, so I told him that you went to college. He asked me when your class will end and took Noah to pick you up," she replied.

"You let him meet Noah when I wasn't around."

"Yes, I let him meet his son under my and your father's supervision."

"He came to pick me up with Noah, and there was Brittney. She created a scene," I said, massaging my head.

"Hailey, you pushed him away three years ago when he came to explain. Now you need to stop hiding and give him a chance to explain himself." Mom squeezed my shoulder.

"Mom, he didn't try to contact me in the last three years. He never asked me about Noah. Now, he is engaged."

"Hailey, you told him not to contact you until you contact him yourself. He has been in touch with me for the last three years. He would ask me about you because he cares for you, honey. Whatever he has done in the past wasn't right, and I am not telling you to forgive him. I am asking you to give yourself a chance. You gave me one when I was the cause of your pain, and I got a chance at redemption," she said as tears trailed down from her eyes.

I wiped her tears and said, "Mom, please, stop crying. I forgive you, and I love you. In the past three years, you were my greatest support. You taught me how to be tough and held my head high in front of the world."

She hugged me, and I rubbed her back.

Yes, she had changed. The woman I knew in the past died when Emily left. This woman was my mother, only mine and I loved her.

In these past three years, she did everything in her power to turn me into a strong girl.

"I will not push him away again," I said, pulling away from the hug.

"Thank you, Hailey."

She turned around, wiped her tears, and started cooking lunch. I started helping her in the kitchen. I took a quick glance in the living room to make sure Dad was not trying to murder Chase.

I was amazed at what I was seeing. My dad was watching TV and doing a great job ignoring Chase's presence. Like he didn't exist, which was better than the murder scene that I was picturing.

After my grandfather's death, Dad had become silent. He would only smile when Noah was around.

Chase was sitting on the couch with Noah on his lap. He was listening to Noah's story about his favorite cartoons.

A smile appeared on my face, looking at them.

That was when Mom decided to look at me. She caught me smiling like a fool, and her face lit up with a teasing smile. I bit my lips to stop the smile and straightened myself, so I didn't appear like a complete fool in front of her.

She raised her eyebrows at me, and I shrugged my shoulders at her.

"I am going to my room to freshen up," I told her, leaving her in the kitchen.

I went to my room to use the washroom. I was washing my face when I caught my reflection in the mirror.

There was a pink hue on my cheeks, and my dull brown eyes were shining. There was a smile on my face without any reason.

I shook my head at myself and dampened the towel under the tap water. I placed the towel on my hot cheeks to make them look normal again. I heard mom calling me down, so I walked out of the washroom. I opened my hair and sprayed some perfume on myself then I went down to the dining room.

Everyone was already settled on the chairs, leaving only one chair empty that was magically beside Chase. Noah was sitting on the right seat beside his dad, and he was already filling his plate. He never ate without me, but the minute his dad showed up in his life, he forgot about his mother.

Mom's mischievous eyes landed on me.

"Hailey, why are you standing there? Come take a seat," she said with a smug face, knowing why I was still standing.

I narrowed my eyes knowing that she planned to make me sit beside Chase. I was sure she was the one who told everyone where to sit.

Chase saw my hesitation and smirked like he was challenging me to take a seat beside him.

I said to myself, "You are not a shy sixteen-year-old girl anymore, and you shouldn't show him that you still feel nervous around him."

He had no idea what he was getting himself into by challenging me.

I settled on the seat beside him without showing any signs of discomfort and started filling my plate with the freshly cooked food. We were all eating silently. I reached for the bowl of mashed potatoes, which was in the center of the table, and at that time Chase also decided to reach for it too.

I was the first one to take hold of the bowl, and his hand was above mine. I gasped at the sensation. We both froze and stared into each other's eyes. My heart beat accelerated when he slid his hand back. He left the electrifying sensation on my skin when his fingers brushed mine.

I took a risk and looked into his eyes, and my heart pounded in my chest, seeing the intensity in them.

Mom coughed loudly, and it brought us out from la la land.

I put the bowl of mashed potatoes back on the table and placed my hand on my lap feeling my skin tingle. My face flushed with embarrassment. The rest of lunch, I didn't take the risk of glancing into Chase's eyes again.

After we were all done with lunch, Chase decided to leave, promising Noah to come and meet him tomorrow.

I walked with Chase to the door.

"Hailey, can you come out with me? I need to talk to you," he said.

I nodded my head and went out.

"Hailey I…Uh I want to take you and Noah out for dinner tomorrow. That is if you don't mind having dinner with me."

"You don't need to take us out for dinner. If you want to meet Noah again, you can come here and meet him. I won't stop you from meeting your son," I said to him.

"I want to talk to you about something important. Please, let me take you both out for dinner."

I glanced at him with curiosity.

Why did he want to take Noah and me out for dinner?

Maybe he wanted to tell me about his engagement with Clara.

I smiled sweetly at him and took a step back.

"You can tell me anything you want right here. I don't go out with strangers," I said, feeling proud for refusing him.

After hearing my words, an emotion similar to hurt appeared on his face, but he masked it quickly with a smirk.

He took a step forward until he was standing close enough to me to whisper in my ear.

"Hailey, if you called me a stranger one more time. I will be forced to remind you how much I know about you," he said, placing a kiss on my ear.

My eyes went shut at the sensation he aroused in me. I remembered the night we ate spaghetti in my room and got to know each other. He placed a kiss on the same spot that night too and left me thinking about him all night.

To a stranger, it would look like he had murmured something in my ear, but in reality, he had made my stomach clench with his kiss.

He took a step back from me, and I opened my eyes to find a sly smile playing on his lips.

My jaw clenched.

Did he think he could just do things like that to make me agree to go out for dinner with him?

I glared at him.

"Did I tell you how beautiful you look?" he asked.

I narrowed my eyes at him and glared harder.

"Dinner is tomorrow at eight in the evening. I will come to pick up both of you."

"I didn't say yes."

"You didn't say no either. See you tomorrow beautiful," he said and winked at me then got inside his car.

My jaw dropped, and I stared at his speeding car.

I went back inside the house and found my mom standing near the window. She must have been spying on us through the damn window.

She gave me her teasing smile. "So what were you guys talking about?"

"He wants to take Noah and me out for dinner tomorrow," I told her in the most boring voice I could manage.

"Oh! That's great." She was so excited. It was like I just told her I was going on a date.

I cursed my stupid brain for not working properly whenever I was around him.

The rest of the day went pretty quick. When night came, I put Noah in bed and read stories with him when he fell asleep.

My cell phone beeped indicating that I had received a message. I unlocked my cell phone and found a message from Chase. It was a simple good night message, but for some weird reason, it put a smile on my face.

[Morning]

Thump, Thump
Thump, Thump

I groaned, hearing the loud knocks on the door.

Who the hell wanted to take my door down?

I got up from bed and opened the door. I rubbed my eyes twice to clear my vision, but the person standing in front of me didn't disappear.

"Julia, what the hell are you doing here knocking at my door in the morning? It's good that Noah is a heavy sleeper or I would have killed you," I said, but she only rolled her eyes at me.

"Oh my sweet, Hailey, it's eleven in the morning. I think you have had enough sleep to look fresh for your date with your ex-husband."

"Excuse me? It's not a date. And how did you know he asked me to have dinner with him?"

"A little birdy told me that you have a date with him, not dinner," she said in a singsong voice.

"Why would I go on a date with an engaged man?" I sat back down on the bed.

"What did you say? Is he really engaged?"

"Yeah, I think so," I said, scratching my head.

"If he is engaged, it's not a problem. You can still make him regret leaving you. You can make him jealous by showing up on dinner wearing a sexy dress and turning some heads around."

"I don't want to make him regret anything. I'm happy with my life. He has moved on with his life and got engaged to another woman. It is not like he wants me back," I said with a sarcastic laugh.

"Hailey, I am not in the mood to hear your depressing talk. Get up and get ready. We are going out." She pushed me in the direction of the washroom.

No one knew how to stop Julia when she set her mind to do something except Oliver, her boyfriend, her neighbor, and the love of her life. But even Oliver couldn't save me at the moment from his devil of a girlfriend because he went to Florida for two weeks to visit his grandma.

I went inside the washroom did my routine and got changed into my simple denim jeans and cream-colored knit sweater.

We went down, and I grabbed the sandwich that Mom prepared for me. I kissed her cheek and left with Julia.

She took me shopping and forced me into buying a sexy black bodycon dress. It was too revealing for my liking, but Julia didn't know how to take no for an answer. The dress was black, floor length, and fitted on my body like a second skin. It was V-neck and backless.

Our next stop was the spa. We both got a manicure and pedicure. Julia told the girl to curl my hair into loose curls, which looked nice on me.

When we came back home, it was already five in the evening. Julia made me sit on the chair in front of the mirror because she wanted to do my makeup. I tried sitting still, but it was not possible for me to sit still while she poked my eyes. I wiggled in my seat a few times and made weird faces in the mirror to annoy her.

After Julia was done, I told Noah that we were going out for dinner with his dad. He jumped up and down and did the happy dance on the way to my room.

I changed him into his white pants and white dress shirt, paired with a black coat and black shoes. He looked so handsome that Julia couldn't resist taking his pictures and uploading them on her profile. Julia loved children in general, and Noah did have a special place in her heart.

Julia entered my room again while stuffing her mouth with cupcakes, which I baked last night before going to bed.

She told me to get changed into the black dress that we bought today.

"Are you out of your mind? I'm not going to wear that dress," I said to her.

She glared at me then picked up my favorite novel.

"I will rip every page of this novel one by one if you didn't get changed into that dress within five minutes." She threatened me.

I knew how merciless she was, so I hurriedly got changed into the black dress.

I glanced at myself in the mirror and gulped. The dress fitted my body perfectly. It showed all my curves, and the slit on the left side revealed lots of skin.

When I was done admiring myself, I turned around to find Julia dangling my stilettos in front of me.

I took them from her hands and wiggled my feet in them. My black stilettos with golden straps matched perfectly with my outfit.

Simple gold loop earrings adorned my ears, and my gold charm bracelet dangled on my wrist.

Mom looked at me with a lovely smile, and Julia winked at me.

We heard the doorbell and went to the door. I saw a sleek black car parked in front of the house and a man dressed in black.

He walked to me when he saw me standing at the door.

"Hello, ma'am. I'm James. This is for you from my boss," he said, handing me a bouquet of red roses and a card.

I opened the card and read it.

Hailey, I'm sorry for not coming to pick you up, but I am sending my driver. I hope you forgive me for not coming to get you myself. I'll be waiting for you in the restaurant.

Yours,
Chase

I smiled after reading his sweet note and bid goodbye to Mom and Julia. When Noah and I were settled in the car, the driver started the car. After the twenty-minute journey, we reached the restaurant where Chase was waiting for us.

James opened my door, and I got out of the car with Noah. I entered the restaurant, and my breath got caught in my throat.

The restaurant was very beautiful and decorated in vintage style. Expensive chandeliers hang from the roof, illuminating the whole place with light.

The lady at the reception walked towards me.

"Welcome, Mrs. Edwards. Mr. Edwards is waiting for you in the VIP section on the rooftop. Please follow me," she said, smiling politely.

I didn't know why I didn't correct her when she called me Mrs. Edwards and followed her to the elevator. Noah was grasping my hand tightly, looking excited to meet his dad again.

*   *   *

Chase

I was waiting anxiously for them to arrive at the restaurant. I kept glancing at my wristwatch every two seconds. I hoped she would like the idea of dining here on the rooftop.

I heard the sound of the elevator and my head snapped in the direction of the elevator. Noah came out from the elevator first and ran towards me. I picked him up in my arms and placed a kiss on his cheeks.

Then my eyes landed on Hailey, striding towards me in a black dress that fitted her body like a glove and showed off her beautiful curves. Her hair was styled in loose curls resting on one shoulder. Every head in the restaurant turned to look at her.

My mind was simply numb, and I put Noah on the ground before I could drop him in shock.

She was the most gorgeous woman in the world I had ever seen.

I wanted nothing more than to kiss her at that moment and tell people that I was the lucky man whom she belonged to. But I controlled my stupid urge before I would do something to make her leave.

"Hi," she said, looking at me with a beautiful smile on her face.

Even her voice sounded sexy after three years.

My eyes strayed on her pretty cherry-colored plum lips, which were moving, saying something to me, but I wasn't hearing her as I was too busy staring at them.

"You're looking gorgeous. Thanks for coming," I said, taking a step closer to her and got hit with the sensual fragrance of her perfume.

She looked me in the eye, and I felt my world tremble. We stared at each other until her eyes landed on Noah who was trying to pluck a flower from the vase. She ran to stop him, and that was when my eyes landed on her smooth back.

Shit! She was wearing a backless dress.

I gripped the table in shock. *When did she start to dress like this?*

She looked so sexy and beautiful, and my eyes were stuck on her then I realized that I was not the only one appreciating the view. I glared at the other men, and they averted their eyes.

I walked to her and asked her to sit.

When we were settled at the table, the waiter approached with menus, and we ordered dinner.

While we were waiting for dinner to arrive, the waiter served us drinks and appetizers.

She put the straw in her mouth to drink the cocktail, and I wished to be that straw so I would be able to touch her beautiful, kissable lips.

I realized that I was falling in love with her more each second.

"You said you wanted to talk to me about something important," Hailey said, staring at me.

"Uh…Yeah. Actually, I have planned something for Christmas." I started feeling little uneasy under her gaze.

"Okay. What have you planned?" she asked me while taking a bite of her grilled cheese crostini.

I gulped at the innocent actions of her lips.

"There is a cabin near the mountains, which is really beautiful. Noah was telling me yesterday that he wants to celebrate Christmas where he can play in the snow. We could go and spend Christmas there. Near the woods and mountains that is if you don't mind," I said, hoping that she would not refuse.

"Oh, it's okay. We can go there," she said.

I was so happy after hearing that, but my smile vanished when I heard her next words.

"I thought you wanted to tell me about your engagement," she said.

"I'm not engaged. Clara lied to you." I cursed myself in my head.

"Really, but why did she lie to me?" Hailey asked me while trying to look nonchalant about the question, but I saw the glint of jealousy in her eyes.

"She is just being funny. She likes to joke around. I have no fiancée. Hell, I haven't been with any girl in the last three years," I said.

Noah's head snapped my way. Hailey sent me a glare.

I looked at them in confusion.

"Daddy, you said a bad word," Noah said to me, and I frowned in bewilderment.

Then my eyes widened when I realized I said "hell."

"Sorry, Noah. I will not use that word again," I said to my son, and he bobbed his head up and down like he appreciated it.

The waiter approached and saved me from Hailey's wrath by serving dinner. We enjoyed our food peacefully while Noah made small jokes, and Hailey and I couldn't stop laughing. He shared his dreams with me and what he liked. One thing I realized was that my son was really talkative and a curious type of kid. He didn't stop talking until he felt sleepy.

After, we were done eating we decided to leave as Noah seemed tired and sleepy. I picked him up in my arms and walked to the elevator while Hailey followed us. My son put his small arms around my neck and placed his head on my shoulder.

When we came out, the valet brought my car from the parking. I put Noah in the car seat at the back while Hailey sat on the passenger side. I got in the car and drove in the direction of her house.

The ride to her house was peaceful and silent. When we reached her house, the lights were out indicating that her parents were asleep.

I turned around to see Noah sleeping soundly in his car seat. Hailey pulled out the keys from her purse and stepped out from the car. I got out and pulled out Noah from the car seat then took him in my arms.

Hailey opened the main door and waited for me to make my way to her. She extended her hand to take Noah in her arms.

"I can help you take him to his room," I said.

She looked at her dress and nodded. When I was inside, she closed the door.

"My room is upstairs, and Noah sleeps with me there," she said, walking toward the stairs.

I followed her upstairs. She told me to put Noah on the bed. I did, and he started snuggling in the pillows. I kissed his forehead and murmured good night.

I turned back and saw Hailey removing her earrings, standing near the vanity table. My legs moved and took me to her. She turned and gave me a confused look.

Before I could stop myself, I put my hands on her waist and pulled her closer.

Her breath hitched, and she stared at me with a questioning gaze.

"Hailey, I'm sorry for what I am going to do," I said and leaned down to capture her lips with mine.

She froze when my lips touched hers. Slowly, I moved my lips to show her how much I had missed her in the last three years and how much I wanted her.

I sighed recalling how she still tasted like strawberries. At that moment, I wouldn't complain if death came and took my life away.

Suddenly, I felt a push on my chest and stumbled back.

"Chase, what the hell are you doing?" She looked very angry.

"I am sorry, Hailey. I am leaving," I said, turning around to hide the pain that I felt in my heart because of her rejection.

"Isn't it what you have always done? It's just so easy for you to leave and make people leave you."

I didn't say anything to her, letting her continue.

"I'm not your wife anymore. You cannot just walk in my life and kiss me like you were not the one who divorced me," she said, coming to stand in front of me.

I said nothing and stared at her.

"I'm not the same silly sixteen-year-old girl anymore who gave you her heart without asking for anything in return." She jabbed a finger into my chest, and I stayed still.

"I will not allow you to come into my life again then break my heart and rip my soul into pieces just like you did before. Do not even try to touch me again. I'm giving you a chance to be with your son, Chase. But it does not mean that I'm giving you a chance to be with me. Keep that in your mind for next time."

Her eyes were blazing with anger. Each word she uttered was coated with hate. I took a step back from her.

Her cries, her busted lips because my mom slapped, her innocent smile, and the day when I dropped her at airport played in my head. That day her eyes were pleading me to stop her, but I let her go.

I knew this would happen if I divorced her. I knew she would always hate me for this, but I still did what I thought was right to protect her and my son.

Maybe it was the wrong thing to do, and now it was too late to tell her the truth.

"I'm sorry. I didn't mean to upset you. I… just… It has been three years and seeing you again today…" I tried to explain to her what I was feeling but failed.

"I don't want to hear it, Chase! It is too late, and you should leave," she said, looking at me in irritation.

After hearing her asking me to leave, I didn't feel that there was anything left to say. I decided to leave because I was pretty good at that.

I took a step back from her and left her house. I got into my car and sped away from her house. I didn't know where I was going. I had no destination in mind as I was driving.

My brain was messing with me again. Suddenly, I was standing at the altar waiting for Hailey to show up. Then I was in the party where she was dancing, and next minute I was watching her with Noah in her arms on the airport, leaving me.

A light flashed in my eyes, and I immediately swiveled left so I wouldn't hit the dog, which was sitting in the center of the road. My car crashed into the tree, making my head bang against the side of the window, and the pain exploded in my head, blinding me momentarily. I opened my eyes and pulled out my cell phone from my pocket. I dialed James' number.

"I think I need your help," I said and leaned my head on the steering wheel.

Tears brimmed in my eyes as her words rang in my ears again.

She was never going to forgive me again. I lost her and the chance to call her mine.

"I should leave," I mumbled and fell into the darkness.

Chapter Twenty-Nine

Jealousy Hurts Like A Bitch

Hailey

I woke up next morning with stiff muscles. I stretched my arms in the air and moved my neck left to right. Then I noticed the culprit of my discomfort. Last night after Chase left I couldn't fall asleep. My mind was constantly reminding me how I felt when he kissed me. So, I got up from the bed and sat down on the couch with my favorite book, but I still couldn't stop thinking.

Why did my body come alive under his touch? Why did his lips soothe the ache in my heart? Why did it feel like home when he kissed me?

I didn't know why I reacted so aggressively and rudely at Chase. I didn't know if I was angry at him for kissing me, or I was angry at myself for still having the same reaction to his kisses after all this time.

I saw the hurt on his face when I told him to leave. I should apologize to him for being unnecessarily rude last night.

"Mommy, I am hungry," Noah said, walking towards me and jumping on my lap.

I looked at him.

"Today is Sunday, Mommy. We need to go to the park."

Almost every Sunday, Noah went to the park to play with Sammy.

Sammy was a very cute kid and Ethan's nephew. He has blonde hair like Ethan, but his eyes were the unique color of brown and honey. It had been Noah and Sammy's thing to meet at the park every Sunday and play around. Ethan and I would keep an eye on the kids while gossiping.

"Noah, listen baby. First, you need to brush your teeth then come down. I will make your favorite pancakes," I told him, and he ran towards the washroom to brush his teeth.

I dialed Ethan's number. He answered on the third ring.

"Hi. Ethan, are you coming to the park with Sammy?" I asked him.

He sighed and said, "Yes. We are coming."

Then he ended the call. I glared at the cell phone and cursed him.

I went down and made pancakes for Noah and coffee for myself. When Noah came down, he ate his pancakes.

Then I went to take a quick shower and got changed into my baby blue long sleeve jumper, and blue ripped jeans. Then I grabbed my black boots and went downstairs in the living room where my son was waiting for me.

I took him upstairs and changed him into jeans and a blue t-shirt. Then made him wear a jacket to which he made a face, but I gave him an angry glare, so he let me zip it up. Lastly, I put a cute beanie on his head, which made him look cuter.

The weather was really chilly as it was winter, so I was taking some extra precautions. I didn't want my son to get pneumonia.

I helped him lace his shoes then we left for the park. The park was only two blocks away from my house, so we just walked. Noah was running ahead while my earphones were plugged in my ears.

After ten minutes of walking, we entered the park. I found Ethan's car parked outside. Noah ran towards Sammy who was playing with Fuzzy. Fuzzy was Ethan's dog, a golden retriever, and he was the friendliest and funniest dog on the planet. Ethan trained him how to play throw ball with kids, and my son loved to play with him. When Fuzzy saw me coming, he started barking happily and wiggled his tail. I patted him lightly on the back and rubbed his ear, after that he ran away to play with Noah and Sammy.

I found Ethan sitting on the bench, and his eyes were on me.

"Hi," I said, slumping down beside him.

He didn't reply and turned his head away. I rolled my eyes at his childish action.

"Ethan, please, let me explain. I know you are angry at me for not telling you everything, but at least hear me out," I said.

I only had a few friends, and I didn't want to lose them because of some misunderstanding.

He turned to me with a bored look on his face.

I started telling him my story.

"One night, I was about to fall asleep when I heard my mom's voice. I followed her voice and found out she was crying because Emily ran away. She ran away because my granddad wanted her to get married to his friend's grandson. In short, I volunteered to get married instead of her so she could come back home," I told him.

"Was that the only reason you agreed to get married?"

"No, it wasn't. My relationship with my mom wasn't great at that time, and I wanted to leave the house. At that time getting married seemed the best way to get rid of my past life. So I got married to Chase and left Oakland and my old life."

"Were you happy with him? Did he love you?"

"At first, I was scared of him then later I fell in love with him. He didn't see me as the girl who he could fall for. He was in college at that time. He had dreams. I was a silly sixteen-year-old girl with basic education and no plans for the future. I was a dork. I didn't even know how to dress up," I said, laughing at myself recalling my taste in fashion

"But somehow Chase and I end up on the bed together, and later I found out I was pregnant. I was happy, even he was happy. We started to get to know each other, and I started to fall harder for Chase. But after one week of Noah's birth, Chase gave me divorce papers and asked me to sign them. After that, I came back to Oakland to my family and started a new life," I told him and stared at Noah who was smiling when Fuzzy jumped on him.

"Julia knows everything because she knows me from high school and she is my best friend. It was her idea to hide my life story from you, Vanessa, and Matt. She thought my past doesn't define me and will not affect my friends when it would come out."

"Julia was right. Your past doesn't define you. I wouldn't stop being your friend even if you tell me you were a stripper in the past," he said, and I slapped his shoulder.

He smiled at me and said, "I was just hurt. I thought you didn't trust me enough to tell me the truth. And I thought you were still with that man".

"Chase and I have been divorced for the last three years," I told him.

"Hailey, I lied to you about something."

"Last time when we were playing truth and dare at Julia's place, and she asked me if I love any girl. I lied to her and said that I don't, but I do, I love you," he said, shocking me.

My mouth dropped open, and I stared at him.

*   *   *

Chase

I woke up and realized I was on the bed of my hotel room. I remembered what Hailey said to me last night, and on the way back to the hotel I lost control of my car, and it crashed into a tree.

I shouldn't have kissed her because I had lost that right a long time ago. And by kissing her last night, I might've ruined any chance for the future.

My eyes landed on James, sleeping on one of the couches.

"James, wake up," I said.

He opened his eyes and stared at me then got up abruptly.

"Sir, are you alright?" he asked me.

"Yeah, I am fine. How did I come back to the hotel?" I felt like I had a headache.

"I brought you back to the hotel. You were unconsciousness that's why you don't remember."

"Why were you sleeping here on the couch?"

"Sir, after what you have done for my family, it's my responsibility to take care of you. That's why I stayed here last night and fell asleep on the couch."

"James, I have given you a job. It is not like I am paying you without taking your services."

"But sir, I'm still grateful to you for giving me this job when I needed it most."

James had no idea what a horrible person I was and how the world would be a better place if I would just leave.

I told James to go to his room then I decided to go to Hailey's house to apologize to her again about last night and to make sure she wouldn't cancel the plan for Christmas.

I thought of taking her and Noah out for breakfast and apologizing to her.

With that plan in mind, I got up from bed and went to the washroom to freshen up. I got changed into some jeans and denim button-up shirt then pulled my black leather jacket from the closet. I picked up my car keys and made my way out.

I reached her house and talked myself into going out of the car to talk to Hailey, but before I could do that, I saw Noah and Hailey coming out from the house.

I was confused and thought they must be going somewhere for breakfast, so I followed them. They went inside the park, so I thought of going inside and pretend like it was a coincidence to meet them here. But when I went inside, I found Hailey sitting with some guy and that made me jealous.

I moved a little closer and heard her asking him to hear her out. I hid behind the tree and started eavesdropping on their conversation.

She told him everything about her life and our past. Then the guy told her he loved her. She stared at him in shock.

I left the park and got inside my car. I wasn't ready to accept that she had no place for me in her heart that she had a new guy who she loved. I didn't want to hear her say she loved him too.

That day, I realized how rejection felt, and that jealousy hurt like a bitch.

Chapter Thirty

I'm Not Losing Her Again

Hailey

I started laughing. I was laughing really hard that I was clutching my stomach and tears formed in my eyes. I was sure that if there weren't grass on the ground, I would be rolling down.

"Ethan, this is the best prank you ever played on me," I said, still laughing lightly.

He gave me a deadpanned look, which made me a little uneasy and I stopped laughing.

"Ethan, please don't tell me you are serious." My face turned pale.

"I'm dead serious, Hailey," he said.

After hearing him, I didn't know what came over me; I slapped him on the left cheek. Not so hard but hard enough to knock some sense into his dumb brain.

"Ouch! Hailey, that is not a nice way to reject someone," Ethan said, glaring at me.

I glared back at him.

"Mommy, why did you slap Ethan? Did he say the naughty word?" Noah asked me with a toothy grin.

I glanced at Ethan for support to tell these little devils something that would ease their curiosity. But Ethan was still busy massaging his cheek

"Uh... Noah, there was a... a fly on Ethan's cheek. I just slapped his cheek to make it fly away before it bites him. Now go play." I then shooed them away.

"Ethan, are sure? I mean are you a hundred percent sure it is love and not some crush or another kind of love like brotherly love, you know?" I asked him with a curious look, waiting for his answer.

"Hailey, you are so going to regret asking me these stupid questions," he said.

He was making the same face he made before tickling Sammy.

"Oh... I think I'm in trouble." I got up and started running away from him.

He was behind me, running like a predator after his prey.

We ran rounds and rounds. Even Noah, Sammy, and Fuzzy were helping Ethan to catch me by blocking every way. Traitors! They were ganging up on little me. When I hid behind the tree to catch my breath, Ethan sneaked up on me from behind and picked me up in his arms. He spun me around.

I felt dizzy and begged him to stop this nonsense. Noah and Sammy were clapping and laughing crazily at my misery. Finally, Ethan stopped spinning me and dropped me on the grass. We were both breathing heavily and grinning like an idiot. Noah and Sammy fell on the grass beside us with toothy grins on their faces.

"Get up. I will drop you home," Ethan said while helping me stand up.

I took his hand in mine for support and got up dusting grass from my jeans. I glanced down at Noah and Sammy and told them to fetch Fuzzy who was walking on the jogging track with his nose up in the air.

"Ethan, don't take it personally. You know how I am. I really like you. I even love you but as a friend," I said.

Ethan sighed after hearing me and said nothing, so I continued my speech.

"I think there is definitely some girl out there who is dying to meet you and is made only for you to love. Unfortunately, I'm not that girl. I can only be your friend. Nothing more because that's what I am made for."

"I don't want any other girl."

"You will want another girl because you will love her more than you love me," I said, and he frowned. "Ethan, sometimes you are a very gullible guy. Let me ask you few questions then we will see if you are in love with me as you say you are. Tell me, does my presence make your heart beat faster? Does my touch make you feel tingly?" I asked him.

"No, I don't feel any of these things, but I just know that I love you."

"I know you love me, but it's not that kind of love where you would feel sparks at a small touch, where your heart accelerates at the sight of me, and where you would want to spend your whole life with me."

"Oh so you feel sparks with Chase, and your heart accelerates when you are with him? Do you still feel like spending your whole life with him?" he asked me, and I blushed.

"Shut up, Ethan. I'm just telling you everything from my past experience. I hope you listen to me like a good boy. Now let's go."

"I was so jealous when I saw your ex-husband and thought that you were still with him. I love it when you laugh Hailey. Your presence calms me down, and the memories I have of you plays in my head. I think I'm in love with you," he said.

I shook my head at his dumb explanation.

"Ethan, love is not that simple. It makes you crazy, and you don't feel calm. You feel like your soul is on fire, and only one person could calm it down. You are my friend, and we have a great friendship, and that's why my presence makes you calm. Friends are supposed to make you feel happy and calm, and that's what I do to you."

He stared at me silently.

"Your words make sense, Hailey. But I know what I feel. It's something different from friendship," Ethan said, and I rolled my eyes.

We picked Sammy and Noah in our arms and placed them in the backseat then buckled them in their seats. Fuzzy hopped in the backseat and sat in the middle of Noah and Sammy.

Ethan dropped us off at our house then drove away.

I went inside the house and got busy with my daily routine. It was evening when I remembered I needed to apologize to Chase. I dialed his number, and he picked it up on the first ring.

"Hello… uh, how are you?" I asked him.

"I'm good." His answer was neutral, and he sounded like he was not interested in talking to me.

"Are we still going to the cabin tomorrow?" I asked him.

"Yes, I'll pick you up tomorrow at 8 in the morning."

"Okay then. See you tomorrow. Bye." I bid him goodbye.

"Bye," he said then ended the call.

I pulled the duffel bag out of my closet and put my and Noah's warmest clothes, some toiletries, and my camera inside it. Then I zipped it up and placed it in my closet.

I told Mom and Dad about my plan for Christmas. Mom was happy and excited for me. Dad didn't like the idea of me spending my Christmas without family and especially with Chase.

*   *   *

Chase

After the park incident, I came straight to my hotel room. My stomach was grumbling loudly because I didn't have any breakfast. I called room service and asked them to send some coffee and scrambled eggs with toasts.

After I was done eating, I realized that I need to do something to get rid of that guy so Hailey wouldn't fall for him. Jealousy was still eating my heart out. I cursed myself for not staying there a few minutes more to hear Hailey's answer.

I heard a notification alert and picked up my laptop. I started at the list of e-mails that I received yesterday. I was reading them to distract myself from thinking about Hailey and that guy. Then I replied to a few important e-mails related to my business. I decided to call Allison for some help. She picked up on the first ring.

"Hi, Allison. How are you and the kids?"

"I'm good, and the kids are fine too, but they are missing you a lot. When are you coming over for Christmas dinner?" Allison asked me.

"I will not be coming over for Christmas dinner this year, but I will send gifts to you all."

"Chase, please for the love of God don't send gifts like last time. The pony you sent for Susan last year is getting bigger each day, and Susan is still too young to ride on it alone," my sister said, reminding me of the small horse that I sent for my niece last year as she was always telling me how much she loved them.

"Al, not again. Okay. I'm sorry for giving Susan a pony, but she liked it," I explained myself for the hundredth time.

"Okay. But tell me where you are. I called you last night, but you didn't answer my call. I panicked and called your office. Your secretary told me that you are not in Boston."

"I-I'm in Oakland, trying to rebuild my family. But I think I have lost all my chances," I said lightly, and she gasped.

"Oh... Chase. You have no idea how happy I am right now. Hailey will forgive you and accept you. Please, try to win her heart." She brought hope to my heart with what she said.

"I hope so, Al."

"You need her Chase, and she needs you even though she doesn't show it and fight against it. Just be honest with her this time and let her trust you. You cannot afford to lose her again. But first, do whatever you need to do to make her yours."

I bid her goodbye and thought about what she said to me. She was right. I lost her once because of the circumstances my mother created. Now I couldn't afford to lose her again to some teenage boy. I would do everything in my power to make her mine.

I was thinking of how I could get rid of that boy when my cell phone rang. I glanced at the caller id, and my eyes widened. Suddenly, my throat was dry as the Sahara Desert.

Why was she calling me?

Then a thought popped into my head that maybe she was calling me to cut all the ties with me because of what I had done her last night.

But I picked up her call.

"Hello... uh how are you?" she asked me and sounding a little nervous.

"Hi... I'm good." My answer was so simple.

"Are we still going to the cabin tomorrow?"

I sighed in relief when I heard her question.

"Yes, I will pick you up tomorrow at 8 in the morning," I said, collecting myself and containing my happiness inside my heart.

"Okay, see you tomorrow then. Bye."

"Bye." I ended the call.

I jumped up in my room with joy. This Christmas I would make you mine again, Hailey.

Chapter Thirty-One

A Day in The Cabin

Hailey

[Day before Christmas]

I felt someone shaking me. I woke up and groaned in protest like a lazy kid on a school day. I opened my eyes and found Noah hovering above me and grinning.

"Noah, baby, why are you up so early? And why did you wake me up?" I asked while my eyes were closing due to sleepiness.

"Mommy, I woke up because of your cell phone. It was ringing very loudly. It's 6:00 a.m. It's not early." He started shaking me again.

I opened my eyes and picked up my cell phone from the bedside table. I checked it and groaned, seeing that it was my alarm that woke Noah up.

"Yes, baby that was my alarm," I said and pulled Noah in my arms and cuddled him.

"Mommy, we need to get ready." Noah hugged me.

"I know, but I'm tired, and I want to cuddle with you," I said, tightening my hold on him.

Sometimes I felt like he was my small teddy bear.

"Mommy, I'm very excited. This is my first Christmas with Dad. I love him," he said and gave me a sloppy kiss.

"I know you are an excited baby." I placed a kiss on his forehead.

After staying in bed for a few more minutes, I finally decided to leave the warmth of the bed. I picked Noah up and placed him on my hip then made my way towards the washroom. I helped Noah in brushing his teeth and changing his clothes.

Chase called me last night and told me there was a slight change of plans, and that he would pick us at 7:00 a.m. instead of 8:00 a.m., so we could stop for breakfast on the way. I didn't complain.

I took a shower and got changed into my black high waist jeans and white top with a black jacket. We went downstairs with the duffle bag.

I didn't wake my parents up and disturb their sleep just to tell them that I was leaving so I wrote a short note to them. I stuck the note on the refrigerator with some magnets and placed their gifts on the kitchen counter.

I heard the sound of a car pulling up outside, so I hurriedly got up and peeked through the living room window. Chase stepped out of the car dressed in jeans and black leather jacket. He was still unshaven, and a five o'clock shadow on his face was making him look sexier. Before I could start appreciating his looks again, I picked up the duffel bag and took Noah's hand in mine then made our way out of the house.

I let go of Noah's hand, and he ran towards Chase. I walked slowly towards the car because of the heavy bag in my hand. Chase leaned down and scooped Noah in his arms then showered his face with kisses. Noah giggled.

Chase put Noah down on his feet then walked towards me. He took the bag from my hand and put it on the back seat of his black SUV.

Chase said, "Let's get in the car."

I nodded and got inside while Chase put Noah in the car seat at the back.

He drove towards the café, and we stopped there to have breakfast.

After three hours of driving, we finally reached our destination. The cute small wooden cabin was nestled between snow-covered trees and surrounded by the hills, which were also covered in snow. It felt like a white velvet blanket was draped over everything. The light fog was giving the illusion of clouds.

"It is beautiful," I said.

I didn't even realize that I had said it aloud until I heard Chase reply.

"Yes, really beautiful," he said.

I looked at him and found him staring at me. I blushed and went inside the cabin to escape from his intense gaze.

I gasped, looking at the inside of the cabin. There was a very stylish kitchen with white and black cabinets on the right side. There was a small living room in the center. The walls were painted in a wood color contrasting perfectly with the black L-shape leather couch and white curtains. There was a plasma TV fixed on the center wall in front of the couches. On the left wall, there was a fireplace made up of dark grey stones. Then, I saw stairs leading on the upper floor, which Noah and I eagerly followed up.

There was a very large and beautiful room. In the middle of the room, there was a king-size bed covered with a pure white bed sheet. A few paintings were hanging on the wall. Pure white curtains were hanging on the glass door, which was hiding the complete view of the balcony. I slid the glass door open and went outside to the balcony. I felt peace and closed my eyes then took a deep breath.

"So, do you like the cabin?" Chase asked me.

"Uh…Yes, it's extraordinarily beautiful. I love it," I said with a smile on my face.

We were staring into each other's eyes. Noah suddenly came running and announced that he wanted to go outside. Chase agreed and placed our bags in the room then picked Noah up in his arms and ran downstairs, telling me to follow him.

I followed them outside. He took us in the woods and showed us the frozen lake near the cabin. I stare at Chase and Noah while they were busy chasing each other, running around and laughing. After that, we collected some wood for the fireplace and went back inside the cabin.

I took Noah upstairs in the washroom and cleaned him. I shooed him out when he was done and used the washroom. When I came downstairs, I saw Noah sitting on the couch watching TV. Then the smell of the cheese made my stomach growl. I looked at Chase and found him standing near the stove cooking something.

"What are you doing?" I asked in surprise.

"I...Uh. I'm making grilled cheese sandwiches for Noah and heating up this homemade pasta for us." He was working around the kitchen like a pro.

"But when did you learn how to cook?" I asked him in surprise. Because when we used to live in the same house, I had never seen him cooking anything except rarely making coffee.

"I...I learned it from YouTube when I moved out." He gave me a side glance.

I didn't know that he moved out from his parents' house. This news shocked me because Allison, Cameron, and William never told me that he moved out.

"When did you move out from your parents' home?"

"Hailey, I will tell you everything, but now is not the right time," he said and glanced at Noah who was watching TV.

I nodded and sat down on the stool. Chase placed the grilled cheese sandwiches on the kitchen counter then called Noah.

My son came running, and I helped him settle on the stool. Chase placed a plate in front of him then poured pasta in the dish. He put the dish in front of me and handed me the plate then sat on the stool across me. We ate silently.

After eating his sandwiches, Noah ran towards Chase and clutched onto his legs.

"Daddy, do we have a Christmas tree?" Noah asked.

Chase made a face like he was thinking really hard. Noah stared at him curiously, waiting for the answer.

"Noah, I might have forgotten about getting a Christmas tree." Chase glanced down at Noah who was pouting.

"Daddy, how can you forget the Christmas tree? There's no Christmas without a tree," Noah said, glancing at me with a sad face.

"We can arrange something buddy. Come along." Chase picked up Noah and placed him on his shoulders, taking him somewhere.

I picked up the plates and utensils then washed them. I heard Noah's excited laugh and saw Chase carrying a small tree and placing it in the corner of the lounge.

Then Chase placed a large white box on the floor, which had every kind of Christmas decoration. Noah clapped excitedly and hugged Chase's legs.

"Mommy, come help us with the decorations," Noah said, looking at me with a happy smile on his face.

We started decorating the tree by placing all the ornaments on it and lastly covering it with small lights. We also decorated the cabin with lights and hanged some Santa caps and socks around the house. It felt like we were actually a family.

All evening we stayed busy with decorating. When we were done decorating everything, we fell on the couch to relax.

"Mommy, I'm hungry," Noah said, sitting on my lap.

I looked at Chase, and he told me there were cookies in the cabinet. I gave Noah cookies with some milk. He ate the cookies and drank the milk. Then I made him brush his teeth and changed him into his pajamas. He watched cartoons then fell asleep. I put Noah in bed and went down to eat something myself.

When I came down, I found Chase asleep on the couch. I went to the kitchen and looked inside the refrigerator and found it stocked with every kind of thing. I was really surprised at first then I pulled out all the ingredients to make spaghetti with meatballs.

After half an hour I was done, I put the dish with the spaghetti on the counter and set the plates.

"Chase, wake up. Dinner is ready."

He woke up, looking me in the eye. He frowned and looked around then sighed.

"You made dinner?" he asked, and I nodded.

He walked to the kitchen with me following behind him.

"I'm sorry for falling asleep like that. You had to make dinner alone," Chase said, sitting on the stool.

"It's fine. You drove us here then Noah tired you by playing with you."

Chase smiled. I sat across him on the stool and put spaghetti on my plate then started eating.

"Noah is great. He is smart and intelligent. Thanks to God he is not a fool like me," he said.

I coughed when he called himself a fool. I didn't know when he started considering himself a fool.

"Noah started reading when he was one year and three months old. He didn't know how to read, but he would pick up his favorite book and tried reading it. I started teaching him after that, and now he knows how to read."

"Wow! I never thought my son would be so smart. Maybe he took after you," Chase mumbled while eating.

I felt my face heat up thinking that unintentionally he was calling me smart.

For the rest of the dinner, we stayed silent.

After dinner, I went upstairs to check on Noah. He was sleeping peacefully. I came back down and found Chase cleaning the kitchen.

"You don't have to clean the kitchen," I said to him.

"No, it's not a problem. You cooked a meal so you must be tired now."

I'm not that tired," I said. A yawn escaped from my mouth.

Chase gave me an amused smile, and my cheeks started to feel a little warm.

"I made coffee. Would you like a cup?" He pulled two mugs out of the kitchen cabinet.

"Sure," I replied to him, feeling a bit nervous.

"Let's sit in the living room."

We sat near the fireplace on the couch. Chase handed me my coffee, and I took a sip from it. I closed my eyes and sighed loudly at the soothing taste of coffee.

"Is it that good?" Chase asked me, staring at my face.

"It's perfect." I was enjoying my coffee very much.

"How was your life the last three years?" he asked me like he was really interested in my life.

"Uh…there was nothing interesting. After I moved back with my parents, I continued my studies. Now I am in college. I'm studying to become a psychologist." I was still drinking the coffee.

"You want to be a psychologist? Why?" He looked at me curiously while drinking his coffee.

"I want to be a psychologist because I want to help people who went through some horrible accidents in life and want to end themselves. I want to pull them out from depression because it is a very deep dark hole, which sucks you in slowly," I said, glancing at the fire in the fireplace.

I recalled how hard my life was during that phase. My hands started to shake a bit, and I gripped the mug tightly.

"Were you in depression, Hailey?" He looked concerned.

"I'm tired, Chase. Good night," I said, standing up.

I was not ready to answer him. I didn't want to tell him how weak I was when he left me. I didn't want to tell him how many nights I had spent crying on my bed. He had no right to know how much I wished to fall asleep in his arms like I used to do when we would watch movies together in my room.

I was not the same girl anymore. I was a strong woman, a single mother living a happy life with her son. I didn't need him in my life anymore to make me happy. With these thoughts swirling around my head, I fell asleep.

Chapter Thirty-Two

Celebrating Christmas

Hailey

I woke up the next morning in a good mood. I went to the washroom to freshen up. After showering, I changed into a red knee-length dress. I stared at myself in the mirror for a few minutes after blow-drying my hair and thought that I looked pretty nice in the dress. Then I decided to go downstairs to make breakfast.

When I reached the last stair, my eyes landed on Chase. He was sleeping on the couch in the living room. The first thought that came to my mind was that I forgot we had one master bedroom in the cabin, which Noah and I took.

Oh gosh! I didn't even ask him if he wanted to sleep on the bed. But it would be so awkward if we sleep in the same bed.

"Like you remember the first time you shared a bed with him," my mind taunted.

My face heated up at the reminder of our past, which was still a mystery to me.

I walked closer to where he was sleeping. His right hand was under his head while the left one was hanging from the couch because of the small space. I kneeled down and picked up his hand then placed it on his chest.

My hand brushed against his chest. I felt the rhythmic beating of his heart and looked at his face. Before I could stop myself, I placed my hand on his jaw and ran my thumb over his stubble. The stubble on his jaw looked great on his face, giving him a matured look.

In the past, I used to stare at him when he wouldn't be looking at me. I used to imagine my future with him.

My mind was again making me imagine how it would be if we became a family again. I knew Noah was still young to understand why his dad never came to meet him, but someday he would come to know that it was because of me then he would hate me.

I didn't want my son to hate me. He was my only family. But I couldn't lose him to Chase.

I should give Chase a chance to mend our broken relationship for the sake of my son's happiness and future. But I was not ready to fall into a one-sided love again and feel how worthless and unwanted I was in his life.

Chase hated me. Now because of our son, he had been tolerating my presence. It didn't mean he wanted me back in his life.

And if I would share this idea with him, he might do it for Noah. I knew he loved his son. But what would happen when he would see me as a burden, baggage, and an unnecessary responsibility in his life. I didn't want to be a burden again.

It was best if we continued to live our lives the way we have been living it for the last three years.

Noah would understand why his father wasn't part of the family.

I removed my hand from his jaw and got up, ready to leave, when I was pulled back with force and fell down on something hard.

My eyes widened when I realized what happened. I looked at myself. My head was lying on Chase's chest while my legs were dangling from the couch.

After completely accessing our position, my eyes made their way from his chest to his face. I found him wide awake, smiling at me while holding my wrist in his hand.

I glared at him and tried to get up, but he placed his arm around my waist and pulled me closer. My breathing was uneven, and I didn't know if it was because of the fall or the closeness of his warm body.

"Good morning," Chase said, staring at me.

"Good morning." I felt uncomfortable because of our position.

"How did you sleep last night?" he asked me, tucking the strand of my hair behind my ear.

His hand caressed my cheek, creating a weird tingly feeling on my skin.

I couldn't believe my traitorous body for having this reaction because of his simple touch.

"I slept fine," I said and tugged my hand free.

Instead of leaving my hand and freeing me, he made a sudden move and flipped us. Now he was on top of me while I was underneath him.

I was shocked at the complete turn of our position and a little flustered that now I could feel his body fully pressed on mine.

His sterling grey eyes were taking me in like it was some kind of dream.

For a few minutes, I found myself lost in his eyes. His face leaned closer to mine while our eyes were still connected then he planted his lips on mine. My eyes went shut at the softness and warmness of his soft lips.

I didn't know why it felt so good to know that he was kissing me.

He was waiting for me to push him away or do anything to give him an indication that I didn't want this. But my mind was too numb to act properly because of the sensation of his lips on mine.

Did I want this?

"You always wanted him to love you," my mind replied.

His lips moved on mine, and my stupid brain decided to completely stop working at that moment, and my body was on fire.

I didn't know when I started kissing him back, but my hands made their way to his neck. I pushed my fingers through the mess of his silky hair and gripped them.

He bit my lower lip, and I gasped giving him access to enter my mouth. His tongue leisurely stroked my tongue, and I felt like I was in heaven.

I tried to win this brutal war but lost my breath and energy. He was winning the damn war with his playful nips. Then I heard light footsteps making its way down.

Chase distracted me by brushing his knuckles on my breast.

I tugged his hair to distract him, but the stupid man thought I wanted him to deepen the kiss.

He was turning the kiss into a passionate one, and I didn't want to let go of him. He was making me feel like I would die if I stopped kissing him.

"Mommy, mommy, where are you?" Noah yelled from the stairs in his cute voice.

After hearing Noah's voice, I got all my senses back that I earlier lost to my devil of an ex-husband.

I pushed Chase away on time, so when Noah came, he found Chase on the ground.

Sadly, the push was quite unexpected for Chase, and he fell down on the floor on his back.

Noah's eyes landed on his dad who was hissing in pain, and he came running to him.

"Dad... Are you hurt?" Noah asked Chase looking concerned.

I was busy with calming my breath.

"I'm good, son." Chase rolled on the floor on his back in pain.

"Mommy, help Dad," Noah pleaded while looking at me.

At Noah's demand, I got up from the couch and offered my hand to Chase. I helped him get back on the couch.

When Chase was sitting on the couch, I let out a sigh.

"Are you alright?" I asked Chase.

He nodded, making a pained face.

I rolled my eyes at his drama.

Was he trying to gain sympathy by acting like he was in pain?

A push couldn't have hurt him that much.

I smirked and decided to tease him.

"Chase, do you know how strong Noah is? One time, he fell down from the stairs and scraped his knees, but he didn't shed a single tear. He told me that boys are strong and they don't cry like babies, so you should stop crying too," I said with a smirk.

Chase's eyes widened, and he straightened up.

"I'm fine, and there is no pain," Chase said, smiling at Noah.

Noah and I erupted into giggles at Chase's statement.

Suddenly, Chase started to look at me with a full smile on his face, and I stopped giggling. It felt strange when he looked at me so intensely.

Noah broke the awkward atmosphere by complimenting me.

"Mommy, you're looking so pretty," Noah said, staring at me with happiness in his grey eyes.

"Thank you, love." I picked him up in my arms and kissed his cheek.

He giggled and planted a kiss on my cheek.

"Dad, tell Mommy how pretty she is looking," Noah said, making my eyes widened.

He always did this. Noah would compliment me then made Mom and Dad compliment me. Even if we were out on shopping, he would ask any stranger how I looked.

Noah's question caught Chase off guard. He glanced at me from my head to my red toenails.

"Your mom is looking gorgeous. She is the epitome of beauty." Chase stared into my eyes.

"What does epitome mean?" Noah asked, staring at Chase.

I put Noah down on the floor before he continued asking Chase more questions.

"Noah baby, let's change you into your Christmas outfit," I said, distracting him from his question.

Noah's face lit up, and he started running back upstairs to our room.

Chase caught my hand. He stopped me then stood up from the couch.

"Hailey, I wasn't lying when I said how beautiful you look," Chase whispered in my ear.

I did let myself slip once again to his charm, but this time I was not going to become a fool again.

"Chase, we are here for Noah. You should remember this and I should too," I said in a curt voice.

Chase's face fell, and he let go my hand.

"I'm sorry," he said.

I nodded and made my way upstairs.

I helped Noah brush his teeth then changed him into his favorite Santa outfit, which he loved to wear every Christmas. He looked so cute in the little red pants and shirt with the Santa cap on his head.

Noah went down to find his dad. I stayed in the room, thinking. The kiss that we shared earlier made me curse myself. It wasn't right. We had been divorced for three years.

I loved him, and I was attracted to him. But after three years, I wasn't expecting the same feelings for him to surface again.. I wasn't expecting my heart to throb again like it used to do in the past.

I went downstairs and found Chase making pancakes.

"Can you help me in arranging the table?" Chase asked me.

I nodded and put the plates on the table while Noah sat on the kitchen counter, telling Chase how every Sunday he and I went out for breakfast and ate chocolate chip pancakes.

I loved the smile on both of their faces, and my heart softened for Chase.

He was making an effort to make our son happy. I should help him too instead of holding a grudge against him.

After having breakfast, Noah dragged us towards the Christmas tree to open his gifts. There were so many gift boxes placed under the tree. I had no idea where they came from. I only put two gift boxes for Noah under the tree and didn't bring any gift for Chase.

"Mommy, look. Santa came last night and placed so many gifts." Noah was so excited and leaned down to pick one box.

"Oh, baby. I think it's not from Santa. They are from your dad," I said, making him look at Chase with his grey eyes.

Noah was literally in love with Chase at that moment. I knew what his little mind used to think when I would tell him that his dad was busy and couldn't come home for Christmas. Now that Chase had showered Noah with gifts and love, my son was happy. Chase had successfully won his heart.

"Thank you. I love you! I love you," Noah said, hugging Chase's legs.

He looked up at him with love in his eyes.

Chase kneeled down and hugged Noah tightly. He kissed his head then pulled away. I noticed tears in Chase's eyes, but he blinked them back.

"I love you too, son. I'm sorry for not coming back earlier," Chase said.

Noah smiled at him and kissed his cheek. I smiled and blinked back my tears.

Noah asked me to help him in opening his gifts. I sat down beside him and helped him. He opened the first gift, and he found an electronic tablet inside from a very well-known company around the world. Noah knew what a tablet was and how it worked, so he got really excited seeing that gift and squealed with happiness.

Chase was smiling ear to ear while watching Noah jumping in excitement.

He opened the second gift, which was an autographed t-shirt from his favorite football player. The third gift was three tickets for Disneyland. After that Noah was over the moon. Chase received another kiss on his cheek from Noah. The fourth gift was a remote control mini helicopter, and that was from me and a new book. Lastly, I got the chance to receive a kiss and hug from him.

I was ready to faint if I would find another expensive gift from Chase for Noah. Two boxes were still sitting under the tree unopened.

I got up from the floor. Noah picked the box up in his hand and looked at it.

"Mommy, this is for you. It has your name on the card," my son said, handing me the box.

I gave him a quizzical look but took the box from his tiny hands. I read the card attached to the box and found my name written on it.

"It's for you," Chase said, staring at me.

"But I didn't bring anything for you." I felt ashamed for being so inconsiderate.

"Hailey, you don't have to give me any gift when you have already given me Noah. Simply allowing me to spend this Christmas with him and you is the best gift for me," Chase said smiling.

I wanted to cry and hug him at the honesty behind his words. I realized how cruel I was to ask him to never come back and show me his face. He missed three years of his son's life because of me.

How could I do this to him?

When did I become so selfish? Why did I punish him by asking him not to come back until I asked him?

This man thought Noah was the best gift in the world that I had given him. If that was true, why did he divorce me and send me back to my parents? This man did look like the Chase I fell in love with, but his words were telling me how much he had changed. And I loved this change.

"If you still want to give me something then you can always give me a kiss as a thank you," Chase said, taking a step closer to me and whispering in my ear so Noah wouldn't hear us.

The smell of his cologne was reminding me how crazy I was about it.

"I can push you the same way I did this morning. That was pretty fun," I said innocently.

"I didn't know you enjoy it rough." Chase had a silly smirk on his stupidly handsome face.

At first, I didn't understand him, but when it made sense, my face turned hot.

"Open it up," Chase said, distracting me.

I opened the box and found a velvet cloth inside it. I removed the piece of cloth and found a small red jewelry box. I took it out and opened it.

A loud gasp escaped from my mouth when I looked at the beautiful sapphire necklace set in front of my eyes. I was literally speechless at the beautiful combination of sapphires and diamonds shining in front of me.

"Do you like it?" Chase asked me, looking nervous.

"I… I'm speechless. It's… It's really beautiful and looks expensive. I can't take it, Chase."

The smile vanished from his face.

"Why?" He asked me.

"It's expensive, and I am your ex-wife. It doesn't look like an appropriate gift to give to your ex." I handed him back the jewelry box.

"When I saw this necklace in the shop, I imagined you wearing it. I would really like it if you put it on for me and accept it," Chase said with a puppy dog face.

Now, I knew where Noah got this habit of making a puppy dog face when he wanted something. It was obviously from his dad.

I wasn't wearing any earrings, so I put the earrings on. I was trying to tie the necklace around my neck when Chase saw me struggling and took it from me. He set my hair on one shoulder.

His fingers brushed on the back of my neck. I felt a shiver, which didn't go unnoticed by him. He placed the necklace on my neck and clasped it.

"Now it looks more beautiful because you are wearing it," Chase whispered in my ear.

I closed my eyes to stop myself from bawling my eyes out. He was confusing me by saying things that I always wanted to hear from his lips.

Why was he doing this to my poor heart?

It took me years to get back to my normal life and stop myself from loving him and crying over the time he divorced me.

My mind was a mess and filled with confusion.

"Hailey, are you alright?" Chase asked with concern.

I opened my eyes and stared at him in the eyes. He cupped my face between his strong hands and touched his head with mine.

"Hailey, please for today, for our son's happiness don't recall the past," Chase said, understanding me.

At that moment, I forgot that he was the same person who snatched my happiness and broke my heart. My stupid heart was once again falling for him, and just like last time, I had no control over my heart and my feelings

I didn't ask him why he divorced me and made me leave with our one-week-old son when everything was going fine between us.

But, I planned to ask him every damn question that had been swirling around my mind for the past three years. I wondered what happened to him that changed him so much. He used to hate me and looked at me like I was the one who destroyed everything and entered his life unwelcomed

It was like he was a completely new person. A different man who was not afraid to show his emotions to me. His tender voice, his honest smile, and the tears in his eyes tell me how happy he was to be here with us.

But every time I caught him staring at me, I noticed shame, sadness, regret, and love in his eyes.

I looked into his eyes, and a mix of all those emotions was still in his eyes, so I threw my arms around his neck.

His arms went around my waist, and he pulled me closer to him, pressing our bodies completely. He snuggled his face into the hollow part of my neck then I felt something wet falling on my neck.

"Was he crying?" I asked myself.

And my question was answered when one after another tear fell on my neck, making its way inside my dress and falling on my breast.

I tightened my grip on him and ran one hand over his nape to provide him some comfort.

"I'm sorry for everything, Hailey. I'm so sorry," he mumbled.

"Chase, it's fine." I tried to make him stop crying.

He murmured something again, which I didn't understand. Then I felt soft kisses on the hollow part of my neck. I closed my eyes and bit my lips to stop myself from gasping or making any noise.

I didn't know how long we held each other in a passionate hug. When we pulled away, I averted my eyes from him feeling my face heat up at what just happened between us.

Chase was quiet for a few minutes.

"Uh… there's another gift for you," Chase said, wiping his eyes then picked up the box from the floor.

I raised my eyebrows at him, and he smiled sheepishly at me. I took the box from him and opened it. There were five books from my favorite authors. I pulled them out and yelled in excitement. I couldn't believe my eyes when I realized they were all new books that I was planning to buy.

How did he know what books I liked and was planning to buy?

Then my eyes landed on the signature of the author.

"Oh! God! Chase, are they... they signed? Am I dreaming?" I asked him in shock.

They were all from my favorite authors.

"No, Hailey. You're not dreaming. I can assure you," Chase said, laughing at my excitement.

Without thinking much, I placed a kiss on his cheek.

"Thank you so much!" I said.

He blushed and stared at me. I was smiling ear to ear.

"Mommy, I need your help." We both looked at him.

He was sitting on the couch surrounded by his gifts and trying to assemble his helicopter so it would start to fly.

We laughed and went to help him. After reading the instructions five times and putting the wrong batteries in the controller three times, we were finally able to make it work.

Chase and Noah went out to play in the snow, and I joined them after preparing lunch for us.

After snow fighting and making a snowman, we had lunch.

Noah asked me to bake chocolate cupcakes, and I baked cupcakes for him.

Thanks to Chase the cabin was stocked with all the necessary ingredients required to prepare chocolate cupcakes.

After the chocolate cupcakes were done, Noah helped me in decorating them, and we ate them while watching a Christmas movie.

"Mommy, this is the best Christmas ever."

It made Chase and me smile.

"I think this is the best Christmas of my life too," Chase whispered in my ear, and I stared into his eyes.

Chapter Thirty-Three

Night of Confessions

Hailey

I looked at Noah's sleeping form and thought that my poor baby wore himself out today playing all day with his father and his new gifts. I put the blanket over him and slipped out from the bed to go downstairs.

When I got downstairs, I found the living room empty.

Hmm... I wondered where Chase had gone.

I looked outside from the window and realized that it was snowing heavily. The hills were covered in white snowflakes, and the view was mesmerizing.

I turned back and went to sit on the carpeted floor near the fireplace. I was staring at the burning flames in the fireplace when I heard the noise of a door opening.

I turned around and saw Chase rubbing his hands together to warm them. He was wearing a thick muffler around his neck and long black coat. His head was covered in numerous snowflakes, and his cheeks were rosy due to the cold outside.

He looked so cute and oblivious to my presence. I took advantage of the situation and stared at him like it was my first time looking at him.

My heart galloped inside my chest at the reality of my feelings.

I might be crazy for still loving the man who would never love me in return.

When he was done removing his coat and muffler, he turned around. His eyes widened at the sight of me sitting on the floor near the fireplace.

He walked towards me and asked, "Why are you still awake?"

"I'm not yet sleepy," I said.

"Okay." He looked flustered.

"Damn! Why did he have to be so cute!" I thought.

"Stop right there, Hailey!" my mind said, making me freeze.

"Why did you go out?" I asked, averting my eyes from his sinfully beautiful face.

"I just went outside to check the car." He sat beside me.

A peaceful silence fell between us.

"Hailey," he said my name hesitantly like I would bite him.

I made a sound of listening to him, but my gaze was still fixed on the dance of flames.

"I... want to tell you something. But first, you need to promise me you won't get angry," Chase said, sounding nervous.

"Um, okay." I looked at him with uncertainty.

"I know we never talked about... that night. Do you remember anything?"

I frowned at his question and looked at him with a questioning gaze.

He was looking at me waiting with a flustered expression on his face.

My eyes widened when I realized what he was asking me. I felt my face heat up.

"N-no, I don't remember much. In the last three years, a few flashbacks occurred but it was too difficult to understand," I said, looking at everything in the room except his face.

"Hailey, when we came home after the party, you were not able to walk on your own to your room, so I carried you."

My heart started beating like crazy at the mention of me in his arms, but I said nothing, letting him continue.

"When I took you to your room, you started crying. You told me that nobody loves you. Then you made me promise to never leave you alone. That night you confessed to me that you loved me," he said, running his fingers through his brown hair.

At that moment, I wanted to throw myself in the crackling fire. I would rather die burning in the fire than die from embarrassment.

I confessed my love to him!

Was I drunk or something? Because truly, I was not that confident to confess something like that unless...

"After your confession, you decided to change out of your dress in front of me, but your zipper got stuck, and I helped you to get out of the dress," he said.

Oh, God! I started changing in front of him.

I should just jump into the fire to save myself from further embarrassment.

"You were looking cute, and I just kissed you. Then one thing lead to another, and we ended up making love on your bed," he said, making my heart pound inside my chest.

"I was drunk that night, and I thought you were too. But we were both drugged, and we had no control over our minds and bodies that night. I woke up and remembered what happened between us. I panicked and left your room without explaining anything. I was guilty and embarrassed with myself for the things that happened," he said, making me close my eyes for a moment.

"That's why I ignored you for a month. I didn't know how to apologize for my shameful actions. I felt like I took advantage of you and robbed you of the chance of sharing that moment with the man you loved."

"Why couldn't I still remember anything?" I asked him.

"You still don't remember anything because of drugs. It was Britney, the girl who liked Sam, and when he was showing interest in you, she got really jealous. She gave you a spiked drink."

Did I regret spending that night with him?

No, I didn't. Because of that night, I had a beautiful son today. But I regretted that it didn't happen because he loved me but the drugs were the reason behind it.

If I weren't so naive, those girls wouldn't be able to spike my drink.

That night due to alcohol and those drugs, I felt lightheaded. The constant worry of embarrassing myself escaped my mind, and I confessed my real feelings for Chase. I was attracted to him and always wanted to feel his love.

He was drunk, and my antics did nothing to help him restrain his desire, and we ended up on the bed. Now the flashbacks made sense. I understood what happened and why

I was just a stupid girl with no sense of responsibility.

"I'm really sorry, Hailey… I ruined your life because I couldn't stop myself from getting close to you that night. I was so drunk to think about using protection and ended up impregnating you. It was my entire fault that you had to take the responsibility of having a child at such a young age," he said, making me snap my head in his direction.

I felt tears brimming in my eyes.

I asked him "Why are you saying this?"

"I'm saying this because I should have stopped that night rather than letting my desire, alcohol, and those drugs took control of my body." He clenched his hands.

"Please, stop. I don't know why you are telling me this now."

"I just want to apologize for taking that special night from you."

"Did I try to stop you that night?" I asked him.

"No… No, you didn't." He shook his head.

"Tell me what I said and did that night."

My voice was suddenly strong and free of any emotions.

Chase was staring at me with his jaw dropped.

"Tell me, Chase. I have a right to know," I said, making him close his mouth.

"You… you told me to keep kissing you." He stared into my eyes.

He wanted me to ask him to stop, but despite feeling my cheeks getting hotter with a new wave of blush, I kept staring at him with a poker face and didn't let my gaze waver.

"Tell me more, Chase. I know there is more," I said.

"You… You told me everything is magical and…" He stopped again.

"And what, Chase?" I asked, and his head snapped at my way.

"No one loved you like that before, and you wanted to spend every night with me making love to you." He gulped and blinked as his breath turned ragged.

I got up from the floor, and he did the same.

"Listen to me very carefully, Chase. I don't want you to think that you took advantage of me. Do you hear me? If you want to call that night a one night stand, tumble on the bed, or one drunken night then call it that. I don't mind but don't ever say that you took advantage of me. I was your wife. I was attracted to you and loved you. I don't know if you were attracted to me or it was only drugs that made you love me that night. Honestly, I don't care about anything anymore. We were both not in the right state of mind, and it happened between us. I accepted it as my faith. I got a son because of that night, and I love him, so please, don't tell me that you are guilty or you regret that night. Because Chase, I don't regret it," I said and took a large breath.

My face was red with anger. I wanted to kill him for telling me that he was ashamed and guilty for spending a night with me.

I turned around to leave, but his hand gripped my wrist and turned me back to face him.

"I'm sorry, Hailey. Please, forgive me for saying stupid things all the time and making you hate me." He looked really sad.

"I don't hate you," I mumbled, looking down.

"Thanks for not hating me because I deserve all your hate for what I have done to you all these years." He grasped my hand.

"You didn't ruin my life, Chase. Stop talking nonsense. I don't want to recall what happened in the past. I just know because of my past I got the cutest son in the world, and I love him more than anything," I said, tugging my hand free from his grasp.

He let go my hand, and I was ready to leave when his words left me frozen.

"That night didn't only happen because we were drunk," he said, taking a step closer.

I turned back and stared at him.

Chase took a step closer and closer until he was standing a breath away from me. He gazed into my eyes directly, and I was completely frozen, not even breathing.

"It happened because I was attracted to you from the very first day I saw you. I was attracted to you more than I have ever been attracted to any girl. That night happened because you were the one I would like to spend every night with. The innocent smile on your face melted my heart. I used to see you as a beautiful innocent girl, and that attracted me, but it also reminded me that we were forced to be together. Your beauty and innocence used to call to me like a siren, but I pushed you away so I wouldn't end up falling in love with you. Then the lie about your age came out and I thought what I have done so far was right, and we were not meant to be together," he said, running his knuckles over my cheek making me shiver.

"Your shy glances, innocent gestures, and sweet smile made me weak. I knew that you were in love with me. Still, I didn't want our relationship to turn into something serious when you were not even close to eighteen. I wanted to keep you the way you were: innocent and pure." He moved closer and put his forehead to mine

His confession was too much to digest. I felt like falling backward but Chase put his arm around my waist and pulled me closer to his chest.

I found my hand gripping the front of his shirt.

"I hated you in the start for coming into my life and destroying my dreams. But when I came to know you and spent time with you, I realized how wrong I was. I fell in love with you, Hailey. I was shocked at myself for not realizing it for a long time, but when I did, it was too late," he said breathlessly.

My body started to tremble, and I knew he could feel it.

"Why did you divorce me? Why did you make me and Noah leave?" I asked him, and he shook his head.

"I already loved our son when he was still inside you, Hailey. The moment he was born, I felt the urge to protect him from everything. How can I not love my own son? Last three years, I spent my days and nights wanting you and my son back in my life. Every day was hell for me without both of you in my life."

"Then why did you make us leave, Chase? Why?" I asked him.

He remained silent, so I continued.

"Before his birth, you were fine and looked excited to welcome our son. You started showing love and care towards me, and it gave me hope that my son would grow up in a loving family."

He sighed and closed his eyes.

"Hailey, one day I walked in on Kate and Mom talking about you. I heard them talking about getting you an abortion." He grimaced.

A gasp escaped my mouth.

"What? But I never asked her to get me an abortion," I said to Chase.

"I know you never asked her. So I confronted her and begged her to leave you alone. You and Noah were never safe in that house."

He started explaining to me.

"When Noah was born, I thought she finally believed me that the child is mine. But I was wrong." He looked sad.

"After Noah was born and you were back home, I got a call from the hospital to collect some test results. I went to the hospital to collect those reports and found out that they were paternity test reports. The doctor told me that my mother asked them to do that test. She didn't believe that Noah was my son. After that, I came home and went straight to my mother to demand answers to her nonsense. She told me to divorce you and claim full custody of Noah or else she would sell her shares of the Edwards Investing Company to someone else. If she did that, I knew I would lose my father, and our family would crumble," he said.

At those words, traitorous tears rolled down from my face.

"I... I never thought she hated me so much," I told him.

He looked so broken with his head hung low and guilt visible on his face when he said, "I... I made the most difficult decision that day, Hailey. I asked you to sign those divorce papers and send you back to your parents with Noah. I fought with my mother for the first time that day because she didn't want you to leave with Noah. I told her that I don't care about you and Noah, and I want you both out of the house so I can continue my life like before. I had no other choice but to make her believe that I don't care about you, because if you both stayed, she would do her best to make your life hell."

He continued when I said nothing.

"I thought of moving out and taking you both with me. But I didn't have the money or job experience to give you and him a comfortable life. So I thought, for the time being, the best place for you and my son to live will be your house. I was sure that you'll stay safe there and live a comfortable life that's why I sent you back to your parents," he said. "After that, I also moved out from my parents' house and went to Boston to complete my internship."

I was just absorbing everything he said.

Many questions were still unanswered, but at least my heart wasn't hurting anymore at the thought that he never loved me.

"Hailey... Please say something." He begged me.

"Chase what... what do you want me... me to say?" I asked him.

He cupped my face and said, "Oh, Hailey, I know. I know I am responsible for your pain... and every trouble you went through in life. If I were strong enough to support you and Noah, you wouldn't have gone through all this shit in life. Please forgive me. I'm really sorry, Hailey." He fell down on his knees, crying like a baby.

It was the second time in my life seeing Chase Edward breaking down in front of me.

I saw so many emotions playing on his face, but the most prominent ones were pain and guilt.

"Chase, why didn't you tell me this before? Why did you wait three years?" I asked him, kneeling down.

"Hailey... when I came to visit you, you refused to meet me. I thought that I will not show you my face until you ask me to," he explained to me, still shaking with tears.

"Oh, Chase." I flung myself into his arms hugging him.

"I'm sorry for keeping you away from Noah," I said, crying uncontrollably on his shoulder.

We both stayed in each other's arms crying for the loss of our happiness. Then Chase pulled away, making me open my swollen eyes.

"Hailey, I still love you," Chase said.

"Chase, please it's too soon to claim that you love me. Let me absorb all these things you have told me tonight." I hugged him again.

Both of our faces were stained with tears and eyes red from crying.

His arms were wrapped around my body pulling me closer. He made me sit on his lap. I tightened my arms around his neck hugging him that was when his body started to shake violently.

"Chase. What is happening?" I asked him worried.

"Ha... Hailey... uh... my... uh... medi... cines... uh, my... bag." His grip loosened.

I nodded and scrambled up from the floor running upstairs to the room and searched his bag for medicines. When I found the small medicine box, I ran back down and fetched a water bottle from the kitchen.

I went to Chase and kneeled down to give him the medicine. He took the box in his shaking hand and searched for the pills. He took out two white pills and threw them into his mouth. I offered him the water bottle, and he took it from me, gulping down hurriedly.

He leaned his head back on the seat of the couch as he was still sitting on the floor.

After five minutes, his breathing turned normal, but he looked tired like he ran a marathon. The energy was drained from his body, leaving his face pale.

I saw the labels of the medicine, and my hands trembled. I looked at Chase's sleeping form and felt the tears blurring my vision.

Rubbing my eyes, I got up and pulled Chase on the couch then pushed him into a lying position. I pulled out extra blankets and pillows from the cabinet. I put the pillow under his head and a blanket over him then I sat on the floor.

I ran my fingers through his soft hair. I didn't know that he was hurting this much inside.

I thought it was only me who had a broken heart. But I guess, we both became broken-hearted after the divorce.

I placed kisses on his forehead, his cheek, and jaw.

"I believe you, Chase Edwards. I believe every single word you told me tonight. I'm sorry for not understanding you and blaming you for everything. I'm really sorry for not being a good partner and a good wife for you when you deserve the best. I love you... I never stopped loving you even when I tried my best. It was impossible for me."

Hearing his even breathing, I felt relaxed. I put my head on the small space on the couch near Chase's chest and laced my fingers with his. And just like that, I fell asleep holding his hand in mine.

Chapter Thirty-Four

Never Let Her Go Again

Chase

I woke up feeling my whole body ache and moved to my left side. My eyes landed on Hailey. She was sleeping soundly, and her head was resting on the couch while the rest of her body was on the floor in a sitting position.

I tried to sit up but realized that her grip on my bicep was quite tight.

I looked at her and saw a frown on her face. I touched her face and smoothened out the frown. Her clothes had creases on them, and her face was free from all makeup, but she still looked beautiful.

But why was she sleeping here?

Then whatever happened last night came to me, and I groaned in embarrassment. I might have scared her last night with my panic attack.

I shook my head and tried to remove her hand. She woke up at the slight movement.

Her head snapped up, and she looked around startled. When her eyes landed on me, she got up from the floor in haste and stumbled. Her foot got tangled in the mess of blankets on the floor, making her fall directly on my lap.

"Uh. Sorry," she said with wide eyes, looking innocent and cute.

"It's fine." I squeezed her waist, and she stopped.

My hands were still placed on both sides of her waist, which she noticed and her cheeks turned bright red.

I smiled internally at her shyness.

She was still the same: beautiful yet shy and cute.

"Are you alright, Chase?" she asked me, nibbling on her lower lip.

I was distracted by her sweet motion, and my focus was completely on her soft lips.

"I'm fine, Hailey," I mumbled, still staring at her lips.

"Chase you scared me last night. I thought you had a heart attack." She looked sad.

"I'm sorry, Hailey. I used to have these panic attacks when I was a kid. They used to appear when I get worried or feel nervous. But they stopped happening on their own when I turned 12. My grandfather helped me a lot in driving my fear away. They just started to reappear after you and Noah left..." I said grimacing.

"Oh... Chase, I didn't know what was happening. I got really scared. I thought you were dying." She started crying.

"Hailey, I wasn't dying. It was just a panic attack so relax," I said, cupping her face in my hands.

"But it happened because of me. I triggered it. I'm sorry."

The tears were still falling from her eyes.

"No. Hailey, you didn't trigger it. The fear started creeping into my mind when I thought what would happen if you won't believe me. I love you," I said, trying to make her relax.

"Chase, I believe you, okay... I believe every word you said last night." She stared into my eyes.

"Thank you for still believing me when I lied to you and hid my feelings and the truth from you like a coward," I said, feeling disappointed in me.

"No. Chase, you're not a liar. I understand why you hid things from me in the past and the reason behind it. We made many mistakes in the past, and it led us here. That day when you came to meet me, I should have met you instead of hiding like a child. I was trying to protect my fragile heart from crumbling down." She was trying everything to lighten my guilty.

"You're perfect Hailey. You didn't make any mistakes. It was all my fault."

"Chase the attack you had last night was really serious. You can't take it casually. You should contact your psychologist or therapist right now." She looked extremely worried.

"You are right, but we are in the middle of nowhere, and it's a day after Christmas. Aren't you studying psychology to become a psychologist? Can I be your first patient?" I asked Hailey in a mischievous tone.

"What?" She looked bewildered.

"I mean you can be my very own personal psychologist. What do you say?" I asked her with all seriousness.

"I am not a psychologist yet. But I think for a patient like you this will work…" She then placed her lips on mine.

It was the first time, she was initiating the kiss. I was paralyzed with shock. My heart was hammering in my chest, ready to leap out any moment.

Before she could pull away from me because of my lack of response, I started moving my lips in sync with her. My hands went to rest on her waist, and unintentionally my fingers started to make circles. I pulled her closer to my body and felt her hand making its way to my neck from my shoulder. I was letting her control the pace. I couldn't help myself from lightly biting her tempting lower lip. A small gasp escaped from her mouth, and I took the risk of diving my tongue into her mouth.

This kiss felt so different from any others that we shared in the past. It felt real. I could feel the passion, the fire, and the need for us growing with every stroke. Now after years I felt alive. I always knew I loved her but doubted that she would feel the same for me after all these years. But the way she was kissing me made me realize how wrong I was. Her every move, her every touch, and her body pressed against mine were making me go crazy. I was burning, and she was soothing me.

I remembered how she used to do anything just to get my approval, and my acceptance. But now I was the one craving for her approval, her acceptance, and her love.

We both pulled away from each other breathless. A shy smile was playing on her lips, and when she caught me staring, she averted her eyes.

I felt like it was a dream or my illusion. I couldn't believe that she was sitting on my lap and we just kissed passionately.

"I... think this is more effective than any medicine. It will keep me numb for a long time." I teased her and winked.

"I... I... uh should go check on Noah," she said shyly and got up.

Her movements were sluggish, and there was a dazed look on her face. She tripped when her foot collided with Noah's toy and cursed.

I got up to give her a hand when she scrambled back. I frowned at her action.

"I... uh. I'm fine." She looked nervous but still cute.

I smiled at her lifting my hands in surrender. She got up and ran upstairs.

Smiling like a fool, I ran my hands through my hair and thought I would never let her go again. I felt happy after sharing the truth with her. I knew there were still many things to tell her, but for the time being, these things were enough for her to know.

When I heard Noah and Hailey coming down, I got up and went to them. Taking Noah in my arms I kissed his head, and he kissed me on the cheek. My heart swelled at his actions. I felt proud of Hailey for raising a sweet kid like her. I looked at his nose that looked exactly like mine, a replica in fact, and his hair that was the same shade as his mother's. He did look a lot like me, but I hoped his life would not turn out like mine.

After taking a shower, I came downstairs, and I told them that we needed to leave within an hour because the weather would be getting worse.

We had breakfast then we packed our things. I placed our bags in the trunk of my car and locked the cabin. Noah wished to take one last stroll around the woods, and after that we drove away, leaving the cabin and the beautiful memories of our life there.

When we arrived at her house, it was five in the evening. She got out and helped Noah in getting out of the car with his gifts. I also stepped out of the car and pulled her bag out from the trunk then followed her into her house.

*   *   *

Hailey

I went inside the house, and Chase was following behind me with my bags.

"Boo." I heard a voice and jumped.

"Ethan, you dirtbag!" I yelled, punching him in the arm and calming my beating heart.

He just stupidly smiled at me enjoying my misery.

"What are you doing here?" I asked Ethan.

"Oh. I see you're not happy to find me here." He made a sad face and jutted out his lower lip.

I rolled my eyes at his childish behavior.

"You know I didn't mean it like that, so stop making that face. I'm just curious to see you here especially on the day after Christmas," I said to him, looking very interested to know why he came here.

"Well, you see, Sammy was nagging me to take him to meet Noah because he wants to show him his gifts. That's why I came here. And I have brought a special gift for you." He placed a key in my hand.

I took it and instantly knew what it was.

I turned around to see Chase still holding my bag.

"Ethan, this is Chase," I said to Ethan.

Though Chase had already done quite a good job in introducing himself to my whole college, I still introduced him.

"And this is Ethan. He studies in college with me, and he is a very good friend of mine," I said to Chase, making gestures with my hand.

"Hi." Ethan was the first one to extend his hand.

I took the bag from Chase's hand but he protested, and I reassured him that I could carry my bags to my room.

"Hello," Chase said and shook his hand.

They both looked extremely awkward, so I left them to go to my room to drop off my bag.

Then I went to the garage and found my car. Ethan knew best which things needed modification in my car, so I asked him once to make my car brand new. He said he would do it, but I knew he was waiting for Christmas to do that.

My car looked new, no scratch, and had the latest car accessories. The new leather covers looked so nice. I checked everything again then went inside to say thank you to Ethan.

When I reached inside, Chase and Ethan were standing nose to nose and glaring at each other.

"Then let's start the game," Ethan said.

Chapter Thirty-Five

Then Let's Start the Game

Chase

Hailey left us to see whatever that boy had given her.

"Hello, Chase. Let me just make one thing clear. Hailey is not yours anymore so stop manipulating her. I know who you are and what you do. Your and Clara's relationship was popularly discussed by Boston magazine last month. Hailey is innocent. She doesn't read magazines about businessmen like you, so I suggest stay away from her," Ethan said, fuming.

"Why are you so concerned about her, pretty boy? Are you interested in her? If that's the case, then I pity you.

And let me also clarify one thing with you. Not every time what the paparazzi or the magazines say is true. You have no right to interfere in my personal life and call me a manipulator. So I suggest you stay away from her because she wants me and I'm the father of her son." I was also getting angry at his claim on my Hailey.

"Oh really, so where were you all these years? Do you think I'm a fool? Three years is a long time man. You don't know her like I do and your son loves me. If you quietly leave my girl and this city, I'll propose to her at the end of the last semester," Ethan said, moving nearer to me.

My hands were clenching with anger, and I also moved an inch glaring at his face.

Sarcastically laughing at him I said, "Go find a girl for you pretty boy because she is my wife, my woman, and my son's mother. You're just her friend. Keep it that way. Don't cross the line. I am her husband, and she loves me and that I know because of what happened between us last night."

I smirked when his face fell.

"You're her ex-husband. What happened last night? Did you have sex with her? You are sick. You are using her, manipulating her. I will do everything in my power to make her mine," Ethan said, looking at me with disgust.

I was ready to pounce on him.

"What we did or did not last night is not your concern. And you can try to make her fall in love with you, but let me tell you, it's a lost battle because she already belongs to me."

"Then let's start the game," Ethan said, standing nose to nose with me.

We heard a voice of a throat being cleared and turned our heads slowly to see Hailey standing there.

Shit, how much did she hear?

"Um, what are you guys talking about?" Hailey asked us.

She glanced at our faces with a questioning gaze.

"I... I... We were talking about a new video game and that we should play it someday," Ethan said while rubbing his neck.

"Yeah, we were talking about a new video game. I think I should leave now." I looked at everywhere but Hailey.

I moved out of the door, and Hailey followed behind me.

"Chase... Chase, what happened?" Hailey asked me.

We had now reached my car.

"Hailey nothing happened. I want to take you somewhere tomorrow if that's fine with you," I asked her, hoping that she would say yes.

"Noah isn't going to leave his toys for a week. He has a habit of getting obsessed with new things." Hailey had a smile on her face.

"Uh... Hailey, I didn't say Noah should come with us. I said I want to take you somewhere," I said smiling at her.

"Oh... I'm free tomorrow."

"Then I'll pick you up at seven," I said to her.

She nodded her head in a silent yes. I was about to leave when I caught sight of Ethan leaning at the door and looking at us.

An evil plan formed in my head and I said, "Hailey, aren't you going to give me the evening dose? You know, I might a get panic attack while driving".

I took a step closer to her and placed my hand on her waist then pulled her closer, leaving no space between us.

She gave me a shy smile and wrapped her arms around my neck then pulled me down.

"I don't think you need the dose now because you look fine to me," she said, unaware how her voice had lowered and turned seductive.

"Well… I'm not fine, Hailey. Leaving you here after spending days with you and Noah is a very difficult thing to do for me." My voice was filled with love and pain.

She captured my lips and our lips moved in sync. The kiss was short but sweet and enough to show Ethan that she was mine. I bid her goodbye pecking her lips one more time before leaving.

*   *   *

Hailey

When I walked into the house, I had a silly smile on my face. Ethan was standing at the door.

I hoped he didn't see us kissing. It would be really embarrassing for me if he did.

"Ethan, how was your Christmas?" I asked him, but instead of answering my question, he glared at me.

"Hailey, I know it's personal, but tell me, did you sleep with him? Did something happen last night between you and him?" Ethan was fuming with anger.

"What the hell, Ethan? It's my personal life. Whether I slept with him or not does not concern you. You have no right to ask me such a personal question," I said, getting angry at his nonsense questioning.

"Oh really, it's not my concern. Noah's safety and your safety is my concern. I know you and Noah for three years, Hailey. Do you know anything about him? I suggest you read about him in the last month's Boston magazine. They'll give you a pretty good idea of that manipulative ex-husband of yours." Ethan left the house after saying those things.

I was angry, hurt, and confused. I might have no idea how Chase spent his last three years, but we were trying to get to know each other again. His confession last night revealed all the secrets of the past. I knew he wasn't a manipulator. I couldn't understand why Ethan called him that.

I never judged people based on what magazines say about them.

Mom came and hugged me.

I said, "Hey Mom. How are you?"

"I'm fine, Hailey. I was in your room with Noah and Sammy watching them play when I saw Ethan storming out and driving away. Did you guys have a fight?"

"No Mom. He remembered that he had again forgotten to lock his apartment door," I said, laughing lightly, but in my mind, I was cursing Ethan. That bitch forgot that he came here with Sammy.

Now, who would drop him off?

My mind sarcastically reminded me, *"Duh… you."*

[Next morning]

After breakfast, I left Noah in the living room to play with his toys. Obviously under my mom's care. I locked myself in the room and spent my day working on my thesis.

My eyes caught the time on the wall clock, and I hurriedly ended my work. I moved towards my closet and rampaged through my closet for a few minutes then finally my hand landed on my black high waist jeans and peach off-shoulder top.

I showered and blow-dried my hair then changed into my jeans and top. I applied minimal makeup. My eyes were looking dull, so I lined them with jet black liner and applied mascara to make my eyelashes look longer.

I took a look at my appearance in the mirror and felt satisfied with my work. Then I went down while trying to put my feet in my black wedges.

I reached down, and mother looked at me from head to toe for a good two minutes.

Then she asked, "Where are you going, getting all dolled up?"

"I... uh I'm just going out with Chase." I felt shy.

"Oh... so I guess Noah is staying with me?" Mom asked me.

"Yup. Can you take care of him for me?" I gave her my best puppy dog look.

"You know, I love my grandson. That's why I am going to take care of him, but you've to promise to tell me what's cooking between you and him," she said, and I groaned.

Noah was really engrossed in watching his favorite cartoon. I kissed his cute cheeks telling him sternly to sleep on his bedtime.

Chase's car appeared outside my house. I ran out saying a final bye to my mom. Chase opened the door for me, and I buckled up myself for the ride.

"Chase, where are we going?" I asked him.

"Nah... That's a surprise. You have to wait to find out." Chase glanced at me amused while driving.

I knew my curiosity was clear on my face.

Chase was looking ahead on the road, and I decided to take advantage of that. I stared at him. He was wearing black jeans and grey button-up shirt. His face was unshaven, making him look older. I used to think he was handsome, but now I found him way sexier than any other man.

I started feeling a little uncomfortable with my own thoughts and glanced out of the window at the passing scenery. We entered in a posh area where large mansion-like houses were built.

Chase stopped outside the white painted big double story stylish house. A man came running out and opened the gate for our car to enter.

Then he opened the door for me and said, "Welcome ma'am."

I nodded my head with a small smile on my face.

"Chase, are you staying here?" I asked him confused.

"Come with me inside, Hailey."

He didn't answer my question. Instead, he took my hand in his, lacing our fingers together.

Chase pushed open the door, and we went inside.

When the lights were switched on, I was beyond shocked. The house was more beautiful inside than it was from the outside. The shining white marbles and long stairs in the middle were making it look like some palace.

Chase dragged me inside with him, showing me the whole house. It was perfect, decorated with extremely expensive and delicate furniture. The house looked like it belonged to some celebrity.

There were two chairs and a table placed on the balcony. The rose petals were spread on the floor. I glanced at Chase and then again at the table.

"I… I know I have never done anything romantic, and it's my first time, so I hope you like it," Chase said to me with hope in his grey eyes.

"Chase, I love it. It's beautiful. Thanks." I smiled broadly at him.

He led me to the table and pulled out a chair for me. I settled down on it. He sat across me.

"Everything is prepared by best chefs. I didn't cook anything myself so you wouldn't get food poison after dinner," he said to me.

I laughed, and a light blush appeared on his cheeks.

"Oh. It's fine. What counts is your effort," I said, looking at the dishes filled with different cuisines.

There was cheesy white pasta, steak, salads, fried chicken, and rice.

"Wow… Everything looks delicious, Chase," I said, filling my plate.

Chase gave me his dazzling smile.

I studied whole day locked in your room and didn't have the time to eat, so I was starving.

We enjoyed dinner in peace with the beautiful view of the evening in front of our eyes.

After we were done with dinner, I asked, "So what did you want to tell me?"

Chapter Thirty-Six

Telling Her the Whole Truth

Chase

When I went back to the hotel from Hailey's place, I was fuming in anger at what Ethan said. My blood was boiling. *How dare he claim what was mine?* I would do anything to make sure Ethan would go to hell before he could manipulate my woman and destroy our relationship.

I was pacing in my room and thinking what I should do to get rid of Ethan. I heard the ringing of my cell phone and picked it up.

"Hello, Chase Edwards speaking," I said.

"Hi, Chase. It's Daniel Adam. The house you requested us to decorate is ready."

"That's the best news you have just given me. Thanks, man." I thanked him for decorating the house on such short notice.

"Don't mention it. You're our business partner and a very good friend. There is no reason I wouldn't do it," Daniel replied with politeness.

We talked for a while about the business then ended the call.

Daniel Adam was a very famous businessman in England, running an interior designing company and five-star restaurants, which he inherited from his father. We had been business partners for a few years now and became very good friends in a very short time.

Suddenly, something clicked in my mind, and I looked for my laptop. I picked it up and placed it on my lap. I opened Google and searched Daniel Adam. His pictures appeared on the screen, shocking me with the similarities between them. Wikipedia showed that he had a sibling. I searched his sibling, but no picture appeared. One article caught my eyes, and I clicked on it.

Ethan Adam, the son of multi-millionaire, Michael Adam, and brother of a famous interior design company holder, Daniel Adam once again stars in another scandal. Lindsay, a former model claims Ethan is the father of her child. She also claims he ran away from his home because his dad wants him to marry her. She said police and private investigators have been searching for him for months, but there is still no news about where he is hiding. She appealed us to help her in finding Ethan Adam. If you know where he is, please call the number mentioned. Hopefully, we will find him and get our answers soon.

The article was one week old. It meant Ethan must be hiding here for the last three years. Now his secret was out. I thought with an evil smile on my face.

After reading the whole article, I was beyond shocked. I couldn't believe he was claiming that he didn't want me to hurt Hailey when he was the one hurting her by lying and manipulating her. I wouldn't let him fool her.

He was so going to regret challenging me. I called Daniel, and he picked up.

"Hey, is there something you didn't like in the house?" he asked me.

"No… I haven't called to talk about that. I know where Ethan is hiding."

"What? Chase, are you sure?" he asked me, sounding unsure himself.

"Yeah, I'm sure. He is in Oakland."

"Oh… Chase, thank you so much man for telling me this. We have been searching for him in England, but he has been hiding in the US all this time," Daniel said angrily.

"What are you going to do now?"

"I'm going to pay him a visit and force him to come with me to England because Dad really wants to meet him, and he needs to clean the mess he left," Daniel told me his plan.

"I am here if you need my help," I said and ended the call.

Then I went to see the house and started to work on my plan for tomorrow.

*   *   *

The next day, I went to pick her from her house at exactly seven. She came out dressed in black jeans and peach off-shoulder top and looked gorgeous. I could clearly see the swell of her breast and her perfectly fitted jeans was not helping much to hide her curves.

I opened the door for her, and when she was inside the car, my senses were filled with the subtle fragrance of her jasmine and vanilla perfume. I started to drive towards the house. All the way to the house she kept asking me where we were going, but I didn't tell her anything. I wanted to surprise her.

When we arrived there, I took her hand in mine and dragged her with me inside to show her the whole house. She was shocked at first, but then she looked at everything with a dreamy look on her face.

After giving her a tour of the house, I took her in the balcony where I arranged dinner.

She smiled broadly when she saw the arrangements.

After we were done with dinner, she asked, "So what did you want to tell me?"

"Can we go to the living room? It's getting pretty cold here," I said to her and stood up.

I took her hand in mine and walked in the direction of the living room.

"Hailey, I don't know how to say this," I said then stopped, still contemplating my decision in my mind.

She got settled on the couch and placed a cushion on her lap. She looked at me, waiting for me to say something.

"Chase, you're making me nervous. Just tell me already," Hailey said to me with an exasperated sigh.

I sighed and said, "I have been living in Boston for the last three years. After I completed my internship with Carrington Enterprises, I started a new office in Boston. And in the past few years, I have become a very well-known businessman."

"That's wonderful, Chase." Hailey looked at me with a smile.

"But it also made my life a little complicated, Hailey. One night, when I was coming out of the restaurant after having dinner with Clara, the paparazzi took our photographs and next day, the news about us getting engaged spread," I said then waited for Hailey to say something.

But she was just staring at me, so I continued.

"I don't want you to find this out from any other source. Clara and I are just friends, nothing more than that. I swear. You... you were the only woman in my mind all these years," I said to her, desperately trying to prove my innocence.

"Chase, I think it's too much for me to take in. I'm not saying that I don't trust you, but Clara told me that she was your fiancée. Then you told me she was just joking and now this." She looked a little jealous.

"I don't know why she did that, but it was a lie. There is nothing between her and me," I said, trying to explain.

"Chase, I think she likes you. Maybe that's why she lied to me."

My heart stopped beating.

Silence fell in the room. I didn't know what I could say to stop her from thinking that she wasn't wrong. In fact, she was right about Clara. She liked me, but my heart belonged to Hailey.

I cut all ties with Clara when I left New York. But one day, we coincidentally met at a charity gala in Boston, and she kind of clung to me and rekindled our friendship again, putting the past behind us. I always saw her as a friend and nothing more.

"Chase, I think I should go. You need time to think about all this. Maybe you feel something for her too," she said and started to get up from the couch.

I gripped her hand and pulled her towards my chest. I placed my other hand on her waist and held her there in my arms.

"Hailey, please don't go yet. I had three years to think, and I don't want more time. I love you, Hailey. I have always loved you. I know we had a very unusual relationship, but we cannot change our destiny. Yes, I know I committed a lot of mistakes, and I have hurt you many times. But with every tear you shed, my heart bleeds. With your smile, my heart beat accelerates. My heart belongs to you," I told her while we were lost in each other's eyes.

"Please, believe me. I only want you. There is no other girl for me. You are my first love, my wife and that's how it is going to stay as long as I am breathing," I said, kissing her forehead lightly.

"Chase, I'm not your wife. We have been divorced for last three years, and you keep forgetting that." She looked down.

Her eyes were brimming with unshed tears.

"Hailey, you're my wife. I... I never signed those papers." Finally, I was able to tell her.

"What... what do you mean?" she asked me with raised eyebrows, looking confused.

"It means we are still legally very much wedded. You are still my wife."

Her cute mouth fell wide open.

"Oh, God. Chase! You mean you never divorced me. We are still married," she said, looking wide-eyed.

"Yes, I never wanted a divorce in the first place. It was just an act to make my mother believe. I did that to make you leave."

She pushed me away harshly. I was in shock. What had I done to make her this angry?

"How could you, Chase? How can you do this to me? All these years, I thought I was worthless, ugly, and unattractive, and that's why you divorced me. I was in love with you, and your rejection broke me. I was depressed. I wished to die because I was hurt. You... you could have told me this before. I hate you... you made me doubt myself. You ruined three years of my life," she said.

Tears were running down from her eyes.

"I'm so sorry."

"You are sorry? Your sorry won't make me forget all those nights when I cried myself to sleep. There were days when I didn't want to wake up. I was tired, sad, and sick. My mind constantly reminded me of all the things those bullies used to say to me. I started believing them. You didn't think about it, did you? Your lie pushed me into a dark cave. And my son brought me back from it. His small cries for my attention brought me back. He saved me from ending myself, and he gave me hope for a future." She was breathing hard.

Tears were rolling from her eyes. I wanted to die at the moment because I was the reason for her pain.

"I thought you were better without me. I thought I was not worthy of your love. I thought I have hurt you enough already and that you wouldn't give me another chance again. I thought I was letting you live your life the way you wanted. I didn't say anything because I thought confessing will make you more confused and depressed. I didn't know I was hurting you more by hiding the truth," I said, trying to explain to her.

She didn't say anything and just stared at me.

"I'm sorry, Hailey. I'm so sorry. I never wanted you to feel that much pain," I said, moving towards her.

I hugged her while she cried, hiding her face in my chest.

That day, I realized that we were both broken and I took an oath to mend our hearts.

Chapter Thirty-Seven

It Felt Like a Dream

Hailey

After crying my eyes out, I moved my face away from his warm, hard chest then looked up at him with my now swollen eyes and runny nose.

"I'm sorry for ruining your shirt," I said, still looking at him and sniffing.

"I don't care about the shirt. I care about you." He caressed my cheek.

"I… uh… I'm just too emotional nowadays," I said, feeling embarrassed.

"I… can understand. I shouldn't have dumped all of this on you today." He looked down.

"Chase I. . ." I started to say, but he interrupted me.

"Hailey... I love you. I really do. But I... uh... I can understand if you don't believe me and want a divorce."

Before he could say something else, I slapped my hand on his mouth to shut him up.

"Mr. Chase Edwards, I will beat the hell out of you if you say another word. I'm still angry with you." I glared at him and removed my hand.

He stared at me with his mouth agape.

"I used to admire you. I used to think you were perfect and very intelligent. Now I think I was wrong. You are the dumbest man alive. If I wanted a divorce, I would've asked you about it a long time ago," I said every word clearly.

"You... you mean you don't want to leave me. You don't want a divorce. You are giving us another chance."

"I'm not giving you a chance, Chase. You have to work hard to get the chance and your time starts now," I said to him, hiding the grin that was threatening to appear on my face.

I was enjoying the way his face turned white like paper. Every trace of a smile vanished.

"Now be a good husband and drop me back to my house," I said to him.

But again he gripped my hand and pulled me towards his chest.

"What?" I asked him irritatingly.

"This is your house." He was staring intensely at my face.

"What do you mean?" I questioned him, confused.

"I bought this house last week but didn't show you because it needed some renovation. I actually wanted to give you this as a Christmas gift. The renovation wasn't complete, so I waited to show you this." He looked at me.

When I didn't say anything, he started to look anxious.

"'It's in your name as well. I know you have to stay here in Oakland until you graduate that's why I bought this house. You can move in whenever you want," he said.

I was just staring at him in disbelief.

"Are you insane? You bought an extremely extravagant two-story house for a Christmas gift. I'm still not over the gifts you gave Noah and me on Christmas. Now, this damn house!" I said.

"If you don't like my gifts then I am sorry. I just want to do so much for you and Noah. I know I overdo things, but I don't know any other way to show how much I love you both."

I was just staring and absorbing every word he said. It touched my heart. I didn't know when he learned to say things like this.

"I'm an idiot, aren't I? I'm doing everything wrong," he said, leaning his head on mine and closing his eyes.

I placed my hand on his jaw and started making circles with my thumb and said, "You are an idiot, but a good one. Noah is still young. He has no idea how costly those gifts were. For him, every one of those gifts was given by his father, and that made him happy."

"And I only did that to make him happy," he said staring at me again.

"I know. But if you will keep doing that he will soon become a spoiled rich kid."

"I understand it. Next time, I'll talk to you before buying something for him." He took my hand in his.

"The good thing is that I can give you anything and everything I want because you won't turn into a spoiled kid," he whispered in my ear.

His breath was tickling me, so I pulled back and smiled mischievously.

"I can turn into a spoiled rich wife. You never know," I said with shrug of my shoulder.

He said, "You are allowed to turn into a spoiled rich wife."

His husky voice sent a shiver to my spine.

I just wanted to throw myself at him and kiss the hell out him for being so sweet and saying the right thing every time.

"I think it's pretty late. I need to go back home," I said.

"I don't want you to go. I want to spend every day and every night of my life with you."

Then I noticed there were dark circles under his eyes like he wasn't getting proper sleep. He looked tired and drowsy.

"Can you stay here tonight with me?" he asked me.

"Okay."

He looked shocked, eyes wide open and jaw dropped.

"Are you serious?" he said, looking like he didn't believe me one bit.

"I'm dead serious. Just let me call my mom and tell her about my plans before Dad freaks out and sends a search party." I picked my cell phone up and dialed Mom's number.

When she picked up, I asked her about Noah. She told me he was already asleep. I told her I would be staying with Chase tonight, which shocked her. I never lied to my dad, so I pleaded her to tell him that I would be staying at Julia's tonight.

"What?" I asked him, raising my eyebrows.

"Tell me if I kiss you right now, would you get angry?" He had a smirk on his handsome face.

"There's only one way to find out, and that's testing your luck," I said, smirking.

He didn't waste a second and smashed his lips on mine. The way he was kissing me made my legs wobble. I could feel his passion, his desperation. The way his lips were moving with mine felt like he was marking my soul. I kissed him back with the same ferocity, same passion, and desperation.

When we broke the kiss, we were both smiling like crazy at each other. Then he gave me one more peck on my lips and scooped me into his arms.

"What are you doing? Put me down this instant. I have legs, and I can walk on them pretty well," I said, glaring at him.

"You… you used to be so quiet and shy. I liked that thing about you. And now you talk too much woman." He had a smug smile on his face.

"Hey... I have changed a lot in the last three years. I have become talkative because I have to answer every question our three-year-old son asks. I have to feed his curiosity," I said.

Chase laughed, and his laugh was music to my ears.

"Can you please tell me why are we going to the roof?" I asked him.

"Oh, God. You just can't wait till we get there." He pretended to be annoyed.

I didn't say anything. After climbing five hundred and fifty steps, well not literally, I just felt that they were too long; he stopped outside the brown wooden door.

He pushed it open with his leg and went inside then put me down on my feet. I was busy staring at the beauty of the place. The rooftop was decorated with different types of flowers. There was a small fountain in the center. Two stylish chairs were sitting in the middle with one small table in the center.

"It's so beautiful here," I said to him, still looking at the view.

"Come, let's sit." He gestured with his hand towards the chairs.

I nodded, and we sat down on the chairs. The cold breeze was tickling our skin while we were sharing almost everything about ourselves. This time we were creating a stronger bond than before. I found out that he knew so much about me already and it was courtesy of my mom.

Then after spending hours on the rooftop, we decided that sitting there longer would make us both sick. We went down and decided to watch a movie. We picked the room which had dark curtains so we could watch the movie with the lights off.

Chase and I got under the comforters after playing the movie on TV. It was a romantic comedy movie. I had not watched it before. When I turned to look at Chase, I found him asleep with his arms folded and a frown on his face.

I picked up the remote control and pressed the off button to turn off the TV. Then I put my head on a pillow and stared at his sleeping form beside me.

I smoothened his eyebrows out then gave him a peck on his lips. It felt like a dream to be here with him and sleep in his arms.

Chapter Thirty-Eight

Then Be My Very Personal Slave

Hailey

Next morning, I woke up feeling featherlike kisses on my neck. Unintentionally, a moan escaped my lips.

"Chase," I moaned his name, making him stop for a second.

Then he started sucking the skin of the hollow part of my neck. I couldn't stop the loud moan escaping my mouth when I felt his tongue massaging the flesh that stung.

He kissed his way from my neck to my ear and placed a kiss behind my ear. I shuddered. My eyes were closed from the ecstasy running through my veins. I had never felt something like this before in my life. His kisses felt heavenly to me, arousing some new feelings inside me for the first time.

I put my hand in his silky hair and ran my fingers through them while he continued to shower my neck with kisses.

"Good morning," Chase said with his husky voice, making my stomach flip.

"Is this a new way of waking up someone sleeping?" My voice came out breathless.

He chuckled and said, "You can say that if you want."

"It was certainly a good way." I opened my eyes with a small smile on my face.

I found Chase gazing at me with such intensity and passion in his eyes. My breath hitched when his hand tucked my traitorous strand of hair behind my ear.

I had never seen anyone looking at me like this before like I am the most beautiful thing and he wanted to devour me. Amazingly, I felt confident under his lustful gaze, so I pulled him closer to me and brushed my lips on his lightly.

"It is not this simple to win me back," I said, staring at him.

He groaned and said, "I know. I will do whatever you want me to do."

"You will do anything?"

"I will do anything for you, my love." He pecked my lips lightly.

"Then be my very personal slave for a week," I said, making him still.

"What, a slave? Okay, whatever you say, princess." He agreed, looking at me doubtfully.

I was stunned with how easily he agreed without even asking me what I would make him do if he would become my slave.

"Well, do I need to call you madam from now on or would you prefer mademoiselle?" he asked me with an amused expression.

"Just call me princess. It would be fine, my personal slave." I smiled sweetly at him.

He leaned closer to kiss me. But I pushed him, making him fall back on the bed, and I got up. I glanced at his confused face and went to the washroom, giving him a teasing smile.

After I was done with my daily routine, I caught my reflection in the mirror and groaned. My hair was sticking in different directions, and my face was flushed. Then my eyes landed on a red mark on my neck.

He gave me a hickey, stupid man. He knew that I needed to go back home. If anyone saw this, I would be dead with embarrassment.

I blushed looking at the hickey on my neck.

I found Chase standing in front of the mirror checking his appearance.

"Where did you get ready?" I asked him.

"You were taking too long, so I went to another bathroom to freshen up." He glanced at me in the mirror.

"I wouldn't have taken this much time in the washroom if you haven't done this to me," I said, removing my hair from my neck showing him his work.

His eyes stared at the hickeys in amusement.

Then he cleared his throat and said, "My mark is looking good on you."

After hearing his stupid reply, my jaw dropped.

Was he serious right now? The nerve of this man!

My calm eyes blazed.

"You think it's funny. Well, no more kisses for today."

The smile dropped from his face.

"That's unfair."

"I don't care, Mr. Chase Edwards. You have to do what I say. You're my slave."

"Maybe I can change your mind." He looked at me with hopeful eyes.

"I'm hungry. Let's have breakfast then maybe I'll change my mind," I said, taking his hand in mine and dragging him out.

We went to the cafe near the lake and ate breakfast there. Then we walked for a few minutes near the lake and even dipped our feet in the cold water, making them numb. Dipping our feet in freezing water was not a good idea because we couldn't stand for fifteen minutes. We laughed at our stupidity but agreed that it was fun.

Then he dropped me at my house, but not without reminding me that he was my personal slave and I could call him whenever I wanted.

I went inside and found Mom and Dad having breakfast. I told Dad that I was with Julia working on the thesis all night, and she just dropped me off. Unexpectedly, he bought the whole story.

I went to my room and woke Noah up. Then I gave him a shower and changed him into his black sweatpants and grey hoodie, which matched with his eyes.

I blow-dried and combed his hair, showering his face with several kisses. I took his picture and sent it to Chase. Within a second, I received his reply.

Chase: Noah is looking really cute. Give him a kiss for me. :-*

Hailey: I know. After all, he is my son. :-P

Chase: That's true, but he looks like me more and that you can't deny

Hailey: Whatever, Mr. MVPS.

Chase: What does MVPS mean?

Hailey: My Very Personal Slave. :-P.

Chase: Only yours, Hailey ;-)

Hailey: Only mine.

I turned beetroot after reading his last text. I replied and went to take a shower.

The rest of the day was boring. I went grocery shopping and completed my thesis. When dinner time came, I went downstairs with Noah. He was on my back because he wanted a piggyback ride from Mommy.

I helped Mom with the last minute preparation and set the table.

I was busy enjoying dinner, and I didn't notice that someone was observing me keenly.

"Mommy you have a bruise on your neck. Did you also fall off the stairs like Aunt Julia?" Noah asked, making me choke on my food.

Mom and Dad stilled and stared at me.

I was coughing like a dying woman, making them get up and rub my back. Mom offered me a glass of water, and I took it, drinking hurriedly.

When I stopped coughing, and my breathing became normal, I looked at my parents who were giving me a we-need-to-talk-alone stare.

I quickly finished my dinner with a red-hot face and tried escaping, but I was unsuccessful.

"Noah, your favorite cartoon is playing on TV. Go watch it," my father said to him, and he ran towards the living room, leaving his poor mommy alone.

Turning to me, my dad said, "Hailey, do you want to tell us anything?"

It was not the right time to tell my dad about Chase and me.

I shook my head and said, "No. No, Dad."

"Okay. Then I'm waiting until you think you are ready to share with me who gave you bruises on your neck." He got up from the chair and left me with Mom.

I groaned and put my face on the table in embarrassment.

"Hailey, is it really a love bite?" Mom asked me with a mischievous smile on her face.

"Please Mom, don't tease me." I looked a bit more flushed.

"I'm your mother. You can tell me this stuff. I can give you a few tips on how to hide them properly if you want," she said, winking at me.

"Oh God! Mom, please stop talking like a teenager."

She rolled her eyes at me.

"I'm going to my bedroom. Good night and use a cold spoon if you want that gone by tomorrow morning," she said and got up.

"Good night and sweet dreams, Mom."

After cleaning the table, I took Noah with me upstairs. Then we read his favorite book until he fell asleep. At almost 1:00 a.m. I heard my cell phone ringing.

Picking up my cell phone, I found it was a call from Chase. My heart started to beat wildly.

"Hello," I said.

"Uh... Hi. I hope I didn't wake you up?"

"No, you didn't. I was awake reading."

"Oh... and here I thought you were thinking about me." He teased me.

Then we started talking about our day and made some plans for tomorrow. I fell asleep with a wide smile on my face that night.

Chapter Thirty-Nine

Something I Wasn't Expecting

Hailey

Today, Chase asked me to get ready at 5:00 p.m. because he had planned something for us.

Chase had been playing the role of my very personal slave for five days. And he had convinced me by literally doing anything and everything on my command. Last night, when he called me, we started chatting normally, but I was craving for ice cream and told him that I wanted to eat some. After fifteen minutes, he was standing outside my house looking disheveled and sexy with a tub of my favorite chocolate and cookie dough ice cream and two plastic spoons in hand.

I went down, and we sat in his car. We talked while eating ice cream until sunrise. For the first time in my life, I realized how it felt when you were in love with someone and that someone loved you back.

We had been spending a lot of time together, stealing kisses while keeping our relationship secret from the world. Noah was mostly involved in our plans, but today Chase asked me to meet him alone.

We had become so close these past few days that now going back to my old life seemed impossible. Our little make-out session here and there felt so thrilling. Sometimes my stupid brain made me think like we were forbidden lovers meeting in secret and that excited me.

Chase had been treating me like a princess, showering me with gifts and surprises every day. He had been playing the role of a perfect husband that any girl dreamed of.

Chase had opened his heart out for me and placed it on my feet for me to take it or stomp on it. He left the choice to me. The thing was that I felt scared of repeating the same mistake. I was hesitant to take the next step.

I sighed, placing my hair on the left shoulder. For today, I selected a simple soft pink dress that reached my knees. I put a little amount of blush and lip gloss then applied some mascara.

I glanced at myself in the mirror and felt satisfied with my look. I put my stilettos on and picked my clutch with my jacket then walked downstairs.

When I reached downstairs, I saw my mom and Noah sitting on the couch and reading newspaper. Mom was teaching him how to read the newspaper, which had recently caught his attention, and he had become very adamant to learn how to read it.

When he saw me, he came running to me.

"Mommy you're looking so pretty," Noah said, looking at me from head to toe.

His reactions were always cute, and he never forgot to compliment me.

I kneeled down and hugged him. Then I placed a kiss on his cheek. I told him that I was going out, and he needed to be a good kid and go to bed on time.

Mom came to me and stared at me with her teasing smile.

"Mom, please stop giving me those weird smiles. I'm going out with Chase, so I really need you to cover for me," I said with my puppy dog face.

She rolled her eyes and said, "I'm very tempted to tell your dad about your secret lover."

My face turned crimson.

"But like a good mother, I will keep it a secret even when you don't share any juicy updates with poor me," she said, making a sad face.

Taking both her hands in mine, I gave them a squeeze and said, "Mom, I promise. I will tell you everything tonight."

"Hailey, you mean tomorrow morning because you hardly have time for us at night." She was teasing me again, making me groan.

She wouldn't let a moment slide without teasing me.

She said that I was a very good source of entertainment. My life story was as good as the TV soaps that she watched on TV. And she enjoyed watching my reaction to her teasing comments. I felt my cell phone vibrate. I looked at it, and it was a message from Chase saying that he was outside my house, waiting for me. I said bye to my mom and went out.

I found Chase leaning on the car wearing a dark blue button-up shirt with black jeans and leather jacket, looking dazzling.

I ran to him and hugged him. He picked me up and spun me around, then placed me back on the ground. He pecked my lips and pulled away from me.

"Hey, where are we going?" I asked him, getting in the car.

"Baby, it is a surprise." Chase buckled himself and started the car.

I shook my head with a smile.

After the thirty-minute journey, he finally stopped outside a place, which looked like a garden. He grasped my hand in his and dragged me into the garden. The first thing I saw was the path made of roses, leading me somewhere.

I looked to my left to realize that Chase had disappeared, leaving me to follow the path alone. My heart was thumping in my chest, but I made my way to where that path was leading me.

I took every step, feeling scared. I started thinking that it might be his new way of giving me a gift

The path ended, making me look at my surroundings. A sudden gasp escaped my mouth.

There was a shape of a heart outlined by the rose petals in the center of the garden and Chase was standing there waiting for me with his hand extended. I stepped into the heart shape formed on the grass.

Chase grasped my hand and pulled me closer to him.

"What?" I asked him, too surprised to form a simple sentence.

"Hailey… I have told you this before. I'm in love with you. I think I had fallen for you when I first laid eyes on you in the chapel in that wedding dress. My first thought was you were an angel sent here to tempt me to make me sin. I tried creating distance between us, but your innocence, your love made me bend my rules. When the secret about your age came out, I thought you were a kid, and you didn't know what love is. But you proved me wrong. You proved to me that age doesn't matter in understanding what love is and that made me fall even more in love with you." He stared into my eyes.

I felt every emotion through his words.

Then he suddenly moved away from me, creating a gap between us and kneeled down on one knee.

"Have you ever heard the phrase that you won't realize the value of something until it's gone? Now, I understand the meaning of that phrase. The day you left me I felt dead from inside. I know, I was the one who made you leave, but it was very painful for me to let you go. I never ever want to experience that pain again. I want to live with you and die in your arms when the time comes, like a true lover. I want to spend my days and nights with you. I can't thank you enough for giving me, such wonderful son. But if you will give me a chance I promise to thank you every day. Hailey, will you marry me again?" he asked, pulling out a rose shape jewelry box from his pocket and opened it.

I was staring at the ring with my mouth agape. It was that beautiful.

He cleared his throat, drawing attention to the fact that he was still down on one knee, waiting for my answer.

Tears started to stream down from my eyes, and I yelled, "Yes."

He sighed and got up then hastily put the ring on my ring finger. I flung myself into his arms hugging him tightly. He chuckled while pressing me closer. I felt roses falling on us from above and looked up to find a helicopter in the sky, videotaping everything and showering rose petals.

"Chase, you made them videotape everything," I said in a shock.

"I did just to prove that you actually said yes." He winked at me.

The man in the helicopter waved at Chase and left us.

I looked at the beautiful princess cut diamond ring with a huge diamond in the center and tiny diamonds circling around making it look more enchanting.

"I feel like a princess wearing this ring," I said to Chase.

He cupped my face between his palms and said, "You're my princess."

Then his head leaned down, and he captured my lips in a toe-curling kiss, making me breathless.

"I love you," I said, making him smile.

"Say it again."

"I love you," I yelled.

"I love you too, Hailey." He leaned down and placed his hands on my waist.

He lifted me up and spun me around. Both of us were laughing, truly happy in that moment.

Chapter Forty

Wedding

Hailey

"Chase, are you sure? I mean, don't you need more time to think?" I asked him, glancing at my house.

"Yes, Hailey. I am sure. Now step out of the car so we can go inside and meet your parents." He was waiting for me to get out of the car.

"As you wish, but if he ends up murdering you, then I will engrave 'I told you so' on the stone of your grave," I said, glaring at him and stepped out of the car.

I started walking towards the door when he abruptly stopped.

"What? Have you changed your mind?" I asked him, frowning.

"No, I'm just nervous." He looked scared.

"What will you say to Dad?" I asked him.

He shrugged his shoulders without making eye contact with me.

"Chase this is so stupid. I'm telling you," I told him.

I tried making him realize that there was no need to immediately inform my dad tonight.

Before he could answer me, the main door opened, and I groaned. My dad was standing there glaring at Chase. He pulled me inside the house.

"Uh… Da-Dad, Chase wants to talk to you," I said, crossing my fingers behind my back.

He nodded his head, making me smile. I ushered Chase into the house and closed the door behind us.

They glanced at me, and I had a hundred watt smile on my face.

"Hailey, come here." My dad called me to join them.

"Yes, Dad?" I asked him.

I was still staring at Chase with a dreamy smile.

"Can you stop smiling like a Cheshire cat for a second and tell me what's going on?" he asked me.

"Chase proposed to me today." I was overwhelmed with happiness and jumped to show him my ring.

My dad's eyes looked ready to pop out any moment. He stood in shock. His hand went to his chest like he had a heart attack.

"Hailey, I have a weak heart. Do not surprise me like that again," he said with a pained face.

"Oh... Dad, I'm so sorry, but I'm just so happy today I... I," I said, trying to tell him something but failing due to the excitement rushing through my whole body.

Chase came closer to me and hissed in my ear, "Hailey, go to your room."

I glanced at him with a pout on my face. He glared at me, and I giggled.

I went upstairs to my room, leaving my dad and Chase to have a heart-to-heart conversation. When I opened my bedroom door, I saw Mom reading a book to Noah.

"Mom, guess what happened?" I walked straight to her.

She looked at me weirdly and said, "What happened?"

"Mom, Chase proposed me." I squealed, making Noah and Mom jump in surprise at my loud voice.

Then I picked Noah up in my arms and spun him around, showering his face with kisses. Mom stopped me by gripping my arm before I would fall.

"Mom, look at my ring," I said, showing my left hand to her while adjusting my son on my hip.

Noah and Mom both started at my ring, stunned.

"It's beautiful," my mom said, kissing my head.

"I'm so happy. He proposed to me. It was so romantic. He videotaped everything. He went down on his knees then said that he can't live without me. Oh, Mom. He loves me so much." I was still high with happiness that I was able to say everything in one breath.

"Hailey, I can understand that you're excited but don't forget to breathe," she said, smiling.

I took deep breaths, and Noah kissed my cheek. I was sure he had no idea about what's going on right now. But he was always happy every time I was happy.

"I'm so happy for you, Hailey." She hugged me.

"Are you drunk?" she asked me, her mouth agape.

She must have smelled the wine.

"I drank just a little to celebrate Mom," I told her while gesturing with my hand and giggling. "Ahhh. I'm so sleepy. Good night Mom." I yawned and fell on my bed with Noah. "Mom, can you please check on Dad and Chase? They're downstairs."

"What? You left him alone with your dad!" she yelled then ran out of my room, closing the door behind her.

I giggled at the thought of her going downstairs and stopping my dad from murdering Chase.

Then I pulled Noah close to me to cuddle with him.

"Good night, cuddle buddy." I kissed Noah on his head.

"Good night, Mommy," he replied in his sweet sleepy voice.

[Next morning]

I woke up feeling someone shaking me madly. I groaned and moved in my bed changing from the position I was sleeping before.

When there was another shake, I said "Let me sleep. Go away."

"Wake up, you lousy friend," Julia said, making me get up at lightning speed.

"What are you doing here?" I massaged my head.

I thought I had a headache from getting up too fast.

"You got engaged to that sweet man last night and didn't inform me. You have been dating him, and you didn't think of sharing any juicy updates with your best friend," she said, hitting me with the cushion.

"I'm sorry, Julia." I sighed.

"No. You're not a sorry bitch," she said, glaring at me.

"Hey, Noah is sleeping beside me. Don't curse!" I glanced at my left to check on my baby, but I didn't find him there.

"Where's Noah?"

"He's with his dad. You don't have to worry," she told me like she knew something that I didn't.

Then I saw three strange ladies standing near my dressing table and placing things on it.

"What's going on?" I asked Julia.

"Today is your wedding." Julia was jumping up and down with excitement.

"Hold on. What did you say?" I asked her again to make sure I heard her fine.

"You are getting married today. Chase has arranged everything, so you don't need to worry. These people are the best makeup artists in the country, and they will help you look like the most beautiful bride in the whole world."

"I think I'm dreaming. Go away, Julia," I said, closing my eyes.

"Hailey, get up before I rip this blanket to shreds and give you a good slap." Julia was getting angry.

"Then slap me because I am having a hard time believing you."

"Okay then. You asked for it," Julia said and slapped me really hard on the back, almost robbing me of my breath.

"Shoot. You don't need to hit me that hard." I groaned in pain. "So it's his surprise. Don't you think it's too soon, Julia? I mean, we just got back together," I asked her, making a sad face.

"No, it's not. You both have waited long enough to be with each other. Now, shut up, and we really need to hurry. Time is running, chop-chop." She pulled my hand and made me stand.

"Hi. I'm sorry. Let me introduce myself. I'm Hailey," I said, extending my hand towards the three ladies. They took my hand and told me their names.

Julia pushed me into the washroom and instructed me to take a shower. When I was done showering and asked for clothes, Julia handed me a silky white robe with a set of white lacy undergarments and a thin garter.

When I came out from the washroom, the ladies started blow-drying my hair.

Finally, Julia came back to my room with my wedding dress. Everyone in the room gasped, and I did a double take when my eyes landed on the dress.

The dress was simply beautiful and elegant. Julia and the ladies helped me into the dress and then started my makeup and hairdo. After spending two hours getting ready, I was done, and they took me in front of the standing mirror.

I glanced in the mirror and gasped at my reflection. The dress perfectly cupped my breast, making them look fuller, and the slit in the middle of the chest showed a teasing amount of cleavage. The skirt was made up of a pure white net and cascading down at my feet with an embroidered bottom, increasing the beauty of the dress. And the long matching veil was attached to the elegant bun on my head. The rest of the veil's material was draped on my back mixing with my dress, making it look more beautiful like some princess' dress.

My makeup was soft and natural. The nude pink lips and light pink blush with shimmer on my cheeks gave them magical life. My eyelashes were clad in thick mascara, making them longer. My eyes were lined with a very thin black liner making them prominent. Lastly, I was wearing the same necklace and earrings Chase gifted me on Christmas.

"You're looking so beautiful, Hailey," my mom said with tears in her eyes.

"Yes you're looking simply gorgeous, my friend." Julia kissed my head.

*   *   *

Chase

Yesterday, when Hailey left her dad in the lounge alone with me, I talked to him. I told him everything. I told him why I left her and Noah and how much I loved them. He understood that I couldn't live without them anymore.

He finally gave me his blessings, and I told him how I plan to marry his daughter again at which his reaction was surprisingly sweet.

In the morning, I went to back to Hailey's house to drop off her wedding dress and pickup my son.

When I was in Paris for a meeting last month, Allison asked me to get her something from her favorite boutique and being the good brother that I was, I went.

After buying a dress for my lovely sister, I was about to walk out when the wedding dress caught my eye. I looked at that dress and imagined Hailey wearing it. So last week, I called that designer and requested her to deliver that same dress in Oakland to my address. She agreed to give me the dress when I paid her double the original price.

Now, I was standing with my son in the same chapel Hailey, and I last got married, waiting for her to walk in the chapel. My son was wearing a tux same as mine. We were both wearing a black tux with a white shirt underneath and black shoes.

Some of Hailey's friends were already here, and we were waiting for her to come. Suddenly, the door of the chapel opened, and I saw her mother and her friend entering.

Then finally, I saw her coming inside. Her eyes were downcast, and she was grasping her father's arm. She was looking magnificent in her wedding gown. Her face was hidden by the veil.

I felt proud of my choice of gown and the woman I was about to marry again. She finally reached me, and her father placed her daughter's hand in mine. I gripped it.

Leaning down towards her ear, I said, "You're looking magnificent."

"But you haven't seen me yet," she said without even knowing how much her words affected me.

"I plan to see you tonight."

I felt her shivering.

Then the priest started the ceremony. We were both smiling, genuinely happy the whole time.

Finally, it was time for our vows.

The priest asked her and, she said, "I do."

I sighed after hearing her. When the priest asked me, I didn't think twice before saying "I do."

"I pronounce you husband and wife. Now you may kiss your bride."

I pulled off her veil and looked at her beautiful face.

"You're beautiful and mine," I said and captured her lips with mine, kissing her deeply as I pulled her closer to me.

In the background, we both heard the cheers of her friends and her mother. When we pulled away, she was breathless, staring at me with love in her eyes, promising to look at me like this always.

One by one her friends and family greeted us.

"Congratulations. I'm Julia, Hailey's BFF," her friend said.

I nodded my head in recognition, and we both replied with, "Thanks."

"Oh, Hailey, you're looking gorgeous. Your wedding dress is so beautiful. Who is the designer?" her friend asked hugging her.

"Oh! Vanessa, thank you! And I don't know who the designer of this dress is. You have to ask my husband." Hailey looked at me with eyes full of love.

I told her the dress was made by a famous designer in Paris.

"Congratulations." A man came and hugged Hailey. Instantly my guards were up.

My mind started thinking that this was another competitor.

"Hey, Matt. Thanks. Let me introduce you to my husband. Chase, this is my college friend Matt, Vanessa's boyfriend," Hailey introduced the man, making me relax.

I hated feeling jealous, but I couldn't stop myself from getting jealous when another man came near her.

I extended my hand, and after a polite conversation with her friends, we decided to go to the restaurant I booked for our guest to have dinner.

We arrived at the restaurant at 7:00 p.m., and had dinner. After dinner, the waiter brought out the red velvet cake with vanilla icing that I ordered, knowing it was

Hailey's favorite. I picked up Noah in my arms and made him hold the knife while Hailey's hand was placed above his and mine was above her. The three of us cut the cake while others clapped.

We stayed in the poolside area of the restaurant, talking and enjoying some wine.

Her friends took a lot of pictures all over the place. Finally, I called my driver at 8:30 p.m and told him to pick us up.

When we were about to leave, Noah came running to Hailey and said, "Mommy, I want a brother okay. Don't make a sister."

I laughed and picked him up in my arms and kissed his cute face. Hailey's face, on the other hand, was priceless. She was completely red with embarrassment and shock. Her wide eyes and wide open mouth were just so funny. I wished I could capture it.

"Noah, we're not... Who said anything about brother or sister?" Hailey glared at Noah.

"Mommy, Auntie Julia said you're going to make a sister for me," Noah said, looking sad.

"Julia, you devil. Come out! Don't hide from me. I told you not to ruin my child's innocence." Hailey was really angry.

Julia didn't come out, so I interfered.

"Hailey, she's your friend. Cut her some slack. And the car is waiting," I said.

Hailey nodded and turned to Noah. She kissed him on the head while he was still clinging to me.

"Just for tonight, you will stay with your grandma and tomorrow we are going to come and take you to our new home," I said told him, kissing his forehead and receiving a kiss on the cheek in return.

But he still looked sad, so to cheer him up, I whispered, "I'll definitely try to get you a brother soon."

I winked at him, and it put a smile on his face.

He gave me his toothy smile and said, "You're the best dad."

Hailey was already sitting inside the car, waiting for me.

"So where are we going?" she asked me when I got inside the car.

"We're going to our house." I took her hand in mine.

She placed her head on my shoulder.

I intertwined our hands and kissed her head.

Chapter Forty-One

Love Me

Hailey

When we arrived at our house, he scooped me into his arms.

"Chase what are you doing? Let me walk," I said to him.

"No. It's a family tradition. The groom has to carry his bride to their room on the wedding night." He continued walking upstairs to our room.

I knew it was no family tradition and rolled my eyes.

When we reached our room, he placed me on my feet. I looked at the beautiful room decorated in white and gold.

The king-size bed in the center of the room had plain white sheets. White rose petals were scattered all over it. The matching pillows and comforter were set on the bed.

The white chiffon curtains were flowing because of the light breeze coming through the open window. The whole room was decorated with roses and white tulips. Some were even spread on the floor. The fragrance of flowers that filled the room was so relaxing. I took a deep breath.

I turned to see Chase staring at me intensely. My face turned red with a blush at the way he was looking at me.

"Have I told you how beautiful you look in this wedding dress?" he asked me, taking a step closer.

"Yes, you have told me how beautiful I look umpteenth times, including now." I took a step closer to him.

He pulled something out from his pocket.

"What's that?" I asked him curiously.

"It's your wedding gift." He handed me the box.

"Chase, you have given me so many gifts already. There is no need for more gifts for the next ten years," I said, scolding him.

"I can't resist buying gifts for you. Now open it." He looked at me smiling and handing me a jewelry box.

I opened the jewelry box and said, "A bracelet."

"No, it's an anklet." He picked it out from the box.

I looked at the anklet in his hand. It was beautiful. It had a thin golden chain, and small diamond shapes were dangling a few centimeters from each other, making it look so delicate.

"It looks very delicate and beautiful," I said in awe, and he smiled.

"May I?"

I nodded my head in a silent yes. I was standing so he made me sit on the bed. Then he bent down and picked my left foot and placed it on his knee. I pulled my gown up to my knees to give him more access.

He clasped the anklet on my left ankle, and I heard him murmured "Beautiful."

Then I felt his lips on my ankle, kissing his way up to my leg.

My heart thumped at the feeling of his lips on my skin. I shivered when his lips reached my knee. My breath started to haywire. He didn't stop there and pushed my gown up to my thigh.

His lips were so soft, kissing me lightly, transferring some kind of electronic wave in my body.

My hands clenched the sheets underneath me with anticipation when he reached my mid-thigh.

A moan escaped my mouth when I felt his tongue massaging my flesh after biting there.

I was anxious about what will happen tonight. He was my first, and I had never been with anyone else in the past three years. The evil thing was that I didn't even remember anything about the night I spent with him three years ago.

He looked up at me, his passion filled eyes making me breathless.

"Cha... Chase, I don't have any experience," I confessed embarrassed.

He got up, placing my foot down on the floor. He sat beside me on the bed.

"Hailey, you are perfect the way you are," he said, taking my hand in his and kissing.

"Was... was I any good that night?" I glanced down at my feet.

He chuckled lightly at my flushed face.

"No," he said with a teasing smile, making my heart drop. Then he whispered, "You were wild."

I got up from the bed in embarrassment and mumbled that I was going to change. Then I stopped mid-step remembering that I was wearing a wedding dress, which had a low zipper that I couldn't reach. I turned back to find Chase standing and unbuttoning his shirt. And I couldn't help myself from staring at his chiseled chest.

He caught me staring then discarded his shirt on the chair near him. He came closer to me and smiled in amusement, making me blush.

"Anything you want, love?" he asked, leaning closer to my ear.

Why did his voice have to be so sexy and husky?

"Uh... yeah... I... I need help with the dress," I asked him, looking into his eyes, as it started to smolder.

"I will be honored to help you." He moved a lot closer.

I turned my back to him waiting for him to start working on my zipper. He caught the zipper, and his fingers brushed the bare part of my back, making my heart beat faster.

Very slowly he started to pull the zipper down. When his hand brushed the bare skin of my lower back, I got even weaker in the knees.

Finally, the zipper stopped above my hip, and his thumb started to make circles, making my toes curl. I didn't know if I wanted him to stop or continue as my mind was getting hazy.

I felt his lips on my shoulder, kissing his way to my neck. Then he took a small part of my skin in his mouth and sucked on it.

Instinctively, I arched my back, pressing my back on his hard chest and giving him more access to continue his torture. His hand came to rest on my stomach, and he pulled me closer, pressing my bare back against his naked chest.

My eyes were shut. My body was lost in the feel of his sweet tormenting kisses.

"I'm going to show you how much I love you, Hailey," he said, placing a kiss on my collarbone. "And I love kissing you here." He bit my neck with a bit of pressure this time.

I was moaning loudly in pleasure.

"I love it when you moan," he said while his hand was making its way to my breast.

His touch was making me crazy. My stomach clenched at the sensation pooling inside of me

"Cha… Chase." I bit my lips to stop the next moan emerging from my throat as he touched the most sensitive part of my body.

"Don't stop your moans, love. I want to hear them, all night," he whispered in my ear, pulling my dress lower.

His words instantly relaxed my body. All the anxiety I was feeling completely disappeared from my body, leaving me craving for more of his kisses. I wanted his kisses on every part of my body. I wanted to feel his love tonight. His lips were starting a fire inside my body that only he could calm.

"Chase, love me," I said breathlessly, unable to contain my feelings any longer.

He whirled me around to face him then captured my lips in a sensual kiss.

His lips were moving softly, yet there was this urgency like he couldn't believe I was standing there, and I would disappear if he let go of me. My hand sneaked up and fisted his soft hair while the other one was on his neck pressing his mouth closer to mine. His hand was resting on my waist, and the other one was pleasuring my body

I didn't know how and when we got rid of my dress and ended up on the bed without anything to separate us from each other.

His lips were frantic, kissing me, tasting me, and devouring me like a starved man. I was in paradise

The whole night we were spellbound with love, as we revealed the unyielding desire that we kept from each other all these years.

I could never forget the passion and love he showed me all night. His every kiss, his every touch, and his every word were imprinted on my memory. No drug or drink would make me forget this night with him.

That night he made me his forever and gave me memories that were mine to cherish and to keep sealed in my heart and mind.

Chapter Forty-Two

A New Life

Chase

Next morning, I woke up feeling fingers running up and down my chest. I glanced at Hailey and saw her head resting on my chest. Her fingers were leisurely moving up and down on my chest. She stirred inside the cover, and I felt her bare legs tangled with mine, making me groan.

"You're going to be the death of me, Hailey," I said, gripping her wrist with my hand to stop her sweet torture.

"You're awake." She looked at my face, startled.

"Yeah. Your torture woke me up."

"When did I torture you?"

"What were you thinking, running your fingers over my chest would make me sleep peacefully?" I asked, hovering above her face.

"Yes." She looked nervous.

"Let me show you what you were doing to me," I said, running my hand from her neck to her bare breast.

A breathless moan left her mouth when my hand reached her navel.

"Now you know how I was feeling earlier," I said, lightly brushing my lips on her collarbone.

She didn't reply. Instead, she pulled me closer to her and kissed me. I responded, moving my lips over hers slowly. I felt her hands running down my bare back then up towards my head. She lightly fisted my hair and deepened the kiss. She bit my lip, surprising me and entered her tongue into my mouth. She explored my mouth with her sweet tongue. I, on the other hand, was enjoying the taste of her mouth, which made me greedy for more

We pulled away breathless, staring at each other.

After last night she still seemed shy, blushing at my mere touch.

But I loved her shyness, her blush, and especially the pleasure filled noises that she made whenever I pleased her and took her to a place where she had never been before.

Last night with Hailey was so good. She was the best for me even if she didn't know a lot of things. I enjoyed teaching her. She was the sweetest thing I had ever tasted in my life. Her innocence increased the passion between us. Every emotion that she showed me last night was raw and pure because of her inexperience. And I was proud that I was the only man who had seen her in the throes of pleasure. Every detail of last night was engraved in my memory.

"Chase. I... I'm hungry," she said, looking embarrassed.

"Okay then. Go get freshen up. I'll make you something, or we can go out for breakfast if you want."

I got up from the bed.

"Oh! God, cover yourself." I heard Hailey saying.

"What? Baby, you have seen, touched, and tasted everything," I said, picking a robe out from my closet and shrugging it on.

She threw a pillow at me looking bright red, and I winked at her.

I pulled out my boxers, jeans, and shirt along with my towel and said, "I'm going to the next room for a shower. I have bought some dresses for you, and they're hanging in my closet."

I walked towards the bed where she was still sitting with the sheets clutched to her chest, and kissed her head.

Then I left her to give her some privacy. I didn't want to make her feel pressured, overwhelmed, or uncomfortable. I wanted her to feel happy and comfortable with me more than she was now.

After showering, I came out of the washroom and changed into the clothes I bought with me. Then I went back to our room to see if Hailey was ready. Opening the door of my bedroom, I entered and felt my breath knocked out from me.

She was wearing a white off-shoulder dress, which clung to her body perfectly.

"You're looking gorgeous. When I bought this, I knew it will look great on you," I said, running my eyes up and down her.

"Thanks. I'm ready."

"Let's go." I took her hand in mine.

I took her to the best breakfast café that was a ten-minute drive away from our house. We ordered a good amount of breakfast and enjoyed it.

Then we decided to go and pick Noah up from his grandparent's house. When we got there, he was awake and watching cartoons.

"Chase, I need to pack my and Noah's stuff. I'll go start on it because it will take time." She told me.

I nodded in understanding. After three hours, she had packed her and Noah's stuff in two large bags and few small boxes. I took them and deposited them in the trunk.

She bid goodbye to her family while I strapped Noah in his car seat in the back. Then I walked back to my beautiful wife.

"Goodbye, sir," I said, extending my hand to her dad.

"Goodbye, and take good care of my girl." He patted my back.

"I promise. This time, I won't disappoint you," I said, glancing down as regret started seeping into my brain.

"I hope so, son." He smiled at me.

"Chase, honey. Promise me, you are going to come here every weekend with Noah and Hailey," her mom said.

"I promise." I hugged her.

I wished my mother would also change and realize her mistakes like Melanie did. Melanie was a changed person now and truly loved Noah and Hailey.

After thirty minutes of driving, we finally reached our destination. I pulled Noah from the backseat then shut the door and took Hailey, hand in mine.

"Dad, is this your house?" Noah had a cute smile on his face.

"Well, son. It's not only my house. It's yours too. Basically, it's your mommy's house. She is the boss of this place," I said to Noah.

He had a frown on his face.

"So we're not going back to Grandma and Grandpa?" he asked me with a sad face.

"No, we are not going to live there. You, your mommy, and I are going to live here. We'll ask your Grandma and Grandpa to come here, and we can always go there too," I suggested while kissing Hailey on the head.

Noah smiled.

"I have a surprise for you," I said.

His face instantly lit up with a smile.

"Where is it?" he asked me curiously.

"Come, I'll show you." I took him upstairs and opened the door of his room.

"Oh thanks, Daddy. It's so cool," he said, staring at his room.

I made sure during the renovation that the theme of his room would be his favorite game: football.

Hailey was smiling at Noah and me. I felt like I had successfully won their hearts. My sole reason for doing everything was to make the two most important people in my life happy, and they were happy.

$$* \qquad * \qquad *$$

Hailey

[Three months]

"Chase your phone has been ringing for the past ten minutes," I said, walking in the washroom where he was showering, hidden behind the blurry glass door.

He slid the glass door a little and asked, "Is it my mom's number?"

"No. It's an unknown number." I rolled my eyes.

He was still hiding from his family the fact that we were married or in the right sense remarried. He even succeeded in convincing me to hide it from Allison and Cameron. Chase had turned paranoid, and he thought that his mother would again do something to separate us.

"Chase, darling. You're getting so paranoid about your mother. She's not going to do the same thing again." I tried reassuring him.

"I know my mother, and I don't trust her," he replied.

"Okay. I'm going to set dinner. Please hurry and come down once you're done."

"I thought you wanted to join me in the shower," he mumbled.

"Maybe tomorrow if you decide to come home early from the office," I yelled and walked out of the washroom.

Chase had transferred his office here and had been working from there for the last three months. If something important came up, he would go to Boston for a day or two. He had hinted that he wanted us to transfer to Boston after my study would be completed here. I liked the idea of moving to Boston because I could see how difficult it was for him to handle his business from here. But I needed a year more to finally graduate.

His cell phone started ringing in my hand again, and in irritation, I picked it up.

"Hello."

"Hello. Can I talk to Chase?" I heard a feminine voice on the other line.

"Um, he is busy at the moment. You can leave a message if you want. I'll deliver it to him," I said to the woman on the line, thinking that maybe she was his colleague or business partner.

"Can I ask you who you are?"

"I'm his wife. You can tell me. Don't worry," I replied.

I thought that maybe she was having trouble trusting me.

"Oh. Then his wife, please, tell him to call his mother urgently," the woman shouted, and the line went dead.

Chase came out of the washroom in a towel wrapped around his lower body and saw me standing like a statue with his phone still pressed to my ear.

"Hailey, what happened? Are you fine?" he asked me concerned.

He took his phone from my hand and threw it on the bed.

He cupped my face and asked, "Hailey, tell me."

"Chase... I answered your phone."

"So what? You can answer it. You're my wife," he said looking nonchalant.

"But it was your mom's call."

He instantly turned pale and looked scared.

"She asked me who I am and I told her that I'm your wife. I thought she was some business colleague." I tried explaining to him.

"Relax Hailey. Don't worry. I'll handle it," he said, hurriedly changing into his sweatpants and shirt.

We walked downstairs where Noah was sitting on the couch. His head snapped up when he heard us coming.

"Daddy, look at my art," he said, showing Chase and me his art paper.

"Wow. It's good."

He turned to me with a hopeful face, waiting for me to compliment him.

"It's really nice. We'll keep it in your art folder, okay? Now come. Let's have dinner," I said, making my way towards the table.

I placed dinner, and we ate in silence. Then I took Noah with me to his room. After changing him into his nightdress, I made him brush his teeth. When he fell asleep, I left his room and went to study. Chase was sitting there on the chair with his hands folded, looking deep in thought.

"Hey, what happened?" I asked him.

He glanced at me and extended his hand. I placed my hand in his, and he pulled me on his lap.

"She wants to meet my wife. I didn't tell her that it's you. She told me to come to New York next week because she has planned dinner for the whole family," he said with a grim face.

"Chase, we'll go. Sooner or later this secret has to come out. We can't hide this our whole lives." I caressed his jaw.

"You're right," he said, placing his head on mine.

Chapter Forty-Three

Attending Dinner

Hailey

My head was resting on Chase's shoulder while he was busy watching a movie with Noah. Noah was becoming so attached to Chase that I sometimes felt neglected. He was always asking him to go and play in the park, not me. But inside I knew he was a kid who just got his father, and if you had a father like Chase, I thought it was very hard not to love him and get attached.

Chase was now completely a changed man. He was very different from the boy I fell in love with. He was so caring towards us that sometimes I was forced to think how I had lived this long without him.

Chase always knew what to say to make me laugh. He always knew how to convince our son to do something or not to do something.

Without even hearing me ask, he understood that I needed his help for my thesis. He would just come to me and help me even if he was tired himself.

When he knew I was on shark week and felt like laughing hard then crying in a blink of an eye, he took care of me like a newborn baby.

He told me I was his princess and now I had really started to feel like one. I regretted the day I wished would die because of what happened in our past. I regretted thinking about death because if I knew that I would get him after surviving all the pain, I would have never begged for it in the first place

I felt a light kiss on my head, making me open my eyes.

"Huh. Thinking about something intense again?" he asked.

That was what I was talking about. He always knew everything before I could tell him personally.

I was starting to get suspicious that he was a mind reader.

"I'm just thinking about us and tomorrow's dinner," I said, giving him a small smile then my eyes went to the sleeping Noah on his lap.

The laptop was still on Noah's small lap; they had been watching a movie.

Chase saw me looking at our sleeping son and said, "He must be tired after the long flight."

I nodded my and picked the laptop up from his lap and kissed his forehead.

"Make room so I could lay him there," Chase said.

I nodded and cleared out some space in the center of the bed. Chase lay him there and kissed his head mumbling a good night.

We were in a hotel room in New York. We decided to come here a day before dinner, just to make sure we would not chicken out. Everyone was coming to this family dinner: Allison, Cameron, and Kate with her husband and son.

No one knew that I would be coming to dinner, and I had no idea how they would react upon seeing me after three years.

"You're thinking again, Hailey," he said, taking my hand in his and pulling me off of the bed.

"Sorry, I just I think I'm a little nervous about tomorrow," I told him honestly.

He dragged me to the balcony that had a view of the sparkling New York night. This city never slept. It was young and filled with enthusiasm like the youth that lived here.

"Hailey, you know I won't force you if you don't want to meet them. I will just go alone tomorrow and tell her some fabricated story then come back to the hotel. We can just enjoy our visit here than go back home," he said, looking ahead.

"Chase, please don't give me ideas. We have to do this, you know that. I'm just nervous about their reaction. I know Allison, Cameron, and your dad would be happy to see me, but Kate and your mom is another story. They are unpredictable." I looked into his eyes.

He cupped my face in his hands and pulled me closer. Placing his head on mine, he said, "You know, I don't give a fu*k what they both think anymore. The day she tried to kill you, and my son then made me leave you was the day she lost all my respect."

I sighed. I could feel his pain with every word, and I understood his feelings now.

"Chase, you can't stay mad at her. She is your real mother. You have seen with your own eyes how Melanie changed, so maybe your mother will change as well. She used to be so sweet to me before she found out that I was pregnant. I don't know what made her hate me."

"I know, Hailey. I wish she could change, but she hasn't changed. Listen here, whatever happens, tomorrow, you keep this in your pretty little head that I am always with you. If they don't accept you and create drama we will leave right away," he said to me, making me nod my head in a silent yes.

"Now tell me, do you want to eat ice cream? All four flavors?"

I blushed.

He remembered my craving during my pregnancy. When I wished to eat ice cream, he came to my door with them.

"I'm not pregnant, so I have no crazy cravings tonight, Mr. Edwards."

"Are you sure?" he asked me.

I nodded my head.

"Then Mrs. Edwards, I think I need to work hard. I promised our son that he will have a brother to play with soon," he said, pulling me to his chest.

"Chase, shut up!" I slapped his chest.

"What? Don't you think it would be nice if he will have a brother to play with him? We will get more alone time to spend with each other," he said again, luring me in with his talks.

"Chase, we have talked about this. You know, I have to graduate from my college first. I'm not saying that I don't want more kids, but I want to finish college first." I glanced at his face.

"I know, Hailey. I am just teasing you," he said, pecking my lips lightly.

Then the small peck on the lips morphed into a heavy make-out session on the balcony.

[Dinner night]

I glanced at Chase in the mirror. He was looking mouthwatering in his casual fitted jeans with a white shirt, and that color just made him look even sexier.

His unshaven face was something I cherished. He knew how much I liked it, so he tried keeping it that way most of the time.

I glanced at Noah who had been trying for the past five minutes to tie his shoes. I got up from the chair to help him, but Chase kneeled down and showed him how to tie his shoes.

I smiled at them and said, "Hey, come on stand up. I want to take a picture of both of you."

Chase picked Noah up in his arms, and they both made the cutest pout I had ever seen. Clicking and uploading the picture, I gave them a thumbs up and turned around to take one last look at myself.

I picked a simple white knee-length dress and applied light makeup to give my skin a fresh look. I had put my hair in a bun on my head, which wasn't looking that bad. Simple diamond studs were adorning my ears, another gift from my handsome husband, and the anklet he gave me on our wedding night was clasped around my ankle.

It made me recall the memories of our wedding night, and a shiver went through my body.

"You're looking magnificent. I would love to ravish you here," Chase said, placing a kiss on my neck while standing behind me.

His kisses made my inside mush. It was usually hard to resist what he offered.

"Chase, please I'm already too nervous, and your antics will make me hot and bothered then we will end up not going to dinner," I said pleading with him so he would stop looking at me with those lustful eyes.

"I don't know how to control myself around you, Hailey. Sorry, if I made you uncomfortable." He distanced himself a little. I hated it when he doubted himself or thought that he was making me uncomfortable.

I moved closer to him and placed my lips on his. I gave him a deep, passionate kiss, which he fully enjoyed.

Then I pulled away breathless and said, "You're looking so handsome and sweet that sometimes I don't even know how to resist you. I would love it if you ravish me, but Noah is here, and we really need to go. Most importantly you never make me uncomfortable. Instead, you make me feel so many other things, which I would love to show you, but this is not the right time," I said, stepping away from.

He was staring at me with his jaw dropped. I thought my little speech left him stunned.

"Wow. You just… Wow. Let's go, woman," he said, dragging me out of our room and my sweet baby followed behind us.

He was looking cute in his small jeans and shirt that was the same color as his dad's.

We reached the hotel lobby and waited for the valet to get our car, and that was when some people stared at us. I even saw some girls checking out Chase, which made me really jealous.

After thirty minutes of driving, we arrived at Chase's house. We got out of the car, and I reminded Noah that this was his grandparents' house and he had to be on his best behavior. Being a sweet and understanding kid, he nodded his head.

I gripped Noah's hand in mine and Chase gripped my hand in his as we walked towards the door.

A man opened the door and looked at Chase wide-eyed then glanced at Noah and me.

"Hailey, this is Evan Thompson. He is Kate's husband. And Evan this beautiful woman is my wife, Hailey and this is Noah, my son." Chase introduces us.

The man, Evan Thompson looked so shocked. He was just staring at us, and for a second I thought he would drop dead.

"Hi, Evan." I extended my hand, which he took it.

"Hi, sorry. I'm just shocked. "Aren't you his ex-wife?" he asked.

Chase glared at him, and I nodded.

"You're really beautiful. I heard a lot about you from Cameron," he said, glancing at me up and down.

I blushed, and Chase cleared his throat. He was glaring at Evan nonstop. I knew Evan used to be a lady's man before he got married to Kate.

"No need to feel jealous, Chase. I just like to appreciate beauty when I see one," Evan said and picked up Noah in his arms.

Chase just clenched his jaw. Then Evan ushered us in and lead us to the back garden of the house.

"Everyone look who we have here," he said loudly.

Everyone's head snapped in our direction, and they looked at us in complete shock.

Cameron was the first one to recover from his shock. He got up from his seat and walked towards me.

"Hailey, it's you. Oh, God," he said and hugged me.

I patted his back, giggling at his shocked face.

"Yes, it's me. Here is Noah," I said, pointing at my left.

"Uncle Cameron," Noah yelled and wiggled out from Evan's arms then jumped into Cameron's arm.

Cameron kissed his head and hugged him, spinning him around making Noah giggle.

Allison got up and came to hug me. Then, Chase's dad came and hugged Noah and me. Everyone was smiling, looking happy except Kate and his mom. Their eyes were filled with disapproval.

His mom got up and walked to us. She stared at our faces angrily.

"Chase, what is this? Is this some kind of a joke? What is this witch doing here with you?" she asked.

Suddenly, there was complete silence.

"Mom, mind your language when talking about my wife. She is not a witch, but you're an evil mother," he said.

I gasped at his cruel choice of words and squeezed his hand.

"Allison, can you take the kids inside?" I said, already guessing what was going to happen next.

She nodded and hurriedly ushered Noah, Susan, and Chris inside the house.

"Please, you don't need to be cruel to each other. It will only make things complicated," I said, trying to convince them to be polite to each other.

"Shut up, girl. Because of you, my son left this house. Now don't act innocent," she shouted at me.

But before I could say anything, we all heard some woman's voice from the back. "Is everything alright here?" she asked us, making me go stiff.

Chapter Forty-Four

Disastrous Dinner

Hailey

Everyone had gone silent and looked at the woman like she was some alien who crashed into our house from a different planet.

Chase's booming voice broke the heavy silence.

"What the hell are you doing here?" he asked the woman, scaring her.

"Your mother invited me." She glanced at Chase and Eva.

"Great. Mom, can you please explain to me, why the hell have you invited Clara here?" he asked angrily.

He was glaring at his mother and was having a hard time controlling his anger.

"I… I thought you married her and you were both keeping it a secret from us. I thought I should invite her to show my acceptance towards your relationship," she said, making me flinch.

It felt like she just slapped me by telling me how she thought Clara was the more deserving one to stand beside her son.

"How generous of you mother," Chase murmured, gritting his teeth.

"Excuse me. I'm a little lost here. Who married whom and keeping it a secret?" She was looking at Chase curiously while asking him.

"Clara, meet my wife, Hailey Edwards," Chase said, placing his hand on my back and pulling me closer to him.

I awkwardly gave her a small smile, but I could feel she was going to explode. Her face was completely red and was giving away how angry and jealous she was at that moment.

Clara stared at me from head to toe and then turned her attention back to Chase.

"Chase, you're joking, right?" she asked him.

"No, I'm serious. She is my wife." He answered her in a monotone voice.

"How can you do this to me, Chase? We were engaged," she said, looking sad.

I felt sympathy for her and her obsession towards Chase.

"Oh, so when did I propose to you? Do you have any ring? No? Did I ever show interest in you? Have I ever hinted that I want anything more than friendship with you?" Chase asked, glaring at her.

Instead of answering him, she attacked me like a crazy woman, pushing me backward. It was because of Chase's arm on my lower back that I caught my balance on time and saved myself from falling.

"You bitch! How dare you steal my man? You whore! You're leaving me just because of some one-night stand. I'm going to kill this bitch." She was out of control and tried to attack me again.

But Chase gripped her arm tightly and dragged her away from me. A whimper escaped her mouth, and her eyes turned glossy as Chase's grip tightened on her arms.

"Listen here, Clara, and listen well because I will not repeat this again. She is my wife for the last four years, and we have a three-year-old son. We had some misunderstanding because of some people, but we have cleared things up now, and we are back together. So I'm warning you to never show your face to me again. And if you ever think of hurting my wife, I will kill you," he said to her.

Clara didn't talk back instead she was crying lightly.

"Do you understand me, Clara?" he asked her, and when she didn't answer him, he tightened his grip on her arms, making her cry in pain.

She nodded her head hurriedly in a silent yes, making Chase release his hold on her arms.

I shivered, looking at Chase. I had never seen this side to him before. He never got this angry at anything, and I never wanted to see this side ever again because he really looked scary. All the softness on his face vanished, and his voice sounded really harsh, making him look dangerous and threatening.

His eyes met mine, and they instantly softened. I saw a glint of regret in his eyes as he glanced at me. He realized how scared I felt finding him this angry.

He was about to walk towards me when his mother spoke, making him stop.

"Chase, you are acting like you have never treated her badly. And if my memory serves me right, you hated Hailey. You were the one who divorced her, and now you are protecting her? Tell me. Is she blackmailing you to make you act like this?" she asked Chase.

After spending so much time with my husband, I could tell by looking at him how much he loathed those memories.

I started feeling uneasy and wanted to say something before everything went out of hand, but Chase's voice stopped me from saying anything.

"Mom, are you calling her a blackmailer when you know very well who blackmailed whom? Yes, I treated her badly because I thought she was ruining the future you planned for me. I was scared of disappointing you, so I pushed her back. But I was so wrong, Mom. She was my freedom. She was my freedom from all the plans you made for me since the day I was born," he said, looking straight into my eyes.

I could understand what he was feeling. The constant pressure to be someone who people would appreciate was too much for him. He was something else, and his mother was trying to make him someone else.

"I fell in love with her, Mom. I tried really hard to stop myself from falling for her, but at the end, my attempts were all futile. I realized that no matter what I do to make her hate me, we would still end up together. I had to make her leave because if she had stayed, you would have made her life a living hell." He continued, making everyone's eyes misty.

Allison and I had tears in our eyes because we understood his pain better than others.

"Oh. Then why did you divorce her? Pray tell me, sweet son?" she asked him.

His eyes turned cold, and he glared at his mom.

"You really want to know why, mother?" he asked his mother, shouting.

I saw a flicker of fear in Eva's eyes before she very skillfully concealed it and nodded. She knew he wouldn't tell the truth in his father's presence.

"I made my wife and child leave because of you, mother. I never wanted to divorce her and get separated from my then one-week-old son. But you made me do that by blackmailing me that you would sell your shares of the Edwards Investing Company and ruin my dad," he yelled.

I wanted to stop him, to leave this place, and to never come back but a part of me also knew that he really wanted it out from his chest.

"Mom, do you know how it feels like to rip a part of your body with your own hands? No? That's what I felt when I told Hailey that I wanted a divorce and made her leave with our son," he shouted.

His mom looked shocked, and her mouth hung open at her son's revelation.

"Mom, if I didn't catch you that day with Kate talking about getting her an abortion, I would've never found out how dangerous you were for my son and wife," he said, making everyone gasp.

"Eva, what's Chase talking about? Is it true? Were you the reason behind their divorce?" William looked at his wife in anger.

"Yes, I blackmailed him. I told him I would sell our company's share just to make him divorce Hailey. I could never hurt you, William. I just threatened him so he would divorce her. And yes, I was thinking of getting her abortion because I thought she was too young to give birth. I had doubts that the child was Chase's," she said, trying to explain.

"I just can't believe it, Eva. I just can't believe that I have spent thirty-five years of my life with you and I still don't know you. Dammit! Hailey was his wife, Eva. She wasn't just any random girl who he knocked up and didn't want to take responsibility for his child. How can you ruin your own son's life?" Chase's dad looked really disappointed at his wife's actions.

"But William, I thought I was helping him get rid of the unnecessary burden," she replied, trying to appear innocent.

"Don't call my son an unnecessary burden, Mom. Don't! He is my son, not a burden, and not a mistake. You never noticed my love for him. You never noticed my connection with him or with her because you were so busy hating her. I spent countless nights talking to my son when he wasn't even born yet and connected with him. But the first thing you did, when he was born, you asked doctors to run a paternity test. Even after, I repeatedly told you that he is my son." Chase was shouting at his mother.

I glanced at Chase and realized how tired he looked. Sweat beads were forming on his forehead, and he was breathing heavily.

I was concerned about him, so I walked to him and hugged him. I felt his hand tightly wrapped around me, embracing me, and he kissed my head.

"I'm sorry, Hailey. It wasn't a good idea to come here," he murmured lightly in my ear.

"Chase… You don't have to say sorry for anything. It's not your fault." I rubbed his back.

Then suddenly, I felt something wet on my cheek and looked up thinking that maybe they were tears falling from his eyes, but I was so wrong. My body became frozen in shock.

Blood was running down from his nose, and he looked dazed. I caught him in my arms in time and shouted for help.

Cameron and Evan ran to us and helped Chase sit on the nearest chair. I kneeled down in front of him and looked at him.

Allison got tissues and kneeled down beside me.

"Chase, your nose is bleeding." I stammered and cleaned the blood with my trembling hands.

"Don't worry, Hailey. Just promise me you will stay with me," he said and pulled me closer to his chest.

I placed my arms around his neck and hugged him. Suddenly, his body went limp in my arms. My heart stilled at that moment, and I felt like someone tilted my world upside down.

Chapter Forty-Five

Never Leaving You Again

Hailey

After Chase fainted, we rushed him to the hospital. Now we were waiting in the waiting area for the doctors to come out of his room and inform us about his condition.

I was sitting on the chair lost in my own thoughts while tears rolled down my face.

We heard the sound of a door opening and then found doctor and nurses coming out from his room.

"Where is Chase Edwards' family?" the nurse asked.

"Yes. I'm his wife. Is he alright?"

She gave me a small smile.

"He is fine, just sleeping at the moment because of sedatives. Dr. Carl will tell you the details if you would follow me," she said.

I nodded my head and followed her. I could feel that Chase's parents and Cameron were also following the nurse.

We all entered the doctor's office.

"I'm Hailey, Chase Edwards' wife, and they are his parents," I told the doctor.

"Yes. Please take a seat."

I sat down on the chair, and Chase's father took the empty seat beside me.

"So we have a scan of your husband's brain, and this point here shows an enormous sized tumor," the doctor said, pointing at the scan.

Did my heart stop beating? It did.

"And I'm really sad to announce that his tumor is in the last stage. We have found some traces of medicine in his blood test, which he must have been taking for a while to treat this tumor, but they are just worsening his condition. We can remove the tumor by surgery, but at this stage, patients have a risk of getting long-term amnesia, and most of the time after surgery, patients end up in a permanent coma or if the condition gets worse, they end up dead. I believe that this kind of attacks like he had today would also increase if we will take more time in making a decision. For now, we have given him some sedatives to lessen his stress, and we are keeping him here tonight under observation."

"What do you recommend we do? When is the right time to do this surgery?" Chase's dad asked him.

"At this stage, we don't recommend surgery because it sadly doesn't go in favor of the patient. But if some patients take the risk, there will be only 20% chance that they will survive. Sometimes people stay alive, but they lose their memory, and that made it difficult for them to live, and some end up in a coma."

His last explanation left me gasping for air.

I pushed my chair back and got up then left the room without saying anything. I went to the room where Chase was admitted. He was resting on the bed motionless. His breathing was even, and his eyes were closed. I felt my heart contracting in my chest and pain exploded, making me take a step backward. I leaned on the nearest wall for support but my legs gave up, and I slid down.

"You can't leave me, Chase... You can't. After, giving me hopes of happily ever after you can't leave me... I will not let you go." I chanted that lightly then my eyes shut and blackness consumed me.

Next morning, when I woke up, I found myself in the room, which I left three years ago. I sat up on the bed and saw Noah sleeping beside me. I kissed his head.

I went down to the kitchen where everyone was sitting and having breakfast. When they saw me, they stopped and stared at me like I was some ticking bomb.

"Why am I here? How did I even get here?" I asked them, feeling confused.

"You fainted last night, and we found you on the floor in Chase's room, so we brought you here," Allison answered me.

"I want to go to the hospital right now." I demanded desperately.

"Okay. Evan will take you but first, have some breakfast. You haven't eaten anything from last night," she said, looking concerned.

"No, Al. I am not hungry at the moment. I just want to go to the hospital to visit Chase." Tears were pooling in my eyes again.

"Chase is fine. Cameron stayed with him last night. He just called me and informed that Chase will be discharged soon and will come back home," she said, wiping the tears from my face.

"Really?" I couldn't believe what she just told me.

"Yes. Now you go get freshened up. I have placed a dress of mine in your room," she said to me, pushing me out of the kitchen.

I went back to the room and freshened up. Then I got changed into a blue long sleeved, knee-length dress. I went downstairs and there he was sitting on the couch, changed into a grey t-shirt and jeans, talking to Cameron.

When his eyes meet mine, he got up from the couch. I ran towards him and flung myself into his waiting arms.

"Oh, God. Chase, you scared me to death. Please, promise me you will not do something like that to my fragile heart again," I mumbled while crying on his chest.

"Hailey, don't cry, baby. You know I hate tears in your eyes." He tightened his arms around my waist.

Finally, after a few minutes, I pulled away from him.

"I'm sorry for lying to you again," he said, looking down at his feet in guilt.

It dawned on me what he was talking about.

"Chase, you knew about the tumor, and you never thought to discuss it with me? I am your wife, your partner, and you hid it from me."

"Hailey, I just I…" He tried to find the right words to explain, but there was nothing he could say to defend his lie.

"Chase, how long did you know about this?" I asked him, making him uncomfortable.

"Hailey. I… I found out two years ago that I have a tumor."

My breath hitched.

He tried to move closer to me, but I took a few steps back creating a space between us. A sudden hurt flashed on his face, making me sad, but at that moment I was way too hurt to care.

"Why? Why did you hide this from me?" I cried.

"Hailey, please. I know I've hurt you but please, hear me out," he said, trying to reach me again.

"Save it. I don't want to hear more lies." I left and went outside to the backyard.

I had been sitting there on the grass under my favorite tree for the past fifteen minutes when he came outside and sat beside me.

"One day, I was working in my office when I felt a sudden pain in my head and fell unconscious. Jack came to visit me that day and found me passed out. He took me to the hospital where they ran a few tests on me. And next day, the doctor informed me that I have a tumor in my brain. He prescribed me some medicines, but nothing worked, my condition got worse. So I decided that I would never contact you again because death seems so near. I thought you will be better without me. But that day, when you called me, I broke all the walls I had put up all these years. I came to you and confessed everything. I never wanted to give you false hope, but I became selfish because I craved your love, and time with my son before death would snatch every chance away from me to be with you. I truly wanted to feel your love and die in your arms, Hailey," he said, placing his head on my lap.

The tears were now falling from my eyes freely. I wanted to hate him for hiding this from me and stay angry. But I couldn't blame him for hiding anything.

I wanted to kiss him and never let him go. I loved him so much that I wouldn't be able to live without him. I wouldn't be able to survive in this world if anything happened to him. This time it would be too difficult to repair my broken heart.

I ran my fingers through his silky hair and placed a kiss on his forehead.

"Nothing is going to happen to you, Chase. You're going to be fine."

"Hailey only 20% of patients survive at this stage. I don't think I am that lucky," he said, staring at the sky.

"I'm sure. I will ask God to take my life instead of yours." I glanced at his face.

"Don't say something like that, Hailey. As long as you are alive, healthy, and smiling, I would be happy too. It doesn't matter if I will be dead or alive. I just want you and my son happy with me or without me." He snuggled his face into my stomach to hide the mist in his own eyes.

"I don't know how. But I promise you, nothing will happen to you. And did you forget your promise about giving Noah a brother?" I asked him, giving him a watery smile.

"Well, that's really a great motivation you just gave me." He smiled and placed a kiss on my stomach, making me giggle.

Then we just sat there for a few more minutes and enjoyed the peacefulness of our surroundings. After that, we got up and went inside where Noah was sitting on the table and eating pancakes. When he saw Chase and me, he jumped into his arms. Chase surprisingly caught him in time otherwise he would surely have fallen and injured himself.

"Daddy, where did you and Mommy go last night?" He asked innocently, glancing at Chase.

"We went to visit some relatives. Now, you tell me, little boy. Did you meet Chris and Susan?" Chase tickled him in the stomach.

Noah's musical laugh made everyone's eyes turned to him.

"Daddy, Chris knows how to play chess. He told me you and he played it all the time. Will you teach me, Daddy?" Noah asked Chase in a hopeful voice.

"Yes. I will teach you, son." He kissed his head.

After that, we had breakfast and went back to the living room.

"We have a flight in three hours, so we need to leave." Chase glanced at me.

"Can't you stay here? We can arrange for the best doctors in New York and ask for their advice before we make the final decision for your surgery." Eva suggested, looking hopeful.

"No. I think we should go back home and I will ask my doctor about surgery."

Chase's voice was firm when he replied to his mother, which left no room for discussion, but she tried her luck again.

"But Chase we are your family. We want to be with you. You're my son. I can't just sit here after knowing the state you are in while you go back to God knows where," Eva said, staring at Chase with tears in her eyes.

"Mom, Hailey has a college to attend, and I have an office to take care of. We are going back home, and for your information, there are also good doctors where I live." Chase angrily answered.

"Son, you shouldn't travel in this state," William stated, concerned.

"No, Dad. I'm perfectly fine. I don't want to stay here in this house where people don't respect my choices." Chase glanced at his mother and Kate.

"Chase, I'm sorry. Please, forget everything and stay here." Eva pleaded, crying.

"Mom, I am not going to change my decision and don't ask me for forgiveness because it's not easy to forgive you. I can't forget everything you did." Chase glanced at his mom, and his face turned soft.

"Chase, I think we should stay here. Don't worry about my college. I will ask for leave, and your office will be fine without you for a few days, I am sure," I said to Chase.

I really wanted him to spend this time with his family.

I knew they wanted us to stay here. I also wanted support from Cameron and Allison. They had been my best friends after all these years, and I couldn't go through all this without them.

"Brother, you can live in my apartment if you don't want to stay here. I just bought it a week ago," Cameron suggested.

"Yeah. Cameron and I want to spend more time with Hailey and Noah. We haven't even got the time to spend with you both." Allison also added.

Now, I knew Chase wouldn't be able to say no because frankly there had was reason left for him to state.

"Okay," he finally said the words we all wanted to hear.

The whole day passed making appointments with the best doctors in New York. When night came, we went to his old room, which Allison and I cleaned earlier.

He pulled me close to his chest until there was no space left between us. Then he planted his lips on mine, kissing me passionately. After a few minutes, we pulled away breathing hard.

"I've been dying to kiss you all day," Chase said, staring into my eyes lovingly.

I didn't reply to him. Instead, I kissed him, pouring my love and my want for him.

"Chase, you're the most important person in my life. I cannot live without you if anything happened to you, so you have to fight and win. I'll die without you. Please, promise me that you wouldn't leave me," I said.

He pecked my lips again and placed his head on mine.

"I will never leave you," Chase said.

I placed my lips on his and kissed him, wishing that time would stop.

Chapter Forty-Six

Taking a Risk

Hailey

Next day, we arranged an appointment with the best doctors in New York and discussed Chase's case with them. They briefed us completely about the pros and cons of the surgery.

The risk of amnesia after surgery was measurably high, but to our disappointment there was no other way to remove the tumor. It was like a do-or-die situation for us.

But I was optimistic about the decision of surgery. There was this hopeful voice in my heart that assured me everything would go fine.

It was decided that tomorrow he would undergo surgery in the presence of five well-known doctors of New York City Hospital.

"Hailey. You have spaced out again," Allison said, making me jump.

"Sorry. I was just thinking about tomorrow." I stared at the lunch table we were setting.

"I can't even comprehend what you're feeling right now. But Hailey you have to be strong for him and your son," she said, giving a light a squeeze to my hand.

I nodded my head, but tears had already started to pool in my eyes, making me blink to stop them from falling.

"Let's go. They're waiting for us," Allison said, dragging me outside.

Chase smiled at me, and I took the seat beside him. He glanced at my face, and his smile disappeared.

"Were you crying again?" he whispered in my ear.

"No." I lied.

"But your eyes are telling me another story," he said, staring at my face.

"No. It's because of the smoke in the kitchen." I averted my eyes from his face.

"I have planned something for us," he whispered in my ear, lightly brushing his lips on the outline of my ear.

The feeling of his lips turned my inside into mush. I looked into his eyes.

Chase's dad cleared his throat loudly to snap us out from our own haze of love. I blushed when my eyes landed on the teasing smile on Allison and Cameron's face. Chase was just grinning stupidly.

The rest of the lunch went peacefully without any more embarrassing moments for me.

[Night]

I was helping Allison in cleaning the table after dinner when Chase came and dragged me upstairs to our room.

"Why have you dragged me here?" I asked him baffled.

"I have dragged you here to tell you that tonight we are going to sneak out from the house." He smiled broadly.

"Chase. You need to rest for the surgery tomorrow. We are not sneaking out and going anywhere. End of discussion," I said, scolding him for even thinking about this stupid plan.

"Baby, grant this one wish from a dying man." He played the dying man card with me.

"You're incorrigible," I said.

The smile reappeared on his face.

After dinner, everyone went to their rooms, and I picked the sleeping Noah from my bed then went to Allison's room. I didn't want him to wake up and get scared if he couldn't find Chase and me. Noah was familiar with Allison so he would listen to her.

"Please take care of him. He has a habit of turning after every hour," I said to Allison, placing Noah on her bed.

"Don't worry about him. Tell me, where are you guys going?"

"I don't know where we are going. Your brother has been really secretive throughout the day," I replied to her with a smile.

"Go enjoy." She pushed me out the room and closed the door behind me.

I went downstairs where he was waiting for me.

"Have you packed everything that I told you to pack?" he asked me, taking the small duffel bag from my hand.

"Yes, boss. Now tell me where are we going?" I waited for his reply.

"We're going to the beach," Chase said, dragging me towards the car.

"Chase! Are you out of your mind? Why are we going to the beach at this time?" I protested, making him stop.

"The beach is only a thirty-minute drive away from here, and it's not even midnight. Don't be a party pooper." He forced me to get inside the car.

He sat on the driver seat and buckled himself then he started the car.

We reached the beach in twenty minutes because of his crazy speed driving, and there was no traffic on the road.

He pulled the bag and basket out from the back seat.

"Is this some kind of picnic?" I asked Chase, confused.

"Yes, it is. Now follow me." He ordered me, walking ahead.

Chase placed the bag and basket down on the sand then spread a thin sheet. He sat down on it, and he pulled me beside him.

"You're acting weird." I glanced at the beautiful stars in the sky.

"No, I'm not," he replied.

He was also busy in admiring the beautiful view of the beach.

"Remind me again why we are here?" I asked, turning my eyes to gaze at his beautiful face.

"We are here because I want to make this night special for us." He glanced at my face then turned his head to see the waves.

"Every night and day is special if it's with you," I said, scooting closer to his body.

He draped his arm over my shoulder and leaned towards my lips. He brushed his lips lightly on mine, making my heart flutter.

"The things that come out of your pretty mouth have some kind of power on me. My heart rate increases and knees go weak when you say things like that," he said, staring into my eyes.

"It happens to me too, Chase. It's the effect of love." I winked and said.

He smiled at me.

"Hailey, if I... I went into a coma or forget everything, promise me you will remind me of everything. You'll make me fall for you again," he said, caressing my cheek.

"I promise. I will make you fall in love with me again." I brushed my lips against his.

"And if I will die. You will move on with your life," he said with a hopeful voice.

"I can't promise something that's not possible for me to fulfill. Even, after our divorce, I never dated anyone," I told him, making his eyes widened.

"Really?" He looked amused.

"Yes, it is because you own my heart, my body, and my soul. So tomorrow, you have to survive no matter what. You will come back to me," I said, placing a chaste kiss on his jaw.

"Hailey, I'll try my best to come back to you. But whatever happens, remember that I love you. You and Noah mean everything to me." He planted his lips on mine.

My lips moved in sync with his. I let him control the kiss and found myself lost in his heavenly mouth. He ravished my lips like I was the last drop of water on this earth and he wanted to have me completely.

After some sweet amount of time, he pulled away, showing me his talented swollen lips.

"We should go back. It's getting cold here, and I don't want you to get sick," I said, getting up and dusting my jeans.

He got up and held his hand out for me to take. I took hold of his hand, and on the other hand, he picked the basket and bag.

The direction he was going made me confused and I voiced out my confusion.

"You're going the wrong way. Our car is there," I said to him, indicating towards the direction we parked the car.

"No. I'm going the right way." He had a mischievous smile.

My eyebrows rose in confusion, but I followed him nonetheless. He stopped outside a beautiful beach house and let go of my hand then took out the keys from his pockets. He unlocked the door and made his way inside, and I followed him.

He switched on the lights, and I felt my breath quicken.

"Wow," I mumbled, staring at the beautiful room.

The room was decorated with some candles and roses, creating a romantic atmosphere.

"Chase, did you plan this?" I asked him wide-eyed.

"Yes, I did. I want to spend the night here with you." He pecked my lips softly.

I broke the kiss and removed my jacket then threw it on the floor and planted my lips back on his. I was kissing him passionately. My body was full of the fervor of love and burning with passion.

Our movements were frantic when we removed each other's clothes. His hands were everywhere, caressing and loving. He placed me on the bed and crawled to me. His lips were back to assault me, and I was a mess.

[Next morning]

I snuggled in the crook of his neck and sighed. He was running his fingers up and down on my bare back, silently staring at the ceiling.

"Chase," I called his name while running my hand over his hard muscular chest.

"Hmmm." He made a sound to tell me that he was hearing me.

"We should get up and leave," I said, placing a kiss on his chest.

"But I don't want to get up."

I heard the sadness in his voice.

"I know, but we have to go back love," I said, getting up and kissed his lips.

After taking a shower and changing clothes, we left the beach house with beautiful memories of last night sealed inside our hearts.

When we arrived at his house, everyone was up and waiting. It felt like no one got any sleep last night. After an hour, we decided to leave for the hospital.

Chase and I went with Cameron to the hospital, and their parents followed behind in a different car.

When we arrived at the hospital, the nurses took him with them to prepare him for the surgery.

Then he came out wearing a long white shirt and a green surgical cap over his head.

"Love you," I said and gave him a peck on his lips.

"Love you too."

Then the nurses took him inside the operating room.

I was pacing like a mad woman and Cameron had enough of it. He dragged me to the chair and made me sit. Chase's parents were sitting opposite us.

"Hailey, you're shaking. Relax," Cameron said, rubbing my back.

"Cam, please pray for him."

"I've been praying for him, Hailey. He's my only brother. I love him even though I hated him when he divorced you. Evan and I taunted him every dinner about being unlucky and destroying his family. Now we regret it," Cameron said, hiding his face in his hands.

"But he... he never divorced me."

Cameron's head snapped in my direction, and Chase's parents gasped loudly.

"What do you mean he never divorced you? He did it in front of us," Eva said.

"Yes, he made me sign those papers, but he never signed them himself and never submitted them to his lawyers. He pretended to divorce me to make me leave with Noah and to show you that he doesn't want us in his life even though he wanted us more than anything. I found out about this on Christmas when he came to spend it with us."

His mother looked ashamed at what she had done to her own son.

"Now I hate myself more, Hailey," Cameron grunted.

"Don't hate yourself, Cameron. Chase loves you and has always admired you," I said, reassuring him.

An hour passed and no one came out from the operating room. We were all sitting in the waiting area waiting for the doctors to inform us about Chase. Cameron got us coffee, but I wasn't able to take a sip due to the anticipation.

The nurse came out, and I rushed towards her.

"How's Chase?" I asked her.

"He's fine. The surgery is going to take more than three hours." She left us again to endure the silence.

After three hours, the doctor came out. His parents and I stood up from the chair.

"Well good news. The surgery went well. He is on sedatives right now and sleeping peacefully. We'll know if the surgery was as successful as we think it is after he wakes up."

"Can we see him?" I asked him hopefully.

"We're transferring him to his room. Then you can see him," the doctor replied.

"Thank you."

The doctor smiled and left.

Chapter Forty-Seven

Expect the Unexpected

Hailey

"Chase. Please, baby, wake up. You can't do this to me, to Noah... Chase, please open your eyes." I was screaming, cupping his face between my palms, but there was no response.

He was lying on the bed, not moving. The only indication that he was still alive was just his beating heart, nothing else. If he could hear me right now, he would have stopped me from crying.

Placing my head on his chest just above his beating heart, I cried. My cries were ringing loudly in the room while my body shook with every sob.

"Ma'am, please. You have to calm yourself, or we will have to give you something to calm you down," the nurse said to me.

My sobs lightened but the tears didn't stop falling. The nurse left me alone. I moved my eyes up and saw his pale face, but I couldn't see his beautiful grey eyes anymore as they were closed.

I heard someone entering the room, but I didn't have the energy to turn around and face anyone right now.

"Hailey, get up. Let's go home. You don't look okay," Cameron said.

"Cameron, please leave me alone. I... I don't want to move from here. He'll ask for me when he wakes up." I took Chase's hand in mine.

"Hailey, don't do this. I can understand what you're feeling, but you have to be strong for Noah," he said, placing his hands on my shoulder.

"No, I don't want to be strong. Now leave me alone."

He sighed and left me.

I kissed the back of his hand and murmured "Chase you... You have to come back to me."

I spent the whole night with him, praying that he would wake up soon.

After two hours of surgery, the sedatives should have worn off. He should have woken up already, but it didn't happen.

Even after eight hours, he stayed asleep. The doctor told us that he had gone into a coma. They said that he could hear me and feel my touch, but he couldn't respond.

His brain was recuperating and had to shut the entire world out.

I knew he couldn't hear me right now because I had been crying for hours and he didn't even stir to show me that he wanted me to stop crying.

[Two weeks later]

The two weeks had passed, and he was still in a coma. My days and nights were spent here in the hospital, staring at his sleeping face. I hadn't left his side except when I needed to change and shower. The entire week he hadn't responded to my voice, not even once. My heart was dying to hear his voice, to see his cute smile, and to feel his lips on mine again.

"Hailey, I'll stay here. Please go home and stay with Noah. He's getting antsy," Cameron said, making me get up from the chair.

He took the seat beside his brother's bed. I kissed Chase on the head and left the hospital.

The driver was waiting outside to take me home. I felt nausea and dizzy spell on the way. I hadn't been eating properly for the past week so it might be the reason why I felt so low and tired.

Eating was not in my to-do-list since the day Chase went into a coma. I still had hope that he would wake up soon. He had to wake up. He promised me that he would never leave me again.

When I arrived at the house, I stepped outside the car and made my way towards the house. Eva opened the door for me. She was waiting for me to inform her about her son.

"He's still the same," I said, squeezing my eyes shut for a second to get rid of the dizziness.

"He'll wake up soon. I know. And Noah is upstairs."

I nodded my head and went upstairs. I pushed open the door of our room and found Noah sitting on the bed, watching his favorite cartoon. I took a deep breath and prepared myself to answer my son's questions today. I didn't want to keep him in the dark anymore.

"Noah, baby," I said to get his attention, but he didn't reply to me.

He looked angry, and his eyes stayed fix on the cartoon. I walked closer to the bed and sat down beside him.

"Someone is mad with Mommy. *Huh*. What should Mommy do to make Noah a happy baby again?" I pretend to think then I picked him up in my arms and started tickling him.

"Mommy, stop. See I'm not mad at you," he replied giggling.

"Why haven't you eaten anything all morning?" I settled him on my lap.

"I don't want to eat anything. I want Daddy. I want to go home," he said, staring at me sadly.

"We can't go back home yet."

"Why? Mommy, did Daddy leave us again?" he asked me with tears in his eyes.

"No, baby. He is sick. He'll come home soon. Now come I'll make you your favorite mac n cheese." I controlled my tears and waited for him to get up from the bed.

He looked somber but nodded his head. I went downstairs to the kitchen with him. When I entered the kitchen, the strong smell of coffee hit my nose and I felt nauseated again.

I ran back to my room and went inside the washroom. I emptied my stomach. My head started spinning, so I gripped the basin tightly to stop myself from falling on the floor.

I closed my eyes for a few minutes and opened them again. I felt a severe headache, and my body weakened, sliding down on the floor. The tears I had been holding back in front of my son started to fall freely from my eyes.

I cried there for how long I didn't remember. I got up and brushed my teeth and washed my face. When my eyes caught my reflection in the mirror, I saw sunken cheeks, a pale face, and prominent black bags under my eyes from lack of sleep.

Cleaning up myself, I changed into a new set of clothes and went downstairs again to see Noah.

"Mommy, Aunt Allison made me chicken noodles," Noah said, showing me his bowl full of noodles.

I gave him a small smile and turned to Allison.

"Allison, when did you arrive?" I asked her.

"I just arrived here after dropping Chris and Susan off to school. I saw you running back to your room. Is everything alright?" She stared at my face.

"Yeah, I felt a sudden wave of nausea," I said, leaning my head on the counter.

"Hailey, look at your face. You look pale. You have to take care of yourself. What are you going to tell Chase when he wakes up and sees you like this?" She looked concerned about my health.

I nodded my head.

"Did you have breakfast?" she asked me, and I shook my head in a silent no.

She scolded me and served me some toast and coffee.

"Allison, can you please take this coffee back? It smells funny to me and triggering my nausea," I said, giving the coffee mug a disgusted look.

She removed the coffee and placed a glass of milk in front me. Like a mother, she stayed in the kitchen and forced me to finish the whole glass of milk.

"I'm going to the hospital," I said getting up.

"No, missy. You're not going anywhere. You are going to bed right this moment, and you will take a nap." Allison ordered me, giving her best you-have-to-do-this glare.

I sighed and went to my room. I slipped inside the covers and started thinking about the time when I first fell in love with him. I never thought it was just infatuation. I knew from the start that I loved him. He had something special in him that called me towards him.

I missed his smile, his touch, his laugh, and mostly his presence beside me. I missed hearing him say how much he loved me. He made me addicted to his care and his presence. My day felt lifeless because he wasn't here to make me blush with his teasing comments. My body ached to feel his love again. I didn't know what was happening to me but I was falling apart like before, and it was scary.

I felt the tears rolling down from my face and making its way to my neck. I cried silently, wishing he would wake up and come back to me.

I needed him to tell me again that he loved me. I didn't know how long I cried, but sometime later I fell asleep.

When I woke up in the evening, I hurriedly changed into my jeans and a clean shirt. I searched for Noah but didn't find him anywhere.

"Where is Noah?" I asked Eva.

"Allison took him with Chris and Susan to play in the park," she replied.

I nodded my head.

"Are you going somewhere?" she asked me.

"Yes, I'm going to the hospital."

She stayed quiet.

After fifteen minutes of driving, I reached the hospital. I went to his room and was shocked to find Cameron with a girl. They were sitting on the couch and looked deep in conversation.

When they noticed me, Cameron got up.

"Hailey... This is Bianca, my girlfriend," he told me while his face turned a little pink with a blush.

I smiled and extended my hand towards her.

"Hi. I'm Hailey."

"I know. Cameron talks about you and Noah a lot. He even showed me Noah's cute pictures with you and him in matching outfits." She shook my hand.

"Well, I make him wear matching outfits a lot," I said smiling then my eyes went to Chase and my smile disappeared.

"I have prayed for Chase. He'll wake up soon. I never meet him before, but whatever Cameron told me about him, it sounds like he has suffered a lot and doesn't deserve to suffer more." She took my hands in hers and squeezed it.

We talked for a while then they decided to leave.

"Take care and keep your cell phone close," Cameron said, hugging me.

I nodded my head.

Bianca surprised me when she hugged me.

She whispered lightly in my ear, "A blessing will always come and take the pain away."

When she pulled away from me and gave me a small smile, I felt some kind of calmness wash over me.

Her words rang in my head even after she left.

I sat on the chair near Chase's bed and started talking to him.

That evening, the nurse entered the room to check on Chase. She was busy with his checkup when sudden nausea hit me. I ran towards the washroom and threw up whatever Allison made me eat in the morning.

I came out of the washroom, and the nurse was still there waiting for me.

"Is everything fine?" I asked her.

"Yes, his heartbeat and temperature are normal."

I nodded my head.

She was staring at me with weird eyes, making me feel uncomfortable.

"How far along are you?" she asked me.

"Excuse me," I gave her a baffled look.

"Don't tell me you don't know? You're pregnant," she said, laughing lightly.

"I'm not pregnant."

"Oh! I know when I see a pregnant girl. I've got a lot of experience working as a nurse, you know." With that said, she left the room leaving me to think.

We hadn't been using protection since the day we landed in New York. *Could I be pregnant?*

My brain replied, *"Yes. You could be because both of you are equally crazy."*

At that stupid thought, my heart started to beat wildly. A layer of sweat formed on my forehead due to the anticipation.

Then suddenly, I recalled Bianca's words. "A blessing will always come and take the pain away."

I kissed Chase on the forehead and left his room to go and see the doctor.

Chapter Forty-Eight

A Surprise Blessing

A baby is a blessing
A gift from heaven above
A precious little angel
To cherish and to love

Hailey

I was pregnant!

No! Yes! No. No! Yes! Yes.

I was pregnant. Again.

The pregnancy test confirmed that I was pregnant again.

"A blessing will always come and take the pain away."

Oh, God. This baby was indeed a blessing in this situation.

Now, who should I tell first?

Definitely Chase.

A smile was plastered on my face, and I ran back to Chase's room. The people in the hospital glanced at me weirdly when they saw me smiling ear to ear. The nurses I passed by on my way to his room looked at me, frowning.

It wasn't their fault. They had been seeing me gloomy and sad for the past two weeks, and now a sudden change was definitely weird for them.

Finally, I reached outside his room and contemplated if telling him was right or not. *Would he respond to this news? Would he hear me?*

He would be happy to know that we were having another baby. I took a shaky breath and went into his room. Taking slow steps towards his bed, I picked up his hand in mine and kissed it.

Slowly, I leaned down to the level of his ear.

"I just found out a few minutes ago that I'm pregnant again and you're going to become a father of another boy or girl. You have successfully knocked me up again, Chase Edwards. Now, what I am trying to tell you is that I am really excited, and I want you to meet your baby. Please, wake up soon or just do something to show me that you have heard me," I whispered in his ear.

When I finished my rant, he was still the same. He didn't twitch or made any movement. He did nothing to show me that he heard me.

The disappointment started seeping into me, making my heart drop to the pit of my stomach.

He had to be happy. It was what he wanted. He couldn't abandon the three of us like nothing mattered.

Tears rolled down my face, and I wiped them. I was determined to make him realize that he had to come back. He just couldn't stay here motionless.

I pulled my shirt up a little and placed his cold hand on my bare stomach.

"Feel it, Chase. It is our baby. Our child will need you. Noah didn't get to experience the love of his dad when he was still a baby. You... you can't be this cruel and do the same with this child. Chase, you have to wake up. Damn it! You have to wake up. Do you hear me?" I asked him while crying.

Suddenly, I felt his hand moving on my stomach.

I was shocked, and for a moment I thought that I imagined it. But his hand moved again.

Oh, God! He heard me.

Suddenly, the room was filled with a loud beeping noise coming from the heart monitor. I became worried and called for a nurse.

The nurses and doctors came running and started checking him. I was watching everything silently. The nurses were scrambling everywhere, and doctors were shouting orders.

One nurse saw me standing and told me to wait outside and closed the door. My body started shaking so I sat on the nearest chair and took out my phone from my jeans' pocket. I called Cameron.

"Cam... Chase... something is not right," I stuttered, and it was enough for him to know that I needed him.

Fifteen minutes later, Cameron arrived at the hospital with his parents, and we waited for the doctors to emerge out from Chase's room. I was so shocked and scared. Secretly, I started thinking that his condition worsened because of me.

"If something happened to him because you pressured him by yelling that he has to wake up, how will you forgive yourself? You're responsible for stressing him out with your rant."

These thoughts started making me sick, and I felt nausea starting to build up again. I got up from the chair, making everyone's attention turned to me, and I puked in the nearest dumpster.

Cameron came running towards me while I was busy throwing up.

The tears were running down my face uncontrollably, and my throat felt raw.

I turned around when I was finished throwing up and glanced at their worried faces.

"You look very pale, Hailey," he said to me, touching my cheek lightly.

Before I could reply to him, I felt my body going limp like there was no energy left in my body. My head felt heavy, and everything was spinning. My eyes rolled back in my head, and I fell down on the floor.

I heard Cameron shout and others also coming to my aid, surrounding me. With my half-open lids, I saw his extremely worried and confused face staring at me.

Cameron picked me up bridal style calling a nurse, but I was losing consciousness.

Finally, I closed my eyes, escaping from all the pain my sensitive heart had been in for weeks.

When I woke up, I found myself in a white hospital room, and tubes were attached to me. The window in my room showed that it was evening, which meant I had been out for hours.

My head felt better, and I wasn't drowsy and weak anymore, so I got up and pulled the tubes off.

There was no one in my room. I was alone. Maybe everyone was with Chase.

"Chase... I want to see him. I want to know how he is doing." With these thoughts, I walked out of the room.

When I reached outside his door, I heard noises and laughter coming from the room.

I pushed the door open and found Cameron, Eva and William, and Noah standing around the bed. Allison and her husband were sitting on the couch at the corner.

When they saw me standing frozen at the door, they stopped talking and stared at me.

"Hailey are you alright?" Cameron asked me.

I didn't hear him. My eyes were stuck on Chase. I was not even blinking just staring at him and thinking that maybe I was still dreaming.

"Cam is he?" I stuttered.

I tried completing my statement, but at that moment it was the most difficult thing to do.

The good thing was, Cameron understood what I wanted to say.

"Yes, Hailey. He is perfectly fine. He has been awake for three hours now. The surgery went successfully. They made him walk, and he will be fully recovered in a few weeks but..." Cameron said then stopped.

"But?" I asked him.

Cameron suddenly took my arm and dragged me towards Chase's bed. He was just staring at me plainly. There was no emotion on his face. No happiness like he didn't recognize me.

Oh, God! He forgot everything.

"Who is she?" Chase asked Cameron, confirming my suspicion.

"He forgot everything about you, Hailey. He doesn't remember you. You're the unluckiest woman in the world. Your husband forgot you," my treacherous mind said.

I stumbled back a little, feeling my heart broken beyond repair.

I should remind him. He would surely remember me. It was just his brain messing around with him.

I opened my mouth to say something, but nothing came out. My throat felt clogged with my emotions, and my mind felt numb. I couldn't stay here and let him look at me like I was a stranger.

I turned to leave the room when his words stopped me.

"My Princess," he said.

Completely stunned, I turned to face him.

He was the only one who called me princess. *Oh, God! It meant he remembered me.*

"Come give me a hug or kiss. I don't mind if you give me both," he said, winking.

My breath hitched.

"You... you remember me?" I asked him confused.

"Yes. I remember you. You're not someone who can be easily forgotten, Hailey. I was just messing with you." He was smiling like he just didn't turn my world upside down a few seconds ago with his stupid prank.

I strode towards him and punched him in the stomach, hard.

"Ouch! Woman! Don't hit me so hard. I just woke up from the deathbed," he said with a teasing smile playing on his face.

"Whatever. I don't care. You played a prank on me, on your wife who has been hell worried about you." I was angry.

He got up and walked to me.

"I know that was a shitty prank and I'm sorry," he said, giving me his puppy dog eyes.

"I know you're not sorry so don't act like you are." I glared at him.

"You know me too well. Can I calm you down with my magical kiss?" he asked me, giving his sweet smile, and it melted my anger.

"You can try." I had a small smile on my face.

He didn't need any more encouragement to plant his lips on mine.

His minty breath and the feel of his lips on mine made me feel like I was home after a tiresome long vacation. Placing his hands on my waist, he pulled me closer to his body and deepened the kiss, blowing my mind away and numbing the pain and stress. His kisses were my very own sedative.

When we pulled away from the kiss, I looked around the empty room.

"Where's everyone? I asked him.

"They left us when I kissed you to give us some privacy." He pulled me closer to his body.

"Chase, I'm pregnant," I told him.

"I know. I heard your pain-filled voice. I felt your skin under my palm. It made me fight. Your voice pulled me out from the abyss I was in. The news of the baby illuminated my empty mind with the light of hope. You're my life, Hailey. But from now on you own my life." He kissed my head.

We stayed in an embrace for few minutes

"It's going to be a boy," Chase said.

"Really? How do you know that?"

"Well, I just know. Father's instinct, you know," he said, shrugging his shoulder.

"Oh. If it will be a girl what will you do?"

"We'll see whose right shortly," Chase said, moving away and dragging me towards his bed.

"What are you doing?" I was baffled by his actions.

"I'm tired, and I have been up for three hours waiting for you," he said, pushing me on the bed and pulling a sheet over me.

Then he moved to the other side and slid beside me in the bed.

"Don't you think the bed is too small to accommodate two people?" I asked pressing myself to him.

"It is small. But if you sleep pressed up against my side, we will be fine." He pulled me closer to his body.

I bit my lip to stop the smile that was threatening to appear and adjusted my head above his chest. The rhythmic beating of his heart was a lullaby to my ears.

"Sleep, Hailey," he lightly murmured in my ear. After the stressful weeks and many sleepless nights, I fell asleep with a wide smile in the arms of my husband, my first and only love.

Epilogue

Hailey

[Five years later]

I was in the kitchen preparing breakfast when I heard loud, angry footsteps coming downstairs.

"Mom, do you know where my soccer ball is? I kept it near my bed last night. I have practice today, and it's missing," Noah frantically said.

Turning around from the stove, I walked to him, and asked, "Did you check under the bed?"

"Yes, Mom. I have checked all the possible places," he answered me upset.

"Well. Then I think you know where it could be."

The realization dawned on him. He groaned and started walking in the direction of Brandon's room.

I pulled him back and said, "Noah honey. You know, you were the one who demanded a brother. Now deal with it." I gave him a teasing smile.

"Mom, I know. Don't remind me again, please. I should have known from the start that he's the little thief in our home. I could have saved fifteen minutes, which I wasted to find that ball," he said, groaning, and I laughed at his misery.

"My poor baby!" I cooed to him. "You have to be polite with him, especially when it's his first day in kindergarten today," I said, placing a kiss on both Noah's cheeks.

Then he went to Brandon's room, and I got busy in making breakfast.

After I was done setting breakfast, I leaned on the kitchen counter and stared at the space. Waiting for them to come and join me for breakfast.

Suddenly, my mind started wondering how fast time flies. It still seemed like yesterday when Brandon was born. My cute little baby brought extreme happiness in my life.

When doctors assured us that Chase's health was fine, we moved back to Oakland for my college. During the pregnancy, Chase took care of me despite being drowned in his business.

When my mood swings wouldn't let me study, he would cheer me up. He was like my hard rock where I could lean on for support. Handling college and the pregnancy together was not an easy task, but I went through it with the help of my husband, and my mom.

Brandon was born at the end of summer. Chase's parents came to visit us when he was born.

After my graduation, we moved to Boston.

Chase took me to visit his beautiful apartment in Boston. I fell in love with the place. He wanted to buy a house again, but I persuaded him to live in the apartment.

Then after a month, Allison with her husband and with their children came for a vacation. Cameron and his fiancée, Bianca also joined us after a week.

All of us went crazy with going out visiting different places and doing nonstop shopping. We were pretty sure that our husbands were going to be bankrupt at the end of the week if we kept spending their money. But they surprisingly assured us that we could do whatever we wanted.

Brandon turned five a few days ago, and it was going to be his first day in kindergarten today. He was pretty active in pre-kindergarten, but there was no match for his excitement in joining kindergarten.

Brandon was my little bundle of mischief. His innocent face melted our hearts, and he always got away with anything by pulling that trick.

Chase didn't possess the ability to say no to Brandon. And also he had done a pretty good job in spoiling this one.

Noah was eight now. His favorite sport, football, had become his obsession, which was now rubbing off on

Brandon as well. Chase thought it was fine and encouraged Noah to join the school football team.

He was doing pretty good in his studies as a third-grade student and taking football training. I just wished every day that both my sons would be successful in whatever they wished to undertake.

I felt a hand creeping around my waist and then a kiss on my neck, making my knees wobble.

I turned around to face him and said, "Chase, what are you doing? You know the kids are up, and that they are going to come here any minute for breakfast."

"I still have time to steal a quick kiss," he said and captured my lips with his own.

After six years of being married to this man, I still felt my knees weaken every time he kissed me. His kisses always sparked an exhilarating sensation of desire in my body.

Our lips were moving in sync reminding me of all the happy moments of my life with him.

My hands were resting on his chest just above his beating heart, pulling him closer while his hand was in my hair and the other one was around my waist providing me support. We were so lost kissing that we didn't hear anyone entering the kitchen.

"Daddy, why are you biting Mommy's lips?" Brandon asked.

Chase's lips froze on mine, and his eyes popped open, gazing into mine in horror. I pulled away breathing hard and rested my head on Chase's shoulder to ease my breathing and recover from the mind-numbing kiss. The way Brandon was staring at us, I felt like we're caught stealing red-handed by the police.

We never kissed so passionately in front of our kids. It was our mutual decision that it was not appropriate to burden them with this much information yet. They would know everything eventually, but right now their little curious minds could lead them anywhere.

If it were Noah who caught us, explaining to him would be easier than Brandon. I was running my mind on how to explain to a five-year-old kid that what we were doing was called a kiss.

"Uh… Brandon, come to Daddy," Chase said, and Brandon came running.

Chase picked him up in his arms and asked, "Are you excited for school?"

"Yes. I am excited." He eagerly nodded his head up and down.

"Good. Then let's have breakfast," Chase said, setting him on the chair.

I sighed, thinking that Chase had distracted him, which was almost impossible in any other situation because he had this annoying habit of asking questions nonstop until he got the answer.

I took a seat and started serving Chase and Brandon their breakfast.

Then Brandon stared at me with a scrutinizing gaze and asked, "Mommy your lips look red. Daddy, why did you bite Mommy?"

Oh shit, oh shit. Apparently, Chase's plan of distracting him was doomed.

"Argh! Why did he have to notice everything?" I thought.

"Uh, Brandon I was kissing your mother," Chase said, and I glared at him.

Like really? That was your way of handling this situation.

"Kissing? Daddy, we kiss softly. You were biting her, hurting Mommy," Brandon said with a scowl.

After hearing him, I wanted to hit my head on the wall.

"Uhm… Brandon, I wasn't hurting your mommy. This kiss only happens between Mommy and Daddy," Chase said, looking pretty distressed himself because of having to explain.

My glare intensified tenfold because unknowingly he just raised another question in Brandon's mind.

"Why does it only happen between Mommy and Daddy?" he asked, looking confused and then curious.

I was ready to interfere and shut them both up by saying eat with their mouths closed when Chase replied, "It happens between Mommy and Daddy because it's a way to show love. And I love your mommy."

"Oh," Brandon said with a huge grin on his face.

Finally, they shut up and quietly ate their breakfast.

Noah came and hurriedly ate the sandwiches. I stuffed their lunch boxes in their bags.

First, we dropped Noah at his school and then Brandon because his classes started a little late.

We bid Brandon goodbye, and he went into his class with the teacher. I was happy that we didn't need to force him to go inside the class like other parents were doing to their kids while they were crying and clutching their parent's leg.

When I was buckled inside the car, Chase asked, "Ready to go to the hospital?"

I swallowed and said, "I don't know."

He didn't answer because he knew what I was feeling at that moment. I was utterly confused yet happy. For few weeks I had been feeling nauseous and lightheaded, so I took two pregnancy tests. One came positive, and the other came negative, confusing the hell out of me. So I repeated the tests with two different kits, and again the same thing happened, making me beyond furious.

Chase suggested that I should confirm it by taking a proper medical test so here we were going to see a doctor and to receive the report of the test I took yesterday.

We both went into the doctor's room.

"Hello. Please take a seat," the lady doctor said.

"Hi. I'm Hailey Edwards, and this is my husband. Do you have my reports?" I asked her while she was reading something, probably my report.

"Yes and it seems congratulations is in order. You are expecting." She had a big smile on her face.

I smiled, and Chase squeezed my hand.

"Is there anything to worry about? I mean her reports are fine right?" Chase asked the doctor.

"Yes, sir. There's nothing to worry about. She is perfectly fine. Well, your wife's history shows that she gets a severe case of nausea during every pregnancy, so I'm prescribing some medicines. I suggest using the herbal tea during the early weeks." The doctor gave us the prescription.

We thanked the doctor and went out. When we reached the parking lot, Chase suddenly hugged me, and I saw his eyes glazed with tears.

"What's the matter, Chase?" I asked him, cupping his face.

"Nothing, I'm just happy that I lived that day or I would have definitely missed this beautiful life with you and my sons, and now with my daughter." His voice was thick due to emotions.

"Uh-huh. You look for sure that it's a girl this time," I said, and a smile appeared on his face.

"Yes. I'm sure."

I rolled my eyes at his confidence.

"I hope so. Because I'm seriously sick playing football with you guys. I think I'm turning into a man," I said pouting.

Chase laughed loudly throwing his head back and said, "You're pretty funny, Hailey. I can assure you that you are a perfect, beautiful woman inside and out. And no one knows that better than me."

"You're always thinking about one thing. Stop being a pervert." I pushed his shoulder and got inside the car.

"You know pushing me away is your first sign of mood swing," he said, buckling himself in the driving seat.

"Whatever." I stared out the window.

When we arrived at the house, Chase lazily lay down on the couch and snatched my hand making me sit on his lap.

"Chase, are you not getting late for office?" I asked him confused.

"No. I'm taking a day off today. We're going to celebrate the good news." He kissed me on my forehead.

His sweet nothings literally increased my love for him. He enjoyed spending time with our kids and me. He never looked bored with us, and he forced us to celebrate small things.

He even celebrated the day Noah got an A+ in his drawing class and when Brandon first started walking. Chase was just a very lovely husband and a friendly father.

He was playing with a strand of my hair, and I was just staring at him.

"What are you thinking, Hailey?" he asked me.

"Nothing."

He rolled his eyes at my silly answer.

"So we have like two hours before we need to pick Brandon. What do you want to do?" he asked me.

"I don't know." I shrugged.

"Uh-huh. I know. We can do something that includes us lying in our bedroom naked between the sheets," he said, wiggling his eyebrows.

I glared at him and said, "Chase, you're such a man."

"No one knows that better than you."

I groaned.

"Now don't groan like that because you know it turns me on then I will become a beast," he said with his teasing smile.

"Shut up." I punched him in the arm.

Then I leaned towards his lips to kiss him when the cell phone started ringing loudly, ruining the mood.

He picked it up and talked for three minutes then ended the call.

"What?" I asked him looking at his worried face.

"It was Brandon's teacher. She asked us to come and pick him." He picked up his car keys.

We locked the house and ran towards the car. After fifteen minutes of driving, we reached Brandon's school.

We walked into the school and went straight to Brandon's class where her teacher took us in a different room.

"What's the matter? Is Brandon alright?" I asked her, concerned.

"Brandon is alright. He just did something that created a riot in the class." She looked disturbed.

At her words, my heart dropped. "What?"

"He kissed a girl," she said, making me frown.

"He did what?" I couldn't believe it.

"He kissed a girl on the lips. A girl named Laura was sitting beside him, and he kissed her. She started crying, and we had to call her parents to calm her down," the teacher said, looking flustered herself.

I felt dizzy after hearing her and held Chase's hand.

"Take him home. Explain to him politely that what he did was wrong," the teacher said, dismissing us.

"Chase, I am so angry at you right now. You know how fast he learns things and copies them." I scolded Chase.

"Hailey, it's pretty funny," he said, smiling at me, and I gave him a death glare in return.

The smile disappeared from his face in a flash.

Brandon came to us carrying his bag.

"Daddy, why are they sending me back?" he asked us, innocently.

"Um… because you're too intelligent and they want you to go home to enjoy the rest of the day," Chase replied coolly, picking him in his arms.

I felt an extreme urge to throttle Chase with his stupid explanation.

We went back to the car and settled in our seats.

Chase asked, "Son, how was your class today?"

"I made some friends and played the piano," he answered very efficiently, hiding the kiss part.

"And?" Chase glanced back from the side mirror of the car.

"Daddy! Laura is my new friend. She is shoo pretty. I loved her and kissed her like you did to Mommy," he said excitedly like we were going to appreciate him.

My face exploded with a blush at his innocent words. He had no idea what he did today, and now he was telling us proudly.

"Brandon, what did Daddy tell you in the morning? That kiss only happens between Mommy and Daddy? You are not allowed to do that with anyone. Do you understand me, Brandon?" I said sternly, making him sad.

The smile vanished from his face, and he curled his lips inside stopping himself from crying.

To change the sad mood in the car, Chase asked, "Who wants ice cream?"

But Brandon didn't reply, making me worry. Ice cream was his favorite. He would never let go of the chance of having ice cream. Now he was refusing it.

Chase stopped outside Brandon's favorite ice cream parlor and got out from the car. He pulled him out from his car seat. Brandon hugged Chase, and when I came to him, he hid his face in Chase's neck.

I felt a pang of hurt in my chest.

Chase saw my gloomy face, and said, "Brandon, baby. Look at your mommy."

"No, she hurt me," he replied, snuggling his face more.

"No, baby. She was just telling you not to do that again."

"Okay, I will not do that again, but I'm not talking to mommy," he said, picking his face from Chase's shoulder and glancing at me.

"Well, that's bad because your mommy has a surprise for you." Chase whistled. Brandon jumped from his arms and came running to me.

"Mommy! Where's the surprise?" he said, jumping up and down curiously.

I pretended to think, then said, "First, you need to promise me you will not do that again."

"I will not do that again. I promise," Brandon said.

"Let's eat ice cream then I will give you your surprise."

Can't get enough of Hailey and Chase? Make sure you sign up for the author's blog to find out more about them!

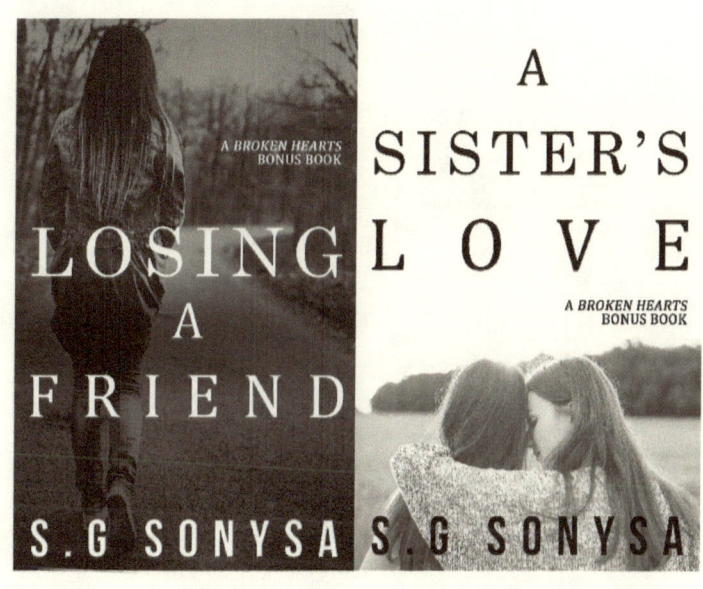

Get these two bonus chapters and more freebies when you sign up at
sg-sonysa.awesomeauthors.org!

A UNIQUE KIND OF
LOVE

JASMINE ROSE

Prologue

Two light grocery bags in hand, she followed her dad to the bright, white family car that caused them many troubles as they struggled to find it in the middle of snow. The girl opened the front seat door and slipped inside the car, completely oblivious to the look her father was giving her.

He sighed. "Lena?" The girl froze because he never called her by her actual name, unless he was serious about something. He always called her Rosie. "We talked about this. On the way here, you'd sit in front. On the way back, you'll sit behind me."

"Daaad! Please?" Lena pouted and widened her eyes a little. He shook his head and pointed to the back seat. He refused to give in to her, not again. Lena groaned and held out a hand to her dad. He took it and supported her waist as she moved to the backseat. She huffed and put on her seat belt.

"Happy?" she asked.

He gave her a smile. "That's my girl."

The car ride was silent, until her dad put a CD in and played it. Lena grinned and sat up immediately. At the first notes of the song, she made jazz hands. Her ponytail swung as she swayed in her seat to the music.

"Love, love me do. You know, I love you. I'll always be true," they both sang loudly. The Beatles had always been their favorite band, even though Lena's mom didn't like them much.

"I love you, Dad!" cried out the girl, her chestnut-colored eyes shining in exhilaration and excitement.

Her father laughed. "You know I love you too, Rosie."

The next seconds were a blur. Between the music, their singing and the momentary happiness, there was a truck that had passed the red light and was heading towards them. Time froze—this was the moment that would turn the girl's life upside down.

Lena turned just in time to see the truck inches away from colliding with the car. Her dad noticed as well, and his eyes widened. She screamed. The car lurched and Lena was thrown forward violently, the seatbelt biting into her stomach and knocking the wind out of her. The sound of her dad calling out her name was the last thing she heard before the world faded away from her.

"Rosie!"

I could hear a vague sound in the background.

I felt myself crying. For a long moment my upper eyelid seemed glued to the lower one, because I couldn't open my eyes. When I finally could, they hurt from my tears.

My gaze settled on Mom's terrified expression, and I watched as her face slowly softened with relief. She wiped the tears on my cheeks, although that didn't stop them from falling again.

She patted my hand. "Was it a bad dream, honey?" she asked. I took deep breaths to steady myself. I nodded.

"I wish I turned earlier, so I could—I don't know," I whispered, watching as the invisible switch clicked in my mom's mind.

"I wish he was here," she said.

Me too, Mom, I thought. I miss him too. How often had I wished that he was still alive, and that I was the one who had died?

I closed my eyes again and felt myself drift away into another dream.

Chapter One

Wonder and Anxiety

"The best is yet to be."
~Robert Browning~

Lena Rose Winter

Sighing, I laid my head down on the unshaven grass. I smiled. Stars glimmered and gleamed at me, assisting the moon's job to light up the sky at night. It seemed to me that there was a snowfall sparkling in outer space and I felt privileged to witness it. With soft, soothing music blasting in my ears, I felt better than I had in a long time. Comfort was something I cherished more than anything. I could feel a slight breeze blow on my neck; it cooled the few beads of sweat that had formed earlier that night.

Mom and I had decided to do a Welcome to the New Home barbecue. We'd eaten until our stomachs were begging for a break. It was always a moment that embellished my relationship with her. She went to sleep about an hour ago, the wine easing the process. So I'd been lying here for what, an hour or two? In those moments, I witnessed the sun disappearing and permitting the moon to rise in the sky; it was a never ending cycle.

Except, of course, for people who lived in the North Pole.

I had come close enough once, though. A few years ago, when I was twelve, Mom's company gave her a post somewhere in Alberta, Canada. We lived there only for about two months, but my, oh my, we had gone there in the middle of January. I still recall fearing that my toes were going to fall off because I couldn't feel them.

Thank God that this time, we moved into a place that wasn't too horribly cold, hopefully. Albany, NY seemed like a pretty cool place so far. I took a walk around yesterday and there was a gigantic park, Ridgefield, where I was sure to spend more time throughout the year. Myrtle Avenue was a considerably calm street and I was content about the small house we rented for the year. Since it was senior year, Mom promised that we could stay here long enough so I could finish my year and do all of the senior celebrations.

I was never one to fear new beginnings, considering this was the seventh home I lived in. In the span of four years, I had gone to seven different schools, met different kinds of people, and lived in unique types of houses. I was aware of what was waiting for me tomorrow.

Pressure.

Questions would be asked and answers would have to be given. I'd have to walk away from the spotlight and fade away from the minds of students who loved the "new girl." I would go back into the turtle shell I built myself.

A particular star in the sky winked at me and it got me thinking about Dad.

I often wondered why life could be so fair, yet cruel. Growing up without a father for the past seven years was hard. I saw my mother cry on his birthdays and, of course, I also carried around the memory of my fellow 4th grade 'friends' practically engraving the idea that I murdered my dad in my mind. Mom often said that I wasn't to blame, that it was his fate to die. Still, it wasn't something anyone can just forget.

A shooting star shot through the sky, and I closed my eyes.

I wish that this year brings me happiness, I thought.

***

I forced a big smile as I looked at myself in the mirror, my reflection looking ecstatic. Letting go of the strain I was feeling, my lips fell back into a straight line. I gave the rest of my features a cursory look. My long, dull chestnut brown hair flowed to my waist, and not even the sunlight hitting it could make it appear any more special than it was.

I wrapped a silver bracelet around my wrist. "Let's do this," I murmured.

"LENA! YOU'RE GOING TO BE LATE!" called Mom, disturbing the moment of peace I was having and making me jump in fright. I shook my head, chuckling absent-mindedly.

You'd think that after 17 years of living with her, I would've gotten used to her yelling that I was going to be late—which I never was—but I could swear that her screaming gets louder every time. I slipped my comfy, soft jean jacket on and hopped down the stairs.

I placed a kiss on her forehead. "Good morning," I said.

I mentally pinched my nose as I did so; I hated the smell of coffee. Mom gave me a small smile, sipping on her black, steaming drink. Her onyx black hair was in an elegant bun and she was in her business clothes, which meant that she was going to work.

"Good morning, sweetheart," she said, checking something on her phone. She looked up at me and gave me a small smile. "You ready?"

I nodded, pouring myself a cup of apple juice.

"Oh, I just remembered," said my mom, lifting her eyes from the magazine. "One of my co-workers' daughter goes to this school. Look for her. Stacy Hennings. Okay?" I noticed the familiar kindness and worry in her gaze. Noticing my absence of response, she prodded, "Okay, Lena?"

I rolled my eyes. Mom always had a fear of me being friendless. But what she didn't understand was that sometimes, I wanted to be alone. I'd gladly choose re-reading Looking for Alaska on a Saturday night than partying with a bunch of stuck-up teenagers. I was just that kind of person.

Saluting like a soldier, I replied. "Yes, mother." She looked at me, raising an eyebrow.

"What?" I exclaimed, feeling self-conscious all of a sudden. She walked over to me and stuffed a waffle in my mouth.

I immediately removed the oversized waffle from my mouth and glared at her, both of us extremely amused.

"I was just wondering what I've ever done to deserve a daughter like you." She winked, poking my nose.

I folded my arms over my chest and pouted. "Is that a compliment or an insult?"

"A little bit of both," she answered, putting her now empty cup in the sink. She pointed at it and I nodded.

"Hey! And I'll do them, I know."

After a few minutes of the daily teasing and fighting, I walked out the door, blowing her a kiss.

"Love you!" I exclaimed, taking a red apple and walking to our front door.

"Take care! Watch out for cars and don't forget to smile and be happy!" shouted Mom. I closed the door behind me and took a deep breath. I felt a smile appear on my face, making me feel just a little bit better.

Sure, it was autumn, but the weather was extraordinary. The sun was out, perfectly shining, but there was a breeze cooling the slight heat. The leaves of the trees surrounding my neighborhood were red, orange, and yellow, making the view breathtaking. I wished I had my camera to capture this moment. My dream has always been to become a photographer, to save every moment of every sunrise, sunset and every scene that takes my breath away.

I began my route to my new school, Albany High School. During the summer, I had walked by the school so many times—I knew the way by heart. I plugged my earphones on and put them in my ears. Lego House was playing, and that was because it had been on replay for a few days. I hummed its tune softly as I walked to the high school where I'd spend my senior year.

It was time to pick up the pieces and build a Lego house.

***

After about 15 minutes, I arrived at my new high school. Unlike all those summer days when there was no one, it was now packed with teenagers. And seriously, it was chaos. As my eyes scanned the scene before me, all I could see were footballs being thrown around, making any path to the main entrance impossible.

Jocks these days.

There was a girl leaning her back against a giant tree, absent-mindedly smiling as she gently rocked her head. I could see ear buds in her ear and I figured she was listening to the music she loved.

A group of girls were gossiping about something, concentrating on that subject. I frowned upon seeing one of them dressed in underwear, or as they called them, short-shorts. It was autumn for God's sake! If you needed to get lustful gazes from guys, you should've done it during summer, instead of risking hypothermia.

I headed to the main entrance, eager to get my schedule. I muttered a few "Excuse me's" along the way. Some students looked at me, as if analyzing me with their eyes.

Why wouldn't they?

I was the new girl.

Out of nowhere, something hard hit the back of my head. Black spots clouded my vision and I felt my body fall to the ground as I lost consciousness.

Well, gosh diddly darn, what a great start to the new school year!

If you enjoyed this sample then look for <u>A Unique Kind of Love</u> on Amazon!

Introducing the Characters Magazine App

Download the app to get the free issues of interviews from famous fiction characters and find your next favorite book!

iTunes: bit.ly/CharactersApple
Google Play: bit.ly/CharactersAndroid

Acknowledgements

I thank my God for gifting me the talent of writing
and expressing my thoughts in inspirational form.

I would like to express gratitude to my mother. She
is the most lovable and caring woman that I know. I admire
the grace and vigor she holds. Her encouragement and
belief gave me the vitality to write this beautiful story.
Without her support, I couldn't have been able to start this
book.

Now, the special acknowledgment goes to my
incredible readers. The completion of this book couldn't
have been possible without their encouragement and huge
support that they displayed throughout the journey of
writing this book. I sincerely appreciate their endless love
and praises, which helped me to progress my writing and to
complete this book.

Lastly, thanks to my younger brother for not
disturbing me while I wrote this book.

Author's Note

Hey there!

Thank you so much for reading Broken Hearts! I can't express how grateful I am for reading something that was once just a thought inside my head.

I'd love to hear from you! Please feel free to email me at sg_sonysa@awesomeauthors.org and sign up at sg-sonysa.awesomeauthors.org for freebies!

One last thing: I'd love to hear your thoughts on the book. Please leave a review on Amazon or Goodreads because I just love reading your comments and getting to know YOU!

Whether that review is good or bad, I'd still love to hear it!

Can't wait to hear from you!

S.G. Sonysa

About the Author

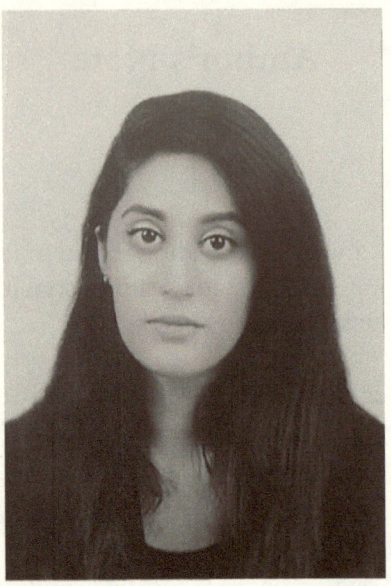

My name is Sarah, but people commonly know me as Sonysa, which is my pen name. I am twenty-two years old and studying in university. After my studies and daily chores, the leisure time I get I spend that time on writing or reading.

Writing is my passion and I love creating stories. I try my best to make readers feel every bit of emotion, love, and drama in the story.

When I'm not writing, you can find me in my room reading my favorite book or gossiping with my mom.